Roz placed her hands on the table, shut her eyes and breathed deeply.

'Move your chairs as close in as you can.'

'Do we have to shut our eyes too?' asked Wallis.

'No,' said Roz. 'I want you to enjoy the view.'

And with that, the room dissolved around them. Steve fel⟨...⟩iff breeze on his face ⟨...⟩ ⟨...⟩ he saw a clear blue s⟨...⟩ over⟨...⟩head ⟨...⟩ an incredibly distant horizon ⟨...⟩.

Roz looked ⟨...⟩ tranquil, in marked contrast to the task-force ⟨...⟩ paralysed with terror. Looking down, ⟨...⟩ way ⟨...⟩ he and the other people seated round the table were perched on top of a narrow pinnacle of weathered rock at least a thousand feet above the plain below. . . The slightest backward movement by anyone would cause them to topple over the edge!

Also by Patrick Tilley in Sphere Books:

THE AMTRAK WARS BOOK 1: CLOUD WARRIOR
THE AMTRAK WARS BOOK 2: FIRST FAMILY
THE AMTRAK WARS BOOK 3: IRON MASTER
THE AMTRAK WARS BOOK 4: BLOOD RIVER
THE AMTRAK WARS BOOK 6: EARTH-THUNDER
DARK VISIONS: AN ILLUSTRATED GUIDE TO
THE AMT___
MISSION

The Amtrak Wars
Book 5:
Death-Bringer

PATRICK TILLEY

SPHERE BOOKS LIMITED

19659

A SPHERE BOOK

First published in Great Britain by Sphere Books Ltd 1989
Reprinted 1990 (twice), 1991

Copyright © 1989 by Patrick Tilley

ISBN 0 7474 0001 6

Printed and bound in Great Britain by
Cox & Wyman Ltd, Reading

Sphere Books Ltd
A Division of
Macdonald & Co (Publishers) Ltd
165 Great Dover Street
London SE1 4YA
A member of Maxwell Macmillan Publishing Corporation

For
Patrick, Freddie and Sean
the next generation
who were into computers
before they were out of nappies
and have now come to grips with karate.
From the way things are shaping up
this looks like a good career move
for anyone with a ticket to the 21st Century.
Good luck, boys. Carry the torch. Hold it high.
Opa

CHAPTER ONE

In the spring of 2991, Mr Snow, wordsmith of the Clan M'Call, faced a difficult decision. Should he accompany the clan's delegation to the trading post on the shores of the Great River – or should he stay behind in the hills of Wyoming in case the cloud-warrior returned with Cadillac and Clearwater?

Two winters had passed since his charges had flown into the Eastern Lands and it was almost a year since the cloud-warrior had gone in search of them. Brickman had promised to help them escape from the Iron Masters but that was easier said than done. The Dead-faces were a fearsome race who lived behind closed borders. No Plainfolk Mute taken away on the wheel-boats had ever regained his liberty. But Cadillac and Clearwater were no ordinary Mutes. They had been born in the shadow of Talisman, and Brickman, the cloud-warrior, was also gifted and resourceful and as cunning as a coyote. And though he did not yet understand why, he too had been touched by Talisman.

If there was a chance to escape then these three would seize it, for between them they possessed the power to overturn nations. That had been their destiny from the day they had been born. But where were they? Day after day, Mr Snow had posted sentinels to keep a special watch over the eastern approaches to the settlement but the long-awaited travellers had failed to appear.

They were not dead. In an uncertain world, that was the only thing Mr Snow was sure of. Cadillac and Clearwater were the sword and shield of Talisman, saviour of the Plainfolk who – according to prophecy – was due to appear in human form. Cadillac was to use his great gifts to prepare the way for Talisman, and Clearwater was to use the immense forces at her command to protect the Thrice-Gifted One until his own powers were fully formed. Which, for instance, would be the case if he entered the world as a new-born child. On the other hand, if he was present in someone already alive, with his powers over heaven and earth lying dormant until the chosen moment, then her given task was to protect that individual until Talisman chose to reveal himself. She would do this instinctively, without necessarily understanding why, because Talisman would draw her to him.

Mr Snow had often wondered if Steve Brickman bore the Talisman within him. The cloud-warrior's descent from the sky into the hands of the M'Calls had been foretold by the Sky Voices. He and Clearwater had been destined to meet, and in giving herself to him body and soul she had broken the solemn vows that bound her to Cadillac – grievously wounding her former lover's pride in the process.

In time, Cadillac would get over it. It was he who had seen their separation in the stones. Clearwater was destined to journey into the dark world of the sand-burrowers that lay beneath the deserts of the south. Home of the iron-snakes that crawled through the land leaving a trail of devastation behind them, and the arrow-heads which carried the cloud-warriors across the skies. Warriors armed with long sharp iron and fire-seeds which erupted into smoke and flame with the sound of earth-thunder. Not the pure flame that swept the tree-spirits up towards the heavens but an evil cousin conjured up by the sand-burrowers. A flame whose thirst could not be quenched by water, that clung to flesh and burned through to the bone.

Yes, these were dark days. The time known as The Great Dying had come. A time when the courage of the Plainfolk would be sorely tested. Mo-Town, the Great Sky-Mother had withdrawn into the Black Tower of Tamla to weep for her people. Many would perish but the Plainfolk would survive and become a great nation under the banner of Talisman. As a Mute, a revered sage and walking history book of the Clan M'Call, Mr Snow knew that the journey through the Valley of Death had to be undertaken with as much good grace as one could muster. The Wheel turned, The Path was drawn. Human beings could not change their destiny; it was the hubris of the unenlightened that fostered the cruel illusion they could do so.

But meanwhile, three of the principal players were missing. Where in the name of Talisman were they? In a few days, the clan's trade delegation would be ready to leave for the annual gathering on the shores of the Great River. Mr Snow had two choices: to go with them, or stay behind. And the cloud-warrior had two ways to return with Cadillac and Clearwater: by smuggling themselves aboard one of the giant wheel-boats due to travel along the Great River to the trading post, or by a more direct, overland route through the territory that had once belonged to the Io-Wa and Ne-Braska.

A year ago, Brickman had stolen aboard one of the wheel-boats at the trading post and had been carried away to the Fire-Pits of Beth-Lem. If he had managed to complete the journey without being discovered he might decide that this was the best way to return. In the bustle of trading activity, with Mutes helping to load and unload the wheel-boats, they would have an excellent opportunity to steal ashore. Once there they could rejoin their clanfolk, becoming part of the delegation which would then travel home across the plains during the period of truce known as 'Walking on the Water'.

That was the sensible way, but the journey from Ne-Issan took many days – perhaps weeks. Finding a place on a wheel-boat where three people could remain undetected for days on end would not be easy. Mr Snow had been taken aboard one for a brief audience with Lord Yama-Shita. They were giant structures but they also carried a large crew who constantly swarmed back and forth like ants on a dunghill. And the wheel-boats only came to the trading post once a year. To return via this route meant boarding the right vessel at exactly the right moment. The cloud-warrior was resourceful enough to gather this information but what if they missed the boat? Or escaped much earlier and were unable to take the longer but safer way home?

Mr Snow's dilemma arose from his desire to be at the chosen point of arrival in case his powers were needed to fight off any pursuers. For they would be pursued. That was certain. Over the years of trading, he had come to understand the character of the Iron Masters and their obsession with 'face', what the Mutes called 'standing'. Because of the status accorded to warriors, it was a concept the two races shared, but not to the same degree. Mutes generally nursed their shattered pride then gave it another shot. To the Iron Masters, loss of face was an unbearable condition which, if the victim's sense of honour could not be regained, often led to suicide. This concern with honour, impeccable behaviour and faultless performance of one's duties only affected the pure-blood ruling classes; the lower orders – the inferior races – were not graced by such concerns. Which, according to his informant, explained why the gods had condemned them to a life of servitude.

Yes . . . Given the nature of Cadillac's mission, their escape would cause a definite loss of face, and the authorities concerned would spare no effort to recapture them. Failure to do so would cause heads to roll. Mr Snow – who knew nothing of the mayhem the trio had caused at the Heron Pool – was unaware that in its bloody aftermath a great many already had. He only knew the Iron Masters were tenacious adversaries who did not admit defeat. That was why he had to be on hand in case they pursued his young charges into the heartland of the Plainfolk.

But he could not be in two places at once and he could no longer hesitate. He now had less than a week in which to make his decision. Perhaps the Sky Voices would consent to guide him. He had consulted them many times during the past year but they had greeted his questions

4

about Clearwater, Cadillac and the cloud-warrior with a baffling silence. He clambered up to his favourite rock, sat down with his legs crossed, took several deep breaths while he admired the view, then raised his closed eyes and opened his mind to the sky.

For a long while it seemed as if the staff of this spiritual advice bureau was out to lunch but eventually a series of pictures appeared before his inner eye. Soul-searing images of death and destruction on an unparalleled scale; a grisly drama in which he had been given a starring role. Mr Snow was renowned for his courage and resolution but even his indomitable heart quailed at this new burden that Fate had thrust upon him. And what made it worse was the knowledge that these fleeting images were merely a foretaste of what was to come. But there could be no turning back. The Sky Voices had spoken – and had left him in no doubt as to what he had to do.

Some two thousand miles to the east of the M'Call settlement, Ieyasu, Lord Chamberlain of the Inner Court, grand-uncle and principal advisor to the Shogun Yoritomo Toh-Yota, absolute ruler of Ne-Issan, was also beset by problems that demanded resolution.

If Mr Snow was old, Ieyasu was ancient, but they had many qualities in common including keen eyes and fire in their belly. Both were shrewd, highly intelligent and infinitely wise in the ways of the world even though the societies in which they lived were totally dissimilar except for their respect of physical courage and the code of honour which formed the basis of the warrior ethos.

Mr Snow could not read or write but possessed gifts of memory and magic: Ieyasu was literate, extremely well educated and although he was unable to summon earth and sky forces to his aid, the skill and cunning with which he outmanoeuvred all those who sought to remove him from power was little short of supernatural.

Before Yoritomo's accession to the throne at the tender age of twenty-three, Ieyasu had exercised absolute power in the name of the Shogun's dissolute father. Yoritomo, now twenty-nine, was made of different cloth. Restrained in his sexual appetites, something of an ascetic in his attitude to food and drink, overburdened with a tiresome morality and obsessed with traditional values, Yoritomo had proved particularly difficult to deal with. And the main source of difficulty was his determination to take sole charge of the nation's affairs and ignore the voice of experience. The voice, of course, being that of his grand-uncle.

It was hard enough trying to keep the government afloat and conspirators at bay without having to re-educate an aspiring saint who was trying to manoeuvre you out of office. In time, Yoritomo would learn. But he would learn a lot quicker and make life a lot easier for everyone by absorbing the distilled wisdom of his grand-uncle. Something he had done with the utmost reluctance.

In part, it was a natural reaction to the moral laxity which had pervaded the Inner Court during his father's reign. As a new broom, Yoritomo wanted to make a clean sweep. A perfectly laudable aim. The court was in need of a thorough spring cleaning. But in politics one never did anything to excess. Yoritomo did not understand the importance of leaving a little dirt in the corners. His puritanical streak – laudable in a monk but utterly depressing in a vigorous, intelligent young man holding the highest office in the land – was blinding him to the realities of power.

The young shogun had not yet grasped an essential truth: exploiting the weaknesses of powerful men – especially powerful opponents – was an important element in the art of statecraft. It was also true that a nation needed honest men of high principle and modest ambition. They made excellent civil servants. The government revenue and customs houses and the postal service were always crying out for more. Sinners, on the other hand, made better dinner companions. And they were a lot easier to do business with.

Ieyasu was also a traditionalist, as opposed to those

who favoured progressive ideals – a group of domain-lords led by the Yama-Shita family. But the progress advocated by this cabal of entrepreneurs was restricted to the introduction of new industrial processes and manufacturing techniques. No one, however radical their ideas were in that direction, was in favour of modernising the feudal system on which Ne-Issan had been built.

The problem – in Ieyasu's eyes at least – was that you could not have one without undermining the other. And none of the seventeen ruling samurai families was prepared to surrender an ounce of power or privilege to the lower classes. It was the merchants who argued the case for an expanding economy and the benefits to be gained by increasing the purchasing power of the masses by – if you please – paying tradesmen and servants higher wages! Some had even suggested setting up trade links with the long-dogs inhabiting the buried cities beyond the Western Hills – but what else could one expect from chinamen who had an abacus where their brains should be?

The greatest bar to progress was the immutable edict which forbade, under pain of death, the re-introduction of the Dark Light. It was also a treasonable offence for lesser mortals to utter its name and such was the dread it inspired, even those at the pinnacle of power only did so with the greatest circumspection. According to the scrolls which chronicled the distant past, the creation of the Dark Light – electricity – had corrupted mankind and led the gods to destroy The World Before with a tidal wave of golden fire. A wave that had engulfed the ancient homeland of the Iron Masters, and which was so high, it had covered the peak of Fuji, the sacred mountain which contained the soul of Nippon. As a result, there was a deeply-held belief that to seek to resurrect the Dark Light would be an act of incredible folly which would once again place the world in mortal peril.

But, as Ieyasu knew, the world of Ne-Issan was bordered by the Appalachians and the Eastern Sea. There was another vaster world beyond the Western Hills, inhabited by grass-monkeys and long-dogs: Plainfolk Mutes and Trackers – the soldier-citizens of the Amtrak Federation. The Mutes were hairy savages, semi-nomadic hunters with no craft skills beyond those needed to support their simple mode of life. All their edged-weapons, crossbows and metal implements were supplied by the Iron Masters. But the Trackers were warriors who had no fear of the Dark Light. It was the life-force of their underground society. It enabled them to send images and voices through the air, it powered their weapons, their giant, caterpillar-like land-cruisers and their sky-chariots – war-machines which entered the cloud-realm of the *kami* with impunity *and were not cast down*.

Their presence posed a threat to the world of Ne-Issan yet Amaterasu–Omikami stood aside and did nothing. Their underground cities were not crushed, and the world beyond the Appalachians was not ravaged by heavenly fire – a theological conundrum that was studiously ignored by the leading sages of the *Shinto* priesthood.

Ieyasu knew the answer. The Dark Light was neither good nor bad. Electricity was a power that lay at the heart of the natural world. It could be captured by special, cunningly-wrought machines and conveyed along special threads from one place to another, or shot through the air like an invisible arrow that flew across plains, mountains and seas within the space of a single heartbeat.

Like all power, it could be used and abused. It could corrupt, in the same way that *sake* addled the brains of drunkards and opium destroyed the will of addicts. But in its pure state, it was not inherently evil. Electricity had been created to be the slave of man. Only if the man was weak could the slave became his master. Ieyasu had certain foibles but he was not a weak man. He enjoyed the attendant luxury his privileged birth and high rank afforded him but he was consumed by nothing except the desire to manipulate the reins of power to the ultimate benefit of the Toh-Yota family and the Shogun. In that order. Ieyasu ate well, drank judiciously, and kept his gaunt, aging body in trim by practising his swordsmanship. He enjoyed male *and* female company and could still produce a commendable erection which a select circle of court ladies -- ever anxious to advance themselves or the careers of their husbands – accommodated by supplying him with a string of pubescent nymphets.

The Dark Light might kill him but it would never enslave him. Ieyasu knew this because it had served him well over many years. Key members of his private network of secret agents had been using high-powered radio transceivers and other electronic devices for the last ten years. The same type of equipment used by the secret agents of the Federation and which, after a series of stealthy contacts, had been supplied by them to Ieyasu's organization under the terms of a secret protocol signed by him and Commander-General Karlstrom, the head of AMEXICO.

Among the items covered was the return of any *mexican* caught by the Plainfolk Mutes and sold to the Iron Masters. Other clauses outlined mutually-beneficial arrangements for the pooling of specific types of information, for example – the kinds of weapons the Iron Masters planned to supply to the Mutes by way of trade and, in return, any snippets of information which could help Ieyasu head off any bid to topple the Toh-Yota shogunate.

A final clause set out the arrangements for joint operations between the two spy networks. It was here that AMEXICO's help had proved invaluable. There were certain locations which, for various reasons, Ieyasu's home-grown agents were unable to penetrate or where they could not operate effectively. The wheel-boats operated by the Yama-Shita family were one example. The vetting procedures were so strict it was impossible to slip an outsider into the crew. The only alternative was to buy the allegiance of someone already serving the family but experience had shown this to be a costly and highly unreliable way of doing business.

Karlstrom had supplied the answer: the insertion of

9

mexicans, disguised as Mute slaves, and armed with a working knowledge of japanese and other asiatic languages into sensitive locations. Ieyasu, after some initial misgivings, had accepted the offer. And it had worked. As non-persons, slaves were regarded as part of the brickwork, and since no outlander was permitted to utter a word of the Iron Master's sacred tongue, people talked in front of them without ever suspecting their conversation was being monitored. Disguised slaves could not, of course, penetrate the secret council chambers of high-ranking plotters but they were the source of a surprising amount of raw intelligence. And many of the council chambers were no longer secret thanks to the electronic bugging devices obligingly supplied by AMEXICO.

So far it had paid off, but it was a dangerous game. A balancing act which placed Ieyasu on a tightrope over a pool of hungry sharks. For not only had he approved the use of devices filled with the Dark Light, he had even sent some of his most trusted men to help perfect the language skills of Karlstrom's agents!

His opposite number, the head of AMEXICO – who also spoke fluent japanese – had never sought to press for an advantage. The emphasis had always been on mutual cooperation but Ieyasu knew that if one of the two copies of the secret protocol with his name and seal attached ever reached the Shogun, his hold on the reins of power would be abruptly severed. And so would his head. His own death in the proper course of events did not concern him, but his precipitate departure from office followed by the elimination of his closest aides would leave a dangerous vacuum in the highest councils of the land. A vacuum that a host of undesirables would rush to fill.

In the few years left to him, Ieyasu had to make the best possible use of this unique contact with a potential enemy state without compromising the long-term interests of Ne-Issan or betraying its most cherished beliefs. A lesser wrong for a greater good.

As a pragmatist, Ieyasu had no problem with that. Like all aristocratic Iron Masters, conspiracy was in his blood.

The history of Ne-Issan was a catalogue of internecine feuds and labyrinthine treachery. Even so, there were times when he found it difficult to reconcile his dual roles as master spy and Court Chamberlain of the Toh-Yota shogunate with his blood-ties to the entire japanese ruling class. This was a primal allegiance that went beyond pure reason and, as such, could not be ignored. Up until now he had been able to override this inner conflict, but in the spring of 2991, he learned of an event which placed him in a considerable dilemma.

In the autumn of the previous year, *mexicans* disguised as slave workers had – with his tacit approval – sabotaged an attempt to build flying horses; a project masterminded by the Yama-Shita and Min-Orota families who were also laying plans to overthrow the Toh-Yota Shogunate. The sabotage operation had been a remarkably bloody affair – and so had its aftermath. Hundreds had perished, foot-soldiers, cavalry, samurai, nobles from both families and Domain-Lord Hirohito Yama-Shita who, by all accounts, had died in a particularly gruesome manner.

Ieyasu's agents had been instrumental in helping the five saboteurs to leave the country but their departure had not been the end of the story. Judged guilty of seeking to resurrect the Dark Light, several leading members of the Yama-Shita family were given the chance to take their own lives; others, of lower rank, were executed, fines were levied and economic sanctions applied.

Armed resistance against the government was out of the question. The judgment against the family had been rendered by its peers; a committee of powerful domain-lords including several of its closest allies – whose neutrality had been purchased by giving them valuable pieces of the Yama-Shita trading empire.

All this had been done yet it had not brought the Yama-Shita to heel. They wanted revenge. Not against the Toh-Yota. Without its two main allies, the Ko-Nikka and the Se-Iko – the beneficaries of the Shogun's *largesse* – the shogunate and the traditionalists now held the balance of power. It would take years to win back its former

11

supporters and longer still before they were ready to even the score. No . . . the family's thirst for revenge was directed against the five assassins – the outlanders who had killed their domain-lord and brought the house of Yama-Shita to its knees. They could not have done their bloody work without highly-placed friends inside Ne-Issan. If this murderous gang could be captured alive, they would soon reveal the identity of their masters . . .

Ieyasu did not need the bug planted inside the council chamber of the Yama-Shita's palace at Sara-kusa to tell him how they had reasoned. He merely had to put himself in their place. The last-minute decision by the Shogun not to attend the flying display at the Heron Pool pointed to his complicity in the murderous onslaught unleased by the assassins. An onslaught which – in the minds of the Yama-Shita family – had been stage-managed by Ieyasu.

Not exactly true, but close enough. Ieyasu had not known in detail what the saboteurs intended to do; he had merely allowed the operation to go ahead. Had he known more, he might have acted otherwise. Using communication devices and 'hired' agents was one thing; allowing those same agents and Mute witches to murder highborn japanese citizens with impunity was something else entirely.

The events which had led to this indiscriminate killing were, arguably, an example of a delicate political problem that could not have been solved in any other way, and with such brutal swiftness. But there were limits beyond which Ieyasu was reluctant to go in his desire to preserve the shogunate. The Heron Pool incident marked the top of a slippery slope he had no wish to descend. And now, in the spring of 2991, the long-dogs had attacked again. Only this time, they had struck first and told him afterwards. A wheel-boat of the Yama-Shita family, carrying a large number of samurai and foot-soldiers towards the western shore of Lake Mi-shiga had been sunk with the loss of all hands

Karlstrom, in sending his apologies, had explained that there had been no time to seek his approval. At the very last minute, AMEXICO had received news that the Yama-Shita intended to launch a military operation against a clan of Mutes that was sheltering the agents who had sabotaged the Heron Pool. No one could condemn the Yama-Shita family's desire for revenge, said Karlstrom, but it was, under the laws of Ne-Issan, an illegal act of war.

True. But even so, regardless of the circumstances, the loss of 250 samurai, 300 red-stripes and 150 officers and crew was an act of violence that was difficult to condone: an affront to the pride of the entire nations. Had the attack gone ahead, it would have been a criminal act for which the Yama-Shita would have been duly punished. But it was equally reprehensible for the long-dogs to take the law into their own hands. To engineer the death of over seven hundred soldiers of Ne-Issan in order to save five of their agents and a clan of grass-monkeys was a totally disproportionate response. Secret agents were treasured assets but their duties also included a readiness to die. AMEXICO's action against the wheel-boat had seriously damaged the existing relationship to the point where Ieyasu was beset with grave doubts about its future.

There was also another problem. Should he tell the Shogun about the illegal expedition mounted by the Yama-Shita? Or should he remain silent about the whole affair and accept the announcement from the palace at Sara-kusa that a wheel-boat supplying the new out-stations on Lake Mi-shiga had been lost with all hands during a violent storm? To reveal the truth – or part of it – would place Yoritomo under an obligation to impose further sanctions.

Ieyasu was reluctant to increase the pressure on the family. The death of Domain-Lord Yama-Shita and the exposure of the plot to resurrect the Dark Light had strengthened the position of the Toh-Yota. Its most powerful rival had been humbled, but they still commanded a great deal of covert support. Applying more sanctions would be seen as an attempt to completely destroy the family – a move that would arouse suspicion and resentment among the other domain-lords.

In their eyes, the deaths of the named conspirators and their closest relatives and the harsh fines had expunged the family's guilt. Any further attempt to crush the Yama-Shita would be seen as a threat to all those who supported its progressive ideals. No one wanted to create conditions that could lead to another civil war. As the first among equals, the Toh-Yota had to be strong but not too strong. And since it could not singlehandedly sweep all opposition aside, it had to maintain the balance of power by a mixture of skilful government and skulduggery – two areas in which Ieyasu was the acknowledged master.

After lengthy reflection, Ieyasu decided to say and do nothing. He would, for the moment at least, leave the dilemma posed by his relationship with Karlstrom unresolved. He had not lost all sense of honour. It was simply that his self-esteem was of minor importance compared with the maintenance of the Toh-Yota shogunate. As long as he, Ieyasu, was alive, Yoritomo could be left in charge of the moral high ground. His task was to underpin the succession by ensuring that the opposition remained fragmented. His legacy would be to imbue Yoritomo with the determination to gradually reduce the Yama-Shita to penury, redistribute their lands and drive them into political obscurity like the once-great Da-Tsuni.

To aid Yoritomo in this task, Ieyasu's successor needed to retain access to the same alien devices that had enabled the present spy network to function so efficiently. The links with AMEXICO would not be severed but, equally, they would not be extended and the existing arrangements would have to be more tightly controlled. Karlstrom would have to understand that the indiscriminate killing of high-ranking Iron Masters by outlanders – no matter what the circumstances – could no longer be countenanced.

The presence of a Mute witch among the team of saboteurs at the Heron Pool and this latest action against the wheel-boat in defence of a clan of Mute fisherfolk

14

were discordant notes in what until then had been a harmonious relationship. Similar, in many respects, to the trading contacts built up by Iron Master and Mute over several decades; contacts which had subsequently received the covert blessing of AMEXICO.

Having invested a great deal of time, money and effort, the Iron Masters regarded the Plainfolk Mutes as their own milch cow. These illiterate animals could never be allies but they had been accorded the status of auxiliaries. That was why they had been armed instead of being enslaved in the hope they could slow down the northwards advance of the Federation. But had the ground rules changed? Were these two disquieting incidents the product of another 'understanding'? Another secret protocol signed by one or more of the competing Mute bloodlines and the smooth-tongued head of AMEXICO?

Only time would tell.

In the palace-fortress of Sara-kusa, built on the site of the pre-Holocaust city of Syracuse, N.Y, Aishi Sakimoto, acting Regent of the Yama-Shita family, had been asking himself more or less the same question and believed he now knew the answer.

In the normal course of events, the domain-lord's eldest son would have assumed his father's title, but on the orders of the Shogun, Hirohito's children had all died by their own hand, or had been killed by their mother before turning the knife upon herself.

In some families, blood-feuds erupted when competing branches disputed the succession but Domain-Lord Hirohito Yama-Shita had ruthlessly eliminated all potential rivals. He had ruled with an iron hand but under his leadership the family, already rich, had prospered even more. Only now, with most of his immediate relatives dead, had come the sombre realization that his murderous reign had eliminated most of the candidates with the necessary strength, ability and drive to take his place.

The qualities of leadership now displayed by Aishi Sakimoto had not escaped the notice of his late nephew but he had survived, partly because he was Hirohito's favourite uncle and a fairly ruthless character himself. But what had really saved him from assassination was the fact that he was old and without issue, and was therefore not regarded as a threat to the domain-lord's own family.

It was also the reason why the shaken survivors had appointed him to head the council now running the family's affairs until one of their number formally assumed the title. In the present climate, the chosen successor to Hirohito would not necessarily be the best man for the job. Ieyasu, the Lord Chamberlain had sent word that whoever was chosen could only become domain-lord with the approval of the Shogun. And everyone knew Yoritomo would not allow a strong candidate to take the helm.

It was a bitter pill. Never before had the family been forced to endure such interference with their affairs. The twin ancestors of the Yama-Shita, the Yama-Ha and the Matsu-Shita had helped the Toh-Yota defeat the Da-Tsuni. They had been allies. As part of the historic Seventh Wave, their blood had mingled on the shore of the Eastern Sea. But with the merger of the two families to form one of the biggest domains in Ne-Issan they had become rivals. And their differences had been aggravated by Hirohito's espousal of progressive ideals.

The domain formed by the merger was not significantly larger than the territory held by the Toh-Yota. The source of their unease lay in its unique geographical position which gave it access to the the Great Lakes *and* the Eastern Sea, borders that could be easily defended and, above all, an enviable trading advantage. Even though the Toh-Yota had filled its own coffers by taxing the family's revenues, the steadily increasing wealth and influence of the Yama-Shita had come to be viewed as a threat to the Shogunate.

Lord Hirohito's overconfidence had led him to act

prematurely. He had been right about Yoritomo. Left to his own devices, the young Shogun would not have been a problem. He was his own worst enemy. But Hirohito had seriously underestimated Ieyasu's staying power. With Yoritomo's accession and his attempted clean sweep, Ieyasu's grip on the Inner Court had been seriously weakened. Many of his cronies had been ousted and his place-men in the *bakufu* had been demoted or pensioned off. Everyone had confidently expected Ieyasu to follow them out through the door to spend his last years pottering about the garden or the library of his large estate.

But the old fox had hung on, and six years later, the foothold he had managed to preserve had become a veritable stranglehold. It had been reported that he not only had the Shogun's ear, he had both ears pinned against the wall. The proof was there for all to see! Yoritomo's fleet-footed manoeuvres in the wake of the Heron Pool massacre bore all the hall-marks of the great conspirator.

Yes. More positive action should have been taken at the beginning. An overt assassination attempt was out of the question but Ieyasu's penchant for juveniles was no secret within court circles. Instead of gloating over the reports of his imminent removal from office on the grounds of galloping senility, Hirohito should have slipped a couple of well-schooled 'spring blossoms' into the old bugger's bed with orders to stay on the job until they had fucked his brains out.

Well, it was too late now. Hirohito had paid dearly for his mistake and so had the family. The account would be settled – with interest. But it would be an uphill task. Ieyasu would not last for ever, but it was clear that the young Shogun could no longer be written off. He had learned a great deal. The Yama-Shita would rise again but it would be many years before they would be strong enough to dislodge the Toh-Yota. He, Aishi Sakimoto, would play his part, but the sweet moment of victory would not come in his lifetime. For the moment, they

17

would have to content themselves with punishing the clan M'Call and the rest of the She-Kargo bloodline.

Thanks to a message sent from the wheel-boat soon after the unmasking of the two Kojak 'guides', Sakimoto now knew that one of them was the cloud-warrior that the M'Calls had sent to Ne-Issan escorted by a female Mute. It was not clear whether this female – who had last been seen in the hands of the Min-Orota – was the unmarked white witch who had murdered Lord Hirohito with her foul magic, but there was a possibility they were one and the same.

When unmasked on the wheel-boat, the cloud-warrior had been disguised as Mute. His companion, whose skin was similarly marked, had been identified as the grass-monkey who had become the cloud-warrior's personal servant and had flown the first rocket-powered proto-type. In view of the expert way he had handled the craft he was probably another skilfully-disguised long-dog. As for the white witch, her true identity remained problematical. Sakimoto knew of the rumours of Mute magic but he had discounted them as Lord Hirohito had. Now he was not so sure. If the witch was *not* a long-dog, then it meant that there were clear-skinned, smooth-boned Mutes who – on the outside at least – looked just like Trackers!

It was all very confusing.

There was, however, one aspect of this affair which was not bedevilled by doubt. A working connection between long-dog and grass-monkey had been clearly established. By piecing together the information gathered from the fisherfolk of Lake Mi-shiga by the agents now stationed on the eastern shore, Sakimoto knew the wheel-boat had been set afire and sunk by flying-horses which could only have come from the Federation. And the first two assassins had arrived in Ne-Issan as emissaries of the Clan M'Call. Under a deal struck by Lord Hirohito and a wordsmith called Mr Snow, the clan had agreed to deliver a cloud-warrior and his flying-horse in exchange for a hundred rifles!

Who could have guessed that this dull-eyed, oafish scum was capable of such duplicity? Never mind. It would not go unavenged, and nor would the crimes of the clan Kojak who – after the sinking of the wheel-boat – had massacred all those who reached the shore. But the first move would be against the M'Calls – the link between the Plainfolk and the Federation. And this time, the operation had to be mounted without any possibility of failure.

The family could expect no assistance from its few remaining friends in an act of war that did not have government approval. And in the present climate, that was unlikely to be obtained without being forced to hand over a large piece of the pie. The only way round the problem was to mask the attack by using Mute clans from the D'Troit bloodline, the fiercest rivals of the She-Kargo.

Sakimoto was aware that slaughtering the She-Kargo trade delegations would net very few of the real offenders. The bulk of the clan M'Call was safely out of reach. But this attack was only the first step in a plan the family had been hatching for some considerable time. The harsh consequences of Lord Hirohito's misadventure had weakened the family's power-base and it could only be rebuilt by implementing the plan to expand its present boundaries.

Recruiting the D'Troit to do the spade work was part of that plan. The present fragmented nature of the Plainfolk which led to clans of the same blood-line fighting each other was pointless and unproductive. And the trading arrangements under which each clan annually supplied varying-sized groups of 'volunteer' slave-workers was an inefficient way of meeting the constant demand for labour.

They killed each other in the same haphazard way. There was no master plan. Warriors who triumphed in a clash of arms did not go on to plunder the settlement of the losers. The victorious clan did not occupy its rival's land or slaughter the survivors. It did not even attempt to enslave them. The winners simply went home and composed fire-songs which extolled their prowess!

Part of the problem was the vastness of the territory at their disposal. There was too much land and too few people. And because the inhabitants were savages with a simple life-style, they did not need to exploit the land's resources. There was enough room for everyone, an abundance of game and more raw material than anyone could possibly need. There was no need to conquer each other. Mutes fought each other because they were wedded to the warrior ethic. It was a test of courage, part of the process of natural selection. Very laudable. But all that ferocious energy should not be allowed to go to waste. It should be directed towards a loftier goal, not frittered away on inconsequential skirmishes.

The Yama-Shita planned to provide that sense of direction by unifying the disparate clans of the D'Troit and C'Natti bloodlines and creating two vassal states. Armed and advised by the Yama-Shita, they would then subjugate their hated rivals, the She-Kargo, and the other lesser bloodlines. When this had been done, they would levy annual tributes in the form of raw materials and able-bodied males and females. Punitive tributes which would force this race of savages to toil from dawn till dusk instead of idling their days away with smoke-filled dreams. Work would be their saviour, not some invisible being called Talisman.

As patrons and protectors of the D'Troit and C'Natti, the Yama-Shita family would be the sole conduit for this new flow of materials and labour. It would generate unimaginable wealth – but only if each move was carefully planned. The treasonous acts of Lord Hirohito had robbed the family of its exclusive right to trade with the grass-monkeys. Licences had been awarded to its southern neighbours, the Ko-Nikka and Se-Iko but it was Yama-Shita who controlled the entrances to the Great Lakes and it was *their* navigators who knew what course to steer through the deeps and shallows. They had the know-how and the contacts, and their fleet of giant wheel-boats dwarfed the vessels owned by the Ko-Nikka. The Se-Iko, whose domain was land-locked, only possessed river craft. For this first trip they had been obliged to lease two boats and their crews from the Yama-Shita at exorbitant rates. Both families had placed orders for larger vessels but the Ko-Nikka's shipwrights – who lacked the expertise needed to construct such large vessels – were still wrestling with the problem of how to lay out the bilges.

Sakimoto was content to let them stew in their own juice. The family's former allies had broken ranks in return for a share of the Great Lakes trade and now they were learning that there was more to it than a pretty piece of paper with the Shogun's seal on it. The Yama-Shita still had the edge on its new partners and they both knew that without its assistance their own crews might return empty-handed.

From the signals coming into Sara-kusa, it appeared that some of the wiser heads in both domains were already regretting the hasty leap onto the Shogun's coat-tails. If these veiled contacts were inspired by feelings of guilt then he, Aishi Sakimoto, intended to exploit such sentiments to gain whatever advantage he could. Given their recent turn-about, he could not take them into his confidence and it was not necessary. They would serve his purpose better by remaining independent witnesses. They would be able to testify that the fighting at the trading post broke out between the rival Mute bloodlines and it was only when the conflict appeared to be getting out of hand that the Yama-Shita family felt obliged to intervene in order to separate the warring factions and protect the Iron Masters trapped on shore. And if, in the course of establishing a cease-fire, one faction suffered heavier casualties than the other then that would be régrettable but unavoidable.

This had been Lord Hirohito's plan, and it was a good one. In making it, he had not been inspired by any particular animosity towards the She-Kargo. On the contrary. Their pre-eminence was something to be admired. He had simply decided to back the D'Troit and

21

the C'Natti because their burning desire to become the paramount bloodlines of the Plainfolk would tempt them into an alliance with the Yama-Shita.

But with his death at the hands of the white witch, the subjugation of the She-Kargo was no longer just the initial phase in the economic development of the Western Plains. It had become an act of vengeance.

And the first tribute to be exacted by the new vassal states on behalf of their master would be the heads of the Clan M'Call.

The M'Calls were also at the top of the hit-list drawn up by the leaders of the Amtrak Federation. The narrow escape of the wagon-train known as The Lady from Louisiana in the Battle of the Now and Then River in June 2989, and the subsequent disastrous attack which destroyed a third of its wagons and crew in the November snows of 2990 had badly dented the Federation's image of invincibility.

It was a challenge that could not be ignored. Such spirited resistance by sub-human savages could not go unpunished. The Clan M'Call, the group responsible for this outrage, had to be crushed. Ground into dust as an example of what happened to those who resisted the might of the Federation.

The decision to annihilate the clan had been the easy part. The difficulties lay in its implementation. The M'Calls were led by an individual called Mr Snow – said to be one of the most powerful summoners ever born into the Plainfolk.

The ability to summon invisible forces present in the earth and sky – dynamic energy which flowed through their bodies and was shaped and directed by their minds – was one of three attributes possessed by certain 'gifted Mutes'. Their rarity was something to be thankful for; the ability to summon hurricane-force winds, 'sky-fire' and 'earth-thunder', and to levitate rocks weighing up to half-a-ton was the most spectacular and dangerous form of what had come to be known as 'Mute magic'.

Summoners, seers – those gifted with the power to read the past and foretell the future with the aid of seeing-stones – and wordsmiths – those born with prodigious memories – displayed mental abilities that belied their primitive appearance and life-style. They were highly intelligent, and the powers they possessed – or could call upon – defied all rational explanation.

In due course an answer would be found through the rigorous application of the recognized laws of physics, but in the meantime, faced with something they could not master or understand, the First Family had officially decreed that there was no such thing as Mute magic. Any public utterance to the contrary was a Code One offence – punishable by death, and any overground unit that found itself on the receiving end of Mute magic could not use it as an excuse for failing to achieve its operational objectives.

Draconian measures which had been ruthlessly enforced. And with good reason. Maintaining a high degree of motivation among units exposed to a hostile environment for months at a time in distant work-camps and way-stations was no easy task. And that included the elite troops known as Trail-Blazers who crewed the wagon-trains. Totally dedicated and highly disciplined, the Trail-Blazer Division was a cross between the battle-hardened WW2 generation of US Marines and the Waffen-SS of the same period. But even they had been known to lose their grip when confronted by the awesome powers unleashed by a summoner able to call upon the Seven Rings of Power.

Mr Snow, known as The Storm-Bringer, was one such individual – perhaps the only one of his kind among the Plainfolk. Thanks to the efforts of Steve and Roz Brickman, Mr Snow's protégée, Clearwater, was now in the hands of the Federation. Well, almost. To be more precise, she was in the intensive care ward of the mobile field hospital hitched to the Red River wagon-train now heading south out of Nebraska.

Clearwater, on past form, was rated as potentially even

more dangerous than Mr Snow, but after suffering massive wounding followed by major surgery she was now under continuous sedation and, in the short term, was not judged to be a threat while in transit aboard Red River or to the Federation where the research staff of the Life Institute were eagerly awaiting her arrival.

That left Mr Snow, summoner and wordsmith of the Clan M'Call, and his other young pupil, Cadillac Deville, apprentice wordsmith and seer. Their capture (at planning level it was called 'their removal from the equation') was to be the final phase in OPERATION SQUARE-DANCE, masterminded by Commander-General Ben Karlstrom.

Karlstrom, a close relative of the President-General, was the Operational Director of AMEXICO, the covert operations unit formed to carry out assignments initiated directly from the Oval Office – currently occupied by George Washington Jefferson the 31st.

In late 19th century terms, AMEXICO combined the functions of the American CIA, the Gestapo of Germany's Third Reich and the British SAS. Intelligence-gathering, state security, commando-style forays and 'judicial terminations' in parallel to, but without the knowledge of, the recognized military police and army intelligence units. Its agents – known as *mexicans* – operated within the subterranean nation-state ruled by the First Family and the blue-sky world above, and its existence was the best-kept secret in the Federation.

The nine members of the Supreme Council were officially aware of the general nature of the organization but they did not know the manpower it employed, the resources it could call upon or the scope of its activities. Only Jefferson the 31st and Karlstrom knew the full score. Others could only speculate. AMEXICO was the President-General's private army and the impenetrable cloak of secrecy was essential because it was sometimes called upon to eliminate potentially troublesome members of the First Family.

To some readers, it may seem strange that disaffection of any sort could exist in an enclosed totalitarian state in which every aspect of the environment and its soldier-citizen's lives was controlled with military precision and computerized efficiency from Day One. But such was the case. Any reader with direct experience of the armed forces or the electronics industry will know that 'military precision' and 'computerized efficiency' are mythical states which bear little relation to what either system is able to deliver.

All monolithic power structures staffed by human beings are bound to be less than perfect – especially one reliant on advanced technology – and the Federation was no exception. Nine hundred years of relentless regimentation had failed to produce a First Family version of 'Soviet Man'. People at every level of the command structure still screwed up and systems crashed with unfailing regularity. Depending on your attitude towards what the First Family was trying to achieve this was either a matter of grave concern or grounds for celebration. Proof of the indestructibility of the human spirit; a ray of hope for the future of mankind.

The founding Father, George Washington Jefferson the 1st, had known this basic truth when he laid the foundations on which his vision of the future was to be built. 'Only people fail, not the system', was one of his two Delphic utterances emblazoned on every available wallspace throughout the Federation and echoed daily on the nine public video channels. A phrase of cunning simplicity which had helped to preserve the status quo by deflecting the blame for any shortcomings in the system back onto the individual who raised his voice in protest against the measures taken in its name.

To prevent these isolated cranks spreading their disaffection like a virus through the body politic over which they presided, the First Family had installed a number of fail-safe systems. By the spring of 2991, these included an acoustic surveillance system code-named HYDRA under which their entire underground empire had been wired for sound.

Any location, at any level, could be monitored by keying its coordinates into a command console. It was possible for human operators to listen in to conversations but the sheer logistics made that impractical. Most of the eavesdropping was controlled by COLUMBUS using a given hit-list of suspects and hourly random samplings known as 'sound sweeps'. Ordinary conversations were monitored but not recorded: it was only when a speaker used a word or phrase listed in a 'subversive vocabulary' that the reels started turning. The taped conversations were then subjected to computer analysis, classified into various categories according to the nature of the cconversation and graded in terms of 'arrestability'. It was only when this sifting process had been completed, that the daily residue of hard cases – known as the action list – was displayed on the screens of the operatives at HYDRA Central.

But the system, and its handlers, missed the big one.

Despite HYDRA and the nation-wide network of undercover agents the Family were caught totally off-guard by the protest strike mounted by the crews of the Federation's wagon-trains. Organized and led by their executive officers it had none of the characteristics of a popular uprising led by dissidents, but it was, nevertheless, a rebellion; the first serious challenge to the authority and wisdom of the First Family for over six hundred years.

The protest, which was confined to Trail-Blazers on active duty aboard the trains, was disciplined and un-publicised and the divisions's so-called grievances were conveyed to CINC-TRAIN in a coded message signed by twenty wagon-masters and their executive officers out of the Federation's fleet of twenty-one. Only the name of Red River – Amtrak's flagship – was missing from the roll.

The protesters had two demands. First, official recognition of the existence of Mute magic. If, for reasons of state, this could not be made public then it was to be admitted in secret session to the wagon-train fraternity by representatives of the First Family. Second, the disciplinary charges brought against Commander Bill Hartmann and the executive officers of The Lady – which had arisen from their inability to combat the power of a Plainfolk summoner – were to be dropped. All crew members were to be fully exonerated and returned to active duty in their previous posts without loss of seniority to privileges.

There was no 'or else' but with 95% of its wagon-train force ranged solidly behind the protest, the White House decided to roll with the punch. In a hurriedly-prepared videocast beamed exclusively to the wagon-trains, Jefferson the 31st agreed to the rebel's requests within forty-eight hours of their receipt.

It was an unprecedented concession; the first time an organized protest had not been brutally crushed, but it was also a victory for both sides. The First Family had been wrestling with the problem of Mute magic for the last two hundred and fifty years.

The decision to deny its existence had been taken by a long-dead and buried Supreme Council. At the time, it had not been a problem. It was the Southern Mutes who had then been the enemy. The rumoured existence of summoners had been reported by FINTEL, but on the few occasions where their presence had been suspected, their intercession had failed to halt the advance of the Federation.

The Family had therefore concluded that the alleged power of these individuals did not pose a serious threat to future operations. The danger came from uncontrolled rumours and wild speculation about Mute magic within their own ranks. But instead of ending all ill-informed discussion of the subject, the imposition of sanctions had merely driven it underground.

With the move north into Plainfolk territory the nature of the conflict had changed. The days of easy victories were over and the earlier blanket denial of Mute magic had left the present leaders of the First Family on the hook. This was a chance to slide off it and score a few Brownie points in the process.

Given the latest situation reports from Wyoming and Nebraska, the call for the reinstatement of Commander Hartmann and his crew could not have come at a more opportune moment. Conceding to the rebel's demands provided the First Family with an opportunity to bring its secret OPERATION SQUARE-DANCE to successful conclusion.

That fact would only become apparent with hindsight, but it did not mean that all would be forgiven and forgotten. Hartmann and his executives had been the catalyst which caused a simmering discontent to crystallize into open rebellion. The protest might have been restrained, short-lived and totally justified, but it was a direct challenge to the First Family's inalienable right to rule from the top down.

What made it worse was the fact that the rebellion had been well-organized and *had not been foreseen*. Such appalling laxity on the part of security services could not go unpunished. Sooner or later everyone concerned would be dealt with. No one got the better of the First Family and lived to tell the tale. And among the first to learn that harsh lesson would be the crew of The Lady from Louisiana.

CHAPTER TWO

Commander James Fargo, the wagon-master of Red River, had seen plenty of Mutes at close-quarters during his time on the overground but they had all been dead, dying, or framed in his gun sights. Killing Mutes was what he had been trained to do. He had never once imagined that a day would come when he was required to play host to two live lump-heads. But they were here. Cosseted aboard Red River.

It was a strange feeling. As far as he knew, this was the first time Mutes had ever sullied the interior of a wagon-train with their poisonous presence, and it was a dubious honour he would have preferred to do without. But orders were orders. Even so, he felt he should have been taken into the confidence of his other guests, a seven-man task-force from the White House complete with their own secure lines of communications. From the moment the two Mutes had come aboard, it was clear they were not true lumpheads and – to judge from the flurry of coded signals flowing between the task force and Grand Central – might be something else entirely.

As the top-rated wagon-train in the Federation, Red River had, for many years, been involved in the delivery and collection of a number of individuals whose reason for being on the overground had never been fully explained but who were clearly engaged in some form of covert activity. Since the soldier-citizens of the Federation were members of one vast army whose chain of command led back to the White House, these individuals had to be working for the First Family but, to date, no one had ever discovered the name or the precise function of the unit they belonged to.

Fargo knew it was unwise to enquire further. No one

reached the top spot on the Federation's premier wagon-train without learning that at a very early age. As an exemplary product of the system, Fargo believed that if a man wasn't party to secret information then he had no business prying into it. The First Family told you everything you needed to know when it was time for you to know it.

This unquestioning attitude did not mean that the commander of Red River was a colourless, mindless automaton. Initiative and intelligence were part of the job profile. Fargo's unswerving allegiance to the Federation was comparable to Reinhard Heydrich's total commitment to the genocidal policies of Hitler's Third Reich. And like the latter, he had a distinctive personality and a mind of his own. But any reservations he had about the way the First Family ran things (and they were very few) was something he kept strictly to himself.

The first of his visitors had been flown in following a night pick-up by the White House task-force using Skyhawks supplied by Red River. One of their number was a 17-year-old Junior Medical Officer named on the detachment order as Roz Brickman. Since she had little experience of battle-field injuries, three members of Red River's own surgical team had flown out with her, riding the buddy-frames attached to the fuselages of the five-plane formation.

The badly-wounded Mute had been brought back lashed to the spare berth and had undergone immediate surgery. In the only direct message he had received from CINC-TRAIN, Fargo had been instructed to put the crew and services of Red River at the disposal of the task-force. He had done so. The female Mute – logged aboard as ALPHA-BRAVO – was now in intensive care with the Brickman girl at her bedside. Mitch – Michelle French, Red River's immensely able CMO, who had performed the major part of the surgery rated her chances at no better than 50–50.

Some thirty-six hours after Red River's first unwelcome guest had flown in, the second had arrived under his own steam. Or, to be more precise, on the back of a four-legged animal that Fargo – like the rest of his crew – had been told was extinct.

Code-named YANKEE-ZULU by the secretive task-force, the smooth-boned, fair-haired Mute had made his approach in broad daylight astride a horse, with two similar beasts in tow. Fargo had relayed the video pictures through the train so that his crew could share the experience of seeing these living relics of a bygone age. Since he was also required to take the horses on board, there was little point in trying to keep their presence secret. But as he watched them being led towards the train, Fargo could not help asking himself the inevitable question. If COLUMBUS held the wrong data on horses, what other errors had it made?

Fargo erased the question and its consequent uncertainties from his mind. COLUMBUS had not made a mistake. The First Family, in its wisdom, had instructed it to withhold the information. And there would be a good reason for doing so.

Although unhurt, YANKEE-ZULU was now in the blood-wagon – the fully-equipped field-hospital that was an integral part of each wagon-train. The medical staff was accommodated on the ground floor along with stores and small lab units, The second floor contained an operating theatre, pre- and post-op, IC, x-ray and ultra-sound units and a clinic for treating minor wounds and ailments. The top floor contained three medical wards, designed to be self-contained if the need arose. The task-force, led by someone labelled as WALLIS, DONALD, E, had taken over aft-section, sealing itself off behind the sound-proofed partitions with its special radio equipment. ALPHA-BRAVO, still unconscious after her ordeal on the operating table, was in one of the cubicles of the intensive care unit on the floor below.

Fargo could not help wishing he knew what was being discussed behind those closed doors. He was too disciplined to display his feelings in front of his crew but he was more than a little put out by the thought that after eighteen years service in the field he was still denied knowledge of secret operations of which Red River was an integral part. And – as if to add insult to injury – the three horses he had obligingly taken on board were pissing buckets and dropping large steaming piles of crap all over one of his spit and polished cargo floors.

Steve gazed down at the sleeping figure inside the sterile plastic tent. A breathing tube that reached down into her larynx had been inserted between her pale lips. Her mouth and nose were covered by a clear oxygen mask. There were drip feeds in her arms, drainage tubes from internal organs, and wires linking her to electronic monitoring equipment. Clearwater was a long way from Mr Snow's herbal mash remedies. Another world . . .

Her olive brown skin had taken on a deathly pallor. She had no head wounds but someone had cropped her long dark hair, and they'd done it badly, leaving it looking like a porcupine who'd blundered into a chainsaw. But she still looked beautiful, her head and neck resting on a single pillow, miraculously untouched by the hail of bullets.

Steve, who had kept vigil over her broken, bloodstained body, tried not to think of the splintered bones and ruptured flesh that lay beneath the covers. A body so fragile, a curved frame had been placed over it to support the weight of the top sheet.

He turned to Roz. The sides of their bodies came into contact as they gave each other a supporting hug. 'Is she going to make it, little sister?'

Roz grimaced. 'At the moment, her chances are no more than even. When the surgical team saw the state she was in they were amazed she'd survived for so long. In fact, there were a couple of times they nearly lost her on the table.'

'And all because of a stupid, fucking argument – that *I* provoked.' Steve broke away and raised his hands in despair. 'Why?! Ohh, Roz! If she's crippled for life I'll never forgive myself!'

Roz flashed him a warning glance and touched her ear to remind him that someone might be listening to their conversation. 'Guilt is a recognized symptom of shock,' she said, adopting her best bedside manner. 'After all you came close to getting killed yourself. It was a pilot from Red River who gunned her down. You and I just did what we had to do.'

'Yeah, you're right,' said Steve, cottoning on. He looked down at Clearwater then eyed the screen monitoring her weak heartbeat. 'Would it be all right if I just held her hand for a minute?'

'Yes, but very gently – okay?' Roz gathered up the side of the sterile tent and lifted the sheet. Clearwater's right hand lay palm up outside the metal frame.

Steve knelt down and sandwiched her hand between his own. The flesh was moist, the fingers limp. He pressed his palm against hers and tried to reach into her mind, tried to channel his life force into her body. He'd done the same thing in the deserted renegade camp in a desperate effort to infuse her with the will to live as they waited for Roz and the Red River medics to arrive.

'We've got to save her, Roz.'

'We will. Don't worry. Everything that can be done will be done.' Then, for the benefit of the hidden microphones she added: 'You and I aren't the only people with a vested interest in keeping her alive.'

'No . . .'

Roz smiled. 'And if you think this happened just because you got into an argument with Cadillac then I should take some of the blame. After all, the argument *was* over me.'

'That's true.' Steve laughed for the first time since they'd been reunited. 'You've been nothing but trouble ever since you were born!' He parried her playful punch and looked down at Clearwater's hand in time to see the fingertips twitch then curl slowly upwards against the side of his hand. 'Roz! See that?!'

'Yes. Take a look at the screen.'

The weak green trace of Clearwater's heartbeat had

changed. Not dramatically, but every fourth pulse was a little deeper, a little stronger than the others.

Steve's spirits soared. 'D'you think she knows I'm here?!'

Roz caressed the back of his head. 'Yes, I'm sure she does.' *But not because you are holding her hand. She knows because I am within her as I am within you . . .*

In the sealed ward above the intensive care unit, Don Wallis motioned Steve and Roz to take the facing seats in the middle of the table where they were sandwiched between the six-man team from AMEXICO. Wallis, the team leader, sat at the head of the table on Steve's right. Jake Nevill, his Number Two, was at the other end.

It was Nevill who had flown out with Roz zipped onto the buddy-frame of his Skyhawk. While she and the Red River medics were busy with Clearwater, he and Steve had given each other the buzz. Satisfied he was talking to the right man, Nevill told Steve he had been assigned the temporary code-name of YANKEE-ZULU while on board the wagon-train: his AMEXICO code-name was never to be disclosed to anyone outside the organization. The task-force of mexicans was disguised as a special detachment from the White House, complete with fake ID-cards, name-tags and the distinctive blue and white badge on the shoulders of their camouflaged fatigues.

It was, explained Nevill, standard procedure when operating alongside regular army units.

As a JMO, Roz was wearing hospital whites with her name tag, surmounted by miniature lieutenant's rank stripes, tacked onto a Velcro patch above her right breast pocket.

Steve, after a long, hot shower and a medical examination designed to make sure he had not contracted some unspeakable overground infection, had been given a set of Trail-Blazer fatigues with no name-tag or badges. Since he still had his long ragged hair, rat-tail plaits and

34

multi-coloured skin markings, the effect was bizarre. The task-force's bewildered reaction on first seeing him in uniform reminded Steve of his painful encounter with Lt. Harmer at the Pueblo way-station. This time however, no one tried to pulverize his liver with the butt end of a rifle.

How much does Roz know about all this? he wondered. In the few brief moments they had spent together since boarding Red River he had been so concerned about Clearwater, he hadn't even asked Roz how she came to be on the wagon-train. He had just been thankful she'd been close at hand when he needed her. It was probably wiser to say nothing at this stage. Her silent reminder that Clearwater's cubicle might be bugged had jerked him back to the reality of the Federation. The fear that whatever you said might be recorded and used in evidence against you.

Maybe, when the time was right, she would come through on their private line. She was the expert. Steve, who had wilfully neglected his telepathic gifts, was still restricted to the channel used for broadcasting May-Day messages.

Wallis aligned his electronic memo-pad with the edge of the table, cleared his throat and began: 'Steve, ahh – this first session is essentially a debriefing. You've met Jake. I don't think we need formal introductions. The names are on the labels.'

Steve said hello to George Hannah and Cal Parsons who sat across the table on either side of Roz, and to Daryl Coates and Tom Watkins who sat on his left and right respectively.

'They're all members of the organization, and in case you feel a little tongue-tied, Roz has been made an honorary member.'

Steve eyed Roz then looked blankly at Wallis.

'It means she doesn't have a code-name or a call-sign,' said Wallis. He fingered his left earlobe in a seemingly absent-minded gesture.

'Got it . . .' Steve smiled at Roz. 'I had no idea.'

'Well, you know what I'm like – always *dying* to know what you're up to.' Roz's face bore just the merest hint of a smile but Steve knew that inwardly she was savouring the exquisite irony of the situation.

'Hey! Come on, you two – snap out of it!' exclaimed Nevill.

Steve ignored him and turned to Wallis. 'You were saying?'

'I've been asked to congratulate you both,' said Wallis. 'That message comes jointly from the Operational Director and the Oval Office. Initially there was some concern that the goods had been damaged in transit but ALPHA-BRAVO's disablement probably makes the task of shipping her back to Grand Central a lot easier. As Roz has probably told you, it's early days yet, but given the level of medical support available here and down the line, I've been assured that if our target survives the next two weeks, she has every chance of making a full recovery.'

'Glad to hear my efforts weren't totally wasted,' said Steve.

'If she needs any other specialists, they can fly out and treat her on the return trip.'

Steve's eyes met Roz's briefly. With six people watching them they had to tread carefully. 'Return trip . . .?'

'Yes,' said Wallis 'We were planning to airlift her into the Federation but Red River's CMO has advised against it. And I agree. We made that night pick-up because we were in a life-or-death situation but it would be crazy to risk losing such a valuable asset between here and Grand Central. This is the safest way for her to travel. So as soon as we know what your plans are, we're going to run for home.'

Steve weighed up the other members of the task-force then came back to Wallis shaking his head. 'No. Sorry. You're going to have to call Mother and tell him you can't do that.'

'Oh? Why?'

'Because I need Red River to stay here with Clearwater on board. She's the bait that will lure the other two into the net.'

Wallis pursed his lips. 'You mean Cadillac and Mr Snow . . .'

'Yes.' Steve looked at Roz, but apart from listening with interest, like everyone else, she did not respond.

'You had Cadillac – knocked out cold – and you let him go,' This was Nevill again.

'I let him go because he's the one who will bring Mr Snow to us,' said Steve patiently. 'I need a month to get things organized. Six weeks at the outside.'

'Six weeks?!' cried Nevill.

'That's not very long when you consider it's taken me a year to put this together.'

'Christo! Just to kidnap three lumpheads? If someone had given me the job I'd have winkled 'em out inside forty-eight hours.'

'With an airborne snatch-squad?'

'Yeah. They'd be back in Grand Central before they knew what hit 'em.'

Steve looked impressed. 'That certainly would have been a remarkable feat of logistics. One of the trio was in Wyoming, the others were in two separate locations in Ne-Issan – held by people opposed to our friends who run the local network.'

'Quite,' said Wallace hurriedly. He was the only person at the table who knew what Steve was alluding too and it was a subject he wanted to put a cap on. Attempting to be diplomatic he added: 'I don't think you've fully appreciated who it is we're dealing with, Jake.'

'Exactly,' said Steve, opting for a head-on collision instead of conciliation. 'Have you ever come up against a summoner? Actually *seen* them channelling earth magic through their bodies?'

'No, but –'

Steve cut across Nevill's reply and addressed the other mexicans. 'Have any of you?'

They all shook their heads.

'Well, I have. I've been on the receiving end when I was on board The Lady from Louisiana in 2989 –'

'I think we've all read the report on that one,' said Wallis, trying to keep his team's end up.

'But I've also *seen* them make it happen. Seen 'em make rocks fly, blow away half a hillside, take control of someone's mind.'

Steve described the death of Lord Yama-Shita. How Clearwater had made him drive his sword repeatedly through his body. And each time, the blade had sunk in right up to the blood-drenched hilt. Eight killing strokes, one for each of the Mutes he had condemned to death on the giant iron-bound paddle of his wheel-boat.

Turning to Nevill, he said: 'Mr Snow's other name is the Storm-Bringer. That's not just a fancy title. It means precisely what it says. He'd have blown your snatch-squad right out of the sky.'

'But you, of course, know how to handle him,' said Nevill.

Sarcastic sonofabitch . . . Steve had run up against guys like Nevill before. There were some people who took an instant dislike to him and no amount of sweet talk could bring them round. They just did not respond to treatment. The important thing was not to get mad. 'Yes,' he replied. 'With Roz's help I think I can.'

Wallis made another attempt to lower the temperature. 'Roz – what shape will ALPHA-BRAVO be in six weeks from now?'

'Clearwater? She'll still be flat on her back. All we've done so far is stabilize her condition. She needs several more ops and at least four months convalescence before she's on her feet – assuming there are no complications.'

'Okay,' said Wallis. 'Let's move on. Steve, why don't you beging by telling us what happened from the time you took off from Long Point.'

Steve recoiled. 'Wow . . . you mean everything?'

'Yes.'

'How long have we got?'

'As long as it takes.'

'Okay, uhh, before I start – do you happen to know if Kelso and Jodi got home in one piece?'

'Jodi did,' said Wallis. 'Someone found the explosive charge strapped to her chest and managed to pull the detonator out a split-second before it was triggered. It was the other that did the damage.'

Steve nodded soberly. 'The transmitter was hidden under Kelso along with the Px.'

'How did you know?' asked Nevill. 'D'you put it there?'

'No. It was a couple of days before I discovered the explosives were missing. That was when Cadillac told me what they'd done. And later, we heard a wagon-train had been blown apart.'

'Yeah,' said Nevill. 'The Lady from Louisiana. Your ex-crew-mates. Nice gesture, Brickman.'

Angered by this jibe, Steve's self-control snapped. 'You wanna know something? I'm getting pretty sick of your smart-assed remarks and your fucking innuendoes! If you've got some beef you wanna get off your chest, come right out with it!'

Nevill's jaw dropped.

'Whoa! Hold it!' said Wallis. 'I think we're getting a little ahead of ourselves. I'm sure Jake didn't intend to accuse –'

'Yeah? Well, he can take his accusations and shove them right up his ass! *I* was the one who was out there risking my neck for the Federation. What the fuck does *he* know about anything? Desk-bound pratt!'

Nevill bounced back, eyes blazing. 'You can spare us the war-torn hero routine. Not one of these guys around this table has less than five overground assignments on his slate. That's why we're here. And as for what I know about anything, Brickman, let me tell you this. I know *I'm* a major and you're a jumped-up ensign whose lieutenant's tabs are still hanging out to dry.' The mexican tapped his chest. 'I earned my promotion in the *field*, not filling gravy-boats on the fucking mess deck. So I'll say what I like, when I like. And when you

39

next address me, *lieutenant*, you'll do so with the respect you have been trained to show a senior officer!'

'Yes, sir, *major* . . .'

'And no dumb insolence either! I saw that look!'

Wallis made a placatory gesture. 'Okay, that's enough. If we're pulling rank, *I'm* the senior officer here. And I'd like to remind you all that this organization, unlike many regular army units, places a premium on intelligence and a spirit of enquiry. A readiness to challenge assumptions instead of the usual knee-jerk responses required from junior ranks. It is mental discipline we look for, not the kind instilled on the parade-ground and our executive body has, traditionally, always encouraged the free and frank exchange of views –'

'Fuck tradition!' Nevill stabbed a finger at Steve. 'He may be billed as a star turn but he's still a fucking wet-back and no wet-back is going to shit-talk me!'

Wallis coughed. 'Okay, Jake, you've made your point.' He made eye contact with Steve. 'Would you like to proceed?'

Steve gave them the full story. With questions and answers, it took over four hours, split into two sessions with a meal break in between. Steve took a rain check on the food, preferring to spend the allotted time in the intensive care ward with Clearwater. It was no great hardship. The trays sent up from the mess-deck of the adjoining wagon contained standard Federation fare, tasteless, processed, vitaminized pap. After the food in Ne-Issan and the strong-flavoured fish and meat served up by the Plainfolk, Steve found it quite uneatable.

Afterwards, when Steve concluded his account, Wallis said: 'Okay, so Cadillac is on his way home. Assuming you're still on the case, what's your next move?'

'I've got to catch up with him. Tell him what's happened.'

Nevill stuck his oar in again. 'Isn't he going to be a little unhappy when he hears you put his pet beaver on a wagon-train?'

Steve swallowed his irritation. 'Unhappy? He's gonna

40

be bouncing off the walls. But that's his problem. He's lucky she's still alive. Don't worry. I'll talk him round.'

How're you going to do that?' asked Wallis. 'If Clearwater's on board Red River it's because you arranged to put her there. How are you going to get Cadillac to trust you when you're obviously working for us?'

'Simple,' said Steve. 'I'll tell him the truth. I didn't contact the wagon-train. I contacted Roz.'

Wallis waved a finger at Steve and his kin-sister. 'Do the M'Calls know about the link-up between you two?'

'No. Only Cadillac and Clearwater. Clearwater was watching from the shore when the planes fire-bombed the wheel-boat. Cadillac was below decks with me so he saw nothing. By the time we surfaced the planes had gone but eventually I had to come up with some kind of an explanation. The only way to remove any suspicion that I was still working for the Federation was by telling them about the link between Roz and myself.

'The fact that the Federation had sent the planes to bomb the wheel-boat meant that the First Family thought I was still working for them. Which, of course, led Cadillac to suspect Roz's motives. So in order to persuade him that we could both be trusted, I told him I'd convinced Roz – who had complete faith in me – that I was still one hundred per cent loyal. Which was why you'd sent the planes to help us escape.'

'Did he buy it?' asked Wallis.

'Yes, in his usual half-assed way. We got away from the japs, I saved his life but – you know what it's like –' Steve gave Nevill a sideways glance, '– he's one of these guys who is never satisfied. He's brave, highly intelligent, possesses the most amazing mental capabilities, but he just hasn't got his shit together.'

'So what story are you going to lay on him?'

'He already knows that Roz came through to tell me she was on board Red River. I'll tell him the shock of seeing them both gunned down triggered another contact between Roz and myself. She knew immediately what had happened and where we were, so I waited until she

41

confirmed that help was on the way then pulled out as the first plane dropped a string of parachute flares.

'And I'll say that in a subsequent contact, Roz told me that Clearwater was out of danger. Cadillac will be suspicious but what the hell can he do? He has to go along with it because the only way he can keep tabs on what's happening to her is through me and Roz. And I will continue to claim that I didn't arrange anything through official channels. I was never here. How does it sound?'

The six-man task force exchanged thoughtful glances. Steve found the silence of the middle four a little unnerving. The guys who listened but didn't say anything were the ones you had to watch out for. More often than not, it was they who were really running the show.

Nevill shook his head dismissively. 'Too clever by half.'

'Jake, ease up will you? Give the guy a break.' Wallis came back to Steve. 'It sounds good but you may have outwitted yourself. Roz couldn't have sneaked Clearwater on board Red River by herself. It could only have been with our full knowledge and cooperation. And the reason Clearwater's still with us is because Red River's surgical team spent nearly twelve hours putting the bits back together.'

'I'm not denying that.'

Wallis threw his hands in the air. 'So we're back where we started. If Roz is working with us, and *you're* working with Roz – why should these Mutes trust you?'

'It's simple,' said Steve.

'I wish you'd stopped saying that,' snapped Nevill. 'You're switching sides so fast I've lost track of who's getting shafted!'

Steve looked at his kin-sister then said: 'Roz is only *pretending* to work for you.' Their eyes met again. The message she had beamed into his mind was so astonishing, none of the others would realise he was telling the truth. He glanced round the table and tried not to smile at his audacity.

'That's what I told Cadillac when he challenged me about her role in the strike on the wheel-boat. And when I discovered she was on Red River, it reinforced my claim that she was a secret ally who, having gained Mother's confidence, had persuaded him to put her on board the wagon-train because she intended to go over the side and join up with me at the very first opportunity.'

Steve's gaze returned once more to his kin-sister. 'A claim that Clearwater confirmed because Roz had already got inside her head and was doing a number on her.'

Wallis' eyes narrowed. In briefing him, Karlstrom had never even suggested such a bizarre possibility. But in emphasizing the need to keep her safe and secure at all times, he had warned him to be braced for the unexpected. Which was why the task-force had been sticking to her like shit to a blanket.

'Go on . . .'

'The next step is to convince Cadillac and Mr Snow that if we can find a way of getting aboard Red River – maybe with the help of Malone's renegades – then we can rescue both Roz *and* Clearwater. And perhaps even capture the train.'

Tom Watkins, the mex on Steve's right broke his silence with a dry laugh. 'D'you really think they'd suck on that?'

'If the plan Malone put forward was good enough, yes.'

Wallis looked perplexed. 'But in the time-frame you're talking about, Roz has said that ALPHA-BRAVO will still be too ill to be moved.'

'I know that, and you know that,' said Steve. 'But they don't. And I'm not going to tell them.'

'Let's run through this again.' Wallis placed his hands together in a prayer-like gesture in front of his mouth and collected his thoughts. 'You're suggesting we let your two remaining targets and a group of Mutes gain access to the wagon-train then we spring some kind of trap.'

'Right . . .'

'And once Cadillac and Mr Snow have been captured,

and the other lumps have been neutralized, we make it look as if the attack has succeeded. All right so far?' enquired Wallis.

'Perfect,' said Steve.

'At which point the rest of the clan will rush the wagon-train to get their share of the pickings and –'

'Get it right in the kisser,' said Nevill.

Wallis contained his annoyance at being interrupted. 'It's going to require meticulous planning. I mean, we want these lumps on the train but we don't want them running wild . . .'

'That's why we need time,' said Steve. '(a) to set it up and (b) for Malone to sell the idea to Cadillac.'

'Why can't you do that?' asked Nevill.

'Because of these personality problems I mentioned. He doesn't wholly trust me. But then, neither do you, major.'

The challenge brought a smile to Nevill's face. 'I wouldn't go as far as to say that. I've read up on what you did at the Heron Pool and I've got to hand it to you. That was a first class operation. And don't think I'm put off by that paint-job you're wearing. I've been down to the dye-works a couple of times myself. But I'm always a little wary about mexicans who get so deep into their covers they end up bouncing beaver.'

Steve controlled his anger. 'Go downstairs and take a look at her, major. Take a long, hard look then come and tell me, hand on your heart how – if you didn't know already – you could tell she was a Mute.'

Nevill laughed. 'By the skin colours, of course.'

Steve pushed his left sleeve halfway up towards his elbow and displayed his hand and arm. 'They're dyes, major. Just like these. Underneath, her skin is exactly the same as yours and mine. All it takes to make the switch is a few handfuls of pink leaves, crushed and dipped in water. Put her under a shower with someone like Roz and you wouldn't be able to tell one from the other.'

'It doesn't matter what she looks like on the outside. On the inside, she's still a Mute.'

Steve didn't let up. 'But doesn't it strike you as strange that a race that's officially classified as sub-human can produce creatures that walk, talk, look and think like real people?'

Wallis looked worried. 'Steve – I don't think this has any relevance to –'

'With respect, sir, I think it's extremely relevant. Major Nevill has questioned my reliability and, for good measure, has thrown out a thinly-veiled accusation of misconduct. My defence to that hinges around the status of Mutes and their place in the scheme of things. They're the enemy. They oppose everything the Federation stands for. There's no dispute about that –'

'Glad to hear it,' muttered Wallis.

'But the presence of Mutes like Cadillac and Clearwater – who far from being sub-human, are actually closer to being super-human – brings into question everything the First Family has taught us about Mutes. The Plainfolk have an answer to that question. They claim that before the Holocaust, Mutes and Trackers were members of the same society. The same race. Humankind.'

Wallis intervened, his voice edged with anger. 'That's enough, Steve! These are very dangerous waters you're getting into.'

'See what I mean about this guy?' said Nevill. 'He tried to peddle the same muddled-headed shit to the Board of Assessors.' He faced Steve with a triumphant leer. 'What did she do to you, lieutenant – suck your brains out through your dick?'

Steve was gripped by a sudden desire to throw himself across the table at Nevill and punch the mex's teeth down his throat but Roz came into his head and willed him to stay calm. 'You're right, major,' he said amiably. 'I guess I asked for that. When you been out on your own for as long as I have, playing both sides of the track, it's sometimes hard to know where the edges are.'

'We're aware of the problem,' said Wallis. 'That's

45

why this temporary lapse of judgement will not go on the record. As for you, Jake, we might be able to get through this a lot quicker and more constructively if you adopted a less aggressive attitude. We are *not* a Board of Assessors, and Steve is not on trial. The eight of us are all on the same team.'

Nevill accepted this with a nod but he was not a happy man.

'Okay, let's get this meeting back on the rails. Steve, you were saying that Cadillac did not entirely trust you . . .'

'Call it a lurking suspicion. His feelings are confounded by the fact that I've got him out of several tight corners. But like you said, he's not an idiot. We couldn't have escaped from Ne-Issan without help from the outside and there came a point where I could no longer conceal that fact. So I came clean – admitted I was an undercover agent, sent out to capture the three of them. And I told him I'd been forced to accept the assignment because the Federation had threatened to kill Roz if I refused.'

'And did he believe you?' asked Wallis.

Steve shrugged. 'He went along with it. It was the only way he could get out of Ne-Issan. I think he finally bought the story when we knocked out Side-Winder and the mex pilots at Long Point and grabbed the airplanes. Things got better from there on in un-'

'Until he and that Mute bitch downstairs blew four of our aircraft out of the sky and planted explosives on Kelso and Kazan!' Nevill's eyes made it clear what he thought of Steve's contribution to the war effort.

Steve took a deep breath before replying. 'I've already been through this. I didn't *know* Kelso and Jodi were primed to explode. They didn't even know themselves! The Clan M'Call got badly burned by The Lady. Cadillac and Clearwater grabbed the opportunity to even the score. But it was more than that. They were testing me. They wanted to see which way I'd jump when they started killing my own kind.

'I objected – violently – but only on the grounds that the strike against The Lady wasn't necessary. Any stronger reaction on my part would have totally destroyed my cover. But I couldn't have stopped Clearwater from using her magic on those Skyhawks even if I'd wanted to.' He turned to Nevill. 'When you acquire some first-hand experience of summoners, you'll understand why. At one point in the battle at the Heron Pool, there were fifty to sixty samurai trying to cut her down. The guys with swords never got within striking distance, and the arrows just bounced off this wall of light she'd wrapped around herself.'

Nevill's mouth twisted into a tight-lipped grin. 'And after all that, some guy in a Skyhawk heading for home, clears the drum on a bunch of breakers – and here she is. Few dozen well-placed rounds. That's all it took.'

'A fluke. A million to one chance that paid off because her mind was engaged elsewhere,' said Steve. 'But don't worry, I know what you're getting at.' His voice hardened. 'You still think these three could have been lifted without all this hassle. Isn't that right, major?'

Nevill caught Wallis' warning glance and held up his hands. 'Just exercising my traditional right to engage in a free and frank exchange of views . . .'

'Jake doesn't like sensitives,' explained Wallis.

Steve smiled. 'I'm not too happy about being one myself.'

'I've always held there's nothing in this world that a bullet won't cure.'

It was clear from Wallis' expression that this was an old bone of contention. 'Yes, well, you keep saying that Jake, but we both know that the committee which is presently studying the tactical use of psionics takes an entirely different view.'

'They would, wouldn't they?' Nevill saw Wallis' brow darken. He turned to Steve. 'So tell us – after the hit on the wagon-train, did relations between you and Cadillac get any better . . .?'

'Yes. When we started our westward run he had other

47

things to think about. By this time he was into his 'I'm the leader of The Chosen routine'. I went along with it. Everything was fine until we ran into Malone, and Cadillac ran out of *sake* then shortly after that I got this flash from Roz.

'Mother had put her on board Red River and had sent her north to help neutralize Clearwater. By sending the train into Nebraska and having it move parallel to our line of advance Mother hoped Roz would be able to help keep my mind clear. To prevent Clearwater from doing to me what she'd done to Kelso and Jodi.'

Nevill laughed drily. 'That's why you were strip-searched before we let you up the ramp.'

'Wise move. Anyway, maybe it was a bad mistake, but I told Cadillac that Roz had made contact and that she was on Red River. And because of the story I'd fed him before about being pressurized into this job by threats to her life I *had* to come out with this idea of trying to rescue her. It would have seemed odd if I'd passed up a once-in-a-lifetime opportunity without making a positive response. I didn't have any clear idea how it could be done, it was all off the top of my head. But I suggested that if the M'Calls got together with Malone's renegades – maybe in some kind of disguise – we might just be able to pull it off.'

'And how did Cadillac react?'

'He said that attacking the train was exactly what the Federation wanted us to do. That was why they'd put Roz on board. She was the bait that would draw me in if I had truly thrown my lot in with the Mutes. And in the next breath he all but accused me of being prepared to sell his people down the river in order to save her skin.

'As I said earlier, the M'Calls had already taken heavy losses in their attack on the Lady. Cadillac wasn't going to repeat that mistake by leading them into a trap. On the other hand, if I was genuine, a true and loyal friend of the Plainfolk, he still wasn't prepared to let his clanfolk be killed trying to rescue my kin-sister. It was a no-win

48

situation.' Steve shrugged. 'From then on it went down-hill, and as he was trying to put a knife in me, we were hit by the Skyhawk.'

'So what the hell are we doing talking about setting up a dummy take-over of Red River?' demanded Nevill. His eyes searched out the other members of the task force then fixed on Steve. 'If this piece of lump-shit wasn't prepared to involve his clan in an attack on the wagon-train then, why in the name of the Family is he going to want to do it now?!'

Steve tried to appear patient and reasonable. 'Because the situation has changed. Clearwater is *on the train!*'

Nevill grinned. 'Boy – I wish I could be there when you break the news. I'd love to see you wriggle out of that one.'

'I'll manage . . .'

'What will you say to him?' enquired Wallis.

'I'll tell him he was right. My idea of trying to spring Roz from Red River was absolutely crazy. And the same goes for Clearwater. There is no way anyone can get on board that wagon-train and rescue her. He just has to be grateful she's alive and accept that she is now a prisoner of the Federation.'

'And what's his reaction likely to be?' asked Wallis.

Steve smiled. 'I know this guy like the back of my hand. If I say she can't be rescued, he's gonna want to prove me wrong. And he'll buy the idea of attacking the train because it won't come from me but from *Malone*. He's the guy who has to sell it to him. And he has to do it cleverly, so that Cadillac thinks it's all his own work.'

Wallis mulled over the idea. 'Sounds as if it might fly. Anyone spot any holes?'

'Yeah,' said Hannah, the mex sitting between Roz and Nevill on the other side of the table. 'I believe our friend here has got these lumps figured but we can't set up an attack on Red River without the approval from the man at the top. Okay, let's say we get that –'

Nevill interrupted again. 'Can't see CINC-TRAIN

agreeing to put Red River on the line – and Fargo ain't gonna be too happy either.'

'If Mother and the P-G give the go-ahead, CINC-TRAIN and Fargo won't have any choice in the matter,' said Wallis with a sudden hint of steel in his voice. 'Carry on, Ray. Assume we've got the green light . . .'

Hannah resumed: 'Okay. Let's say we then come up with a workable plan. One which has a reasonable chance of success from the Mute's point of view, but which we can turn around when the time comes to spring the trap. The question is – how can we be sure that the lumps will (a) swallow it and (b) follow it?'

'That's where I come in,' said Steve. 'The moment I get wind that Cadillac is serious about rescuing Clearwater, I'm going to oppose the whole idea. That will only make him more determined to go through with it. But to play my part properly, I will have to know exactly what the plan is.'

'Point taken,' said Wallis. 'If we manage to get this thing off the ground Malone will be in touch.'

Steve shook his head. 'Too risky. He and I have got to stay at arm's length. Malone must take his cue from Cadillac and appear to mistrust me. Nothing heavy – otherwise his boys will wonder why he hasn't put a bullet through my throat. He just needs to display a reluctance to let me in on what they're planning. It'll encourage Cadillac and Mr Snow to believe he is totally genuine.'

'So how do we reach you?' asked Wallis.

'Through Roz.'

Nit-picker Nevill came off the sidelines. 'What's wrong with the normal channels of communication?'

'You mean a radio-knife? Too risky,' said Steve. 'I was caught out once before. If we're going to nail this bunch I have to win their absolute trust. I'm well on the way to doing that. Cadillac is a separate problem. A personality clash. We're rivals. Anything I can do, he wants to do better. I don't have this trouble with Mr Snow. He's razor-sharp and he's shrewd but I've managed to establish what you might call a "working relationship". He likes me – and that's another reason why Cadillac has this down on me. He's jealous.'

'How is Mr Snow going to react to the news that you've lost Clearwater?' asked Parsons. He was the mex sitting between Roz and Wallis.

'Well, he's bound to look upon it as a set-back, but it's not a major disaster. Thanks to Roz, I will at least be able to tell him that she's alive and in good hands.'

'But will he support Cadillac's plan to go for Red River?'

'He has to. The clan won't attack a wagon-train if he isn't there to lead them.'

Parsons insisted. 'Yes, but how do you know he *will*?'

'Because he's old. He's near the end of the line, with maybe only a couple of big shots left in the locker. Summoners die a little every time they call up the power. These guys don't get a free ride. Each time they pull down the really heavy shit, their own lives are on the line. I'm not kidding. I've seen it. Their eyes are dead, their bodies are empty shells. It takes time to recharge the batteries.

'The M'Calls will make an all-out effort to rescue Clearwater because she's Mr Snow's successor. Without a summoner, they can't hold onto their position as the paramount clan of the She-Kargo bloodline. They're finished. That's why he will lead them against Red River.' Steve smiled. 'And as honorary member of the Plainfolk, I'll be right alongside him.'

'Haven't you overlooked something?' said Nevill, clearly underwhelmed by Steve's assurances. 'Something you told us a while back? About your friend Mr Snow – the Storm-Bringer? Isn't that the name the Mutes give to someone who holds seven of the nine so-called Rings of Power?'

'Yes . . .'

'Terrific. This is the guy, who according to you, could have blown me out of the sky. And you're suggesting we just let him loose inside Red River. You must be out of your fuckin' mind!"

'Red River won't be in any danger.' His kin-sister's mouth was closed but Steve could her her other voice whispering to him. 'Roz is not just a telepath. She has the power to completely disorientate Mr Snow's mind – put it into neutral gear, if you like – so that he can't use it to channel the power he draws from the earth and sky.'

'Oh, yeah?' scoffed Nevill. 'Since when?'

'Ask her,' said Steve.

Wallis, anxious to take the heat out of the situation, adopted a conciliatory tone. 'If this was true, it could be a very interesting development. Is there, ahh – any way you could validate the claim your kin-brother has just made?'

Roz looked a little nervous. 'You mean . . . now?'

'Well, yes. I realize we're not under threat from a summoner, but if you could give us some tangible demonstration of the, ahh – mental powers you would use on such an occasion it –'

'– would be very helpful,' said Steve.

Nevill laughed. 'For crissakes, Dan! You don't really believe this bullshit, do you?'

'Jake – just shut your mouth, okay?' Wallis nodded to Roz. 'Is this how you want to do it? With us sitting around the table?'

'Yes, that's fine.' Roz placed her hands on the table, shut her eyes and breathed deeply. 'Move your chairs as close in as you can.'

'Do we have to shut our eyes too?' asked Wallis.

'No,' said Roz. 'I want you to enjoy the view.'

And with that, the room dissolved around them. Steve felt a stiff breeze on his face. Looking up, he saw a clear blue sky above his head, stretching away to an incredibly distant horizon rimmed with clouds. They were sitting around the table in the open air! It was an hallucination, of course. But one they all shared, and the detail was absolutely amazing. So real! It was fantastic!

Roz looked incredibly tranquil, in marked contrast to the task-force who sat paralysed with terror. Looking down, Steve saw why. This hallucination was not only fantastic, it was absolutely horrific. He and the other people seated round the table were perched on top of a narrow pinnacle of weathered rock at least a thousand feet above the plain below. The flat top of the rock was just large enough to hold the table and the tubular metal chairs. The slightest backward movement by anyone would cause them to topple over the edge!

Oh, shit . . . Steve sneaked a quick glance down at the terrifying drop then decided this was one demonstration he could have done without. He had no fear of heights when flying but being perched precariously on the edge of a sheer drop made him feel quite sick. This isn't happening, he told himself. I'm sitting in a hospital ward on the top deck of a wagon train. But his mind told him otherwise. The sky, the breeze, the pinnacle of red rock was *real*. And so was the giddying force that was drawing him like a magnet towards the plain below!

Mastering the impulse to throw himself into the void, Steve slid his hands carefully across the table. His first idea was to secure himself by grabbing hold of Roz's wrists but as his right hand brushed across her left hand he received a violent electric shock which threw his arm in the air. Fortunately the jolt twisted him sideways and not backwards. He managed to get his left hand over the far edge. There wasn't a lot of room because everyone around the table had had the same idea.

Don't panic, Brickman. Nothing's going to happen to you. Your little sister is just showing this bunch of assholes what she can do . . .

Steve heard a strangled cry from Nevill's end of the table. Looking between the heads and over the out-stretched arms of his companions, he saw the reason for Nevill's distress. The pinnacle of rock had two points. Nevill's chair was poised on top of the second, smaller peak, about six feet away from the table. The top was just wide enough to hold the base of the chair. Nevill sat there, rigid with terror, clutching the seat, with his feet hanging in the air. Just looking at him made Steve even worse than before.

He closed his eyes and tried to contact his kin-sister.

Okay, Roz, you've made your point. Now get us out of this nightmare . . .

'Hey, guys! Please! Help me!' Nevill's gruff, macho delivery had dissolved into a strangled bleat.

Are you kidding? One false move and we'll all be over the fucking edge!

Nevill's voice became a shrill squawk. 'Aaghh! AAghh' AAGHH!'

Steve forced himself to look in his direction. The top of the second rock needle had started to crumble. Nevill's chair was tilting over backwards. The mex didn't dare lean forward for fear of overbalancing in the other direction. He was frozen to the chair, eyes bulging, his open mouth twitching grotesquely in horrified anticipation—

Steve glimpsed the rubber sole of Nevill's boots rise into the air then shut his eyes as the chair went over, pitching the mex into the void. The sound of Nevill's scream made his blood run cold—

There was a heavy thump and a crash of metal. The breeze which had been buffeting Steve's face ceased abruptly. He opened his eyes and saw Roz looking at him. The table was back in the hospital ward but those seated around her could not quite believe it. They looked at each other, stunned, speechless, then all eyes went to Nevill's end of the table. His chair lay on the floor; Nevill was sprawled on his back beside it. Ray Hannah and Daryl Coates, the mex on Steve's left, righted his chair and helped him to his feet.

Nevill was shaking uncontrollably and there was a spreading dark patch around the crotch of his fatigues where he had fouled himself. He gripped the table to steady himself as Hannah and Coates eased him back into the chair. 'Christo! I had the most terrible –' He broke off as he saw their tense faces. 'Wh-what happened?!'

'Good question . . .' To judge by Wallis' total lack of colour, he'd had a bad trip – like everyone else. He eyed Roz nervously, and when he spoke, his voice wavered. 'Thank you. Yes . . . that was, uhh . . . most instructive.

I had no, uhh –' He cleared his throat and in doing so, forced his voice up half an octave. 'Why don't the two of you check on how your patient is doing, while we, uhh . . .?'

'Of course,' said Roz.

The task force watched in total silence as Steve followed her out. Hannah shut the door behind them.

As they went down the stairs, there were a million questions buzzing around in Steve's head. It had been a shattering experience. His legs were like jelly but he tried to sound casual. 'That was quite a stunt you pulled back there. I'm impressed.'

Roz, two steps below him, glanced back and smiled. 'This is just the beginning.'

The smile was the smile he had always known. but the look in her eyes belonged to a stranger. And there was something else. He had done all the talking while she listened, but for most of the time he had been nothing more than a mouth-piece. Roz had put the words into his head.

There are forces at work here I don't understand, thought Steve. And for the first time in his life he felt frightened of his kin sister . . .

CHAPTER THREE

Cadillac stirred as the effect of the sleeping-pills began to wear off. Griff, the breaker who had been guarding the smooth-boned Mute, stood up as Malone approached. 'Another five or ten minutes and he should be on his feet.'

'Good. Get saddled up. I want to make the most of this moonlight.'

'If it's okay with you, I'd prefer to walk and just use it to carry my gear.'

'I don't give a lump's ass for what you prefer,' snarled Malone. 'You'll get on that fuckin' horse and learn to ride like the rest of us!'

'Wilco!' Griff stepped back out of range of Malone's fists and feet then ran towards the line of tethered horses they'd inherited from a strange trio of travelling Mutes. These three, who had come out of the east, didn't act like your normal run-of-the-mill lump-head. In fact, to judge by the amount of time Malone had spent talking to them before the air strike, they were something extra-special.

Griff's curiosity about the matter ended there. Malone was one tough *hombre*, and if, for some reason, he'd decided to cosy up to a bunch of Mutes then that was strictly his business. The guy knew what he was doing and anyone who poked his nose where it wasn't wanted got a short, sharp lesson he never forgot. Any breaker foolish enough to forget the first lesson, didn't survive the second.

Like most breakers, Griff didn't like Mutes but he'd learned to live alongside them. And provided you didn't kill 'em. they left you pretty much alone. The clans preferred you to stay off their turf but if you went on through their boundary markers and were challenged by a posse of warriors you could usually buy 'em off by giving them a few bits of junk to hang on themselves. And if you handed over any crossbow bolts you'd found – because they did sometimes miss when out hunting – then you really made their day.

The bolts, like the crossbows that fired them, were highly-prized items made by a bunch of ginks over in the east. Mutes even traded their own people to get hold of them, so a handful of free bolts was a big bonus. They'd start laughing and leaping around, shouting and crowing. But in amongst all the jibber-jabbering, they used *real* words, strung together – and which made *sense*.

That had been his biggest surprise on encountering Mutes during his first tour of duty as a service engineer in a Kansas work camp. And ever since becoming a breaker – the moment when he'd been obliged to treat Mutes as equals and not as sullen slaves – Griff had been constantly amazed to discover how *normal* they were. Okay, they had lumpy skulls and multi-coloured hides, but they were like Trackers in so many ways. Griff could never figure out how they could act the way they did and yet not be human beings. It was a real mystery.

This trio who'd come riding out of the east at the head of a whole bunch of horses was a good example. They spoke regular Basic and their brains were as sharp as a knife. And if you stripped away the dark to light brown patches on their skins with your mind's eye and stood 'em alongside three good ole boys you'd be hard put to tell the difference. And when Griff thought about the time he'd spent watching the training videos about bug-ugly Mutes – poisonous savage vicious animals that had to be ruthlessly exterminated – he couldn't help wondering why the First Family hadn't told Trackers the whole story: like the fact that a bunch of breakers could live alongside Mutes and not end up with their heads on a stick.

Yeah . . . it was a puzzle right enough – like trying to figure out why anyone would want to sit on top of one of these four-legged freaks they'd been landed with. Especially when they had teeth that could bite right through your hand and back legs that kicked like a fuggin' jack-hammer. Okay, this bunch had come complete with a seat on their backs and leather straps for steering 'em round corners but it was a helluva way to travel.

Griff could see that horses would be useful for carrying gear but even that had its drawbacks. Leading a string of pack-horses just made you a bigger target and there was always the risk that the beasts might decide to bolt with your precious possessions. Better to travel light than start relying on a transportation system that a passing Skyhawk could blow away in nought seconds flat.

On the other hand, if he put his own feelings to one side, Griff could see what Malone and his new Mute friends had been getting at. If you managed to stay in the saddle and figure out how to get the thing in gear, you could cover a lot of ground pretty fast. Fast enough to outrun a Mute. Some of the guys had already cracked the problem and when he watched them show off in front of the others, Griff could see it gave the riders a real buzz.

There was no two ways about it. It was impressive – but it wasn't natural. Or practical. You just had to take the problem of maintenance. Horses weren't like wheelies. If one of those broke down you just ran the on-board diagnostic programme and ordered whatever new part was required. With horses, you were totally screwed. To begin with, nobody knew what went on inside and you couldn't bolt on new legs like you could wheels. If one of those broke that was it. You couldn't even cannibalize the unit to create a stock of spare parts. You had to ditch the whole bundle.

Griff picked up the wood and leather saddle, admired once again the handiwork of the unknown craftsman then positioned it on the back of his horse. 'Steady, friend,' he muttered. 'I know you hate this as much as I do but the boss-man wants us both back on the trail . . .'

He drew the girth tight around the horse's belly then pulled another notch through the buckle. He'd already done one slow roll off his mount to the raucous cheers of his companions and he didn't intend to make that particular mistake again.

Malone experienced similar misgivings as he gazed down at Cadillac. The Mute was one problem he could have done without. Although he parlayed with Mutes and observed the ground rules of peaceful co-existence, he did not share Griff's qualified forbearance. Malone didn't like Mutes. Period. But then Malone wasn't a renegade, a breaker on the run from the Federation. Some of the men he led were genuine deserters – brave enough to seek an independent existence on the overground but also a treacherous heap of garbage. Malone didn't mind. That was what he been sent out to run: a garbage disposal unit. Malone and the core of his renegade band were *mexicans*, agents of the undercover organization controlled by Commander-General Karlstrom.

Trapped between the worlds of Tracker and Mute, renegades were basically scavengers; wanderers who roamed the overground with no particular destination and no home to return to. Death was the only welcome they could expect from the Federation. Fortunately there were large areas which had not yet attracted the attentions of the Trail-Blazers and where Mutes were thin on the ground. Like the Rocky Mountains for instance. But there was a good reason why the lumpheads gave the Rockies a wide berth. For six months of the year it was so cold, and the snow was so deep, no one could survive there. Unless of course you were well-organized and properly equipped. Karlstrom had made sure his groups had the expertise and equipment they needed but each item was carefully selected and given a worn, weathered look so as not to strike a false note.

Like any species fighting for survival, renegades were subject to the process of natural selection. The strong prospered, the weak perished. A large group offered safety, continuity and companionship. Malone's organization also provided the other vital element – strong leadership. Within months of its formation, it had become a magnet, attracting smaller groups and individuals who, up to that moment, had opted for a hermit-like existence. And within the Federation, Malone's name was deftly inserted into the information network run by known subversives.

To many in this twilight world, Malone had already assumed the status of a folk-hero. Someone who had beaten the system. It hadn't taken long for his name and approximate whereabouts to surface in the way-stations and work-camps. His wasn't the only name that was passed along in whispered conversations. There were several others obligingly provided by AMEXICO for the benefit of potential defectors – all of them fostering the notion of a growing rebel movement and a relatively safe haven.

Only very few who managed to join Malone realized they had fallen back into the hands of the Federation and they were quickly eliminated. It was a sweet operation – one of several similar overground 'stings' which enabled the First Family to keep its finger on the pulse of the protest movement. And it also ensured a steady supply of candidates for the televised show trials. If the wagon-trains failed to flush out a sufficient number of breakers, Malone and his counterparts made up the balance by sending unsuspecting candidates into a carefully-coordinated ambush.

Had the matter been left to him, the Mute at his feet would now be on his way to the Federation. This Cadillac Deville character was on the wanted list. He'd been nailed. He should have been shipped out *pronto*. End of the story. Neat, clean and simple to arrange. But that wasn't how HANG-FIRE wanted to play it. HANG-FIRE was the operational code-name for Steve Brickman, a wet-back who had graduated from Rio Lobo the previous year after serving briefly as a wing-man aboard The Lady from Louisiana.

Malone knew these background details because he had been selected to give Brickman his final test. A potentially fatal ordeal designed to measure a candidate's courage and endurance. Brickman had been 'posted'

– tied in a kneeling position against a stake, face to face with the corpse of a Tracker he'd killed in the line of duty. He'd come through it, earning himself full marks in the process. There was no doubt about it. Brickman had the makings of a real operator and his latest trick had been to get in and out of Ne-Issan, bringing two important Mute targets with him: Clearwater, a female Mute and Cadillac, the lump now at Malone's feet who was taking forever to shake off the double dose of Cloud Nines.

Clearwater had been seriously wounded in a surprise air attack by a stray Skyhawk. At Brickman's request, Malone and his renegades had struck camp and ridden off, leaving them behind. If she hadn't died in his arms, Clearwater was now on board Red River. Cadillac had been superficially wounded and knocked unconscious by the same hail of fire.

To Malone, it seemed like an ideal opportunity to ship them both out together. Two out of three wasn't a bad result, but Brickman wanted a full house. By leaving Cadillac free, he hoped to entrap his third target – Mr Snow, the power behind the Clan M'Call. Which was the reason why he, Malone, had been lumbered with the task of escorting this lumphead as far as navref Cheyenne, Wyoming. A journey which placed his band of renegades in considerable danger.

This was the wrong time of year to be moving around. April was the month when the Mutes hunted 'red-skins' – breakers; the annual round-up of strays which were handed over to the Iron Masters in exchange for goods and shipped east. Malone hadn't planned to leave the camp that Brickman and his friends had ridden into until mid-May. The site was in a commanding position, with good cover and running water: ideal for a long stay. It had been chosen because AMEXICO knew which way Brickman was heading and he was expected to pass close by. At which point Malone – quite by chance – was to pop up and renew their acquaintance. Everything had gone according to plan and then – thanks to some asshole in a Skyhawk and two scumbags who hadn't seen it coming

61

– everything had gone wrong, forcing him to head west when every sensible breaker was lying low.

The only solution was to travel at night. Mutes, for some reason rooted deep in their collective past, were only active between sunrise and sunset. After that, the hunting posses and turf patrols went home or bedded down for the night. It wasn't the ideal time for travelling cross-country but after umpteen years in the field, Malone had become adept at reading the terrain and moving men across it under the most adverse conditions.

Even so, he was sorely tempted to call up a sky-hook to take Cadillac off his hands. But this was not his operation. The orders from Mother had been clear and unequivocal. He had been detailed to intercept Brickman at a given point during his journey, assess his reliability and – with Mother's approval – to render assistance if and when required. Brickman had said and done all the right things but he'd set Malone's internal alarm system ringing. There was something about him. Maybe it was just Malone's instinctive antipathy towards clean-cut blue-eyed golden boys, but Brickman was too smart for his own good – and just too good to be true.

In the previous year, six of Malone's people, including a class-mate of Brickman's, had been sent north to provide him with the back-up he'd requested to help kidnap the same three Mutes. In the last radio contact made by a mex called Donna Lundkwist, she reported the squad had been sighted by a posse of M'Call Mutes – recognizable by the colour of the feathers in their headgear. The Mutes had put up a smoking arrow – a sign they wished to parley. End of message. No one had ever heard from those six *mexicans* again. Brickman had been running with that clan. Painted up, grassed-out and leathered. His degree of involvement in the back-up squad's disappearance was a question that had plagued Malone ever since.

He glanced up at the clear moonlit sky and saw a bank of dark cloud building up on the northern horizon.

Malone was astute and resourceful but patience was not one of his virtues – especially when it came to unwanted guests, and even more so when that guest was a Mute. Following the shooting of Clearwater, Cadillac had not regained consciousness. To avoid any hassles, he had been kept in a drugged stupor for the past two days. Helped by clear night skies, they had covered some seventy odd miles. One way or another, Clearwater was now beyond reach. It was high time for this lump to stand on his own feet instead of having to be carried around everywhere. When Mother had asked him to help Brickman, he hadn't figured it would mean having to namby-pamby an uppity Mute. That was the bit that really pissed him off – not the move.

He dug his boot into Cadillac's side. 'C'mon! Wake up you sonofabitch! We haven't got all night!'

Cadillac stirred drowsily. 'Uh-humm, yeah . . . sure . . .' His eyes fluttered open then closed again as his mouth opened in a huge yawn.

Malone unhitched his water bottle and emptied it over Cadillac's face. Some of it went down his throat causing him to gag. He rolled about choking and coughing then eventually sat up clutching his head.

'On your feet! C'mon! We're moving out!' Malone slid a hand under his left armpit and hauled him upright.

Cadillac steadied himself and rubbed his face. His body seemed gripped by a strange lethargy. 'Mo-Town! I feel –' His eyes widened as he focused on Malone, then he quickly took in his strange surroundings. 'Where's Clearwater? And Brickman?' A jab of pain from his various flesh wounds caused him to frown. He looked down at his left side and saw two bloodstained rips in his walking skins on the outside curve of the thigh. There was also a deep graze in his belly. An expression of alarm crossed his face. 'Who shot me?!'

'You don't remember? Must have been after you hit the ground.' Malone told him about the Skyhawk that had appeared out of the blue, making a single strafing run across the campsite before turning for home.

Some premonition of what he was going to say next made Cadillac howl with grief. He wrapped his arms around his chest and rocked from side to side. 'Oh, Sweet Sky-Mother! Clearwater! Is she dead?'

'Not when we left. But she was hurt pretty bad.'

'Oyy-yehh! This is all my fault! What about Brickman?'

'He's fine. Came out of it without a scratch.'

The news caused Cadillac to grind his teeth. 'He would! Hah! How typical! So what did you do?'

Malone did his best to conceal his irritation at being questioned in this peremptory manner. *Who the fuck did this guy think he was?* 'Do? The best we could. State she was in she couldn't be moved. So we dressed the wounds with what we had then got the hell out. No point in staying there once the camp had been spotted. We've had 'hawks over our heads for the past couple of days.'

Cadillac's mounting anger boiled over. 'Are you telling me she was shot *two days* ago?!'

Malone checked his watch. 'Exactly fifty-four hours and twelve minutes ago.'

'Why didn't someone tell me before now?!'

Malone resisted the impulse to smash Cadillac in the mouth. 'Because there was nothing you could do, friend.'

'Hahh!' Cadillac became aware of the metallic after-taste on his tongue. 'Was it Brickman's idea to pump me full of drugs?!'

'Yeah. He said you'd be hysterical, and he was right. Pull yourself together for crissakes!'

'I *am* together! He had no right to take matters into his own hands like this! We've got to go back for her!'

'Are you crazy? The only thing that could've saved her was major surgery. Federation-type medicine – not the mumbo-jumbo you monkeys mess around with. She'll be dead and buried by now –'

'No! Don't say that!'

Malone ignored the interruption. 'My job is to help you get back to your own people. Isn't that what Brickman promised to do?'

'Yes, but –'

'There are no "buts". That's what we're gonna do, friend. It was two of my guys who let that plane take us by surprise. So quit blaming yourself for what happened. I can understand Brickman bein' upset at losing a neat piece of ass but what the hell have you got to cry about?'

Cadillac brushed away the tears of rage and grief with shaking hands that longed to fasten themselves around Malone's throat. 'She didn't *belong* to him!'

'Could have fooled me. Is that what the fight was about?'

'No. We were fighting because Brickman is a treacherous, lying toad!'

'That seems a mite ungrateful. Didn't he help you and Clearwater get out of Ne-Issan?'

'He didn't do that to help us! He got us out in order to hand us over to his masters in the Federation! He's not a renegade! He's been working with a network of undercover agents for over a year!'

'I see . . .' Malone ruminated on this for a moment. 'Did he tell you anything about this network – like it's name for instance? Or who was running it?'

Cadillac realized he had said too much and was already regretting his temporary loss of control. His antagonism towards Steve had not diminished but Malone was a virtual stranger. A cipher whose mind, for the moment at least, was inaccessible. 'No. But we couldn't have escaped without outside help – which he organized. If he turns up again, ask him about it. All I can say is, no one's safe when he's around.'

'I'll bear that in mind,' said Malone. 'Meanwhile forget we've had this conversation. If Brickman *does* rejoin us, I may decide to let things ride for a while. If you're right, and he *is* an undercover Fed then it may be to our advantage to let him think we trust him completely. Know what I mean?'

'I think so . . .'

'Good. Let's hit the trail.' Malone gave Cadillac a friendly slap on the back then ushered him over to the waiting horses. He would have preferred to have broken the back of this snivelling piece of lumpshit but – like Brickman – he had a job to do and a role to play. That of big-hearted Matt Malone, friend and protector of abandoned Mutes.

Some six hundred miles to the south of Malone's present position close to the Platte River, Nebraska, The Lady from Louisiana wagon-train had emerged from the repair bays and was back in what was known as 'the roads', being readied for action in the vast underground depot at Nixon/Fort Worth.

In June 2989, The Lady had narrowly avoided a major disaster in its first encounter with a Plainfolk clan aided by a summoner. Caught in a flash-flood, The Lady had managed to extricate herself virtually undamaged but in doing so, she had lost nine out of the ten wing-men posted aboard and their aircraft, plus over eighty line-men. Close on double that number had been wounded.

In November 2990, when The Lady had been sent out into the snows on a special mission, it had been even worse. The explosive charges planted by Cadillac and Clearwater had totally destroyed the blood-wagon and flight car, and the tidal wave of fire that erupted from the stock of napalm canisters and liquid methane tanks stored beneath the hanger deck had rolled through three more cars, incinerating the crewmen in its path.

Abandoning the five gutted cars, The Lady reformed and set course, as directed, for Monroe/Wichita, the still-uncompleted divisional base in Kansas. Arriving at the interface, the wounded crewmen had been off-loaded and rushed to hospital. Commander Hartmann and his team of execs, including Trail Boss McDonnell had been placed under close arrest and shuttled to Grand Central to await trial. The surviving members of the crew who had escaped the same 'dereliction of duty' charge were placed under the temporary command of an executive team drawn from the training staff at Fort Worth. It was they who had brought The Lady – defeated and disgraced

– southwards through Oklahoma into the relative safety of the Home State and back down the long incline into the depot.

The winter months – whose high point was the celebration of the New Year – were, by tradition, spent on 'rest and refit' (R & R). A period when Trail-Blazer crews enjoyed a welcome spell of leave after eight to nine months on the overground, and when the depot engineers began their task of overhauling the trains, readying them for their next assault on the blue-sky world.

The Lady was in need of more than a refit. The missing wagons had to be replaced, fire-damage to several others had to be made good, the crew had to be brought up to strength and their shattered morale restored. Bringing The Lady back to operational status was a major undertaking but it proved easier than raising the crew's spirits. Despite the damage and the casualties The Lady had sustained, Hartmann and his executive team – with perhaps one exception – were held in high regard by the Trail-Blazers who served under them. The exec who failed to inspire the troops to the same degree was Captain Baxter, the Flight Operations Officer. He had died in the blast that ripped through the packed hangar deck of the flight car, killing Gus White and the other wing-men, the mechanics, deck handlers and a score of Trail-Blazers.

The Lady's Trail Boss, Buck McDonnell, whose alertness and quick reactions had saved the forward command car and its crew had been released after two months detention. In a brief appearance before a Board of Assessors, he was informed that all charges had been dropped and was ordered to report for active duty at Nixon/Fort Worth. Exiting from the court room, he was met by a Staff-Commander from CINC-TRAIN who welcomed him back into the ranks of the Trail-Blazer Division. His first task would be to knock the new crew of The Lady into shape and he was to begin immediately. Due to operational requirements, there would, explained the

Commander, be no chance of the four weeks base leave to which he was entitled.

In his usual blunt but respectful fashion, the big Trail Boss told him it didn't matter. After eight weeks on the shit and bucket detail he was just happy to be soldiering again.

The decision to release McDonnell had paid off. From Day One there had been a noticeable rise in the spirits of the veteran crewmen and the transferees and wet-feet – the uninitiated replacements – soon discovered that Big D's reputation as a fire-breathing disciplinarian was, if anything, an understatement. A second stand-in team of execs from the depot's permanent staff helped the crew go through their on-board drills but as the weeks passed, even McDonnell became concerned about the deafening silence surrounding the appointment of a new wagon-master.

Finally, one day in early April, when the crew had assembled for the usual morning parade alongside the wagon-train, McDonnell strode along the ranks behind the duty officer with a noticeable gleam in his eye. When the DO completed his formal inspection of the battalion and passed control over to McDonnell, it was clear to old hands like Bad News Logan that something was up.

Somethin' good for a change. Ol' Big D was practically burstin' . . .

McDonnell braced himself. 'Wagon-train-n-n-n EASY!' he boomed.

The battalion stood at ease with a thunderous stamp of boots, the palms of their hands crossed in the small of their backs.

'Okay, hear this!' he said, in the same foghorn voice. 'I have been reliably informed that The Lady has a new commander and he will shortly be arriving with his team of execs!'

The announcement provoked a subdued murmur.

'And as soon as they're settled in – and we've shown them the ropes –'

A ripple of laughter.

'– they'll be taking The Lady out for a shakedown supply run to Abilene, San Angelo and Brady!'

This news raised an audible groan. Abilene, San Angelo and Brady were way-stations to the south-west of Fort Worth in the Home State of Texas. Territory under the total control of the Federation where there was no chance of a fire-fight.

'And then we're goin' north – to hunt Mute!'

The battalion responded with an exultant shout, punching the air with their fists. 'HO!'

McDonnell caught sight of an approaching wheelie. It was a four-car enclosed model: the type used by hire-wires. He called The Lady's crew to attention. 'Wagon-train-n-n-n READY!'

Close on a thousand pairs of boots came together with a synchronised thud. The Trail Boss made a smart about-turn, his brass-topped drill stick braced stiffly under his left arm, and parallel to the ground.

The wheelie whined to a halt in front of him. The doors on both sides opened and disgorged the team of executive officers who were to take charge of The Lady from Louisiana. There was an audible gasp from the veteran crewmen as they glimpsed the bushy white moustache of the officer with the yellow commander's rank bars on his lower sleeve.

It was Hartmann, their old commander. Buffalo Bill – back in uniform and back in charge, and eight of the twelve smiling faces around him belonged to the executive officers who had served with him up to the moment the Provos had come aboard to arrest them all.

Buck McDonnell's right hand snapped into line with the brim of his stetson, fingers and thumb aligned in a perfect drill manual salute. 'Eight Battalion, Trail Blazer Division, mustered aboard The Lady from Louisiana, ready for your inspection, SAH!'

'Thank you, Mr McDonnell.' Hartmann returned the salute, as did the twelve execs lined up in two staggered rows behind him. The formal greetings over, Hartmann exchanged a warm handshake with his Trail Boss.

'Welcome back, sir.'

'It feels good, Buck. When did you hear we were on our way?'

'Last night, sir. Had quite a job keeping it from the boys.'

'Well, they look happy enough,' observed Hartmann. 'I thought they might be a bit leery about serving under a two-time loser.'

'Sir! Are you kidding?!' McDonnell turned towards the men lined up in three ranks in front of The Lady. 'Okay, you clapped-out, time-serving bunch of slack-assed mothers! Let's hear it for the commander!'

The six hundred veterans that formed the core of The Lady's crew cut loose with the time-honoured chant: 'Buffalo Bill! Buffalo Bill! Just say the word and we'll kill, kill, kill! Give us a rifle, helmet and pack, and we'll follow you to hell and back!'

'Are we ready and able?! Are we fit to show?!' demanded McD.

Everyone, including the execs behind Hartmann, joined in the traditional response: 'You bet your ass! Let's GO – GO – GO!'

Hartmann, noticeably moved by the warmth of his reception, signalled McDonnell to stand the men down.

'Wagon-train-n-n-n EASY!'

The nine hundred men and women making up the crew of The Lady were mustered in individual groups in front of the cars to which they were assigned: medical staff in front of the blood wagon, 'fire-men' in front of the power cars, and so on. As Hartmann led his team of execs along the ranks, each squad or section leader called his individual group to attention. The wagon-master paused to exchange a few words when he encountered a familiar face and the veteran execs did the same. Those drafted in as replacements would each get the customary one-on-one interview with Hartmann, and the executive officer in charge of their particular specialization, once they were on board.

When the inspection and greetings were over, Hartmann

sought out his deputy, Lt.Commander Jim Cooper. 'Mount up, will you Coop? I have to place a call to a friend of mine . . .'

The first two video-phone booths had plasfilm notice strips stuck diagonally across their screens bearing the words 'LINE FAULT – VID-COMMSERV NOTI-FIED'. It meant a service engineer was on his way. Sometime between now and the millenium . . .

The third booth he found was working. Hartmann inserted his newly-returned ID-card, keyed his way through the on-screen call menus, entered the state-code for Colorado (09) followed by the three-digit code for the Pueblo way-station (012) and the x-listed number he had memorized.

The Amtrak logo on the screen was replaced by the head and shoulders of Major Jerri Hiller, one of Mary-Ann's junior battalion comanders. Hartmann noticed her hair was considerably longer than when he had last seen her. He also couldn't decide whether she was surprised to see him or annoyed – or both.

'Is Colonel Anderssen available?'

'One moment, Commander . . .' Hiller moved out of view of the tv camera mounted immediately above the screen carrying his image.

There were muted voices off then Colonel Marie Anderssen moved quickly into the empty seat. 'Bill!' She too was surprised, but the pleasure at his call was evident in the broad smile that came beaming across the ether. 'Christo! You're wearing active duty OD's!'

OD was the abbreviation for the olive-drab, military-style fatigues he was wearing.

'Yeah. They let me out of detention yesterday morning. Plus Coop and the rest of the guys. All charges have been dropped. We've been re-instated – and we'll be rolling The Lady up the ramp at 0700 hours tomorrow.'

Mary-Ann interlaced her fingers and squeezed her hands together. 'Oh, Bill, that's wonderful! It's the best news I've had all year!'

'You and me both.'

'I tried to get permission to see you . . .'

'Yeah, I know. Your message got through to me. Thanks. It helped a lot.'

'Is there any chance of you heading this way?'

'Can't say. We're warming up with a home state supply run. After that I'm not sure what they've got lined up for us. The hire-wire from CINC-TRAIN in charge of the welcome-back party hinted we might be given another special assignment.'

Mary-Ann looked concerned. 'Oh, gosh, I hope it's not –!'

Hartmann cut in. 'Honey – we just have to take what comes.' He smiled. 'You're looking great. This picture quality's very good.'

'It is now it's tuned in properly. VID-COMM had no end of problems trying to set up the link with Santa Fe.'

'How long have you been on-line?'

'Not long.' Mary-Ann smiled back at him. 'You're the first personal call I've had. Up to now they've either been test transmissions from VID-COMM or from HQ-P-DIV. How did you get my number?'

'Through a friend. Amazing as it seems, I still have a few.'

'I'm one of them.'

'Oh, you're more than just a friend. You're something special. Let's hope the next time we meet there won't be a piece of glass and an ocean of red grass between us.'

Mary-Ann smiled wistfully as she recalled the comfortable intimacy of their past encounters. 'Amen to that.' Then, on a more cheerful note she added: 'I'm so pleased for you, Bill. Every night I've prayed that somebody somewhere along the line would have the good sense to realize you were innocent.'

'Well, as you can see, your prayers have been answered . . .'

'And not only that, you're back in charge of The Lady. How does it feel?'

'Like coming back from the dead,' said Hartmann.

72

Wallis and Malone rose from their chairs as Commander-General Karlstrom entered his wood-panelled office. As the metal door of his personal elevator closed behind him, a matching section of wood descended over it, sealing it from view. Karlstrom skirted his desk and advanced, right hand extended.

As senior operatives, holding the military rank of Commander, Wallis and Malone had earned the right to warm handshakes and use of their given names in meetings with the Operational Director. This relaxed atmosphere (enjoyed by everyone with more than four years successful service) did not permit them to address Karlstrom as 'Ben', but they weren't required to include the word 'sir' every time they spoke, and there was none of the jumping to attention or parade ground saluting required from wet-backs fresh out of Rio Lobo.

'Don . . .'

'Morning, sir . . .'

Karlstrom turned to greet Malone. 'Matt! Glad you could make it. Hope it wasn't a problem calling you in at such short notice.'

'No, sir. I managed to cover it. Took off with four of the boys to check our southern flank.' He smiled. 'With so much air activity in our sector, I thought we might have a wagon-train on our trail. Provided I'm back by dawn tomorrow, there shouldn't be any problem.'

'We've got enough as it is,' said Karlstrom. 'This particular operation has become so complex I felt we should talk it over face to face.' Karlstrom waved them into their seats and settled into the high-backed chair behind his desk. 'Don, uhh, before you give us your sit-rep, where is Mr Brickman at this moment in time?'

'Still on the wagon-train, awaiting the outcome of this meeting. If he gets a green on the next phase of the operation he intends to head west with his three horses towards the junction of the North and South Platte Rivers in the hope of catching up with Cadillac and, uhh . . .?' Wallis' eyes questioned Malone.

'Don't worry, I'll be there. I don't know how good he is at following trails but I reckon it'll take him at least four days. Karstrom nodded, then turned back to Wallis. 'Run us through what happened on the train.'

'From when Brickman first came on the air?'

'Yes. I want Matt to have the whole picture so that he knows exactly what we're up against.'

Malone looked puzzled. 'Am I on the wrong track, sir? I was under the impression Brickman and his kin sister were working for us.'

'It's not quite that simple, Matt. In theory, yes, they are. Unfortunately, in practice, some doubt has arisen over the question of who is manipulating who. Let Don say his piece and you'll understand what I'm getting at.'

Wallis gave a crisp, coherent account of the rescue operation that had been triggered by the telepathic contact between Brickman and Roz: an operation which Karlstrom had approved over his direct radio link with the task-force. He then gave a brief *résumé* of the surgical treatment Clearwater had received and her present state of health, described Steve's arrival on board, played back the tapes of his conversations with Roz, and concluded by describing her terrifying demonstration of mind-control.

'Don't ask me how she does it. All I can tell you is it works, and she can turn it on just like that.' He snapped his fingers. 'When you imagine what she *could* have dreamed up, you may think that sitting on top of a rock tower is not all that bad –'

Malone held up his hands. 'I didn't say anything, Don.'

'No, but I can see your face. I'm telling you it was absolutely horrendous. And when Jake fell off that fucking . . .' He tried to shake the memory away. 'I hope and pray I never have to go through anything like that again.'

'How is he now,' asked Karlstrom.

'Jake? Having trouble sleeping.'

Malone grunted. 'He'll get over it. Sounds like he got what he had coming.'

'He always did tend to run off at the mouth,' agreed Wallis. 'I don't think he'll do it again while she's around.' He turned to Karlstrom. 'The question is – if she was able to take control of our minds then, is she in control of them now?'

Malone laughed. 'How the hell can she be? You're not on the wagon-train.'

'Why should that make any difference? The telepathic link between Roz and her kin-brother works just as well even when they're thousands of miles apart?' He appealed to Karlstrom. 'Right, sir?'

'It would appear so, yes. But with all due respect, Don, I think you're over-reacting. It was obviously a bad experience but you asked for a demonstration and you got it. Technically she may have taken control of your mind but she did not actually make you *do* anything rash or foolish. As I understand it, apart from Nevill, none of you budged from that table.'

'That's true, but –'

'What she did was induce what psychologists call a positive hallucination. Which you *all* shared. That's the interesting bit. Mass hypnosis is not unknown. You appear to have experienced a sophisticated "instant" version, and a very effective one too. If she can warp someone's perception to that degree and at that speed, I have a feeling she really *could* neutralize Mr Snow.

'But that's not really mind control – at least not the kind that worries me. Roz has no reason to turn against the Federation. Her rival for Steve's affections is now wired to a life-support system – and at her mercy.

'Brickman may still be mixed up over the two of them but he's not going to jump ship if we've got Clearwater and Roz in Grand Central. It would be absolutely point-less. He is a natural undercover agent. He's almost impossible to read but there is one thing I *do* know about him. He's hungry for power. And this is where the power is. No . . .' Karlstrom paused reflectively. 'He and Roz will come through for us. I'm sure of it.'

'So we don't need to worry about her, uhh –?'

Karlstrom smiled, apparently satisfied with his reasoning. 'Don – if she was planning to betray us, would she have shown us what she could do?'

Wallis conceded reluctantly. 'No, I suppose not.'

Malone caught Karlstrom's eye. 'Excuse me asking, but this guy Brickman – is he all right in the head? I mean, does he still know where the edges are? It's no secret he's been bouncing beaver and you've just hinted he's been jacking up his kin-sister.'

'They're not related, Matt. But that's classified, okay?'

'I understand, sir.'

'Okay, let's get down to the real business – setting up this attack by the M'Call Mutes on Red River. I've got approval for the idea from the Oval Office. It could be a good way of finishing off the M'Calls but what we have to do is figure out how to get our two remaining targets on board a wagon-train and safely under lock and key without losing the whole shebang.'

'Sir, I'm not saying it can't be done, but do we *have* to bring these other two in? asked Malone. 'You've got Clearwater. Why don't we just close down the file by putting three triples through their heads?'

Wallis nodded in agreement.

Karlstrom responded with a thin-lipped smile. 'That might take care of Cadillac but from what I've heard about Mr Snow, you could find the bullets coming back at you.'

'Sir – with respect – nobody's *that* fireproof.'

'Don't count on it. I know it's tempting, Matt, but there are other factors to be taken into consideration. High-level strategic objectives that I'm not at liberty to disclose at this moment but which I'll bring you in on as soon as I'm given clearance to do so. Brickman's idea *seems* unnecessarily complex but it could give us the set-piece engagement we're looking for.'

'Ahh . . . I didn't know that.

'And there's something else,' continued Karlstrom. 'I'm not prepared to jeopardize the relationship you've built up with the Mutes in your sector. From past experience, we know that some mutes are able to communicate over long distances. As wordsmiths, Mr. Snow and Cadillac may have that capability.

'Yeah. Don't ask me how. It just does.'

'Exactly. As we speak, the M'Calls may be organizing a Welcome Home party. Could make things very awkward if we suddenly lost him overboard. If you followed that up by the on-site removal of their wordsmith – hell! That would *really* shake the shit loose.'

Malone grimaced ruefully. 'You're right, sir. I hadn't figured it that way. Guess I was just tryin' to cut a few corners.'

'Nothing wrong with that. Just for the record, I sent Brickman out with a dead-or-alive option on these two. But since then I've acquired a better overview. Believe me. Icing Cadillac and Mr Snow at this point in the game would cause more problems than it would solve. Especially for you.'

When Wallis and Malone had left for the airfield, Karlstrom remained in the office he used for meetings with his operatives. Slumped in his upholstered swivel chair, his left elbow resting on the padded arm, he reflected on what he had heard, pulling slowly at his nose, lips and chin with thumb and forefinger as he did so.

He had maintained an up-beat mood throughout their discussions but that had been a front. Don Wallis' account of Roz Brickman's hallucinatory powers filled him with alarm. Despite the soothing assurances he'd laid on Wallis, this *was* mind control – of a pretty spectacular kind. The kind that could plunge them all into deep shit.

Karlstrom didn't give a toss whether Roz had taken temporary control of Wallis and his team; the only mind *he* was concerned about was his own. Was she only able to distort reality and thus induce total disorientation – or was she capable of something far more sinister? And anyway, how the hell did you define reality in the first place? Could she have manipulated him into putting her aboard that train? It had been her suggestion, yes, but had she *forced* him to go along with the idea?

No – that was impossible. The President-General had had the final say. In all matters concerning Steve and Roz Brickman, Karlstrom had been careful to cover his ass. Unfortunately that was not sufficient to remove him from the line of fire. If OPERATION SQUARE-DANCE went down the tube, *he* would be the one taking the flak, not G.W.J. the 31st. Yes, sir . . .

But was she planning to go over the side, or was that just something that Brickman had pulled out of the air to lay on the lump-heads? It had to be a bluff. A wind-up. What the hell would she do out there? No. With Clearwater out of the way Roz had what she wanted. Steve Brickman. Karlstrom was convinced he was back on the rails. The psychologists who selected, shaped and supervised the people on the Special Treatment List knew what made that young man tick. He wanted power, and he wanted to get even. That was why the results of his final exams at the Flight Academy had been fixed, giving him fourth place instead of first and the honours he merited. Yes . . . that had *really* lit a fire under him. And the Federation was the only place his needs could be satisfied.

These thoughts provided Karlstrom with scant comfort. Roz and Brickman were both telepaths, sensitives of a remarkable kind. Did Brickman possess the same latent powers to bend reality out of shape? Right from the very beginning, Karlstrom had been reluctant to meddle with the grey area the Life Institute called 'psionics'. But faced with the threat from such people as Mr Snow, the Federation could not afford to ignore what little home-grown talent it possessed. Karlstrom knew of Steve and Roz; only the P–G and COLUMBUS knew who the rest were. If there *were* any others. Karlstrom hoped not. The P–G had likened Steve and Roz to a weapon-system. But what was the point of a weapon-system whose workings no one fully understood and whose destructive potential was incalculable?

No one in their right mind would launch such a weapon. But the appropriate target data had been fed into Steve and Roz Brickman and the button had been pressed. They had been fired towards enemy lines. Were they, as Karlstrom sometimes feared in the small hours of the morning, beyond recall? Was this weapon they had unleashed about to veer off course – turn back on its makers? That was what Karlstrom feared the most. And he wondered if the handful of quacks who had elbowed themselves into an unassailable position as the sole experts in the so-called 'science' of psionics had had the foresight to fit their charges with a self-destruct mechanism.

Probably not. How could they when none of them could explain in words of less than three syllables (that any normal person could understand) how and why someone like Roz Brickman could fall to the ground with a hole punched through her upper arm by a phantom crossbow bolt? A real hole, with real blood, that healed and disappeared without leaving any scar tissue within eight hours!

They had no answers because they didn't know. There *was* no science, only jargon. Psycho-babble. The Department of Psionics at the Life Institute was an empty shell providing nothing but a few quick promotions, some cheap prestige. A scam. He had never wanted to get involved. He had been pressed into using Steve and Roz, and as a result he was marooned in the middle of a fucking minefield – with the President-General watching from the other side of the warning tapes.

Faced with the possibility that the decision to deploy Roz alongside her kin-brother might backfire with sufficient force to remove him from office, Karlstrom decided to take some avoiding action of his own. He would agree to Steve's request to leave Red River in Nebraska. Clearwater, in any case, could not be moved. There was no danger of losing her: any rescue attempt mounted by force of arms would be fatal. And despite the risk that she might – just might – defect, he would leave Roz there too.

To bring her back into the Federation after this demonstration of new, uncharted powers would be an act of criminal folly. If there was going to be any heat, Wallis and the task force could take it. Karlstrom was aware that his decision placed the entire crew of Red River in jeopardy but there was, for the moment, no acceptable alternative. He had no desire to find himself sitting on top of a dizzying pinnacle of rock, or whatever other horror she might produce from the depths of her mind. And until some way could be found to deal with the problem he, for one, did not intend to get within a hundred miles of her.

If she was the loyal soldier-citizen he believed her to be there would be no problem. But until she proved that beyond all possible doubt it was wiser not to take any chances. As long as she was marooned in Nebraska she could not warp his own mental processes or affect his deliberations in any way. And he would circumvent any treachery by cutting Wallis out of the planning process they had begun that very day. He would continue to receive documentation but it would not be the real thing.

Only Malone and the other units would know the final plan. Roz and Steve would be left in the dark. If they played their parts, all well and good, if not, well . . . Amtrak could survive the loss of a wagon-train. Sensitives like Roz and Steve were a lurking cancer; a menace to the system. Their elimination – by death, or permanent transfer to the overground – was the only way to secure the future of the Federation. The Department of Psionics would be discredited, disbanded; Karlstrom's doubts would be vindicated. AMEXICO could return to the tried and tested ways of secret warfare, and its director would sleep more soundly in his bed.

It was a neat, satisfying scenario, but Karlstrom knew from experience that things never went entirely to plan. Somewhere along the line somebody always fucked-up. The reason why he had held his job for so long was because he was also an expert in containment – the art of damage limitation.

Disclosure was a central feature of that art. You never told anyone anything they did not need to know, and you never *ever* gave them bad news when good news might be just around the corner. That was why Karlstrom had decided not to tell the President-General about Roz Brickman's new and alarming capability. If challenged, he would defend himself – like all canny administrators – by saying he was waiting for a fuller report.

CHAPTER FOUR

After the violent confrontation that preceded the wounding of Clearwater, Steve had not been looking forward to telling Cadillac that she was now on board Red River, but when he finally caught up with the Mute and Malone's renegades, it did not go as badly as he had expected. Cadillac – still crippled with guilt over his part in the affair – was so relieved to learn that Clearwater was alive, he brushed aside the awkward fact that she was in the hands of the Federation.

Having come prepared for a bitter wrangle, Steve found the Mute's fatalistic reaction somewhat disconcerting.

Malone, of course, was still posing as the stalwart leader of a renegade band and Cadillac – while appearing somewhat less than overjoyed to find himself in their company – gave no sign of being aware that Malone and his henchmen were undercover agents or that, during Malone's brief absence, he had been picked up by a Sky-Rider of Air-Mexico and flown into the Federation for a head-to-head with Karlstrom and Wallis.

Steve, who had been one of the main items on the agenda, was also unaware of Malone's flying visit to Grand Central. Wallis had merely told him that Karlstrom had approved his outline plan. He was to proceed on the assumption that an attack on Red River would take place; the final game-plan would be conveyed to him when all the pieces were on the board.

Cadillac already knew he and Roz could communicate telepathically. Steve was now obliged to repeat the story for Malone's benefit, unaware he had already been briefed by Karlstrom. And Malone, alerted by Cadillac's ill-considered claim that Steve was an undercover agent, had to appear to accept his story whilst pretending (for Cadillac's benefit) to secretly mistrust him!

As Jake Nevill had observed on the wagon-train, there were so many layers of deception it was difficult to keep your place in the script. The swirling cross-current of lies threatened to become a vortex which, if they were not careful, could send them and the whole operation down the tube.

Given the no-nonsense character which he had adopted for his role as a renegade, the agent code-named HIGH-SIERRA was put into some difficulty by the revelation of the telepathic link between Roz and Steve. As 'Malone' he couldn't just let it pass without comment; on the other hand, as Steve's covert ally, he didn't want to make a big deal out of it. Having talked to Karlstrom, he had anticipated this topic entering the conversation and had been searching for a way to deal with it since boarding the Sky-River for the return trip. He decided to maintain a healthy scepticism bordering on the dismissive, tempered with a spirit of enquiry.

'You telling me you can speak to each other without a radio?'

'Well, we don't actually speak but we *can* communicate specific items of information. It's like hearing a voice inside your head, but that voice isn't *real*. The sound doesn't physically travel through the air. It's the same principle as a radio transmitter, but these are *thought* waves. The voice I've mentioned – you don't actually *hear* it, you just imagine you do – like when people speak to you in dreams. You can see their lips moving; what you are saying to each other makes sense, you are conscious of their voices but *there is no sound*. Because, by itself, your brain can't make a noise. It needs a tongue, lungs and a larynx to tell you what it's thinking, and it can't decipher external noise without filtering it through an ear.'

'I think I've got the message,' said Malone.

'On the other hand,' continued Steve, 'If you're trans-mitting a feeling – joy, pain, terror – or the image of a particular place, you don't need words. You experience the same sensation, images registered by their mind are transmitted simultaneously into your own. You see what they see – as it happens. The way part of your mind can picture all kinds of things while you're listening to somebody talk – the way you're doing now.'

'That's what bugs me,' said Malone. 'How d'you know it's someone *else's* thoughts and not your own?'

Steve shrugged. 'You just do. There's a kind of tingling, a coolness. I can't explain it, but if it happened to you, you'd know what I mean.'

'Could it happen to me? Can your kin-sister beam this junk to anyone she chooses?'

'No. That would be like COLUMBUS trying to transmit data to someone whose work-station wasn't equipped with a VDU. Your brain has to be able to make the right connections. Just don't ask me what they are. We discovered we had this ability because we were brought up together. I suppose I must have been about five or six years old when it started. To us then, it was just a game. There may be others but no one has come through to us. Roz is my only contact and vice versa.'

'So what's she doing now?'

'Can't tell you. The truth is, as I got older, I became scared about what we'd been doing. In the Federation, it doesn't pay to be too different from everyone else. Especially in that area. It's too much like Mute magic. Besides – who could you tell without getting into trouble? That's why I shut down that side of my mind, didn't answer and tried my best not to let her through. Eventually it worked. Either that or she gave up trying.'

'So how come you're back in touch?'

Steve realized that Malone wasn't just extending this conversation for the benefit of Cadillac and himself. He was quizzing him on behalf of Karlstrom as well.

'It happened when I came up for my first overground solo and caught my first glimpse of the blue-sky world. The shock reopened the link between us. But then a lot of strange things happened to me that day.'

'I know what you mean. It can be quite a moment.' One which, given his allegiance to the Federation, Malone was still trying to come to terms with. 'Still no joy with Roz?' He demanded.

'No. If she needs to come through, she will.'

Malone laughed dismissively. 'I'll believe it when I see it! You've got what it takes, Brickman, but like a lot of guys who are fast on their feet, you're full of bullshit!'

'Yeah, I know it sounds that way. If we have time, I'm hoping to convince you you're wrong.'

Malone jerked a thumb at Cadillac. 'This is the guy you've got to work on. Know what your so-called friend here thinks you are? An undercover Fed!'

Steve met this news with a dry laugh. 'Does he . . .?'

Cadillac, who was totally unprepared for this embarrassing disclosure, stammered: 'Now, uhh – w-wait a minute! I didn't put it exactly like that –'

'That's okay,' said Steve amiably. 'I should have expected you to try and get even.' He turned back to Malone. 'We have a few personal problems that need ironing out.'

'Yeah, so I gather,' chuckled Malone. 'Somethin' to do with you jackin' up his beaver.'

The use of that word riled Steve but there was little he could do about it. Malone was too big and too mean and Steve needed his wholehearted cooperation. 'It's a long story . . .'

'Save it,' said Malone. 'I'm all smoked out.' It was a phrase coined by users of rainbow-grass, which meant they'd had a surfeit of psychedelic fantasies.

As Malone turned on his heel, Steve put a hand to his forehead. 'Wait a minute! Roz is coming through!'

The renegade paused with evident irritation. Cadillac rose from the rock he'd been sitting on.

'It's a message for you. From Clearwater.' He frowned as he mouthed the next few phrases, then repeated them to Cadillac. 'She wants you to rescue her from the wagon-train –'

'From Red River? Nothin' to it!' scoffed Malone.

'– Roz too. She wants to join us.' A pregnant pause then – 'The wagon-train has been ordered to stay in Nebraska . . . and patrol westwards . . . along the line of the Platte River.'

'Are you sure they are going to keep Clearwater aboard?'

'Yes.' Steve concentrated again. 'It's too risky to fly her out and . . . they can't off-load her because . . . all the other wagon-trains are committed elsewhere.'

Malone decided to ask an awkward question. He had to pick at Steve's story in order to enhance his own credibility and also to build up Steve's. 'There's something fishy about all this. I know this kin-sister of yours is working both sides of the track but why would Red River waste time on a wounded Mute? One more, one less – what does it matter to them? Why are they keeping her alive? Is there something you haven't told me?'

Steve appealed to Cadillac and received his permission to speak. 'They're keeping her alive because they know she's important to the Clan M'Call. She's a summoner. A very powerful one. And that's not bullshit. She is *dynamite*.'

'How do they know that? Did you tell 'em?'

'No. I told Roz when we met in Grand Central early last year. I found out later our conversation was bugged.'

'So . . .?'

Steve closed his eyes again and worked his fingers across his brow. 'Roz says the decision has come from Grand Central. They think that if they leave Clearwater on board Red River, the Clan M'Call will try and rescue her.'

'Nahh,' said Malone. 'They ain't gotta hope in hell.'

'On the face of it, no. But the clan is led by another summoner called Mr Snow. He's old but he's still big trouble. I was on board The Lady from Louisiana when he almost wrecked her in 2989.'

Malone looked suitably impressed. 'You mean that Battle of the Now and Then River? Even I've heard of that. Jeez! Was that him?'

'Yes it was!' exclaimed Cadillac. 'And I took part in that battle too!'

Malone looked at the Mute with new respect. 'Is that so? Well, I've gotta tell you. It's no secret I've never been overly fond of you people, but that's somethin' to be proud of. It's not often the Federation gets a hiding like that. Hell, I wish I'd been there.'

Cadillac squared his shoulders. 'The Plainfolk fight their own battles!'

'Sure. But that's no reason why we couldn't put our heads together. I know how those goddam things work. Fact is, quite a few of the boys put in time on the trains. Who knows? Might come up with some ideas . . .'

Cadillac didn't respond.

Malone looked at Steve. 'Let's say – just for argument's sake – you captured a train. More or less in one piece. What would you and your Mute friends do with it once you've got Roz and Clearwater away?'

'That's for Cadillac to say. But if you're asking me, they won't do anything with it. By the time they've finished, there'll be nothing left.'

The news provoked a sigh of regret. 'Seems a shame – a top-class fighting vehicle like that. It's a pity you can't figure a way to get your friends out and leave it more or less in one piece. If the M'Calls took over Red River and let my boys help them run it. Hell –', Malone grinned, '– the Federation really *would* have a fight on their hands!'

'Yes, they would,' agreed Steve. 'And if you laid hands on a few Skyhawks, Cadillac here knows how to fly.'

'No kidding . . .'

'Yup. He's a real ace.'

Unaware that Steve was watching him closely, Cadillac drew himself up, his chest swelling like a mating cockbird. 'And not only that! I designed and built rocket-powered planes for the Iron Masters of Ne-Issan!'

'Did you now?' Malone turned to Steve. 'How come you didn't tell me about this back at the camp site?'

'I did mention he was something special.'

'Yeah, but I didn't realize he was *that* special.'

Steve shrugged. 'Like I said, it's a long story.'

'Yeah, well, I think we've got a good thing going here.' Malone laid a fatherly hand on Cadillac's shoulder. 'How does this sound, good buddy? Cut us in for a slice of the pie, and if we manage to grab this wagon-train, you can be head of the air force!'

Steve laughed disgustedly. 'Aww, c'mon, guys, stop jerking off! This is a pipe dream! There's no way the M'Calls could capture a wagon-train. I'm not saying Mr Snow couldn't wreck one. He came pretty close to doing that at the Now and Then River. But capturing one in working order . . . hell!' He laughed again. 'Can you see a wagon-master lowering the ramps to let a screaming bunch of Mutes on board?'

Malone's brow furrowed. 'No . . .'

'Exactly. It's a total waste of time to even think about it. Cadillac and I have already been through this. That was what started the argument which brought out the knives. I wanted to try and rescue Roz. He said it couldn't be done. And he was right.'

'I didn't say it couldn't be done,' said Cadillac. 'I said I wasn't prepared to waste the lives of my clanfolk trying to rescue your kin-sister.'

'Whatever you say, Caddy. I'm not gonna argue with you any more. I broke my blood-oath once and look what happened. I lost Clearwater.'

'We both lost Clearwater. But she is not lost forever. Thanks to you, she is alive – and has asked us to deliver her!'

'Aren't you forgetting the prophecy? Isn't she supposed to go into the Federation? She asked Mr Snow if she would die in the darkness of their world and he said, "No, you will live".'

'I am a wordsmith as well as a seer,' exclaimed Cadillac. 'I forget nothing. And only a seer can interpret the images he draws from the stones. In speaking of you I said this: *He will come in the guise of a friend with Death hiding in his shadow and he will carry you away on a river of blood*. I said nothing about her going into the Federation. Clearwater just assumed that. In replying to her question – *Am I to die in the darkness of their world, or will I live to see the sun again?* – the Old One merely said she would live. He said nothing about the dark cities.'

'So she's *not* destined to go into the Federation . . .'

'Not in my reading. For me, the images apply to our time in Ne-Issan. You came in the guise of a friend, offering to help me, but you were really planning to wreck my work.' He held up a hand. 'No! Don't interrupt! The death hiding in your shadow was your secret link with the Federation who supplied the devices you used to destroy the Heron Pool. The slaughter surrounding our escape was the river of blood on which you carried Clearwater away.' Cadillac smiled disdainfully. 'You see how it all fits together?'

'Yeah, it's neat. Okay, so I blew you out of a job. And yes, I conned the Federation into thinking I was working with them. It was the only way to get you out of there. I'd promised Mr Snow I'd do my best to rescue the pair of you – and that's what I did. Your place is with the Clan M'Call. And if you're still peeved because I forced you to face up to reality, well tough on you!'

'The reality, Brickman, is that Clearwater is now a prisoner of the Federation, held on board Red River. And until she is rescued, you have only kept *half* your promise to the Old One.'

'Sweet Sky-Mother! Caddy, for crissakes, be practical! Okay, Clearwater is not dying but she needs medical attention! That's why all this talk of storming the train is sheer lunacy. She can be moved, yes, but you're not going to be able to walk out with her thrown over your shoulder!

'She'll have to be evacuated properly – preferably not in the middle of a fire-fight – and for a while she'll need to be cared for by a doctor. The only person we can rely on to do that is Roz. Which means we have to get her out in one piece as well, plus some of the drugs, dressings and equipment that are stored in the blood-wagon –'

'We have no need of such things. The Old One can heal her.'

'The Old One didn't save everybody after the battle with the wagon-train. He can set simple fractures and use plant-based substances to keep some types of wounds free of infection but he's not a miracle worker. You might as well stuff his herbal remedies up your ass for all the good they're going to do Clearwater. You are right, I goofed – but at least I managed to save her life.'

'And I'm grateful for that . . .'

'Good. All you've got to do now is get used to the idea that we can't get her off the train. *I'm* the only person who can rescue her.'

'Oh? How?'

'By switching sides – talking them into believing I'm still the straight arrow they thought I was. I'll have to go back to the Federation with Clearwater and then, when she's better, try and find some way to get her and Roz out into the blue-sky world.'

Cadillac looked dismayed. 'But that could take months, years!'

'It could do,' admitted Steve. 'You got any better ideas?'

'I don't know – surely there must be some way we could –'

'Caddy! For the last time! Forget the fucking train! What are you gonna do? Hang around in the hope that someone's gonna leave a door open? There's absolutely no way your people can get on board! I've served on one of those things! The spectre of Mutes running wild inside a wagon-train is the nightmare all Trail-Blazers share. But it doesn't keep them awake at night because they know it can't happen. That's why the trains are designed the way they are. Even if you got past the guns and the steam jets there's still no way you can get inside. When

90

those ramps are up, those wagons are shut tighter than a gnat's ass!'

Malone came out of his reverie. 'The wagon-master . . .'

Steve had almost forgotten he was there. 'What?'

'The wagon-master. He wouldn't lower a ramp for a bunch of Mutes, but he might lower it to let a group of Trail-Blazers on board – 'specially if they had some lumpheads in hot pursuit.'

Steve saw Cadillac's interest quicken. 'Meaning . . .?'

'Well, it's just an idea but . . . if we were somehow able to get hold of enough helmets, uniforms and rifles . . .'

'Disguise ourselves as Trackers?' asked Cadillac.

'There'd have to be enough of us to seize control of the ramp and hold it long enough to get more of your people aboard.'

'You're crazy,' said Steve. 'D'you think the guys running Red River are just gonna sit there and let it happen? As soon as you show your hand at the top of the ramp, they'll close the fire doors at either end, unhitch the wagon then pull away and reform, leaving you sitting there with nowhere to go!'

'They could do,' admitted Malone. 'But I'm hoping this Mr Snow character might be able to do something about that. But if you think he can't deliver then forget it. To pull this off, we need brains, brawn *and* magic.' He grinned sheepishly. 'Never thought I'd hear myself say that.'

'The Old One has the power,' said Cadillac. 'He will know what to do when the times comes.'

'Does that mean we're in business?' asked Malone.

'No. It means I'll think about it.'

Cadillac had tried to sound non-committal but Steve knew exactly what was going through his mind.

And so did Malone. *The lump had taken the bait. He was on the hook . . .*

Later, as dusk fell, Steve caught Malone sitting by himself in front of a small camp-fire. He hunkered down beside

91

the brooding renegade and stretched his hands over the flames.

'How am I doing?' asked Malone.

'With Cadillac?' Steve smiled. 'Great. Just keep oiling him up. You'll have him eating out of your hand.'

'Brown-nosing ain't exactly my style,' said Malone. 'But if that's what it takes to get a result . . .'

'It's a relief to be working with someone of your experience.'

'Don't get smart, Brickman.'

'I wouldn't dare. The last time I spoke out of turn, you loosened a couple of teeth and almost broke my jaw.' He glanced over his shoulders. 'I'd better go. We shouldn't be seen too often with our heads together.'

'You're right. But listen – these seeing-stones . . . are they for real? Can that lump actually tell what's gonna happen?'

'You'd better believe it,' said Steve. 'He saw both of us going down under the water, and a week or so later we were trapped on a sinking boat and nearly drowned! Creepy, huh?'

'Yeah.' Malone shifted uneasily. 'I hate all this magic shit.'

'You're not the only one,' replied Steve. And he was not just thinking of Nevill. Steve liked situations where you could figure all the angles, plan several moves ahead. The trouble with magic was it was so fucking unpredictable. People were bad enough, but magic was unfettered by the rules of logic, the scientific laws that governed cause and effect. 'But don't let's knock it,' he concluded. 'It's saved my ass several times already.'

'That's what worries me,' growled Malone. 'Bouncing beaver may have softened your brains a little but you're no dick-head.'

'Thanks . . .'

'If a guy like you takes it seriously then we could be in big trouble.'

'You mean with Mr Snow?'

'Yeah. It looks like our friend here will run him up the

ramp but how the fuck do we put the brakes on someone like that before he puts a bolt of lightning up everybody's ass?'

'That's where Roz, my kin-sister comes in.'

Malone accepted this with a nod. 'Mother mentioned something about a demo. Is she a summoner too?'

Steve laughed at the idea. 'Of course not. She's a straight-A like you and me. But being a telepath, her brain – like mine – must have some extra capability, or be using circuits we all possess but which most of us never plug into. And now, suddenly, another part of her brain has been switched on, giving her the ability to take temporary control of other peoples minds – by altering their perception of reality.'

'Whatever that is,' grunted Malone '– but how's this gonna fix Mr Snow?'

'Jeez, what a question! This new power's come as much a surprise to her as it had to everyone else.'

'C'mon, Brickman! If I've gotta put my ass on the line to nail Mister Magic, I wanna know what she's providin' in the way of back-up. You were *there* when she spooked Wallis and the other guys. You tryin' to make out you and she didn't connect over this?'

'No. But all I got were a series of sensations, not the workshop manual.' Steve hesitated. 'The best way to explain it is to imagine Mr Snow is a radio transceiver and she's a heavy burst of static. When he switches on, she's gonna swamp the air-waves and block out all incoming and outgoing signals. If she can prevent his brain from functioning coherently then, in theory, he won't be able to draw in these forces or direct them outwards on to a specific target.

'Sounds plausible. Question is, will it work on the day?'

'That's something we're gonna have to take a chance on.'

'Great. That really builds up my confidence. One last thing. That business with Roz and the message from Clearwater. Was that for real? Did she really come through then or were you just juicing our feathered friend?'

Steve smiled knowingly. He warmed his hands one last time then rose to his feet. 'No point in answering that, is there? You don't believe in all this magic shit.'

Malone's eyes narrowed but his battered face was not unfriendly. 'Gidd-outta-here!'

Since leaving the Clan Kojak on the shores of Lake Mi-Shiga, Steve, Cadillac and Clearwater had followed, wherever possible, the line of the ancient hardway listed on Federation maps as Interstate 80. In the pre-Holocaust era it had been part of a continuous east-west ribbon of concrete that began in the Big Apple and ended at Denver, Colorado, passing through Ohio, Indiana, Illinois, Iowa and Nebraska on the way.

They had long since gone off the left hand edge of the map that Steve had found on board the aircraft they had stolen at Long Point, but the clans they met along the way all agreed that if they continued towards the setting sun they would reach the edge of a wide endless river. Since they had already crossed the Mississippi, Steve knew from the maps he'd seen during his training at Rio Lobo that this had to be the Miz-Hurry – the Mute name for the Missouri.

The crumbling weed-covered remains of Interstate 80 had finally petered out some miles from the river, but eventually they found themselves on the edge of a one hundred foot high bluff overlooking the east bank. On the far side lay the buried remains of Omaha. The headquarters of Strategic Air Command, sited at Offut AFB just south of the city had made Omaha a prime target in the global nuclear war which brought 20th century civilization to an abrupt end.

In the public archives which could be accessed via COLUMBUS, the blame for the Holocaust was laid firmly on the Mutes; the role played by the Russians was ignored, the very existence of the USSR, along with all other nation-states beyond the borders of the USA, had been erased from the records and the minds of the Federation's soldier-citizens.

According to COLUMBUS there was only one continent, America: only one race, Trackers – born to inherit the blue-sky world once it had been cleansed of the sub-human scum spawned in the hell-fires of the Holocaust, the incendiary tidal wave of murder and mindless destruction that had burned every city, township and hamlet to the ground and which – as everyone knew – had been the work of the degenerate, drug-crazed hordes who had fathered the Mutes.

It was an agreeable fiction: the historical fact, insofar as it concerned Omaha, was that the air base, the city and its riverbank neighbour, Council Bluffs, Iowa, had been obliterated by a multiple strike which included both air and ground bursts.

A single H-Bomb would have sufficed, but despite the endless attempts (some genuine, other entirely fraudulent) to reduce the stockpiles of nuclear weapons, the politicians and the generals who held the fate of the planet in their hands were still wedded to the concept of over-kill. The first missile obliterated its target, the remainder merely rearranged the glowing ashes and ensured that the key personnel sheltering in SAC's bomb-proof bunker beneath Offut AFB stayed there – permanently.

The initial fire-flash which, in its first few milliseconds of incandescent life was hotter than a solar flare, had vaporized all the timber-frame houses and reduced their brick-built neighbours to cinders. The four bridges linking the two cities, scarred and riven but still standing after the first blast, had disintegrated in the second, their steel-work fusing with stone and concrete into huge red-hot gobbets of volcanic lava which had been hurled into the boiling river below.

Half-submerged in the wide shallow waters, they had fused and cooled to form irregular clusters of giant stepping stones, their jagged edges worn smooth by the slow-moving, endless flow of the river. Over the centuries, ash and dirt, settling on the exposed surfaces had provided a fertile bed for airborne seeds, and debris floating downstream had become entangled with the rockpiles, forming a ragged gap-toothed weir thatched with wild grasses and a scattering of trees and bushes whose trailing roots were draped with river weeds.

Driving what remained of their herd of captured horses into the tranquil waters upstream of the highest weir, the trio crossed over into Nebraska. In its early, troubled history, the territory had proved so unappealing to would-be settlers, it had become known as the 'corridor state'. Thousands of pioneering families passed through it on the Oregon and Mormon Trails which converged at Fort Kearney then tracked westwards along the line of the Platte River. The Mormons kept to the north bank and were later followed by the riders of the Pony Express; those bound for Oregon stayed on the southern side until the river split into its main northern and southern tributaries some two-thirds of the way across Nebraska.

From here, the trails angled north-westwards, each convoy of covered wagons and handcarts keeping to its chosen side of what was now called the North Platte on the long haul up towards the high plains of Wyoming. It was only after they had passed through Caspar and had turned away from the river that their parallel paths finally came together at the South Pass through the Rockies before going their different ways again at Fort Bridger in the south-west corner of the state.

At this point, those on the Oregon Trail were only just over half-way to their final destination, but the Mormons, whose millennial fervour had roused their more orthodox eastern neighbours to violence, were close to their journey's end – the great salt lake in whose fertile valley they were to build the city that would become a monument to their unshakeable faith in a God who had not only walked the shores of Galilee but also the plains of North America.

A faith which had not saved them: a monument which the Holocaust had turned into a tomb.

Steve, Cadillac and Clearwater had been intercepted

by Malone some forty miles east of Kearney, just north of the river near navref Grand Island. On the fatal afternoon when the Skyhawk had made its strafing run, Red River had been a hundred and fifty miles south of the renegade's campsite. Acting under the orders relayed by Wallis – head of the AMEXICO task force – Commander James Fargo had kept her rolling northwards while his aircraft had gone out to pick up Clearwater, closing the gap between the wagon-train and his second visitor – Steve.

After leaving the train and crossing back over on to the north bank of the shallow river, Steve had re-traced the route taken by the Mormon leader Brigham-Young and his flock of zealots. By the time he caught up with Malone, the renegades were over a hundred miles west of the ill-fated campsite and had already passed beyond the fork in the river at navref North. Platte – a long-vanished city whose name came from its location on the slim point of land between the convergent tributaries.

Cadillac knew the place well. It was burned into his memory. He had journeyed here with Mr Snow and a posse of M'Call Bears led by Motor-Head. And at the Old One's bidding he had searched for and found a seeing-stone. A stone full of terrifying images, heavy with blood, death, sorrow and utter desolation.

This was the Old One's dying place. The memory of that revelation brought back the crushing weight of guilt and grief the act of foretelling had laid upon him. Urging his horse into a gallop, he pulled ahead of his companions to hide the bitter tears streaming down his cheeks. He wanted to distance himself from this dreadful place, but he knew it had already laid claim to his soul and was content to await his return.

The central and western thirds of Nebraska consisted of a vast treeless plain, rolling uplands thinly seeded with buffalo grass and sage, scored here and there by river valleys and streams that drained into the Platte or the Missouri. These valleys were the only shelter from the howling blizzards which had driven out the early 'sod-busters' after the sleet storms had levelled the crops they'd planned to live on through the long winter. And it was here that the trees lay hidden, cottonwood, willow and elm huddled side by side out of reach of the cutting winds.

From North Platte, the river plain varied in width from one mile to fifty, narrowing then broadening, then narrowing again as it squeezed through the surrounding uplands in its gentle climb towards the Goshen Hole on the state border.

At Scotts Bluff, Cadillac encountered another familiar land-mark, a huge yellow-ochre wedge of barren rock rising eight hundred feet above the surrounding land-scape. This was the only signpost that now remained to tell the traveller he was about to leave Nebraska and enter Wyoming. No other evidence that these two states had once existed as legislative and economic entities remained. The traffic signs and roadside buildings had gone, the abandoned, pillaged hulks of the last few Highway Patrol cars had long since crumbled into powdery flakes of rust; the more resistant parts of the engine and chassis disappearing beneath the creeping carpet of vegetation. Day by day, year by year, century after century, the planet had set about the slow task of healing itself. Now, on the eve of the third millennium, apart from the fading lines of the hardways and the few weathered ruins of collaps stone bridges, little remained of what once had been. Twentieth century America had been buried with the same relentless efficiency as the ancient cities of Sumeria.

Now at four thousand feet above sea level and still climbing, Cadillac led the way along the river trail. Malone, after privately consulting his well-concealed miniature map (printed on a square of silk supplied to AMEXICO by Ieyasu's contact men) and a tiny electronic device that took bearings from navigation beacons and converted them into map co-ordinates, found that the nearest navref point was a township called Torrington, on the old US Highway 26.

For Cadillac, visual confirmation that they were back in his home territory came in the shape of the Laramie Mountains whose densely forested slopes were home to a variety of conifers including the towering ponderosa pine. Rising like the sloping ramparts of an overgrown fort to a high point of ten thousand feet, the Laramie range forced the river to run around its northern flank like a moat, passing through navref Caspar before turning southwards and snaking uphill towards its source among the snow-melt streams of the Rockies.

It was on the plain beyond the western flank of the Laramie range that the M'Calls had made their first costly attack upon The Lady, and when Cadillac reached the shrunken lake where the river had been dammed to form the Glendo Reservoir, he turned left and led Steve and Malone's band of renegades towards a trail that wound up and over the pine-covered slopes.

Halfway between the river and the hills they came across a M'Call turf-marker – a tall pole adorned with carved plaques of wood, bones and eagle's wing feathers. A mile further on, Cadillac halted the column as a large posse of Mute warriors with the same golden feathers attached to their leather helmets emerged from the trees and formed a line across their path some two hundred yards ahead of the lead horses. Some carried the revolving-drum rifles given to the clan by the Iron Masters under the deal struck between Mr Snow and Lord Yama-Shita, the remainder were armed with cross-bows.

Malone eased his own rifle from his shoulder and laid it across his lap, a finger on the trigger. 'Friends of yours?'

'Yes.' Cadillac had already made preparations for this encounter. Pulling the elegantly curved Iron Master bow from the quiver attached to the left side of his saddle, he notched an arrow to the draw-string and presented its spear-shaped metal point to Malone. A small bundle of dried red leaves was tied to the shaft immediately behind it.

Malone applied a battery-powered hot-wire to the tips

of several leaves. They started to smoulder, emitting a dense white smoke. Pinching them together, Cadillac blew on them until the whole bundle was alight then aimed his left arm at the sky and sent the arrow soaring high into the air.

The slender arch of smoke formed as the arrow fell to earth behind the line of warriors was the sign used by the Plainfolk when they wished to parley with an opposing group. The warriors responded by raising a clenched fist which they then opened to display the palm of their hand. The invitation had been accepted.

Cadillac dismounted, planted his green flag in the ground and strode forward as a group of Mutes in the centre of the line ran to meet him. Their leader was Purple-Rain, one of the Bears who had come to the aid of Clearwater and Cadillac after the latter's duel with the fearsome Shakatak D'Vine. Cadillac embraced him warmly then grasped the outstretched hand of his excited companions. When the first flurry of greetings had been exchanged, Cadillac invited Steve and Malone to join him.

Introducing them, he said: 'You already know Cloud-Warrior. It was he who rescued me from the Iron Masters. And this is Malone, chief of the redskins who took us under their wing and journeyed with us across the great plains. They have the bodies of sand-burrowers but their hearts are with the Plainfolk and they have but one wish – to fight side by side with us against the iron-snakes!'

'Heyy-yahh! chorused the warriors, brandishing their rifles and crossbows in the air. As the rest of the posse came forward to join them Steve encountered several familiar faces. Most belonged to warriors who had attended his quarter-staff classes or had been part of the delegation that had travelled to the trading post and they greeted him with equal warmth.

The uninhibited way in which Steve responded to the bear-like hugs and ritual hand-slaps turned Malone's stomach. He could not abide physical contact with Mutes but he could not afford to be the odd man out. Forcing a smile onto his face, he shook hands with each member of the posse, disguising his desire to murder every single one of them behind a convincing display of camaraderie.

Purple-Rain ran his eyes over the assembled horsemen and foot-soldiers. He had never seen horses before but he had something far more important on his mind. 'Where is Clearwater?'

Cadillac's smile vanished. 'She was struck down by the sand-burrowers.' His words drew a mournful groan from the posse. 'But she is not dead!' he cried. 'She lies not far from here in the belly of an iron-snake and it is from there we must rescue her!'

Purple-Rain winced at the prospect of storming a wagon-train. 'Can she not use the gift of earth magic to free herself?'

'No. She is too weak. The power will not return until her wounds are healed. Attacking the iron-snake will be a daunting task but,' – he indicated Malone and the renegades with a sweeping gesture – 'we are not alone. Our friends here know its secrets and are willing to fight by our side. The M'Calls proved their bravery in the Battle of the Now and Then River but raw courage is not enough. This time we will use cunning and stealth. The power of the Old One allied to the secret knowledge of these redskins will free Clearwater and bring the sand-burrowers to their knees!'

'But the Old One is not here,' replied Purple-Rain.

Cadillac blanched. 'Not here?!'

'No. He has gone to the trading post.'

Steve was equally appalled by the news, and he could see that Malone was not too happy either. 'When did he leave?'

'Three days ago.'

Shit, shit and triple shit . . . This was a major setback. Mr Snow's presence was absolutely vital. Roz's newly-revealed powers were frightening but they were virtually untried: an unknown quantity. No one could dispute Mr Snow's powers as a summoner. He was the great equalizer; the spearhead of their attack and their first line of defence, the only sure means they had to turn the tables on Malone and the forces who would be lying in wait for them aboard Red River. And they had missed him by three days! What a pill!

The trade delegation would not return for at least five weeks. Steve had asked for and obtained six weeks in which to set up the attack on Red River. They had already used up eight days of that on the present journey to Wyoming. If the delegation was not delayed it now meant that Mr Snow would return just as the present deadline expired – leaving him no time to come up with a game-plan in which his magic would be the trump card!

They needed more elbow room. He would have to ask Malone to arrange an extension. But that was not as simple as it sounded. It was to the Federation's advantage to keep the pressure on the M'Calls – forcing them to attack the train without adequate preparation within a time-frame and in a specific location which was not of their own choosing. But how could he delay the inevitable confrontation without making Mother suspicious . . .?

Cadillac turned to Steve and Malone, his new-found confidence waning visibly. 'What are we going to do?'

Good question . . .

'I'll tell you what we ain't gonna do,' growled Malone. 'An' that's attack this goddam wagon-train of yours without a summoner up front. You sold me on this magic shit and that's the deal. If the old man don't show, we don't go!'

'He'll be back in five weeks!' pleaded Cadillac. 'Four and a half!'

'Good. Give us a call then an' we'll think about it. Adios, amigo!'

Cadillac caught hold of Malone's arm as the renegade turned towards his horse. 'Wait –'

Malone halted and broke Cadillac's grip with a knuckle-crunching squeeze. 'Don't ever lay hands on me, good buddy. Next time I'll break your fuckin' arm.' The threat was delivered with a smile for the benefit of the watching warriors.

Steve intervened. 'Hey! C'mon you guys! Cool it. I know how we can get out of this bind. I'll ride after him – bring him back.'

'It's too late!' said Cadillac. 'Didn't you hear what he said? The delegation left three days ago! They'll be at the trading post by the time you catch up with them!'

'I can try, can't I? Anyway, so what?'

'Isn't it obvious? They're not going to drop everything and come back here after going all that way. They'll stay there and trade. And it's no good thinking you're going to persuade the Old One to get on the back of the horse, because you won't!'

'So what is it you're trying to tell me?'

'It's no good going after them because you won't bring them back any sooner.'

'You underestimate me, Caddy. Especially my powers of persuasion. We've got to try. Can't you see that? Okay, maybe I won't be able to bring them back in time but someone has to go – to warn them.'

'About what?'

'About the Yama-Shita! Have you forgotten what happened on the wheel-boat? Those japs know that you and I were part of the group that destroyed the Heron Pool and that we're linked to whoever blew that boatload of samurai out of the water!'

Cadillac hesitated, unwilling to come to the inevitable conclusion. 'The commanders of the boat knew but –'

'Supposing they sent word to Sara-Kusa by carrier-pigeon?'

'You mean before the boat went down . . .'

'There was plenty of time. We were locked up for several hours.'

'So if they did . . .'

'The family will have linked you and Clearwater to the M'Calls. And Mr Snow, the man who set up the deal with Lord Yama-Shita to send a cloud-warrior to Ne-Issan is on his way to the trading post with five hundred M'Calls. If I were a member of the Yama-Shita family I'd regard this as a golden opportunity to get even – wouldn't you?'

Cadillac paled even further. 'Sweet Sky-Mother. It never occurred to me –'

'That's because you had other more important things to think about,' said Steve diplomatically. 'Truth is, we've both been wrong-footed. I was hoping we'd get back in time.' He shrugged. 'Never mind. We're still in with a chance.' He eyed Malone. 'I'd better get moving . . .'

'You're going now?!' cried Cadillac.

Steve mounted his horse. 'No point in wasting any time.'

'But what about food?'

'Caddy! I wasn't planning to go totally empty-handed. Can you rustle up some flat-bread and a pouchful of meat-twists?'

'I'll do better than that. I'll come with you!'

'Uh-uh. No way. You and our friend here have got some urgent business to attend to. You'll be able to see things more clearly if I get out of your hair for a while.

'All right. But you must have an escort. A hand of warriors, at least.'

'Caddy! I'm going on horseback! They'll never be able to keep up with me!'

Cadillac's confidence curve made an upswing. 'You might be able to outrun them in the first two or three hours, but at the end of the day, a Mute warrior will be still be running when your mount is on its knees!'

Steve capitulated. 'Okay. Go on ahead with Purple-Rain and get things organized. I'll wait here with Malone.'

'Don't you want to come into the settlement?'

'And get caught up in the celebrations? It'd take a week to get out of there!'

An hour later, Cadillac returned with six M'Call Bears led by a warrior called Cat-Ballou and a She-Wolf, the ever hopeful Night-Fever. They were all volunteers who realised the importance of their mission but apart from Night-Fever – who clearly had a more private celebration in mind – Steve could see they were somewhat cheesed

104

off at having to miss out on the party which, apparently, had already got underway.

Having profited from Cadillac's absence to square things with Malone, Steve took the Mute aside for a final word while his escort loaded the provisions they had brought onto the two pack-horses.

'Take care – and watch those breakers, huh?'

'I will . . .'

'And don't do anything rash while I'm gone.'

'I don't intend to. But let's get one thing clear, Brickman. These are my clanfolk, this is my land, attacking the wagon-train is *my* idea, and from now on, *I'm* in charge.'

Steve gathered the reins of his horse and climbed into the saddle. 'Caddy, I wouldn't have it any other way . . .'

CHAPTER FIVE

Du-aruta, the Iron Master's name for the trading-post, was a derivation of Duluth, Minnesota, the pre-H port situated at the western end of Lake Superior. But this was, in fact, something of a misnomer. As the accompanying maps show, Duluth had been built on the northern side of the Lake whereas the trading post had been planted on the opposite shore near its vanished trading partner, the port of Superior, Wisconsin.

In the days when they were both thriving transit points for the Great Lakes freight trade, Duluth and Superior were separated by the St Louis River which snaked down from northern Minnesota then turned east into a meandering estuary whose southern bank was eaten away by inlets and bays. A triangular chunk of land – on which the town of Superior stood – pushed the estuary in a north-easterly direction, but on rounding the point it made a sharp right hand turn into a long narrow lagoon bisected by the state line.

The lagoon itself was separated from Lake Superior by two low needle-like spits of sand and gravel which reached out from the opposing shores to form an almost unbroken line running from the north-west to the south-east.

In pre-Holocaust days the upper and lower sand-bars were separated by a three-hundred foot wide shipping channel kept open by dredgers. With the passage of time, the channel had silted up, narrowing to half its original width, and was now only thigh deep. The land to the south and west of the trading post consisted of rolling plains sloping gently upwards away from the lake, but on the Duluth side, the estuary sand-bar and the lake beyond were dominated by six-hundred foot high bluffs that rose steeply from the narrow shore.

The first thing that struck Mr Snow on reaching the trading post was the size of the D'Troit and C'Natti encampments. Traditionally, the delegations from the six bloodlines were camped around the outside of a huge octagon marked out by a line of stones. The She-Kargo and D'Troit – who were both allocated two segments – faced each other across the central reservation, flanked on each side by the supposedly neutral, lesser bloodlines – the M'Waukee, C'Natti, San'Paul and San'Louis. This arrangement was designed to minimize the violent confrontations which, despite the general truce and the restraining presence of marshals and capos, always flared up as groups of young bloods from both sides prowled around the outer edge of the vast encampment looking for trouble.

This year, the dispositions of the various groups was the same, but not only were the individual D'Troit and C'Natti delegations much larger than usual, there were a great number of turf-markers belonging to Clans who had never been represented before.

Discreet enquiries through intermediaries elicited the reason: the Iron Masters, because of some internal upheaval, had withdrawn the boats which normally called at Bei-Sita, the second trading post serving the Mute clans inhabiting the plains close to the Eastern Lands – the pre-Holocaust states of Ohio, Indiana, and the broad peninsular bordered by Lake Erie, Huron and Michigan – the original home of the D'Troit.

As a result of this temporary closure, the delegations had made their way to Du-aruta. No one wanted to miss the once-yearly opportunity to exchange skins, furs, dream-cap and rainbow-grass for new knives, crossbows, tools, woven cloth and utensils. And, of course, there was always the hope that more clans would be able to obtain examples of the rifles supplied to the clan M'Call the year before.

To understand what went through Mr Snow's mind it

THE TRADING POST / DU-ARUTA

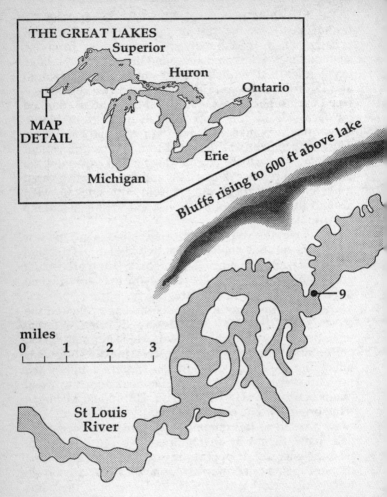

THE GREAT LAKES

Superior

Huron

Ontario

MAP
DETAIL

Erie

Michigan

Bluffs rising to 600 ft above lake

9

miles

0   1   2   3

St Louis
River

KEY TO MAP
1 - Trading Post
2 - Campsite (Lines)
3 - Bull Ring
4 - Lower Sandbar
5 - Shipping Channel
6 - Upper Sandbar
7 - Spur (Headland)
8 - Fording Point
9 - Second Fording Point
10 - Mr Snow's Battle Position

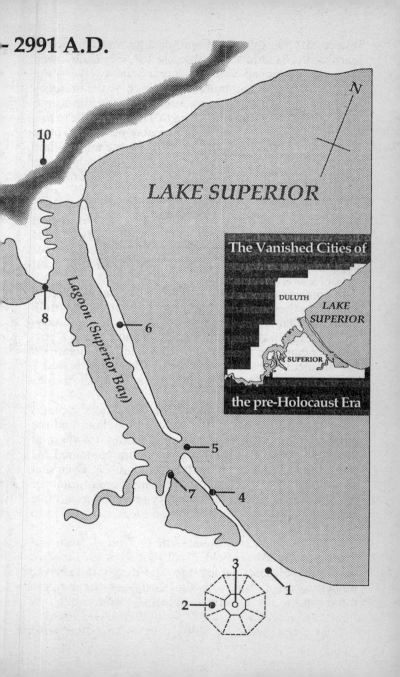

N

LAKE SUPERIOR

10

Lagoon (Superior Bay)

8

6

The Vanished Cities of

DULUTH

LAKE SUPERIOR

SUPERIOR

the pre-Holocaust Era

5

7

4

3

2

1

is necessary to explain that mathematics was a branch of learning the Plainfolk had little use for, especially when the sums embraced numbers larger than twelve – the number of fingers and thumbs possessed by the majority of Mutes. It had always been accepted that the She-Kargo were numerically superior to the D'Troit but prior to this fateful gathering the rival factions had never carried out a head-count of their supporters. This also meant they had no clear idea of the number of warriors their opponents could muster. On this occasion however, the D'Troit had received some outside help.

Over the years of trading with the Mutes, the Yama-Shita family had amassed a great deal of information about the various bloodlines and the multiplicity of clans grouped within. And with the Iron Master's passion for paperwork, everything had been duly recorded in great detail by a battery of scribes.

In some respects, such as the size and breakdown of each clan, they probably knew more about the Plainfolk than the Plainfolk themselves, and like any military-minded organization gathering intelligence about a pot-ential enemy – or client-state – they had even identified the distinctive headgear and turf-markers that placed a clan within a particular bloodline but set it apart from its neighbours.

As part of the larger picture the wheel-boat captains knew the relative size of the various bloodlines and the numbers they could expect to find waiting for them at the trading post. The She-Kargo bloodline contained 242 clans, the M'Waukee 103 and the San'Paul 38. Each sent an average of 150 delegates – making a grand total for the She-Kargo faction of some fifty-seven thousand five hundred delegates – adult males and females from 15 to 55, all fit and able to fight.

Under normal circumstances the D'Troit, C'Natti and San'Louis would have fielded, collectively, some fifty-two thousand delegates giving the She-Kargo faction the numerical edge. But with the closing of the Bei-Sita trading post, the D'Troit faction had been swollen by another 92 delegations from the clans whose turf lay to the east of Lake Michigan. The total number of C'Natti and San'Louis delegations had also increased for the same reason.

Added together, this should have produced a grand total of some seventy-six thousand warriors – large enough to confer a comfortable margin of superiority. But each clan had sent an above average number of delegates. Reinforced by the unexpectedly large numbers of 'journey-men', the D'Troit, C'Natti and San'Louis had fielded a staggering one hundred and sixty-three thousand warriors – giving them an advantage of almost three to one. With that number of people milling about the camp site, it was hardly surprising that the She-Kargo faction thought the odds were even greater.

Since they had no independent means of checking out the state of play at the Bei-Sita trading-post, the She-Kargo were obliged to accept the explanation they were offered. It seemed plausible enough but it did not justify the inflated numbers of journey-men which the D'Troit and C'Natti had brought with them to trade for goods and weapons. Some surreptitious head-counting by the same intrepid intermediaries established that some D'Troit clans known to be only half the size of the M'Calls were proposing to exchange over one hundred men and women whereas the M'Calls themselves had never sent more than fifty down the river in any one year.

The situation was unique and potentially explosive. A hastily convened meeting of elders from the She-Kargo delegations could only envisage two possible explanations: one – by offering so many 'guest-workers', the D'Troit and C'Natti hoped to elbow their rivals aside and grab the lion's share of whatever the Iron Masters had come to trade or, two – the army of journey-men with their yellow headbands were *not* destined to sail away across the Great River *but were here for some other purpose*. Either way it spelt trouble.

The M'Call delegation, some seven hundred miles from their settlement, were too far away to send for reinforcements but some of the other She-Kargo and M'Waukee delegations whose homes were within a day's run promptly despatched messengers to summon reinforcements.

All this was done in great secrecy. Mr Snow and the other wordsmiths had decided that there was to be no provocation and no outward show of suspicion. The explanation furnished by the D'Troit wordsmiths had to be taken at face value. By their own sacred tradition, wordsmiths – even from opposing bloodlines – never lied to one another. If they had not betrayed their oath, then the Iron Masters must have closed down Bei-Sita. The question everyone in the She-Kargo camp was asking was – why?

A hint as to what the answer might be came with the arrival of Carnegie-Hall, wordsmith of the Clan Kojak from the bloodline of the M'Waukee. Entering the bull-ring where the other wordsmiths habitually gathered to exchange news and gossip, he sought out Mr Snow and under cover of the formal greetings exchanged on such occasions, passed over a whispered request for a meeting when darkness fell.

Several hours later when a thousand camp-fires pierced the darkness like orange blossoms scattered on black velvet, Carnegie-Hall, accompanied by five Kojak warriors, was led by a M'Call guide into the small wood west of the camp-site where Mr Snow and his own body-guard stood waiting.

The two wordsmiths sat down on talking mats, their faces lit by the solitary flame of a fire-stone which lay between them. Its glow which sharp eyes could have seen from the camp-site was masked by the cloak Mr Snow had thrown over a nearby bush and the dense undergrowth beyond. As a person, Mr Snow would not have given Carnegie-Hall the time of day, but as a fellow wordsmith he had to be treated with the courtesy traditionally accorded to all practitioners of the ancient art.

'What say you, brother? Do you bring me good tidings or bad?'

'I bring news of great happenings. It is for you to judge whether they are good or ill. But first let us speak of The Chosen. Did your clansmen return safely and in good spirits?'

Mr Snow was familiar with the term 'The Chosen', but for some reason, didn't catch on immediately. 'Clansmen . . .?'

'Cadillac, Clearwater and Cloud-Warrior.'

Mr Snow's present anxieties vanished under a great surge of elation. 'They escaped from the Eastern Lands?!'

'Escaped and more! They are The Chosen – the first of the Lost Ones whose return heralds the coming of Talisman!'

'It is true that these three were born in the shadow of Talisman. By what token do you know them as The Chosen?'

'The words were born on my lips!' exclaimed Carnegie. 'The Thrice-Gifted One appointed me to be the first to recognize them and name them! And when the history of the Plainfolk is retold in the ages to come, the Kojak will be remembered as the clan that first gave them shelter, and whose valiant warriors played a decisive part in the victories achieved by their mighty powers!'

'Victories . . .?'

'Over the arrowheads, the iron-snake and the wheel-boat!'

'Sounds like they've been busy,' grumped Mr Snow. 'Tell me more.'

Carnegie-Hall gave him the whole story including – to his credit – the treacherous deal struck with Izo Wantanabe which, as events unfolded, had reinforced his belief that his steps had been guided by Talisman. And as might be expected he laid great emphasis on the part the Kojak had played in the destruction of the wheel-boat.

As Mr Snow sat listening to Carnegie's graphic description of how the Kojak had massacred the horse-borne samurai, red-stripe infantry and sailors who had struggled ashore, his sense of foreboding increased. All this had

113

happened weeks ago. Since when, Cadillac, Clearwater and Brickman had departed in triumph, with a pile of booty and more than a hundred head of horses – the four-legged beasts which the dead-faces had tamed and learned to ride but which, up to that moment, Mr Snow had never seen.

The trio had last been reported heading westwards towards Nebraska. The southern route! Mr Snow silently cursed the Sky Voices for sending him in the wrong direction. No doubt, by the immutable perverseness of Sod's Law, his protégés would – barring some mishap – have arrived at the settlement within a day or two of his departure!

Never mind. Carnegie-Hall's story had amply confirmed Mr Snow's belief that his two young charges and the cloud-warrior were destined to achieve greatness. They were indeed The Chosen, recognized and hailed as such not just by the Kojak, but by the clans they had encountered in crossing the Central Plains. Whatever misfortune might befall them, they would survive and grow ever stronger, for the power of the Thrice-Gifted One was upon them. An invisible force which, if not an impervious shield, would preserve and heal their earth bodies and the spirit within.

Once again Mr Snow regretted that he would not live to see the saviour of the Plainfolk revealed. But he now understood why the Sky Voices had directed him towards the trading post. It was here the immediate danger lay, and it was here that his gift of power and his courage would be sorely tested.

Perhaps to the limit – and beyond . . .

'What you have said explains a great deal.' Producing a pipe charged with rainbow grass, Mr Snow lit it, taking a soothing puff before offering it to his visitor. 'Old Golden Nose is not going to let such a catastrophic reverse pass unavenged.'

Old Golden Nose was a nickname derived from the elaborate black and gold mask which Domain-Lord Hirohito Yama-Shita wore whenever he appeared at the trading post. Depending on their rank, all Iron-Masters wore masks of one sort or another when dealing with the Mutes – a practice which had given birth to the generic term 'dead-faces'.

'Lord Yama-Shita is dead,' announced Carnegie-Hall.

The news took Mr Snow's breath away. 'How do you know this?'

'Cadillac told me. Before escaping from the Eastern Lands, your clansmen fought a mighty battle with the dead-faces.'

Mr Snow listened with a mixture of pride and dismay as the Kojak wordsmith repeated Cadillac's spell-binding story of death and destruction at the Heron Pool including, in all its gory detail, the moment when Clearwater had compelled the domain-lord to kill himself several times over.

The loss of the wheel-boat with all hands, coming hard on the heels of the mega-debacle that Carnegie-Hall had just described merely added insult to injury. Lord Yama-Shita might be dead – and that removed one formidable adversary from the field – but his successors would be honour bound to strike a devastating blow in return.

The first opportunity to do so would be when the wheel-boats ran their noses aground on the beach by the trading post. It was going to be a strange feeling, watching the vessels appear over the dawn horizon and knowing that this time, as they grew larger and larger and the dread sound of their engines reached the ears of the waiting Mutes, there would be no obsequious welcoming ceremony, full of false smiles and bogus cameraderie. This time, the rising sun would mark the beginning of a countdown that would end in an explosive confrontation; an orgy of blood-letting whose limits could not be foreseen and whose consequences were incalculable.

After a long moment of reflection Mr Snow said: 'I think I can see how this is going to play. The Yama-Shita won't attack us directly. To do so would jeopardize their whole trading operation. That's why the D'Troit and

C'Natti are here in such large numbers. The family is going to use them to put the knife in.'

Mr Snow smiled as he took back the pipe and inhaled some more smoke. 'You're probably on the hit-list too. I'm surprised you came.'

Carnegie-Hall bristled. 'You dare to call the Kojak cowards – after all we have done?!'

'Calm down, Carney. No one's calling you anything. The M'Calls have never backed out of a fight, but if I'd known what we were walking into, I'd have been severely tempted to stay at home.'

'We came because we thought The Chosen would be here!' exclaimed Carnegie-Hall. 'We have seen their power! With them at our side we have nothing to fear. The dead-faces are powerless against them!' Then, with engaging candour, he added: 'Had I known they weren't going to show, we might have had second thoughts too. But where could we go?'

'It's a big country,' replied Mr Snow. 'But if someone's determined to find you, there's no place you can hide. If you have to make a stand, you might as well make it here – amongst your own kind.' He paused and appraised his visitor. 'The M'Calls can count on their blood-brothers. Can the She-Kargo count on the M'Waukee?'

Carnegie-Hall shifted uneasily. 'At this moment I cannot say.'

'You trying to tell me you've found a way to get your head off the block?'

'No! It's just that –'

'– by standing aside, you hope to save your own skins.'

'Never!' cried Carnegie-Hall. 'The M'Calls may be the paramount clan of the She-Kargo. but it is the Kojak who have proved their worth in battle with the dead-faces!'

'With a little help . . .'

'How generous of you!' sneered Carnegie-Hall. 'It takes little courage to face the enemy when you know you are protected by the mantle of Talisman! Your clanfolk emerged unscathed. Mine paid for their triumph with their own blood! How dare you impugn the honour of the Kojak! This conversation is at an end!'

Mr Snow laid a restraining hand on his visitor's knee as he moved to get up. 'Nice try, Carney. You always were good at the old huff'n puff. But don't give me this honour nonsense. Everyone knows you as a man with his eye on the main chance. You've admitted as much yourself. You were prepared to sell my people down the river for a boxful of geegaws!'

Carnegie-Hall dropped the self-righteous anger and adopted the air of a honourable man who has been sorely wronged. 'That was before Talisman revealed his purpose to me! Yes, it is true that when he put his words onto my tongue my heart was full of treachery, but all that changed when he filled my mind with his presence! It is easy for you to look down on us from your safe haven in the far mountains. We live on the front line! The dead-faces now have men and boats on the far side of the waters which were once our own! You seek our help now – what help can we expect from you once you have journeyed beyond the Black Hills?!'

'Not much, I grant you. That's why we have to stand together now. If there *is* a fight, we have to win it. Do you want to live under the heel of the D'Troit?'

'It is a fate many of the M'Waukee already endure.'

'Then now is your chance to get out from under. We can count on the San'Paul. You are the only people who can talk to the San'Louis.'

It was obvious that Carnegie-Hall did not relish the prospect of getting embroiled in a potentially fatal confrontation with the D'Troit. 'It will not be easy,' he muttered. 'Is there no hope that The Chosen will get here in time?'

Mr Snow drew down some more smoke. 'Carney, I could make the right kind of noises in order to string you along but I'm not going to. The answer is – I just don't know but from what my gut is telling me, I'd say the chances are virtually nil. We're going to have to manufacture our own miracles. The only consolation I can offer is the news that Clearwater, the young lady whose performance has so impressed you, is a pupil of mine. She's good – but I'm better.'

'The D'Troit have summoners too.'

'The D'Troit?! Don't make me laugh! Their best man can't even move a pile of buffalo shit unless he has a shovel!' Mr Snow waved the threat away. 'Go back to your lines and talk to your blood-brothers. Contact the leader of each delegation and persuade them to come to a meeting with their paramount warrior plus every available wordsmith and summoner. I want them here within two notches for a meeting with their opposite numbers from the She-Kargo.'

A notch was a standard measurement of time marked on candles made from animal fat and represented one pre-Holocaust hour. The system had originated with the Iron Masters. Having obtained some of these candles at the trading post, the Mutes had made copies of their own. In their normal daily lives, Mutes were not clock-watchers; the candles were only used in situations which were time-critical – such as the present gathering at the trading post.

'Two notches! Sweet Mother, that doesn't give us much time.'

'We're as short of time as we are of people. That's why we've gotta move – fast!'

As they both got to their feet, Carnegie asked: 'What about the San' Louis.'

'Sound them out. See which way the wind's blowing but don't tell them about the meeting.'

Carnegie-Hall nodded, his eyes full of doubt. 'I hope we're doing the right thing.'

'Trust me,' said Mr Snow. He gave Carnegie's arm a reassuring squeeze. 'I too am guided by Talisman. This is what he sent me here for. To preserve the freedom of the Plainfolk.'

Between dawn and nine o'clock on the following day, the last of the trade delegations arrived and set up camp in the area allotted to their own bloodline. Most of them were new faces belonging to the D'Troit. Their appearance caused the heavily-outnumbered She-Kargo and M'Waukee to feel both beleaguered and belligerent and by mid-morning, when all the wordsmiths had gathered in the bull-ring for the opening round of their annual talk-fest the atmosphere had become electric. Everyone was filled with that oppressive sense of foreboding you get when a violent storm is about to break.

In order to appreciate what follows it is necessary to explain that while most but not all clans possessed wordsmiths, very few of these gifted individuals were summoners. Mutes born with two gifts – such as Mr Snow (wordsmith and summoner) and Cadillac (wordsmith and seer) – were extremely rare. And summoners as powerful as Mr Snow and Clearwater were rarer still.

The same degrees of professional competence applied to wordsmiths. The M'Calls had enjoyed the benefit of an unbroken line of wordsmiths stretching back through successive generations to the War of a Thousand Suns. This distinction, shared by only a handful of clans, enhanced Mr Snow's standing but also engendered a great deal of envy.

In many respects, wordsmiths resembled any group of Pre-H professionals. Like lawyers, they came in all shapes and sizes and while they all possessed what was once known as 'the gift of the gab' their performance – as 20th century clients often discovered to their cost – spanned the ratings from the peaks of excellence to the troughs of incompetence.

Like the plethora of personal computers of the pre-H era that came fitted with differing amounts of hard-disc storage, some wordsmiths' memories were better than others. Compared to the ordinary Mute armed with the equivalent of 256K RAM, your average wordsmith with a hundred gigabytes on line was a mental giant – a walking reference library.

However, as with all people-based systems, there was one drawback. Memory is not a product or function of character: the most able brains do not necessarily reside inside the heads of charismatic human beings, or even just plain nice ones. The greatest data-bank in the world is not worth a row of beans if there's a dildo manning the front desk. But when a few zillion gigabytes of memory was allied to an exceedingly acute mind – as in the case of Mr Snow – the result was an outstanding personality whose opinions and influence extended far beyond the narrow confines of their own clan or even their own bloodline.

But while Mr Snow might be regarded as the star of the She-Kargo, there were other noteworthy contenders among the D'Troit and C'Natti ready to pit their wits against his. And they were present on that fateful morning.

Last year, Mr Snow, by virtue of his age and experience, had been selected to chair the proceedings; this year, his place had been awarded to a senior wordsmith from the rival faction – Prime-Cut, leader of the Clan R'Nato from the bloodline of the D'Troit.

Because of Cadillac's triumphal progress through Illinois, Iowa and eastern Nebraska – where the trail had run cold – the hottest topic among the wordsmiths from those areas was the appearance of The Chosen, the trio from the Clan M'Call. The news of their exploits and their escape from the Eastern Lands was not confined to the bull-ring. Exaggerated reports of their prowess passed on by those who had witnessed their travelling road-show were now spreading like a bush-fire through the whole encampment.

To the wordsmiths from the various delegations it was both a source of satisfaction and alarm. Apart from Carnegie-Hall and Mr Snow, none of those present were aware of any prophecy which bore a reference to these individuals and no seer had found their image in the stones. The prediction which came closest referred to the return of The Lost Ones – the generations of Mutes who had been taken away by the dead-faces to the Fire-Pits of Beth-Lem and their off-spring, the Iron-Feet – born into slavery in the Eastern lands.

Invited to take centre-stage, Carnegie-Hall launched into a colourful explanation of how he had met Cadillac, Clearwater and Cloud-Warrior – carefully omitting the details of his treacherous deal with Izo Wantanabe. Guided by Talisman he had despatched a posse of Kojak warriors through the winter snows to a rendezvous with the select band of individuals who were to herald the coming of the Thrice-Gifted One.

A graphic account of their powers – which Clearwater had used to destroy four arrowheads with one wave of her hand and which, later, had been employed to rip the belly out of an iron-snake – made a deep impression on his attentive audience. When he had finished, he appealed to Mr Snow. Had the Sky Voices not told him that Cadillac, Clearwater and Cloud-Warrior were born in the shadow of Talisman?

Rising to his feet, Mr Snow agreed that this was so.

His affirmation of Carnegie's claim sparked off a heated argument. Individual wordsmiths from the D'Troit and C'Natti camps leapt to their feet to protest. Out of all the Plainfolk why should three warriors from the Clan M'Call have been chosen to herald the coming of Talisman? It was just another ploy by the She-Kargo and their lackeys amongst the M'Waukee to further inflate their already exaggerated importance.

No wordsmith, claimed the protesters, had ever spoken of The Chosen in this bull-ring until Carnegie-Hall had coined the phrase. It was all a put-up job; something concocted on the flimsiest of evidence by the Kojak and the M'Calls. At best it was a well-intentioned mis-reading of the events in question; at worst, a total fabrication.

Carnegie-Hall vigorously defended himself but the carefully orchestrated outburst had achieved its aim, splitting the gathering into three camps: the pro-She-Kargo faction who supported the proposition, the pro-D'Troit faction who rejected it, and the uncommitted who were waiting to see who was going to get the better of the argument.

Mean-Machine, a C'Natti wordsmith, made his voice heard amid the hubbub and threw down a challenge. If Carnegie-Hall and those who supported him were speaking the truth where was this mysterious trio? Why had the Clan M'Call not brought them to the trading post where they could display their powers and spread their message to the assembled representatives of the Plainfolk?

Good point, thought Mr Snow. He cursed himself for not having a ready answer.

Carnegie-Hall leapt up angrily and confronted Mean-Machine, his menacing bulk towering over his smaller opponent. 'Do you dare to call me a liar?!'

Prime-Cut – an equally imposing figure – rose and stepped off the low mound which the chairman trad-itionally occupied. 'No!' he cried. Pushing Carnegie-Hall and Mean-Machine apart, he aimed an arm between them, an accusing finger pointed at Mr Snow. 'There sits the man who has lied to us all!'

His words drew a shocked gasp from the uncommitted and an angry roar from the She-Kargo wordsmiths. Half of them got to their feet, exchanging accusations and abuse with their more aggressive counterparts on the other side of the ring.

Prime-Cut spread his arms in a commanding gesture. 'Cease this noise!' he thundered. 'Sit down and parley in the proper manner or leave this place!'

The uproar subsided as the more vociferous protestors and counter-protestors resumed their seats but the murm-uring continued, becoming a sullen underswell of sound.

As Mean-Machine and Carnegie-Hall settled into their places, Mr Snow got to his feet and appealed to his supporters. 'Let peace descend! Let your minds be tran-quil. I am the one who stands accused here. My con-science is clear! Let the charges be heard!'

The murmuring gradually subsided under the fierce gaze of the Plainfolk's two most prestigious wordsmiths.

When silence had been obtained Mr Snow turned to face Prime-Cut in the centre of the bull-ring. Attracted by the violence of the argument, the open space between the inner and outer rings was now crowded with clan elders and other members of the various delegations.

As the R'Nato wordsmith circled him with a wolfish grin, Mr Snow muttered: 'I hope you know what you're doing.'

'Oh, I do, my friend, I do.' Prime-Cut halted by Mr Snow's shoulder and thrust his mouth close to the Old One's ear. 'You are in deep shit,' he whispered. 'I'm going to bury you!'

'You're not the first man to try and do that.' Mr Snow's voice had a confident ring but he felt cold and sick inside. Already outnumbered on the ground, the She-Kargo was in danger of losing the battle for hearts and minds and he could see no way to reverse the situation.

Drawing back, Prime-Cut pointed a finger at his victim and addressed the ring of wordsmiths in a voice loud enough to carry to the expectant crowd beyond.

'You have heard our brother speak! His name is renowned, his memory legend! Yet even he is bound, as we are, by the wordsmith's oath to forswear all falsehoods, to faithfully chronicle the deeds of the Plain-folk and reveal, in their full majesty, the revelations of the Sky Voices!

'To relay the truth, adorned and embellished by his art but sure and solid as a rock, clear and pure as a mountain stream' – his voice hardened – 'not buried beneath shifting sand, or muddied by deceit! You were witness to his claim that the Sky Voices had told him that Cadillac, Clearwater and Cloud-Warrior were born in the shadow of Talisman. Is that not so?!'

'Aye!!' chorused the wordsmiths.

'Were those your words?' demanded Prime-Cut.

Mr Snow sensed the trap but could see no way out. 'They were.'

Prime-Cut could hardly contain himself. 'You hear?!' he thundered. 'He stands condemned out of his own mouth! The young brave known to the Kojak as Cloud-Warrior, and who our revered brother' – he indicated Mr Snow with an elaborate gesture – 'claims as one of the three M'Calls chosen to lead the Plainfolk towards nationhood is not a Mute at all!'

The charge provoked roars of anger and cries of disbelief.

'"Cloud-Warrior" is a name as false as the colour of his skin! He is a sand-burrower from the dark cities – known to his masters as Brickman!'

More shouting. Prime-Cut demanded silence and faced Mr Snow. 'How do you answer?!'

Mr Snow eyed his accuser calmly. 'Is that it?'

'No, there is more!'

'Then I'll wait till you've finished.'

Prime-Cut appealed to his audience. 'Evasions! You see how his serpent tongue wriggles to avoid the truth?! Well I shall reveal it! All of you seated here who played host to The Chosen have been cruelly deceived! Cadillac, Clearwater and Cloud-Warrior are agents of the Federation! And they are not alone! Mr Snow – who would have us believe he is our brother – and the entire clan have sold their souls to the sand-burrowers!'

Once again the meeting erupted with cries of protest and condemnation. Charges and counter-charges were hurled back and forth by the opposing camps and the D'Troit and C'Natti wordsmiths set up a strident chant: 'OUT-OUT-OUT-OUT!' The confusion and bitterness spread amongst the spectators outside the bull-ring, leading to angry exchanges and physical violence. Fortunately there were enough line-capos on hand to restrain the D'Troit hot-heads who were clearly out to cause trouble. Mr Snow had foreseen this and following his midnight meeting with the leaders of the She-Kargo and M'Waukee delegations, their clanfolk had been given strict instructions not to succumb to any provocation from the rival camps.

In the midst of this commotion, Mr Snow stood firm. Seemingly oblivious of the jostling mass of bodies crowded around him, he radiated a deceptive calm like the eye of a hurricane.

Prime-Cut's accusations were highly damaging but Mr Snow could not allow himself to be drawn into answering specific accusations. By remaining silent and allowing the torrent of charges to wash over him, he hoped to tempt Prime-Cut into revealing all his cards and – with luck – the R'Nato wordsmith might even end up as the accused instead of the accuser.

But it was hard to resist the cries of 'Answer! Answer!' from his own camp, and it was clear from the anguished expressions on all sides that many of his friends were in despair at his failure to defend himself.

Prime-Cut ran through a devastating list of questions to which Mr Snow had no answer. Had the sand-burrower not descended from the skies? Did the clan not harbour him in their midst and treat him as one of their own – to the point of even giving him a bedmate? Did they not release him? Had he not returned the following year on a new mission for his masters? Had Mr Snow not brought him to the trading post where he had stolen aboard a wheel-boat to join his two accomplices in Ne-Issan?

And once there, had they not wreaked bloody havoc at a place called the Heron Pool – slaughtering the true friends of the Plainfolk? The Iron Masters who furnished them with weapons and the necessities of existence? But even that was not enough! These ingrates had murdered Domain-Lord Yama-Shita, Captain of all the wheel-boats and master of the Great River! The visionary who over the past years had sought to deepen the links and friendship between Mute and Iron Master.

It was a long time since Mr Snow had heard such sycophantic rubbish but it was clear that Prime-Cut's share of the audience were swallowing it whole. And they were cheering him on!

The calumny reached its climax. The M'Calls had betrayed their brothers, but that was only to be expected. Such treachery was in the blood of the She-Kargo. No longer able to maintain their superiority by force of arms,

125

they were now seeking to bolster their position by secret deals with the sand-burrowers!

Again there was uproar, each side trying to howl the other down. It was a serious charge and it confirmed Mr Snow's reading of the situation. His knowledge of what had happened in Ne-Issan was limited to what Cadillac had told Carnegie-Hall. But at Mr Snow's request, Carnegie-Hall – when addressing the wordsmiths in the bull-ring – had not mentioned the battle at the Heron Pool or the death of Lord Yama-Shita.

Prime-Cut could have only gotten this information from the Iron Masters. The D'Troit and their allies the C'Natti were acting as mouthpieces for the Yama-Shita, but how deep did their involvement go – and how long had they been getting their act together? Long enough to put the She-Kargo on the spot. The degree of coordination between the D'Troit and She-Kargo and the inflated size of their delegations was proof of that. The Iron Masters intended to take their revenge here, at the trading post. Tomorrow. And they were using Prime-Cut to set the stage with his accusations.

It was time to begin the fight-back. He had to defend himself, his clan and the good name of the She-Kargo. And he had to do so publicly in a way that was effective but did not provoke an immediate and violent response. The battle, if there was to be one, had to be on a ground of his own choosing.

By putting him in the dock and trying to make scapegoats out of the M'Calls, Prime-Cut seemed to be trying to isolate the clan from the rest of the Plainfolk. Having achieved that, it would not be too difficult – in view of the enormity of their crimes – to persuade the gathering to hand the M'Call delegation over as a sacrificial offering to appease the Iron Masters. But it hadn't worked. The vociferous support he had received from the other She-Kargo wordsmiths was proof that the M'Calls had not been abandoned. Which was, Mr Snow realized, just what Prime-Cut intended. The blow, when struck, would be aimed at the entire She-Kargo faction. The hand of the D'Troit would be on the knife but they would be acting for the dead-faces. And by this unparalleled act of treachery they hoped to fulfil their long-held ambition to become the paramount bloodline. It was ironic. The D'Troit had become the running dogs of the Iron Masters and yet it was the M'Calls who were accused of betraying the Plainfolk.

But it was not over yet . . .

The focus of Mr Snow's attention turn outwards as the noise subsided. Prime-Cut stood in front of him, trembling as he cranked up the required level of indignation. 'How do you answer?!'

Mr Snow chuckled then raised his voice to address the assembled wordsmiths. 'How do I answer?' He turned full circle, arms out-stretched. 'My brothers under the sun, you have heard what passes as the truth fall from the lips of the D'Troit. You have seen their spokesman circle me like a hungry jackal around an ageing bull. Why? That is the question you must ask yourselves – and which I attempt to answer!

'Why does he choose this moment to accuse me of treachery? Why does he attack the honour of the She-Kargo at a time when the Plainfolk have come together in peace and fellowship? Are his words as pure and clear as a mountain stream or do they mask some dark ambition of the D'Troit which they have yet to reveal?'

'Heyy-yaahhh. . .' The She-Kargo and M'Waukee wordsmiths and their supporters massed beyond the bull-ring voiced a sombre chorus of approval.

'And you must also ask yourself *how* he knows these things. Who else is aware of the events of which he speaks?'

The question, aimed at those around him, met with no response.

'Reflect on what he has told us. He speaks of Mutes who are not Mutes, of secret journeys through the clouds and across the seas to the Eastern Lands! Of battles between Mute and Iron Masters in which the noble lords of Ne-Issan perished in their hundreds! Of wheel-boats sunk by red-eyed nightbirds!

'Are these inventions of a fevered mind? Dreams inspired by envy of his betters? If they are not, how does he know – in such detail – what took place far beyond the Great River, beyond the Running Red Buffalo Hills?! He does not speak, like you or I who only a short while ago listened to our brother Carnegie but as someone with foreknowledge of these events! He has never *met* The Chosen yet he speaks of their great battle at the Heron Pool and the death of Domain-Lord Yama-Shita as if he had *been* there!

'How can he know of such things! There can only be one answer! These words through which he seeks to bring disgrace upon me and the She-Kargo were put into his mouth by the dead-faces – an alien race that would make slaves of us all!'

'Heyy-YAHHH!' This time it was a full-throated cheer. And it came from all sides of the ring.

Mr Snow raised his voice. 'Well, they will not make slaves of the She-Kargo! The weapons they provide are not *given* to us. They are exchanged for goods we gather through sweat and blood and our most priceless possession – our Clan-brothers and sisters! Think back to when this all began. Have you forgotten how they killed those who refused their offerings?! And yet this man stands before us and says we must show gratitude? For what?! We trade with the dead-faces not by choice but by necessity! But there is one thing we will never trade – our freedom!'

This ringing declaration was greeted by a tumultuous cheer.

Mr Snow pointed to Prime-Cut. 'He charges me with treachery! He tries to tell you that The Chosen are agents of the Federation because they were born to the bloodline of the She-Kargo! What will his hatred and envy lead him to do next?! Deny the power of Talisman?

'The Chosen do not belong to the Clan M'Call or the She-Kargo *or* the D'Troit! They are of the Plainfolk! The first of the Lost Ones to return from the Eastern Lands – as it was prophesied – to herald the coming of the Thrice-Gifted One! Under his banner we shall become a mighty nation! We shall crush the dark cities and drive the dead-faces back into the sea!

'This should be a time of rejoicing, not anger! Are we not all brothers under the sun?'

The ground shook as ten thousand voices chanted their response. 'Heyy-YAHHH! Heyy-YAHHH! HEYY-YAAHHH!!'

Mr Snow pointed to Prime-Cut. 'Then beware of those who seek to divide us, for it is they who are the *real* enemy!'

The wordsmiths leapt to their feet to avoid being trampled down by the excited crowd pressing in around them. Those from the D'Troit camp looked sullen and frustrated but everyone else, including many of the C'Natti were cheering and raising their fists in a gesture of solidarity.

Prime-Cut gave it one last try. 'You ask us to believe in The Chosen, but they are not here! Are they frightened to appear before us in case their so-called feats of bravery on behalf of the Plainfolk are revealed for what they *really* are – criminal acts sanctioned by the sand-burrowers who wish to destroy our friendship with those who give us aid and support?!'

His booming voice cut through the surrounding noise, bringing a sudden hush.

Mr Snow closed his eyes, raised his face briefly to the sky then said the first thing that came into his head. 'The Chosen do not fear the truth! They are not here because they confront an enemy the warriors of the D'troit have yet to face! At this moment, as I speak, they battle against the iron-snakes of the Federation!'

The bull-ring erupted with thunderous cheers. Prime-Cut looked as if he was about to bust a blood-vessel, but it was all over and he knew it. He stepped forward, teeth bared, and came nose to nose with Mr Snow. 'You lying sonofabitch!'

'Easy for you to say,' chuckled Mr Snow. 'But can you prove it?'

Before Prime-Cut could frame a reply, several of the She-Kargo wordsmiths hoisted their hero onto their shoulders and carried him in triumph from the ring.

In the afternoon, with the help of the M'Waukee, who provided them with a suitable disguise, a group claiming to represent an important number of C'Natti trade delegations sought an audience with Mr Snow. Essentially, what they had to say was this: they were greatly concerned that the actions of certain members of the She-Kargo might jeopardize the existing trading arrangements (and they left Mr Snow in no doubt as to who they were referring to) but – and it was an important proviso – they were not prepared to lend their support to 'those elements who were actively contemplating a joint action with the Iron Master against certain of the Plainfolk'.

Having stated their position, the disguised spokesmen proceeded to ask questions. Did the She-Kargo have any plans to resist a surprise attack by a rival faction? If so, they were prepared to help in any way they could.

Once again, they did not name names, but there was no doubt who the C'Natti spokesmen were referring to. Their veiled expressions of solidarity could well have been genuine but Mr Snow could not be sure. They might have been sent by the D'Troit in the hope of discovering what, if anything, the She-Kargo had up their sleeve.

Framing his reply as carefully as he could to avoid spurning what might be a bonafide offer, Mr Snow said: 'There is no plan. We have put our faith in Talisman. Let those who believe in him stand by us. The She-Kargo will never be the first to draw sharp iron against their brothers.

'The last thing we wish to do is divide the Plainfolk, especially now when The Chosen are amongst us. All of us must put an end to our ancient blood-feuds. We must cleanse our hearts and minds, sweep away our

130

petty rivalries and rally to Talisman's bright banner. If you believe that He is our Saviour, strike down those who insult His Name by giving aid to our enemies.'

'Yes, but when and where do you expect all this to happen?' enquired one of the C'Natti wordsmiths.

Mr Snow threw up his hands. 'Who can fathom the workings of poisonous hearts? If betrayers revealed their hand treachery would never flourish as richly as it does today! It is the assassin who chooses the place and the hour, not his victim! Look about you! Danger surrounds us! Go and prepare yourselves! And be vigilant!'

Nitwits . . .

Mr Snow spent the remaining daylight hours in head-to-heads with the leaders of friendly delegations, securing pledges of support and a firm promise to attend a mid-night council of war in the depths of the wood which was now ringed by sentinels posted by the She-Kargo. All this should have left the M'Call delegation in an upbeat mood but their earlier exuberance had been dampened by the unprecedented number of clashes between groups of hot-heads from the rival bloodlines.

The use of weapons in these encounters – which by tradition were strictly forbidden – was a sign that the fragile truce governing these occasions was under threat. Despite the efforts of the line-capos and camp-marshals, the ugly brawls continued throughout the day, causing death and injury to both sides.

Faced with a steadily deteriorating situation, a high-level meeting proposed by the M'Waukee and C'Natti brought representatives of the D'Troit and She-Kargo face to face in the bull-ring. But this too failed to ease the tension. By prior agreement, neither Mr Snow nor Prime-Cut was there but it was clear that the D'Troit were still angry that their spokesman had been made to look like a prize asshole and despite the mutual expressions of respect and willingness to reconcile their differences by amicable and reasoned debate the meeting broke up amidst angry recriminations from both sides.

The D'Troit, and to a lesser extent the C'Natti, were

clearly spoiling for a fight. And they had imported the muscle to make sure they won it hands down.

The last major conflict in the history of the Plainfolk had been the Battle of the Black Hills when two entire clans – the M'Calls and the B'Nardinos from the D'Troit bloodline had fought each other to a finish in a running encounter that lasted from sunrise to sunset.

Thunderbird, Clearwater's father, had fallen in that battle from which the M'Calls emerged bloodied but unbowed – a victory which confirmed their position as paramount clan of the She-Kargo.

But that was fifteen years ago. There had never been a clash of arms on that scale before or since and, more important still, there had never been *any* occasion where clans of the same, or competing bloodline had submerged their traditional rivalry to stand shoulder to shoulder against a common enemy. Until now. And having had less than 48 hours in which to cobble together a temporary alliance and hammer out a concerted plan of action, no one in the She-Kargo faction was sure how long it would hold together.

The Mute warrior ethic was similar in many respects to that of the samurai – the military class that ruled Ne-Issan – but there was one important difference. The Mutes were gang-fighters, not battlefield soldiers. Their skills, and the supremacy of the knife were derived from their pre-Holocaust ancestors – the ghetto people who, by some miracle, had emerged indelibly scarred but alive from the nuclear blasts that levelled and torched America's great cities. Desperate, impoverished individuals whose entire lives had been a struggle for survival in the urban jungle. An underclass whose sense of right and wrong had been warped by deprivation and injustice. Whose moral nerve endings had been dulled by the callous exploitation and dog-eat-dog indifference that was the hall-mark of the pre-Holocaust era.

They had survived then by the quickness of their wits, feet and fists, a combination of animal cunning and hair-trigger aggression, a readiness born of desperation to

132

take what they wanted: the very qualities needed to survive the aftermath of a global nuclear war.

Abstract philosophizing, the art of debate, the intellectual flatulence of the educated classes, the privileges of the mega-rich secured by acres of prime real estate and Swiss bank accounts, the well-meaning advocates of charity, compassion and the fellowship of man were buried beneath the smouldering ashes. Literacy went up in smoke as the unschooled burnt the remaining books to keep warm.

It was not the meek who inherited the earth but the traumatized remnants of the bread-line poor, the muggers, pushers, the sewer-rats and hoodlums, along with the Rambo-style, Soldier of Fortune gun-crazy fire-power freaks who had prepared for Armageddon in the backwoods of America.

Stranded amid the wreckage of the 20th century, like flotsam and jetsam left high and dry on an alien shore, this residue of humankind had separated into their different ethnic groups, like snails of different species placed together in a cage. At a time when everyone was a potential predator, the only security was within a group sharing a common language, customs and racial origin.

During the next nine centuries and through numberless generations, they had gathered strength and multiplied. Around countless camp-fires they had recreated the past, mixing fact and fiction in the same way that jazz musicians improvise on a well-known melody. Dimming memories of distant events had given birth to a new mythology, a new identity; mutated genes had spawned a new, mishapen but strangely gifted breed of humankind. And when the grey curtain of clouds that brought the Great Ice-Dark retreated, revealing the sun and stars in all their glory, the first of a race of warrior clans emerged – the Southern Mutes and their northern brothers who later became known as the Plainfolk.

Later, when the delegates to the midnight war council had agreed on a joint plan of action and returned to their own lines, Mr Snow toured the M'Call encampment, bringing hope and encouragement to his clanfolk like Shakespeare's Henry V on the eve of Agincourt. His last call was upon Blue-Thunder, Rolling-Stone and Boston-Bruin who sat around one of the many fires with the other leading lights of the M'Call trade delegation.

As he squatted down and warmed his hands, Rolling-Stone threw some more wood onto the glowing embers and stared moodily into the leaping flames. 'So tomorrow's the big day . . .'

'Yes, when the wheel-boats get here.' Mr Snow's voice was racked and hoarse from countless hours of argument and persuasion.

Blue-Thunder tested the edge of the blade he was sharpening. 'I don't understand it. The D'Troit must know *we* know what they're up to. Why are they waiting? Why didn't they attack us today?'

'Psychology.'

Blue-Thunder frowned at the unfamiliar word.

'They're trying to unnerve us by letting the pressure build up. Keeping us in suspense. The way the numbers are stacked up they know we are not going to attack *them*. In theory, they can strike when and where they please. But it will be on the beach at dawn tomorrow. That's what I'm counting on.'

'But what makes you so sure?' insisted Blue-Thunder.

'Because it's the dead-faces from the Yama-Shita family who want to get even. They'll use the D'Troit and maybe the C'Natti to make the opening play but they'll be in at the kill. You've seen them at work. Chopping people to pieces is what Iron Masters like doing best. They're not going to come all this way just to watch from the sidelines.'

Doctor-Hook, a M'Call warrior who often acted as a bodyguard to Mr Snow, approached the fire. 'It is time to leave, Old One.'

'Good.' Mr Snow rose to his feet. The others followed. After exchanging farewell handclasps with each of them, he said: 'If any of you have any questions about who's supposed to be doing what come the dawn now's the time to ask. We may not see each other again.'

He ran his eyes around the ring of mishapen firelit faces. No one spoke.

'Good.' He turned to go.

'There is one thing,' said Blue-Thunder. 'That stuff in the bull-ring. Was it true? Did Cadillac, Clearwater and the cloud-warrior kill hundreds of dead-faces like Prime-Cut said?'

'They may have done. According to Carnegie-Hall, Cadillac said they were involved in a big battle in which many died. If it's true then it's something we should be proud of.'

'Yes. But did the sand-burrowers help them win it?'

Mr Snow shrugged. 'Who can say? Talisman moves in mysterious ways.' He drew his dark-hued cloak around his body with a showman's flourish. 'Now! I suggest those of you who form part of the beach party should try to get a little sleep. When you wake up you'll find the weather is to our advantage. Make the most of it because we won't be able to hold it in place for long.' He backed away, his hand raised in a last farewell. 'And for goodness sake, try to look more cheerful! We're going to win!'

The M'Call elders and the other members of the She-Kargo war council who shared their misgivings as the small hours ticked away might have gained some comfort had they known that the leaders of the D'Troit faction were also plagued by doubts and difficulties.

Every D'Troit clan, by the cherished tradition of their bloodline, was a mean bunch of mothers – which meant, inevitably, that they were scornful and suspicious of any attempt to moderate their behaviour. They were governed by only one discipline – violence. They were takers, not makers. They preferred pillage to husbandry. The hunting and killing of meat on the hoof was an acceptable pastime, but why grow breadstalks and green-stuffs when the winter larders of weaker clans could be ransacked at The Gathering?

In a violent world where every male and female of fighting age was expected to carry sharp iron, the D'Troit were the supreme predators, feared, hated and despised by all. In the brief period when peace was supposed to reign at Du-aruta, they were the chief trouble-makers and much of it was caused when they were caught trying to augment their own stock of tradeable items by stealing from the baggage trains of other clans. They came to the trading post as spoilers, and during the rest of the year they cruised the ocean of red grass like blood-crazed killer sharks.

Given their reputation, one might reasonably wonder why they were not the paramount bloodline. Perhaps only Talisman knew the answer to that. By some quirk of fate, the clans of the D'Troit bloodline were less fecund than those of the She-Kargo. In overall terms, they had remained numerically inferior. The ratio of gifted Mutes to the rest of the population was also lower amongst D'Troit clans. There were some eminent wordsmiths but very few summoners, most of whom were only gifted with the first two Rings of Power.

The knowledge that their rivals were more favoured in this respect was a constant source of envy and resentment. Talisman's apparent lack of even-handedness had caused the D'Troit to regard this saviour figure with increasing contempt. The Plainfolk had been waiting nine hundred years – how much longer would they have to wait? To the D'Troit, this endless waiting had become futile and pathetic. It was time for those who could to help themselves.

These festering grievances, the innate capacity for violence and the basic indiscipline which had caused many of the D'Troit to abandon their belief in Talisman had also bedevilled the forward planning of their leaders.

Having primed their warriors for a joint attack on the She-Kargo, the chieftains and elders had come close to fighting amongst themselves as they accused each other of failing to control the hotheads under their personal command. Why – they asked – in the name of the Great

Sky-Mother could the mad-dogs they led not understand they were only to attack the She-Kargo *when* the Iron Masters got there?!

Since they all posed the same question whilst denying that their own delegation was at fault the discussion, as might be expected, soon became overheated.

The D'Troit war council, which included representatives from the C'Natti and San'Louis, had counted on seizing and holding the initiative from the very beginning, but Mr Snow's robust defence in the bull-ring had thrown them off balance. His rallying call for the Plainfolk to unite and his invocation of Talisman had caused many of the C'Natti delegations to waver.

Despite the rumours of a mass defection, they would not switch sides. They were too spineless for that, but they might hold back when the fighting broke out. So be it. When the D'Troit emerged triumphant, as the paramount bloodline with the sole right to trade with the Iron Masters, the C'Natti would come crawling like whipped dogs to lick their feet.

And would be crushed like all the others . . .

CHAPTER SIX

Mr Snow's prediction about the weather proved chillingly correct. In the wake of his departure, the air turned cold and damp. A mist began to form. At first, it lay only ankle deep above the ground but within two hours it rose, blotting out the night sky. Sixty minutes later, when the D'Troit, C'Natti and San'Louis rose to make their final surreptitious preparations, the huge encampment, the trading post, and a five mile stretch of the adjacent shoreline was wrapped in a clammy pale grey blanket.

Every year, the clan delegations made their way down to the shore in the pre-dawn twilight to await the moment when the wheel-boats appeared on the horizon, silhouetted against the incandescent disc of the rising sun. To the impressionable unscientific mind of the average Mute the wheel-boats appeared to issue from the sun itself; an impression that the Iron Masters had been at pains to reinforce. This year, the normally well-ordered migration from the lines to the trading post was marked by scenes of unparalleled confusion. The mist was so thick, the D'Troit and their allies were obliged to set up a line of warriors standing at arm's length from each other to find their way to the trading post and the beach below.

When they arrived to take up their alloted positions, they were surprised to discover that the She-Kargo, M'Waukee and San' Paul had already staked their claim to the north-western end of the shoreline and were spread out across the entire width of the lower sand-bar from lake to lagoon. With visibility reduced to three or four yards, the disposition of the entire She-Kargo faction could only be guessed at. Any further reconnaissance was barred by several, densely-packed lines of warriors.

This pre-emptive move on the part of the She-Kargo

left the leaders of the D'Troit-C'Natti-San'Louis war council in some disarray. By denying access to the part of the lower sandbar they now occupied, the She-Kargo faction had neatly blocked any outflanking manoeuvre by their opponents. Any attempt to force a way through would have immediately led to a pitched battle in swirling mist, which at times was so thick you could barely see beyond the end of your knife arm. The present poor visibility was not the only limiting factor: by prior agreement, the attack on the She-Kargo was not supposed to take place before the Iron Masters arrived on the scene. In the circumstances, the D'Troit and their allies had no choice but to position themselves along the remaining section of the beach, between their rivals and the tall, ornately carved trading post. And wait.

The original plan had called for the She-Kargo faction to be sandwiched in between the C'Natti and D'Troit. A twin pincer movement on the landward side – easily achieved by their numerically superior forces – would have left the She-Kargo and M'Waukee surrounded with their backs against the sea and with no possibility of escape. At the same moment, a secondary action was to have been launched by the San'Louis against the camping grounds occupied by the She-Kargo, M'Waukee and San'Paul. With the majority of the delegations crowded onto the shore to await the arrival of the Iron Masters, the lines would only be thinly defended.

But this part of the plan had also misfired. As the D'Troit war council hastily rejigged their general plan of attack a breathless messenger despatched by the San'Louis arrived from the lines. In the mist-shrouded pre-dawn twilight the cooking fires of the She-Kargo faction had been seen burning with shadowy figures seated or sleeping beside them. At the boundary between the M'Waukee lines and the San'Louis and the C'Natti and San'Paul, everything had seemed perfectly normal. It was only some time after the last of the warriors slipped away to join their companions on the sand-bar that the ruse was uncovered.

The lines occupied by the She-Kargo faction were empty. The seated figures were made of hooded cloaks hung on a framework of sticks, the sleepers were rolled straw mats stuffed with grass. Everything of value, all the trade goods and chattels brought by the She-Kargo, M'Waukee and San'Paul delegations had been quietly carried away by baggage-handlers during the night. But they had not vanished without trace. An examination of the ground revealed tracks leading away from the campsite towards the western shore of the lagoon.

Even though they were doomed to fail, the She-Kargo's efforts to avoid defeat were impressive. Prime-Cut unrolled the map given to him by one of the Iron Masters' agents on Lake Mi-Shiga and after a few minutes' intensive study the enemy's intentions became abundantly clear. If forced to give ground, the main force of the She-Kargo would retreat across the shallow channel onto the upper sand-bar in an attempt to seek refuge on the higher ground beyond. The steep bluffs would form a good line of defence against a frontal assault but it could be quickly turned from the west. Prime-Cut also discerned the tactic underlying the midnight retreat of the baggage trains along the western side of the lagoon. The She-Kargo faction were obviously reluctant to abandon their valuable merchandise but, more importantly, they intended to put a considerable body of men across the first fording point on the river estuary and hold the northern shore to prevent a pursuing force from crossing over and blocking the exit from the upper sandbar.

Further examination of the map revealed a second fording point across the estuary, some three miles further west. This would provide an alternative route if the first was denied to them. There was also another point from which an attack could be launched: a spur of land on the western shore of the lagoon came to within four hundred paces of the channel separating the upper and lower sandbar. If bowmen were stationed on the point of the spur they could fire into the left flank of the retreating column while the advancing D'Troit cut their way through from the rear.

At the urging of Prime-Cut and Judas-Priest the war council quickly agreed to split its forces. The D'Troit delegations would remain on the beach ready to move along the sandbar against the main force of She-Kargo and M'Waukee warriors. The C'Natti would despatch a strong force of bowmen onto the spur; the remainder of its warriors would follow the route taken by the fleeing baggage trains and its escort – believed to be the weakling San'Paul stiffened by elements from the two stronger bloodlines. The C'Natti warriors were to destroy everything in their path, seize the first fording point then wheel right onto the upper sandbar, trapping what was left of the She-Kargo and M'Waukee.

Result – total annihilation.

Prime-Cut rubbed his hands jubilantly as the runners departed with the movement orders – orders that were to be put into effect immediately.

Easier said than done. As the She-Kargo faction had already discovered, organizing the movement of thousands of combatants and their assembly into coherent formations is extremely difficult without a proper chain of command – especially when the orders are conveyed down the line by word of mouth. And it was an even bigger problem for the D'Troit faction because they had three times as many warriors to deal with.

All of which meant that the orders to the C'Natti to leave the beach and move off along the western side of the lagoon took some while to get through to the various delegations. The cloying mist slowed the process even further and the planned manoeuvre almost fell apart when several groups of warriors, anxious to get into the fray, rushed off – mostly in the wrong direction – without waiting to hear what exactly it was they were required to do.

Prime-Cut cursed and fretted at the delay and silently berated himself for making what he now realized was a serious tactical blunder. The enlarged D'Troit and

141

C'Natti delegations had appeared at the trading post too soon. Instead of arriving over the two previous days, the extra delegates and 'journey-men' should have delayed their appearance – joining their clansmen in the hours just before dawn.

Had they done that, the She-Kargo faction would, as always, have outnumbered the D'Troit. His verbal attack on Mr Snow might have caused them some disquiet but they would not have felt threatened. Secure in their strength, they would have gone to bed, slept soundly – and woken up to find themselves hopelessly outnumbered, with no time to make a coordinated plan to defend themselves.

On the other hand . . .

Prime-Cut angrily drove these last-minute regrets from his mind. What was done was done. The battle would be harder but that would only make the winning of it more worthwhile. Death, if it was to have any meaning, should be a memorable occasion.

As dawn broke the situation changed rapidly. The warming rays of the rising sun burnt away the blanket of mist revealing the disposition of the opposing forces along the shore. And as the sun lifted clear of the eastern horizon, the wheel-boats of the Iron Masters came into view. But this time, the flotilla consisted of five vessels instead of the usual three.

Mr Snow and the other wordsmiths heading the She-Kargo faction did not know that the two extra wheel-boats had been leased by the Ko-Nikka and Se-Iko families. To them, the approaching vessels meant only one thing; the Yama-Shita had come back in strength – and that spelled trouble.

Steaming in V-formation, with smoke belching from their twin funnels, the five wheel-boats headed towards the trading post, their stern-mounted paddles churning the blue sun-struck water into wide swirling ribbons of green and white foam. The relentless thump-thump-thump of their engines, the boom-pound-boom of the revolving blades plunging into the water which then cascaded noisily and by the ton off the rising blades, merged into one endless barrage of sound, a continuous roll of thunder that reached out across the vast expanse of the lake, striking terror in the hearts of those who stood watching and waiting on the shore.

Sky and earth-thunder were sounds which triggered a primal fear within a Mute's soul. Within the folk-memory of their race, passed down through the generations like their warped genetic code, it recalled the terror inspired by the unbearable brilliance of The War of a Thousand Suns when the earth and sky was riven by fire.

Oshio Shinoda, supreme commander of the punitive expedition despatched by the Yama-Shita family, stood on the bridge of the leading vessel next to its captain, Kato Yukinagi. Both men had polished brass telescopes trained on the approaching shore.

On their rear starboard quarter was the boat crewed by the Ko-Nikka. The Se-Iko boat lay to port. These, in turn, were flanked by the two other boats belonging to the Yama-Shita. Their commanders also had telescopes trained on the crowded shore, and outside the wheelhouse of each ship stood a flag-officer and his men, ready to relay messages to and from the expedition's commander.

On its last visit to the trading post, Yukinagi's vessel – its huge black superstructure relieved with red and gold trim – had carried Domain-Lord Hirohito and Clearwater to their secret meeting with Mr Snow. This time, the elegantly appointed stateroom occupied by the late lamented domain-lord had been left empty, a shrine to his memory, with flowers and various other prayer offerings placed before the dais on which he sat when giving audience. And it would remain so until his death had been well and truly avenged.

With the aid of his powerful spyglass, Samurai-General Shinoda was just able to identify the different bloodlines. The She-Kargo, and M'Waukee were grouped together on the right hand side of the beach. The D'Troit and

143

San'Louis were ranged in the centre and to his left. Normally, the Mutes gathered in one huge throng in front of the trading post, but now, the centre of gravity had shifted noticeably to the right, with the She-Kargo and M'Waukee spread out quite thinly along the lower sand-bar.

This was not what Shinoda had expected to find. The plan had been for the She-Kargo to be separated from the M'Waukee and sandwiched between the C'Natti and D'Troit. But there was no sign of the C'Natti, or for that matter, the San'Paul. Something must have happened to cause the original plan to go awry. Something drastic – like the She-Kargo discovering what lay in store for them. If that was so, then the vital element of surprise had been lost.

Samurai-General Shinoda consulted the map spread out on the navigator's table and conferred with the wheel-boat's captain, Kato Yukinagi. The channel separating the upper and lower sand-bars was now a shallow fording point. It would slow down any force retreating towards the northern shore but it would not prevent them from doing so. Using the powerful spyglass mounted on a gleaming brass pillar outside the wheel-house, he slowly scanned the long upper sand-bar that ran away to starboard. It was completely deserted, but when he focused on the escarpment that dominated the northern shore he glimpsed figures moving about on top. Figures that seemed to be trying to conceal their presence.

After Captain Yukinagi had taken a look through the spyglass and confirmed his suspicions, Shinoda made a careful survey of the escarpment and spotted several lines of men – they could only be Mutes – hauling baggage up the steep slope west of the sand-bar. Their distance from his ship made it impossible to tell which group they belonged to but they had no reason to be there. If they had come to trade, they should be on the beach. On the other hand, if they intended to join those already on top and cover the retreat of the She-Kargo they were heading in the right direction.

144

Shinoda was only guessing at their intentions. The distant figures might be the missing C'Natti moving to cut off the She-Kargo but in that case why were they humping back packs? He could not afford to take any chances. After the sinking of the wheel-boat on Lake Mi-shiga, everyone in the expedition knew that further failure would not be tolerated. As a precautionary measure he decided to land some of his men onto the upper sandbar to seal off this possible escape route. He conferred briefly with Captain Yukinagi, the Flag Officer was summoned, and the appropriate signal was sent to the starboard flank-boat.

On the shore, Rolling-Stone, Mack-Truck and Blue-Thunder saw the wheel-boat detach itself from the flotilla and angle away to their left. They didn't need to be master-tacticians to understand the reason for the move. It was as obvious as it was unexpected.

The plan hatched by Mr Snow and the war council called for the She-Kargo faction to give ground as soon as the D'Troit began to stoke up the present atmosphere to the point where the two sides came to blows. But while exchanging the usual swaggering taunts with the warriors on the She-Kargo right flank, the D'Troit front-liners had kept the situation below boiling point. The She-Kargo *had* to begin their withdrawal before the wheel-boat got into position but was denied the reason for doing so!

The D'Troit, having come to a similar conclusion as to the Iron Master's strategy, had quickly issued instructions to their warriors to cool it, thereby forcing the She-Kargo into making the first move.

The leading delegates of the She-Kargo faction who formed the top echelon of the hastily-formed chain of command on the sand-bar put their heads together.

'Treacherous toads!' exclaimed Rolling-Stone. 'Yesterday they tried to blame us for everything, and now they're trying to force us into a position where we have to attack them!'

'We don't have to pick a fight,' said Wind-Walker, a

145

M'Waukee wordsmith from the Clan T'Maso. 'We could just withdraw.'

Black-Sabbath, paramount warrior of one of the biggest of the She-Kargo clans reacted angrily. 'The Clan K'Rella has never backed away from any of these jackals from the D'Troit and is not about to do so now!'

Several other members of the war council expressed the same view with equal force.

'We're not running away from a fight!' exclaimed Wind-Walker. 'We're running into one! Do you think the D'Troit are just going to stand there and watch us fade away? They'll be right on our heels with the sharp iron out!'

Mack-Truck said: 'If we're going to move, we'd better do it now.' He pointed to the huge straggling pack of C'Natti warriors heading around the western side of the lagoon. 'We have to get to the north shore before they cross the river. Otherwise we're done for.'

'We'll also be done for if we don't get across the channel onto the upper sandbar before that wheel-boat reaches us,' grunted Rolling-Stone.

They all looked at the boat. Dark-Star, a M'Waukee summoner who had been given the task of aiding the 'strategic withdrawal' asked the question that was in everyone's minds: 'Can we outrun it?'

'Not if we stand here arguing,' said Rolling-Stone. 'I propose we move. En masse. Now. All those in favour?'

The motion was carried by eleven to four.

Rolling-Stone turned to Dark-Star. 'Besides yourself, how many summoners do we have who can raise stones?'

'I know of at least thirty. There could be more.'

'Good. Pick nine of the best and spread yourselves out so as we've got the full width of the sand-bar covered. Position yourselves two hundred paces behind the front rank. The signal to withdraw will be three blasts on the buffalo horns – repeated twice. When you hear that, the front line will fall back towards you, and as they reach you –'

'We hit the beach . . .'

'With everything you've got. Raise a wall of shit that will slow them down and give us a head start.' Rolling-Stone patted Dark-Star on the shoulder. 'Take a group of your own clansmen to guard you and as soon as you've got lift-off, pull back but keep the magic flowing for as long as you can. Our second line will cover you.'

Dark-Star eyed the old mute sceptically. 'What with?'

Rolling-Stone gave him a comradely slap on the back. 'Have faith, brother. Talisman looks after his own.'

Yeahhh. Tell me something new . . .

When Rolling-Stone called for the bull-horns to be sounded, the diverted wheel-boat was about four miles from the mouth of the channel between the sand-bars.

The eerie sound drifted across the water to reach the ear of Samurai-Major Akido Mitsunari and Captain Umigami. Mitsunari was the commander of the military force now assembled on the through-deck below: a combined force of cavalry and infantry, ready to charge down the gangways as soon as the boat reached the shore. Umigami was Master of the vessel but when carrying troops he was obliged by tradition, to follow the orders of their commander. As in ancient Japan, the army took precedence over the navy. Umigami, an officer in the *merchant* marine, ranked even lower in the pecking order.

Mitsunari swept his powerful spyglass over the thousands of Mutes that seemed to be milling about aimlessly along the lower sand-bar. Although vastly outnumbered, his tiny force would make mince-meat of them. No discipline! he lamented inwardly. No organization!

As this judgement passed through his mind, the lines of She-Kargo warriors positioned nearest to the D'Troit wilted then fell back rapidly, opening up a wide gap between the opposing factions. The open stretch of beach erupted with explosive force and an instant later Mitsunari became aware of a high keening sound.

Through his spyglass he saw sand, stones, grass and gravel being sucked up into moving funnels of air which then snaked forward at great speed into the leading

147

ranks of the She-Kargo. Dust devils! A stream of mini-tornadoes that scythed through the advancing troops, knocking men off their feet with a vicious hail of rocks and stones and momentarily blinding others with whirling clouds of sand.

It was amazing. Mitsunari had never seen anything like it before. And during the two or three minutes this barrage lasted, the entire She-Kargo army had turned tail and was running towards the channel that separated the two sand-bars.

The next sound Mitsunari heard was an angry roar from seventy thousand throats as the massed delegations of the D'Troit launched themselves in pursuit.

Like his commander, Oshio Shinoda, Mitsunari would have dearly loved to know the battle plan of the D'Troit. The chain of agents stationed in the outlands who had acted on behalf of the Yama-Shita family in setting up this 'arrangement' had tried to persuade the D'Troit to accept the help of a small team of advisors – including a flag signal unit which could have maintained contact with the advancing flotilla.

The idiot monkey-faced chieftains who led the D'Troit had spurned this offer, giving as an excuse the difficulty of concealing IronMasters among their own ranks. The discovery of such individuals by their rivals would, they claimed, have brought an immediate charge of collaborating with the enemy – a charge the D'Troit intended to make against the She-Kargo.

As a result, Oshio Shinoda, his junior force commanders and the boat-captains had no way of knowing the on-shore situation beyond what they could see through their telescopes. And under the strict policy of non-belligerence imposed by the Toh-Yota shogunate – to which they were obliged to adhere because of the unwelcome presence of the wheel-boats crewed by the Ko-Nikka and Se-Iko – they could not lawfully intervene until they had run the boats ashore and had received a formal request for assistance!

Responding to Mitsunari's request for more speed,

the wheel-boat captain sent the traditional signal to the sweating stokers in the engine room. Off his rear port quarter, smoke belched from the funnels of the rest of the flotilla as they responded to a similar order from Oshio Shinoda.

On shore, having recovered from their surprise, the massed clan delegations of the D'Troit raced after the She-Kargo like a howling lynch-mob. Moving with them were their own summoners, but they could not reply in a similar manner. In order to do so, they would have had to place themselves of were their own warriors – exposing themselves to a well-aimed cross-bow bolt. A summoner could only call up the forces from the earth and sky *when he was standing still*. The very act rooted him to the spot until the forces had passed through him. That was the second drawback to being a summoner.

The deadly hail of stones raised by Dark-Star's team had cut down hundreds of warriors. The D'Troit were not prepared to wait for a similar cloud to smite the fleeing She-Kargo. Some of the pebbles on the beach were bigger than a man's fist but a direct hit could not be guaranteed. Knives, on the other hand, always found their target.

The She-Kargo faction had been ordered to cover the three miles to the channel at the fastest possible speed. Those who tripped and fell, or lagged behind for whatever reason were to be left to their own devices. They could either try to catch up or make a stand in the few seconds that remained before they were engulfed by the screaming horde now racing towards them. A brave but futile gesture which failed to slow the pace of the pursuit. The leading ranks of the D'Troit simply ran around the stragglers, leaving them to be hacked to pieces by the tens of thousands of warriors packed into the middle and rear of the column.

The time taken to cover the first three miles was a little under eighteen minutes – well outside the world record for that distance, but this race was run over an uneven

149

bed of sand and shingle, not a rolled Olympic-class cinder track. Even so, the leaders were still travelling at over ten miles an hour, equal to the speed of Mitsunari's wheel-boat.

Fortunately, the wheel-boat had further to go and it was still out of range when the front of the column reached the three hundred yard wide channel and pounded across in a cloud of spray.

Mitsunari realized that there was no chance of placing his wheel-boat in the channel – thereby cutting off the She-Kargo's line of retreat. And having seen the violent sandstorms raised against the D'Troit, he was reluctant to get too close for fear of losing the vessel. The stories of Mute magic had been discounted, but he had now seen evidence of it with his own eyes! Already one wheel-boat with a noted commander and carrying many of his own comrades had gone down in Lake Mi-shiga. He did not propose to be on board the second.

Mitsunari did not fear death, but as a samurai his whole life had been geared to one end: to die in the heat of battle on behalf of his domain-lord. Drowning – even in the line of duty – was a quite ignoble way of departing from this life. He asked Captain Umigami to alter the ship's heading fifteen degrees to starboard. The bow of the wheel-boat was now aimed at the long upper sand-bar, but the approach angle was much shallower, allowing the cannon mounted in the port side galleries to brought to bear against the retreating column.

M'Call elder Rolling-Stone had seen the wheel-boats discharge their cannon in a ceremonial salute but he had never seen them fire in anger. Others, in the early days before the Mute clans agreed to trade with the Iron Masters, had been given a practical demonstration. Being in the target area of a broadside from one of these vessels had proved an unforgettable learning experience and the news had been passed on.

But this was not the only new threat. To the She-Kargo's rear, the deadly pursuit had not slackened and now, as the middle and rear segments of their straggling formation headed towards the channel, they came under fire from the first of the D'Troit bowmen to reach the spur of land jutting out from the western side of the lagoon. Volley after volley of crossbow bolts flew across the four hundred yard stretch of water, cutting down warriors right, left and centre.

Rolling-Stone and Mack-Truck urged the last of their clansmen into the channel then turned to greet Dark-Star D'Mingo. His escort – two giant M'Waukee warriors – had hoisted him up by his armpits, leaving his flailing legs barely touching the ground.

They set him down in front of Rolling-Stone. He crumpled like an empty sack then straightened up. 'I know, I know, I know. They weren't supposed to pick me up. But don't be angry at them. They are my sons.'

He quickly embraced them both then turned his eyes skywards. 'Bless you, Sweet Sky-Mother, for the loan of two strong arms!' He turned back to his sons. 'Right! Off you go! I've got work to do!'

The two young warriors paused uncertainly. Dark-Star shoved them into the water. 'Go on! Get moving!'

His sons raised their hands in a farewell salute then ran on and were lost in the clouds of spray raised by the other fleeing warriors.

Dark-Star crouched at the water's edge between Mack-Truck and Rolling-Stone as hundreds of warriors sprinted past. Muscled thighs lifting and driving their flying feet, pounding the water to foam as they passed across to the other side. Foam that was already tinted with the blood of those slain by the bowmen on the nearby spur.

'Are you out of your mind?!' exclaimed Rolling-Stone. 'Go after them!'

'Pwwahhh! I've done enough running for one day!'

'So have I,' admitted Mack-Truck. 'There's no way I'm ever going to make it to the top of that bluff.'

Rolling-Stone eyed the distant high ground that overlooked the seven mile-long sandbar their warriors had to cover before they reached safety. 'Me neither . . .'

'Better make ourselves useful then,' said Dark-Star.

Running back and forth across the curved point of the sand-bar he recruited two of his earlier colleagues as they stumbled to the water's edge and ordered Rolling-Stone and Mack-Truck to arm their crossbows and gather as many bolts as they could from warriors who had fallen to the incoming fire from the nearby spur.

Working their way through the dune grass on the lagoon side of the sand-bar, they came opposite the point where the D'Troit bowmen were massed. Dark-Star turned to his two colleagues. 'I know it's asking a lot but I want you to raise some more whirlies as the last of our people come through. I'll try and spoil the aim of these toads over here.' He gripped their hands in the traditional gesture of farewell. 'Give it everything you've got. This is as far as we go.'

The two summoners accepted their imminent death with the calm resignation that all Mute warriors strove to achieve and hid themselves in wind-scooped hollows between the spiked tufts of grass.

'And what do we do?' enquired Mack-Truck.

'Do your best to cover us. The longer we can keep going, the more chance our brothers will have of getting out of this alive.' Dark-Star glanced over his shoulder at the wheel-boat in the lake beyond as it crossed the mouth of the channel, almost sideways on to their position. 'See how those yellow runts are trying to cut us off? They're working hand-in-glove with the D'Troit!' He ground his teeth together. 'Oh, Talisman! When the guilty are judged, make them pay in blood!'

Breaking away from Rolling-Stone and Mack-Truck, Dark-Star waded into the water seemingly oblivious of the incoming volleys of crossbow bolts. He concentrated for a moment as if gathering his inner strength, then threw his head back and spread his arms out sideways with the palms facing downwards. A shrill piercing cry burst from his lips and in the same instant, a small whirlpool formed in the water directly below each of his outstretched hands.

Flexing his arms, Dark-Star pushed the whirlpools

out of reach then, as they grew in size and increased their speed of rotation, he swept his arms upwards. Responding to his unspoken command, the whirlpools became two huge spinning columns of water that rose into the air – and kept on rising until they were about a hundred feet high. The noise was deafening – like the buffeting roar of gale-force winds tearing through the tree-tops.

By now, Dark-Star's hands were high over his head. He swept them forwards, the two index fingers aimed across the lagoon at the warriors massed on the opposing shore. The tall, snaking columns of water surged forward like unleashed hunting dogs. Behind them, Dark-Star raised another pair, then another.

Before they had time to grasp what was happening, the C'Natti bowmen on the point of the spur found their view of the sand-bar obscured by twelve huge undulating columns of water, each one now twenty to thirty feet in diameter and bearing down on them with the speed and menace of an approaching express train.

The wind circling each column whipped their faces and tore at their clothing then, as the first waterspouts reached the shore, the huge columns of water collapsed with a thunderclap of sound.

Those immediately below were knocked senseless to the ground, others on the shoreline were swept into the lagoon. More spouts followed in their wake, swamping the spur from all sides. To many of the terrified Mutes it was as if the heavens had opened and the Sky Voices were venting their wrath upon the C'Natti for challenging the will of Talisman. Hundreds turned tail and fled inland. The hardier souls stood their ground but the torrential cascades of water falling out of the sky and the continuous advance of newly-formed waterspouts masked their view of the retreating She-Kargo.

Running in their clan groups, spread out across the whole width of the sand-bar, the forty-five thousand warriors of the She-Kargo faction – or to be more accurate those still up and running – took about ten minutes to pass the point where Rolling-Stone, Mack-Truck, Dark-Star and the other two summoners were making their last stand. The D'Troit had been tearing savagely into the tail end of the column and despite the order to keep running, many of those in the rear had decided to stand and fight rather than face the ignominy of being cut down from behind.

As a consequence of these desperate struggles, a slight gap – no more than thirty yards at best – had opened up between the She-Kargo and their pursuers. It was this approaching gap that Dark-Star's colleagues – Silent-Running and Condition-Red – proceeded to exploit, each raising a power vortex that sucked stones and sand into the air then hurled them at murderous speed towards the advancing D'Troit.

Once again the front ranks wilted and fell back under the onslaught, but as before it only caused a temporary delay. Those behind continued to leap over the prostrate bodies of their comrades, some falling in their turn, others circling round the lake-side of the sand-bar, under cover of the central ridge.

The power given to summoners did not pour endlessly like water from a tap. It came in finite bursts, and like a battery that needed to be recharged after use, it quickly ran out if constant calls were made upon it. That was the third drawback to being a summoner.

The howling sandstorms faltered then died. Sand and stones rained vertically out of the sky and seconds later the water around Dark-Star became ominously still. Totally exhausted, he staggered in the waist-deep water then pitched forward, face down. Two crossbow bolts struck the upper half of his body as he sank beneath the surface. Silent-Running and Condition-Red went down unresisting under a flurry of knife-thrusts. Rolling-Stone and Mack-Truck threw aside their empty cross-bows and met death knife in hand and a cry on their lips.

'Drink, Sweet Mother!'

They had been doomed from the start but their defiant stand had gained a few vital minutes of respite which allowed the tail end of the retreating column to get across the channel onto the upper sand-bar without further losses.

But the chase was far from over. The She-Kargo and their allies had another seven miles to run before reaching the safety of the northern shore, followed by a steep, six-hundred foot climb up the face of the bluff to where Mr Snow now stood, guarded by a phalanx of M'Call Bears and ten of the She-Kargo's most powerful summoners.

It was not his life he cared about. Mr Snow was aware he might not survive the battle. The warriors and summoners were there to protect his *magic*.

Only *he* had the potential to redress the balance; to counter the combined strength of Mute and Iron Master ranged against them. He had made a spectacular stand against the The Lady from Louisiana but his prodigious efforts on that occasion were dwarfed by the scale of the task that now confronted him. He was not even sure he could deliver what he had promised the delegates to the midnight war council.

Immense powers lay hidden in the earth and sky, but the gift that enabled him to summon them was given to him by Talisman – and it was exercised with *his* blessing *to do his Will*. Would he allow his power to be used to tear the Plainfolk asunder? Mr Snow, who had spent virtually every moment since his arrival trying to plan for every eventuality finally gave up worrying and turned his red-rimmed eyes to the sky.

We offer our spirits into your care, Sweet Mother. Let his Will be done . . .

From his present vantage point, Mr Snow had a bird's eye view of the evolving struggle and he could zoom in close on the action with the aid of the compact but powerful viewing device found on Brickman after he had been shot down during the Battle of the Now and Then River.

To the left he could see the long sand-bar with the mass of She-Kargo and M'Waukee Mutes moving along it from the far end. He could also see the wheel-boat closing in

155

on their right flank. Beyond the channel, the first waves of the D'Troit were entering the water.

Immediately below him, defending the northern end of the sand-bar and the steep slope the last of the baggage train and the exhausted runners had yet to climb were several thousand reinforcements summoned from nearby She-Kargo and M'Waukee clans. Arriving in batches all through the night, some had been running Mute-fashion for twelve hours non-stop. These breathless latecomers asked for and were given no respite. They acknowledged the shouted greetings and directions of the battle-marshals with a wave and ran to their allotted positions without breaking their stride.

Swinging to the right, to the western side of the lagoon, Mr Snow could see the C'Natti 'army' advancing along the route taken by the She-Kargo faction's worldly goods. Having stolen away two hours after midnight, the baggage train and its escort of San'Paul warriors were now safely across the narrow point of the river estuary. Half their number had reached the top of the bluffs, but a long jostling line of porters trailed back down the path onto the shore below.

Come on, come on, come on! Move! Move! Move!

It was a nail-biting moment. The C'Natti were closing the gap at an alarming speed, but because of the initial confusion surrounding their departure and the circuitous route they were obliged to follow, the leading groups were still some way behind the She-Kargo column on the upper sand-bar. Mr Snow prayed they would not succeed in drawing level. If his plan was to succeed the She-Kargo faction had to reach the shore and scale the bluffs *before* the C'Natti crossed the river estuary and turned to cut the She-Kargo line of retreat – a danger Mack-Truck had already foreseen.

O, Talisman, our Saviour on high, give wings to the feet of our warriors, and give us the power to defeat our enemies!

By this time, the four remaining boats in the flotilla had

run the square-cut bows of their vessels onto the gently shelving beach below the trading post. The joint D'Troit and C'Natti war council led by Prime-Cut, Judas-Priest, Screaming-Tree, Flesh-Eater, Corpse-Grinder and War-Machine had kept back some ten thousand delegates to provide an impressive welcoming committee. Taking their cue from Prime-Cut, all of them cheered wildly as the masked, richly-dressed samurai came hurrying ashore in their curious bandy-legged fashion as soon as the wide gangways had been lowered into place.

Cutting short the usual formalities, Samurai-General Shinoda dispensed with the services of an interpreter-spokesman and demanded a direct explanation of what was happening.

His boat-captain, Kato Yukinagi, stood nearby, flanked by the worried commanders of the Ko-Nikka and Se-Iko vessels. Neither had expected to find themselves in the middle of a war-zone.

Prime-Cut had already worked out the crucial elements of his reply with one of the Yama-Shita's forward agents. After delivering a brief, highly-coloured and totally biased account of what had happened the day before, he formally requested the assistance of the Iron Masters in punishing the treacherous She-Kargo. Had it not been for the vigilance of the D'Troit, he declared, these hired lackeys of the sand-burrowers would have attempted to seize the wheel-boats and murder their crews!

Hawwwwhh! The leading samurai from the Yama-Shita family crowded behind Shinoda and the wheel-boat captains reacted with a convincing degree of shock and horror, striding to and fro, and posturing in a warlike manner to express their outrage.

If the noble Iron Masters were willing to come to the aid of their loyal friends, cried Judas-Priest, they must do so quickly!

Oshio Shinoda went through the motions of consulting the Se-Iko and Ko-Nikka captains, but while they were formulating their answer, the first of the Yama-Shita's mounted samurai came clattering down the gangways of their two beached vessels.

As strangers in a strange land, the Se-Iko and Ko-Nikka could do little else but agree. They had not come prepared for trouble but having come this far – at great expense – they did not want to return empty-handed.

By the time they had conferred and given their reluctant agreement tŏ the proposed military action, the first two squadrons of samurai cavalry had already departed at the gallop; the first along the sand-bar, the second around the western side of the lagoon. And seconds after the Se-Iko and Ko-Nikka had penned their assent to the bottom of a document that Shinoda had thoughtfully prepared to cover just an emergency, a volley of green rockets soared skywards from the roof of his wheel-boat.

This was the signal that Samurai-Major Mitsunari and Captain Umigami on the bridge of the flank-boat had been waiting for.

B-BA-BBOOOMMMM!! The port side of Mitsunari's wheel-boat erupted with smoke and flame as the thirty lower cannon were fired simultaneously, hurling a salvo of 20lb iron balls at the retreating Mutes. Watching through their spyglasses, Samurai-Major Mitsunari and Captain Umigama chortled gleefully as the cannonade ripped bloody gaps in the column, sending bodies and great gouts of sand and smoke flying into the air.

'B-BA-BBOOOMMMM!!' The guns ranged along the first, upper gallery fired in their turn. More hits. Umigami ordered the helmsman to bring the vessel closer to shore so that the cannoneers could load grapeshot and cause even more casualties. Wounded soldiers ran slower and were easier to kill.

The noise of the first two salvos bounced off the rocky rampart and reverberated across the lake towards the trading post. Noting the increasing bewilderment of the Se-Iko and Ko-Nikka, Shinoda explained with studied courtesy that these opening shots had been the signal for the cavalry to draw their swords in support of the friendly tribes of grass-monkeys. A signal which, of course, could not have been given without their consent.

Inviting the two captains and their chief lieutenants to accompany him, Shinoda boarded the red and gold vessel which had once carried his domain-lord and ordered the captain to cruise along the sand-bar so that he and his guests could survey the carnage. The ingrained streak of cruelty that all Iron Masters possessed made the invitation impossible to resist.

The third Yama-Shita wheel-boat followed, leaving the Se-Iko and Ko-Nikka vessels beached by the trading post, under the command of their junior officers.

From the top of the bluff, Mr Snow watched helplessly as repeated broadsides from the upper and lower decks tore great gaps in the columns of running warriors. And on the flank-boat, the sweating, smoke-blackened gun-crews poured buckets of water over their muzzle-loading cannons to cool the heated barrels.

To aid the retreating She-Kargo and M'Waukee delegations, four lines of bowmen had been stationed across the sand-bar at regular intervals. As the last men passed through the first line, the bowmen fired into the advancing D'Troit, then fell back. And as they and the retreating troops pass through the second line the operation was repeated.

By the time the fourth line had fired their lethal volley, the first line had taken up a new position as the fifth line, and so it went on, mile after mile, all the way along the sand-bar. But the plan had not taken into account the repeated cannonades from the wheel-boat – and now Mr Snow could see that two more were steaming in the same direction!

Fortunately, the firing from the western side of the lagoon had ceased. Through Brickman's viewer, he could see the hunting packs of the C'Natti running flat out in an effort to draw level with the She-Kargo.

Behind them, gaining fast, were the leading horses of the second squadron of samurai. Each rider carried

159

the tall black and silver house-flag of the Yama-Shita mounted on a slender pole fixed to the back of his armoured tunic. With their horned, wide-brimmed helmets, snarling iron battle-masks and other warlike accoutrements they were a fearsome sight.

'B-BA-BBOOOMMMMM!!' The sound of another broadside thundered across the lake as thirty muzzle-loads of grapeshot scythed down several lines of running Mutes. Unable to bear the one-sided slaughter any longer, two She-Kargo summoners, gifted with the Third Ring of Power, ran into the shallows and called up huge waterspouts as Dark-Star had done.

Before this moment it had not been practical to do so. There was a limit to the power that flowed through the Third Ring. The towering columns of water the summoner was able to raise and move in a chosen direction could not travel very far – half a mile at the most and somewhat less if the summoner was generating a series of them. Beyond a certain point, the dynamic thrust that kept the twisting column up in the air and moved it forward simply petered out and the whole thing just collapsed in a cloud of spray.

But now, the wheel-boat had steamed closer to the shore and within seconds of being summoned into life, four towering waterspouts were snaking across the lake towards Captain Umigami's vessel and more were being brought to life behind them.

Seeing what was happening, a large number of warriors broke off from the retreating column and formed a human rampart around the summoners to protect them for as long as they could.

Samurai-Major Mitsunari and Captain Umigami stared in horror as the line of waterspouts came spinning across the lake towards their boat. The wheel-house perched on top of the third floor gallery was already some fifty feet above water-level – these huge roaring white snakes were higher by at least half as much again, maybe more!

A raging wind tore through the portside galleries and buffeted the wheel-house then the boat shuddered as the first four columns of water slammed into it. Water cascaded out of the sky and burst into the side cabins, flooding through the transverse passageways to empty over the starboard side. Again and again the ship was struck. Interior partitions were swept away as torrents of water poured down the maze of stairways onto the through deck and into the holds below.

The basic structure had been built to resist the worst of storms but no one had envisaged moving walls of water as high as this! Two more, top-heavy spouts struck the port side of the wheel-boat just forward of midships, snapping off both funnels and sweeping them into the sea beyond. The next seemed to be aimed directly at the wheel-house.

Before anyone inside had time to react, the hundred foot high column of water struck the corner of the forward galleries. Several tons of water fell out of the sky, flattening the wheel-house and its occupants.

Samurai-General Shinoda, on the bridge of the following boat, watched speechlessly as the tumbling mass of water hit the roof of Mitsunari's vessel and exploded, hurling the splintered wreckage of the wheel-house and the rag-doll bodies of his comrades into the sea. Finding his tongue, he invoked the protection of Omikami-Amaterasu, the supreme deity. Like all his compatriots, he had discounted the half-baked tales of Mute magic, but it was true! He had seen it with his own eyes. These grass-monkeys had summoned a horde of evil *kami* to their aid!

And as if to underline the awful truth of this conclusion, the huge boiler in the bowels of the stricken vessel exploded with a muffled roar. For a brief instant of time the damage was contained then, with a thunderous boom, billowing clouds of smoke and steam burst out through the roof and the ruptured side galleries.

The cannons fell silent. And the last waterspouts faltered and died before reaching the wheel-boat as the two She-Kargo summoners went down under a dozen flashing knives. The bodies of their defenders littered the water's edge, staining it with their blood.

The run continued, the death-toll mounted. But now, with only three lung-stretching miles between the retreating column and the face of the bluffs, they entered the last defensive zone where, in the hours between midnight and dawn, feverish preparations had been made to delay the pursuit.

Six-foot square lattices of poles, lashed together with sharpened stakes fixed at right-angles to every join had been scattered along the bar, sharp end down. As the column passed by, the frames were turned over by the tail-enders to expose the lethal points and tossed into the path of the oncoming D'Troit.

Their size made them too risky to leap over. The fleet-footed dodged around while other more public-spirited individuals attempted to diminish the risk even further by overturning them. But the immense pressure exerted by the middle and rear ranks caused the column to steam-roller over anyone who stopped at the front.

Those who stumbled and fell usually brought a tangle of bodies down on top of them. If they were lucky, those behind ran past or leapt over them, but if there were too many choke points, they were simply trampled into the ground.

Some distance behind the spiked mats were a collection of twenty-foot long barriers made out of a simple framework of poles to which more sharpened stakes had been lashed at an angle facing the enemy like the steel girders in pre-Holocaust tank traps. These too were swung across the sand-bar by the last men to pass.

Compared to the number killed and injured by the wheel-boat's cannon, the casualties suffered by the D'Troit through these hastily-prepared devices were pitifully few. There had not been enough time to prepare and position enough of them, but with the lines of bowmen still firing then falling back, it was enough to break the momentum.

The sand-bar was five-hundred yards wide – enormously wide if you have to defend it, but exceedingly narrow when you have sixty thousand screaming warriors

162

from groups who don't particularly like each other, all chasing the same quarry – and all trying to elbow their way into the front line. Added to which there were now dozens of dead-faces mounted on strange four-legged beasts demanding passage through their ranks from the rear!

When Aishi Sakimoto, the acting regent of the Yama-Shita had resurrected Domain-Lord Hirohito's plan, he had never considered the possibility that the D'Troit might regard the Iron Master's assistance as an interference. But from the angry reactions of the grass-monkeys now surrounding them it was clear to the officer in charge of the first cavalry squadron that they bitterly resented being forced to stand aside. It was their brothers who had fallen. What right did the dead-faces have to push to the front and take all the glory?!

The resulting melee in which Iron Master and Mute ended up brandishing their weapons at each other brought the rear third of the D'Troit column to a standstill. What began as a spontaneous reaction became a deliberate ploy to hold back the Iron Masters so that their clansmen could finish the job they had started, but it gave the She-Kargo and their allies an unexpected respite.

The possibility of Iron Masters giving chase on horseback had been foreseen by Carnegie-Hall. The ultimate line of defence consisted of five staggered rows of forward-sloping stakes running across the sand-bar from lake to lagoon. They were spaced wide enough apart to allow a warrior to slip through, but any horseman attempting to ride through it would immediately find himself in difficulty. The pointed stakes were too close together and too high, and because they were staggered in depth, they could not be cleared in a single jump.

The job of gathering, sharpening and planting the stakes, begun as soon as darkness fell, had continued after dawn and was still being completed as the She-Kargo began to pass through.

The lines of bowmen now formed into two groups, one on either shore to protect the rear of the column, but stocks of the precious crossbow bolts were now dangerously low. When a bowman emptied his pouch, he joined the retreat.

The pursuing D'Troit thought it was a rout, but they were wrong. It was a strategic withdrawal. And that was not a play on words to hide a bitter truth. Every man and woman in the She-Kargo faction would have preferred to stand and fight regardless of the odds. To face an enemy who outnumbered you by 3 to 1, knowing that you were bound to die demanded a very special kind of bravery for which the She-Kargo were renowned. But Mr Snow's stern message had been passed to the leaders of all the threatened delegations. Talisman had spoken through him. The D'Troit, the C'Natti and San'Louis had to be punished for their renunciation of the Thrice-Gifted One and their betrayal of the Plainfolk. And the dead-faces who had inspired their treachery had to be taught a lesson they would never forget.

That was why the She-Kargo faction had to endure this costly and ignominious withdrawal – *to draw their enemies onto the killing ground*.

And the time was nigh . . .

Mr Snow surveyed the scene below him once more. The leading ranks of the retreating column were now splashing across the silted-up bed of a narrow access channel cut through the sandbar close to the northern shore. Soon they would begin to pass through the line of defenders at the base of the bluff.

To his right, the last of the baggage train were toiling up the slopes under the weight of their loads. Their pursuers, the C'Natti, in their tens of thousands, were on the far side of the river estuary, preparing to cross the narrows. Further back still, samurai horsemen moving over open ground between the lines of Mutes were catching up with the leading warriors.

Mr Snow swung the viewing device back towards the lake.

The lead vessel of the Iron Master's flotilla had now drawn alongside the stricken flank-boat. The third boat

164

lay stationary in the water some way behind the first two, a thin line of smoke curling lazily upwards from its funnels. In the distance, the two remaining vessels were beached below the trading post.

Handing the viewer to Awesome-Wells, a M'Call clan-elder and long-time friend, Mr Snow closed his eyes, took a deep breath and steeled himself for what lay ahead. For over an hour he had watched the flower of the She-Kargo and M'Waukee fall under the knives of the D'Troit, had witnessed the bravery of Dark-Star and the other summoners. Now it was time to put his own life on the line – and maybe lose it in attempting to save the Plainfolk.

He could not think of a better reason for having lived until this moment.

Commending his spirit to Mo-Town, he stretched up his arms and silently prayed to Talisman to grant him power over earth and sky.

Let me be your dark, avenging angel!

The earth shivered under his feet. High above his head a dark cloud formed in the clear sky and spread rapidly in all directions. A cry burst from his throat. A cry so terrible, those around him fell to the ground, vainly trying to cover their ears. Some who dared to look upon his face said afterwards that his eyes became two points of blazing white fire.

Drawing the invisible power down from the sky and upwards from the earth with sweeping movements of his hands, Mr Snow hurled it downwards towards the lake, his fingers aiming at a point midway between the northern and southern shore, some three miles beyond the sand-bars.

Samurai-General Oshio Shinoda, on the bridge of his flag-ship, watched the dark cloud form with growing disbelief. A distant rumble of thunder seemed to come from within the bowels of the earth and was followed by an answering peal from the darkening sky.

The lake became ominously still, with scarcely a ripple disturbing its surface. The air had ceased to move. It was as if the whole world was holding its breath.

As a soldier, Shinoda was without fear, but the inexplicable moods of the *kami* who inhabited the natural world filled him with unreasoning terror which – as supreme commander of the expedition – he had to do his best to hide.

The spreading cloud blotted out the sun, casting a shadow across the lake. The ground trembled bringing a hushed silence as the warring Mutes paused uncertainly, pursued and pursuer united in their fear of earth-thunder.

The Mutes in the defensive line at the foot of the bluffs were equally alarmed but they, at least, had been warned about what was to follow. Scrambling back up the slopes, they urged the panicky She-Kargo warriors to follow them as fast as possible. Those now lined along the top called down to their companions, urging them not to look back. Whatever happened, they must keep climbing.

Their exhortations were lost under a longer and much louder, stomach-clenching rumble of subterranean thunder which caused loose earth and stones to slide down the fissured slopes. Some of the exhausted warriors lost their footing, the rest clung on grimly until the mini-avalanche ceased then clawed their way upwards with a new sense of urgency.

A circular depression appeared in the lake at the point on which Mr Snow's powers were focused. For a moment, the water appeared to be draining down a huge plug-hole then the depression became elongated, spreading quickly to either shore. Now it seemed as if a vast bottomless trench had opened up into which the whole lake was emptying itself.

The three Yama-Shita wheel-boats began to drift helplessly towards it, like empty matchboxes being carried along a rain-filled gutter towards a cavernous drain. Then there was another clap of thunder. But this one was mind-splitting not just ear-splitting, and it was twinned with an even more violent earth-tremor that threw everyone who was standing to the ground.

Only Mr Snow remained upright, surrounded by an eerie vertical shaft of light composed of shifting planes that changed colour as they intermeshed. To those who dared to raise their heads from the ground, he appeared to be standing on the threshold of the world beyond, in thrall to the spiritual powers that flowed through his rigid body.

Another rumble of thunder. The trench-like depression splitting the surface of the lake filled abruptly and rose to become a vast wall of water as the sunken bed was pushed upwards by a convulsive subterranean eruption. Rising two hundred feet into the air, the wall of water tilted and fell forwards towards the shore, creating a giant tidal wave whose foaming edge dwarfed the wheel-boats that lay in its path.

Neither the frenzied orders of Samurai-General Shinoda, nor the seamanship of Captain Yukinagi could save the vessels or their crews. Picked up and pinned at an impossible angle against the curving front of the wave, the wheel-boats were carried at sickening speed over the sand-bar and the western shore of the lagoon then smashed and ground to pieces in the breaking surf that spread for several miles over the land beyond.

The beached wheel-boats of the non-belligerent Ko-Nikka and Se-Iko suffered the same fate. Everyone on shore, Prime-Cut, Judas-Priest and the other collaborators in the war-council, the advancing hordes of D'Troit, C'Natti and San'Louis, the samurai cavalry – all were swept away and drowned or battered to death in the vicious undertow.

Only those who had reached the top of the bluffs, or had managed to scramble more than a hundred feet above the shoreline were spared. The tidal wave, sweeping down on the sand-bar had gained extra height as it was forced against the bluff, carrying the stragglers away as it passed.

The bulk of the force who managed to reach the northern shore escaped with their lives but there was no cheering, no celebration. The circumstances surrounding their deliverance were so awesome, the scale of death so overwhelming, the survivors fell wordlessly to the ground, overcome with grief and sheer physical exhaustion.

Mr Snow was one of them. Awesome-Wells and Boston-Bruin ran towards him. For several agonizing minutes they thought he was dead. The lighter parts of his skin were greyish-white, and his almost weightless body, cradled in their arms, felt like a sack of loose bones. Eventually his eyes fluttered open, but they too were drained of life.

Awesome-Wells took hold of Mr Snow's hands and squeezed the unresisting fingers. 'Old One! Old One! Do you know who I am?'

Mr Snow's eyes searched slowly for the speaker but seemed unable to focus on the faces of those who knelt over him. His lips moved soundlessly.

Awesome-Wells placed his ear against them to try and catch what looked like the last words the Old One might utter.

'Is it . . . over . . .?'

'Yes. Most of the She-Kargo and their blood-brothers have survived but everything else has gone. The D'Troit, C'Natti and San'Louis, the wheel-boats, the trading post . . . all have been swept away.' He paused but there was no response. Awesome looked up at those around him then sought the answer to one last question. 'Tell us, Old One – was this the Great Dying the Sky Voices spoke of so long ago?'

'Part . . . of it, yes. Talisman has . . . has cut . . . the poisoned . . . branches from . . . the . . . tree that is the . . . Plainfolk. We who . . . have . . . been chosen must . . . must make sure . . . they never . . . grow . . . again.'

'He did more than cut the poisoned branches!' cried Boston-Bruin. His voice was harsh with anger and grief. 'The She-Kargo, M'Waukee and San'Paul will never be able to count their dead! We alone have lost close to half our clanfolk! If, as you say, we're supposed to be Talisman's chosen people why did he not spare all of us?!'

Mr Snow closed his eyes. 'Ahhh, Boston . . . Boston,' he whispered. 'Why must you . . . always . . . ask questions to which there . . . is . . . no . . . answer?'

CHAPTER SEVEN

Two days later, when Steve, Night-Fever and the band of M'Call Bears came in sight of Lake Superior, the water carried inland by the tidal wave had not yet drained from the dips and hollows in the terrain.

Ranging in size from large puddles to miniature lakes, the farthest pools were up to seven miles from the fatal shore. Bodies and debris littered the entire triangle of land enclosed by the estuary of the St Louis River but the eye was drawn to the shattered remains of the five wheel-boats which rose out of the waterlogged grass like the dismembered carcasses of beached whales.

Moving mechanically through this sombre landscape were groups of scavengers; the numbed survivors of the She-Kargo, M'Waukee and San'Paul. It was clear there had been a major catastrophe with massive loss of life, and to judge from what was left of the wheel-boats, the Iron Master trading expedition had been virtually wiped out.

Steve dismounted and used a length of cord to fasten the front and rear left leg of his horse together. This allowed the animal to walk and graze freely but stopped it from straying too far. Until they found out what had happened and who had won, it would have been unwise to proceed further on horseback. It could raise questions that might prove difficult to answer – especially if they were posed by a bunch of bellicose nips facing a long walk home.

Leaving Night-Fever to guard the roped horse against jackals and other predators, Steve's party made their way down the slope and met up with a small group of She-Kargo Mutes. They were from the Clan M'Kormik, a close neighbour of the M'Call's. All of them looked pale and subdued. Cat-Ballou, the leader of Steve's escort, exchanged formal greetings then, in hushed tones, asked what had caused such devastation.

For a moment none of the M'Kormik warriors replied then, one by one, beginning with a Bear called First-Blood, they took turns to describe what had happened with a kind of dazed weariness. There was none of the elation which, as victors, they might have been expected to display. Mutes were no strangers to pain or sudden death but the tidal wave had claimed nearly two hundred thousand lives. No one had witnessed destruction on this scale since the legendary War of a Thousand Suns.

Rough-Cut, the last to speak, concluded the harrowing tale with a sweeping gesture that took in the empty shoreline which, as Steve suddenly realized, had lost its familiar landmark.

'Even the trading post has gone! Torn from the ground and snapped in two by the wrath of Talisman.'

'Oyy-yehhh!' groaned the M'Call Bears.

'And the Iron Masters?' enquired Steve.

Rough-Cut's face darkened. 'We have killed all those in which a breath of life lingered.'

'And the treacherous dogs from the bloodline of the D'Troit have suffered the same fate,' added First-Blood. 'But all those from the C'Natti and San'Louis who could still walk were sent away unharmed.'

Steve frowned. 'I thought they were in this together.'

'They were,' replied First-Blood, 'But our elders said they should be allowed to go free to bear witness to the fate reserved for those who deny Talisman and seek to divide the Plainfolk!'

'And what of our wordsmith, Mr Snow?' asked Cat-Ballou. 'The Storm-Bringer, whose body served as the hammer which Talisman used to smite the D'Troit? Where can we find him?'

Rough-Cut exchanged glances with his companions then pointed towards the high ground north of the lagoon. 'His body lies above the Great river. There, where you see the smoke rising.'

Steve's stomach turned over. 'His body?! Is he dead?'

'It is hard to say,' replied First-Blood. 'The elders say he crosses over then returns. With so many dead, Mo-Town's cup must be filled to overflowing. Perhaps there is not yet room for him on the other side.'

Terrific . . . So much for the master plan. Steve tried to sound cool, calm and collected. 'How can we get there?'

First-Blood directed him to the river crossing then he and his companions moved past them in search of another untouched heap of debris.

Steve hurried back to where he had left the horse, climbed into the saddle, told Night-Fever where he was going, and galloped back to Cat-Ballou. 'See you guys up there – okay?'

The M'Call Bears watched him ride away then looked at each other in silent agreement. Having walked and run seven hundred miles, sitting on the back of a horse and letting *it* carry you where you wanted to go was beginning to look like an interesting idea.

After leading his horse up the face of the bluff, one of the first persons Steve came across was Carnegie-Hall. Before he could open his mouth, Steve took the wordsmith aside and explained that he was travelling incognito. Talisman did not wish him to be identified as one of The Chosen at this particular moment in time.

Flattered to be the sole guardian of such an earth-shaking secret, Carnegie-Hall readily agreed to keep shtum. He led Steve over to Mr Snow's makeshift bed where he was greeted by the surviving clan elders from the M'Call trade delegation – Awesome-Wells and Boston-Bruin. Blue-Thunder, the paramount warrior was there too; wounded, but still mobile – along with several other Bears that Steve recognized.

Steve sat cross-legged for over an hour by Mr Snow's side willing his eyes to open. Eventually they did. All the colour and sparkle had gone out of them, but there was a faint flicker of recognition when they finally alighted on Steve.

172

'What kept you?' The Old One's face was thin and drawn – aged almost beyond recognition, his voice barely audible.

'Oh, this and that.'

Mr Snow's eyes wandered past him then gave up the search. 'Where's . . .?'

'They couldn't make it.' Steve forced a lightness into his voice. 'You going to lie there for ever? Your friends here want to invite you to a big party.'

Mr Snow's lips twitched in a pale imitation of his mischievous smile. 'You . . . may have to . . . start . . . without me.' Stringing more than three words together seemed to drain all his strength. He paused for a while and tried again. 'Are they . . . safe?'

'Cadillac is.' Steve outlined what had happened after leaving the Kojak. Having spoken to Carnegie-Hall, he knew there was no need to repeat the whole story. It was difficult to know how much Mr Snow was taking in. He took hold of a withered hand. It felt so fragile, he dared not squeeze it for fear of crushing the bones. 'That's why we need you back on your feet. You're the only one with the power to get clearwater off that train.'

Mr Snow sighed and closed his eyes. The forefinger of the hand lying on his chest twitched, beckoning Steve to come closer.

Steve leant over to catch what he was trying to say.

'What are you . . . trying to . . . do . . . kill me?'

In the days following the Battle of the Trading Post, the clan elders and warriors of the victorious delegations conferred on what to do next. Clearly nothing could be as it was before. When the D'Troit, C'Natti and San'Louis clans learned of their defeat there would be great bitterness. The enmity between the opposing bloodlines would deepen, the character of the fighting would change. Not the traditional clashes between rival bands of warriors but large-scale confrontations – and perhaps a permanent state of war.

It was a gloomy prospect. The She-Kargo, M'Waukee

and San'Paul had made common cause against the D'Troit faction but that did not mean their own traditional hostility to one another had evaporated. In a sense, this year's journey to the trading post had been the Plainfolk's road to Damascus but there had been no miraculous conversion. The atmosphere was not now filled with harmony and light. Each clan, while sharing the bond of a common bloodline was still fiercely protective of its own identity and its turf.

What had brought the She-Kargo, M'Waukee and San'Paul together on that fateful day and the desperate hours preceding it was their unshakeable belief in Talisman and their willingness to accept the advent of The Chosen, whereas the D'Troit and its fellow-travellers were apparently ready to ditch those self-same beliefs in exchange for a deal with the hated dead-faces.

All the clans wished to trade with the Iron Masters if only for the simple reason that no one wanted to find themselves living next-door to a better-armed – and thus stronger – clan. But the Mutes were under no illusions about the impact these trading contacts would have on the traditional life-style and belief-system of the Plainfolk. From the very beginning, they knew they were getting the worst of a deal. And the fact they had been forced to trade by the threat of armed invasion by highly-organized predators had offended their sense of honour.

But it was the best and only offer available. And by accepting it, the Mutes had been able to delay the advance of their other enemy – the sand-burrowers. Everyone knew they were being ripped off but the point was *all* the clans from the six major bloodlines had accepted the conditions laid down by the Iron Masters. It was a collective rip-off and that, in some strange way, made it bearable. The mistake the D'Troit had made was in appearing to have come to a more favourable arrangement with the dead-faces in a way that would give the D'Troit extra power and advantages the other bloodlines would not share.

They had come close to succeeding, but their attempt to

win hearts and minds by isolating the M'Calls and the She-Kargo had been foiled by Mr Snow's rousing defence. In implementing Lord Hirohito's plan, his successor, Aishi Sakimoto, had overlooked the crucial flaw in the domain-lord's strategy. The endemic hostility between individual clans and bloodlines imperilled the long-term future of the Plainfolk but the She-Kargo, M'Waukee, San'Paul, San'Louis – and to some extent the C'Natti – were united by their fear and hatred of the D'Troit.

The majority of the C'Natti delegations had submerged these feelings in the hope of gaining the advantages that would accrue from being on the winning side – and had suffered terrible losses as a result. Whether they would now change sides remained to be seen. The few C'Natti who had survived the tidal wave and had been spared in the subsequent mopping-up operation were still too shocked to think rationally about the future.

It was a future which no one taking part in this first council could contemplate with any great pleasure. It seemed unlikely that the Iron Masters would return cap-in-hand to apologize for instigating the attack on the She-Kargo. They had obviously intended to punish the M'Calls and the entire bloodline for the actions of The Chosen in the Eastern Lands. This could not be allowed to happen. No one who believed in the Talisman Prophecy could fail to defend those who had been sent to herald the coming of the Thrice-Gifted One.

The dead-faces would return, but not to trade. From now on, the Plainfolk would have to rely on their own resources. Still stunned by the massive and merciless blow Talisman had struck on their behalf, few relished the prospect of defending themselves against marauding bands of dead-faces armed with an endless supply of long sharp-iron.

At the outset it seemed an impossible goal. Mr Snow, exhausted and at death's door, was unable to lend his reasoned eloquence or wisdom to the debate but at the end of five argumentative and sometimes acrimonious days a fragile consensus emerged. All agreed that the

Battle of the Trading Post marked the end of an era. From henceforth, the interests of individual clans would have to take second place to the protection of the Plainfolk. Warriors who, over the centuries, had been blooded by challenging and killing their peers from neighbouring clans would now have to earn their standing in combat with the *real* enemies of the Plainfolk – the dead-faces and the sand-burrowers.

It was this issue – inter-clan blood-letting – that aroused the most controversy. To deny this right of challenge struck deep into the warrior ethos. The courage to brave close, single-combat was – for the Mutes – absolutely fundamental. It was the corner-stone of their existence, the means by which an individual and the clan to which they belonged measured their worth.

The history of the Plainfolk was the history of heroes. Those who had 'chewed bone' stout hearts whose sharp-iron had filled head-poles. Before the Battle of the Trading Post, no warrior worthy of the name would have used a crossbow in combat against his peers. Long sharp-iron was used solely for hunting game; the rifles and other weapons used by the sand-burrowers were proof of their cowardice, their lack of honour. They were animals whose blood-lust knew no bounds. That was why it was permissible to use the cross-bow when fighting them.

The Iron Masters used a different kind of bow and arrow made of wood. It had a shorter range than the crossbow but a much higher rate of fire. They also possessed other fearsome sharp-iron, long curved swords that could slice through flesh and bone and the heavy black pipes on the wheel-boats that spoke with the voice of sky-thunder and whose fiery breath could tear a man to pieces at five hundred paces.

Their readiness to use such weapons plus the fact they were an alien race placed them in the same category as the sand-burrowers. A category to which – because of their denial of Talisman – the D'Troit and their co-conspirators had also been consigned.

The use of long sharp-iron had always aroused strong

176

emotions. Following the battle with The Lady from Louisiana, Mr Snow had stressed the need to develop not just new tactics but a totally new concept of making war. His radical proposals had not gone down well with the traditionalists within his own clan. There had been further objections following the gift by Lord Yama-Shita of a hundred repeating rifles. Cut off from further supplies of ammunition, they were now useless – as his opponents had predicted.

Such deep-rooted differences of opinion over such a wide range of issues could not be resolved in the space of five days, but there was general agreement that the discussions should continue. The number of the issues on which they were united was greater than the sum total of those on which they remained divided.

Each delegation made a solemn pledge to come to the aid of any clan attacked by the D'Troit faction or the dead-faces, but before this could happen the present patchy bush-telegraph had to be replaced by a more effective nation-wide system of communications. The discussions on how this could be set up would continue within each bloodline, and it was agreed that delegates from the clans now present would consider any proposals put forward when the first Plainfolk Council was convened at Big Running White Water (Sioux Falls, South Dakota) in three months' time.

Meanwhile, the five-week truce which came into effect during the trading period was to be extended through the summer and would embrace any clans of the D'Troit and C'Natti who were prepared to recognize The Chosen as the heralds of Talisman and pledge their allegiance to the Plainfolk.

In his guise as a simple warrior from the Clan M'Call, Steve took no part in the discussions and his interest in the emerging alliance was, at best, academic. His overriding concern was the health of Mr Snow.

The M'Call delegation were also concerned but not to the same extent. They were governed by the fatalism that coloured the Mute view of death. After his experiences on the overground, Steve was increasingly drawn to the idea of a continuing cycle of existence, but in his present predicament the prospect of Mr Snow re-entering the world at some future date in a new body offered little consolation. What he needed was Mr Snow up on his feet and able to call down some heavy shit in the here and now.

As a wordsmith, Mr Snow could be replaced by Cadillac. He did not have the Old One's stature but even Mr Snow had been a young man once. Cadillac's appointment would give him standing within the clan and in time he would grow into the job, but he was not a summoner. There was only one person who could replace the Storm-Bringer – Clearwater.

In urging the clan elders to do their utmost to keep Mr Snow alive, Steve described the powers Clearwater had revealed during their escape from Ne-Issan – powers that might one day surpass even those of the Old One. Aroused by his tales of derring-do the elders promised to do all they could to help rescue her from Red River – even if Mr Snow died. If it was the will of Talisman, they assured him, the whole clan would lay down their lives for her.

A nice gesture but one which would make her rescue a totally pointless operation. In trying to sound helpful, the elders were blinding themselves to the fact that, without Mr Snow's presence and the use of his power Clearwater could not be rescued. In his many arguments with Cadillac, Steve had hammered on about not relying on earth-magic but this time their lives depended on it. Only a summoner with the power and presence of Mr Snow could give them the edge they needed.

It was not just practical considerations that were involved; there was a moral dimension. Despite the promise made by the clan elders, Steve knew that without Mr Snow, the M'Calls would not attack the wagon-train. And if Cadillac tried to persuade them to do so, Steve would do his utmost to prevent it. He had witnessed the reckless bravery of the Bears at the Battle of The Now and Then River when they had been aided by Mr Snow's earth-magic. His powers had been awesome but in the end, the M'Calls' irrational desire to throw themselves headlong upon the enemy regardless of the cost had led to a senseless slaughter and eventual rout. After the losses suffered at the trading post he was not prepared to support any ill-prepared adventures that could lead to even greater sacrifice.

Not even for you, little sister . . .

Over the next few days, as the talks between the delegations continued, Mr Snow gradually recovered some of his strength. He could not sit up unaided, and he was far too weak to walk, but his spirit had returned from that twilight zone between this world and the next and was once more anchored firmly in his physical body. His face was still pale and haggard but the colour and some of the sparkle had come back into his eyes, and the famous smile, though tired, occasionally contained a hint of its old mischief.

His voice now seemed to be set in a husky whisper and he spoke only when necessary using as few words as possible, but as time passed, his powers of concentration increased, and from what little he said it was clear that the brain inside the wizened, white-haired skull was as sharp as a razor.

During these longer periods of wakefulness, Steve related in greater detail his adventures in Ne-Issan with the *ronin*, his high-risk, heart-stopping involvement with the Herald Hase-Gawa, the conspiracy against the Shogun, and the final battle and escape from the Heron Pool.

'I'm not surprised the Yama-Shita . . . went . . . for the throat,' husked Mr Snow.

'Yeah, but it's not entirely my fault,' protested Steve. 'The Heron Pool was blown apart because the Shogun wanted to crush the conspiracy against him. And the reason we got mixed up in it was because of *your* deal with Lord Yama-Shita. If you hadn't sent Cadillac and Clearwater over there none of this would have happened!'

'Just doing what I was told . . .'

'You mean by the Sky Voices? Talisman?'

'The Path is drawn, Brickman. Someone once said: "All the world's a stage, and all the men and women merely players".'

'Yeah . . .' Steve was unaware of the immense legacy of dramatic art and literature that had been buried by the Holocaust so the quotation made little sense.

'Anyway,' he continued, 'Cadillac fell on his feet, but for a while she had a really bad time. So when we blew up the Heron Pool, she took the opportunity to even the score – saving our necks in the process. Do you blame her?'

'No.' Mr Snow gave a breathy laugh. 'Life isn't fair is it? Poor old Prime-Cut –'

'The big-noise from the D'Troit?'

'Yes. Apart from us having done a deal with the Federation, every charge he levelled against us was true.'

'And in spite of that you ran rings round him.'

'So everyone says. But I didn't lie.'

'Well, except for that bit about The Chosen.'

'That wasn't a lie. You *are* one of The Chosen.'

Steve frowned. 'But I'm not a Mute.'

'No.' Mr Snow closed his eyes and let his head fall onto the furs that covered the sloping back-rest.

Not yet, Brickman. Not yet . . .

Having reached a measure of agreement, the delegations spent the sixth and seventh day trading amongst themselves. In addition to preserving most of the goods they had brought with them to trade with the Iron Masters, everyone who was not engaged in deciding the future of the Plainfolk had been busily scouring the battlefield for whatever they could find: crossbows, bolts, knives, items of clothing, Iron Master swords, helmets and body armour, ship's cannon – the list was endless. The dead - even their own – were too numerous to cope with. Unable to give them the usual burial rites or collect them in heaps for burning, the corpses were stripped and left for the circling death-birds.

Those who decided they had too many crossbows and not enough bolts, or preferred to exchange both for samurai long-swords, set up an impromptu arms bazaar. Their initiative was quickly followed by their rivals and it was not long before each delegation set out its other wares – food, furs, dried fish and buffalo meat, dream-cap and rainbow-grass.

It proved to be a novel and rewarding experience, and everyone promised to bring similar goods to the pro-posed meeting of the Plainfolk Council at Sioux Falls. Why, they asked each other, had no one ever thought of this before? Nobody suggested trading the surviving journey-men. The idea that males and females from one clan might take partners from another was so radical it simply never entered anyone's head.

Laden with their booty, the clan delegations bade each other farewell and went their various ways. The happiest were the journey-men and -women who had been chosen to make the journey down the Great River and were going home instead. But their joy at returning to their families was muted by the loss of their clan-brothers and sisters. The general mood was one of sombre optimism. There could be no going back, and no one looked back as another wheeling flock of death-birds, drawn in from all corners of the sky, swooped down to join those already gorging themselves on the fallen.

When Mr Snow woke up and looked around him, he saw the surviving members of the M'Call delegation preparing to join the general exodus. Steve, sitting cross-legged by his side did not appear to have moved an inch.

Their eyes met. 'You still here?'
'I've got a problem I need to talk to you about.'
Mr Snow sighed. 'Who hasn't? Okay . . shoot.'
Steve explained the set-up on board Red River, and

how Cadillac and Malone were working on a plan to free
Roz and Clearwater.

'The thing is . . . Malone is an undercover agent – a
mexican, like me. We're supposed to be working together
to capture you and Cadillac.'

'Helped by your kin-sister . . .'

'Yeah. Roz smart-talked the Federation into thinking
she was their secret weapon. An anti-summoner device.
She's managed to get this far but until she and Clearwater
are free and clear, I have to pretend I'm still a one hundred per cent solid, dependable soldier-citizen. Otherwise . . .'

'Yes, yes, I've got the picture . . .'

'Good. The people on board Red River think they've
got the drop on us, but of course with your help we'll
have the drop on them. I still have to work out the way
we're gonna swing it but if we all put our heads together
we should be able to come up with something.'

'I see . . . so what's the problem?'

'How do I tell Cadillac that Malone's a phoney without
him blowing his top? When he finds out I've been
stringing him along he's gonna go apeshit. We've already
crossed knives over Roz and I don't want to get into that
again.

'But more important still I don't want him sending a
bunch of Bears out to collect Malone's head. We need
him alive and working with us because *he's* the key to
getting on board the wagon-train.'

Steve paused then said: 'It'd made things a lot easier
all round if you told him. I mean – you *are* his teacher.'

'Yes . . .'

'I'm sorry. What exactly is it you're saying? "Yes" you
are his teacher, or "Yes" you'll tell him?'

Mr Snow's left hand waved feebly. 'You're throwing
too much at me, Brickman. Give me some . . . some
time . . . to think about it.'

Steve cursed silently as the wordsmith closed his eyes.
Time! That was the one thing they didn't have!

Mr Snow's hand slipped off the stretcher. Steve took

hold of it and laid it across the old man's chest.

The wasted flesh felt cold. Too cold . . .

Seven hundred miles south and to the west of the now-ruined trading post, another pawn moved a stage further towards its final position in the game as The Lady from Louisiana rolled into the loading bay of the way-station above the almost completed divisional base at Monroe/Wichita. The fuel hoppers that fed the power-cars were topped up, and vital electronic components that had been shuttled northwards in response to an urgent radio message were installed and tested in an effort to get the trouble-prone communications system back into full working order.

The Lady also took on some other unexpected items of freight: a large sealed cargo skip whose contents were not listed on the external manifest docket, and sixty hooded defaulters wearing wrist and foot shackles and the usual black fatigues with the yellow diagonal cross stripes on the chest and back.

But that was not the end of the surprises. A major from the White House, dressed in the same red combat fatigues, came on board with a diskette sealed with an "EYES ONLY" label bearing Hartmann's name.

CINC-TRAIN usually sent top secret instructions by radio in coded blocks that were converted by The Lady's communications unit into a video signal and fed into the work-station in Hartmann's private quarters. Only Hartmann himself, using his ID card and a special key sequence could screen the blocks and turn them back into the original message.

Sealed diskettes delivered by high-ranking couriers from the White House usually contained *ultra*-secret material; orders so sensitive they could not even be transmitted in code through the normal channels. Hartmann used his ID card to 'sign' for the diskette and considered it at some length, holding the small, slim square silver package by his fingertips as he turned it this way and that. This had to be hot stuff . . .

It was.

After locking his door, Hartmann broke the seal, slipped the diskette into the drive slot of his PC, unlocked the system with his ID card and hit the keys to screen and decode the signal from the White-House. The jumble of digits and letters rearranged themselves into lines of clear text. Scrolling carefully through the secret signal the wagon-master discovered why he had been given custody of sixty defaulters – all of whom were under sentence of death. He also learned what was in the cargo skip, when it had to be opened and the reason why a tight-lipped group of service engineers were making certain external modifications to his wagon-train.

The diskette contained precise instructions on when he was to brief his executive officers and crew on the nature of their mission, and ended by informing him that the flight section of The Lady was to be re-equipped with Skyhawk Mark Two's.

In order to allow his wing-men to familiarize themselves with this new machine in the field, Hartmann was ordered to fly off five of his present complement of ten Mark One's to Red River who would replace them with five Mark Two's and their pilots. Half of the flight-deck crew riding on buddy-frames would also be exchanged, allowing the necessary training of air and ground personnel to proceed simultaneously on both wagon-trains.

To Hartmann, the prospect of receiving a new batch of aircraft combined with The Lady's involvement in a secret mission was a sure sign that he and the surviving members of his original crew were on their way to complete rehabilitation. This time at least, the outcome would not be affected by the baleful influence of a Mute summoner. This time, the crewmen who had lost their lives in the past two near-catastrophic encounters would be avenged. The Lady would emerge with her head high.

Third time lucky. Wasn't that what they said . . .?

* * *

About the same time that Hartmann was reflecting on his good fortune, a soldier-citizen of the Federation by the name of Jake Olsen was taking stock of his surroundings and wondering whether he was dreaming or if, in some mysterious way, his luck had taken a turn for the better.

It could hardly get much worse. Arrested and charged under Code One, Olsen had been sentenced to death for the illegal recording and trafficking of blackjack tapes. The severity of the sentence reflected the scale and success of the operation. Olsen and his partners had set up a Federation-wide network of dealers and had avoided detection for over seven years by buying off provost-marshals with bagfuls of top-quality rainbow-grass supplied by overground contacts in the Mines & Mills Division.

The same techniques had been used to secure the cooperation of AmExecs in the Black Tower and low-ranking members of the First Family. They had helped stall and side-track investigations, and had secured plush apartments in the new luxury tower-deeps for the ring-leaders.

It had all gone well. Too well. As an electronics expert, it had been Olsen's task to assemble the necessary equipment and oversee the recording and duplication of the illegal music tapes. There had been a lot of work cleaning up the sound quality because his raw material consisted of *nth* generation copies of the original pre-Holocaust masters. He had even re-recorded entire sequences, matching the originals as faithfully as possible using a synthesizer built from components filched from the First Family's own music workshops.

Yeah, that had been sweet. The mistake had been to branch out into the manufacture of alcohol. In a society where almost everything is controlled by computer, illegal electronic items are easy to hide. Hook 'em into some official circuitry and they're hard to distinguish from the real thing. Crates of plastic containers full of straw-coloured liquid with a distinctive aroma proved to be a whole new ball game and the problem was not eased by some bright spark who labelled a consignment destined for the junior medical staff at the Life Institute as 'urine samples'.

Looking back, it was clear the operation had been penetrated by undercover Feds for some time, but it was after that particular consignment was intercepted that everything started to unravel at the speed of light. Nation-wide, over three hundred people were arrested, charged and tried. But after six televised executions by firing squad, the judicial process had suddenly been put on hold.

For the last five weeks, Olsen had been sitting in his cell on death row, wondering what had caused the delay. Despite his sudden downfall, Olsen was as cheerful as might be expected in the circumstances but he was also a realist. A reprieve was out of the question. The operation in which he'd been involved had caused the high-wires too much embarrassment but in the seven years before his arrest, Olsen had discovered that the First Family was running its own illegal operations – scams to trap potential subversives and budding law-breakers. The possibility that the Family might have decided to recruit him into their own 'bad-hat' brigade was the only plausible explanation for the unexpected stay of execution.

If so, there was several questions to be answered. His brain felt muzzy and seemed to working at half-speed but the last thing Olsen remembered was going to sleep in his small over-warm nine foot by six foot cell in his black T-shirt and underpants, on a narrow bunk with a thin coverlet on top of him, and with the light behind the grille in the ceiling cut to a third – the level of night-time illumination known to Trackers as "twilight".

Now, the biggest and brightest light he had ever seen was beaming down on him from a blue ceiling whose height was beyond computation. And the narrow confines of his cell had been replaced by vast, seemingly limitless horizons. John Wayne Plaza was big and brightly lit but what now met his eyes on all sides was . . . something else.

Yessirrr . . .

Olsen knew that if he was still asleep, this was a dream. On the other hand, if he was awake (and despite the utter impossibility of him being where he was, he had an alarming feeling that he *was* fully conscious) then he had been plunged into a nightmare from which he knew, with mind-numbing certainty, he would never escape.

Despite his intelligence, technical skill and flair for organization, Jake Olsen had never been overground. Indeed he had used that same intelligence to arrange 'soft postings' within the earth-shield, to the units which provided him with the contacts he needed to gain access to the equipment that interested him, and the most rewarding 'career opportunities'.

Now, on a day whose date he was unable to determine, he was sitting supported by his hands with his feet out in front of him in a clearing on a forested hillside which afforded a view over a vast panoramic landscape which stretched away to the east, south and west. Olsen was able to determine this because he had seen video-pictures of the overground and knew the difference between a rising and setting sun.

Behind him, was an upward slope with more red pine trees and rocks peeking out of the tangled undergrowth. He was on a hill, or some kind of mountain. The air had a strange smell and a sharp cold, but not unpleasant, cutting edge to it when he drew it down into his lungs. Where the hell was he? And what the fuck was going on?!

Olsen looked down at his feet and saw that the lower half of his body was inside a camouflage sleeping bag. A further inspection revealed that he was dressed in a set of the standard red, pink, orange and brown camouflaged fatigues issued to overground units and on his right shoulder was a woven fabric badge.

SIG-INT . . . What was he doing wearing a uniform of some guy in the 5th Signals Intelligence Squadron?!

Olsen pulled out his tunic and peered down at the name tag above the right breast pocket. 693 OLSEN J.E . . . Shit . . . This wasn't someone else's uniform, it had his

187

name on it! There was a carbine lying alongside his sleeping bag and a visored helmet. That had his name on it too. He rubbed his forehead and swallowed, trying to rid himself of a sudden dizzying wave of nausea.

Focusing his attention on his immediate surroundings, Olsen was comforted by the fact that he was not alone. Scattered around the clearing and under the trees beyond were a considerable number of recumbent figures in hooded sleeping bags. Too many to count. And there were small heaps of equipment, ration packs, the burnt-out remains of several campfires, and the lower section of some kind of tower made out of slim, red-painted aluminium girders and mounted on a small concrete base. More half-assembled sections lay nearby.

It looked like a UHF radio beacon. That would explain the SIG-INT shoulder badge on his arm. But why did he have no recollection of being transferred from death row into an overground signals outfit? He checked the digital watch someone had strapped on his left wrist: it was nearly 11.00 hours. Why hadn't he and the other sleepers been rousted from their beds? Why was no one awake and on guard? Gripped by rising panic, Olsen tried to get up. It was more difficult than he expected. His legs felt leaden. Stooping down to pick up the carbine and helmet made his head swim. He dropped to one knee to steady himself and had to wait a while for the giddiness to clear then tried again, using the carbine as a prop to haul himself upright.

The short barrelled weapon had a magazine inserted into the lower chamber in front of the trigger guard. Olsen released it and weighed it in his hand. It felt about half full. The air pressure read-out was above the red line. Good enough. Olsen clipped the mag into the chamber, eased off the safety and fired a single volley into the air.

Chuww-wiittt! Chuww-wiittt! Chuww-wiittt!

'At least something's working,' he grunted.

A flak-jacket with its interlaced webbing harness, magazine pouches and air-bottles lay beside his sleeping bag. Olsen knew it was something people on the overground should wear at all times but he didn't want to load himself down. Ever since he put the helmet on it had made his neck ache. It was like a ten-ton weight pressing on his spine.

His present wretched state was not unlike the hangover that came from smoking sour grass and drinking joy-juice at one and the same time. Olsen knew he hadn't done either. The last meal delivered to his cell had been spiked. And while he had lain unconscious – for an undetermined period of time – someone had injected a cocktail of drugs that had left him physically and mentally hamstrung.

With his rubbery legs splayed in an effort to keep his balance Olsen shambled over to the nearest of the sleeping figures and prodded it awake with the butt of his carbine. And he was not at all surprised to find that the occupant of the bag was someone he knew. The bleary face that appeared out of the hood belonged to Marv Dandridge, a close colleague, one of the top men running the blackjack ring and one of his neighbours on death row.

Dandridge hoisted himself up on one elbow and tried to get his sodden brain into gear. He looked around him with growing amazement then shook his head. 'I don't believe this. What the hell are you doing dressed up like –' He broke off as he realized he was wearing a similar outfit. 'Ohh, jeezuss . . .' He turned an anguished face towards Olsen. 'Jake – is this for real?'

'You'd better believe it.'

Dandridge sat up. 'Where are we?'

'How the fuck do I know?! I ain't never been over-ground! All I know is we're in deep shit.'

Dandridge's drugged brain was slow on the uptake. 'Why? Wass-happnin'?'

'Fer crissakes, Marv!' cried Olsen. 'D'you think they dressed us up in these uniforms for fun?! *This* is why we all got that stay of execution! We've been set up! Well and truly shafted!'

'Christo!' Dandridge scrambled to his feet and threw

an arm out to steady himself against Olsen. 'Hey! My arms and legs feel kinda funny.'

'Mine too. That's cos they doped us up to the eyeballs before they dumped us out here.'

The words took time to register. 'You mean . . . to be killed?'

'What d'you think they're gonna do – pin a fuckin' medal on us?! This is a scam set up by the First Family, and we're the meat on the hook! *Dead* meat if we don't move fast!'

'Christo . . .' The threat restored a measure of lucidity to Dandridge's brain and put some life back into his leaden limbs. 'How are we gonna get outta this mess?'

'We have to find where we are first.' Olsen patted Dandridge on the shoulder. 'There's a load of equipment lying around. See if you can find a map case while I check out who else is here.'

Dandridge surveyed the sleeping figures, some of whom had begun to stir. 'These are . . . our people?'

'It wouldn't surprise me.'

'Evil bastards . . .'

'Yeah,' laughed Olsen. 'Y'gotta hand it to 'em. A nice twist, huh?'

He didn't know everyone who'd been involved in the blackjack operation but among those he found awake, or managed to rouse were fifteen people he'd worked with or met when many of those arrested had shared communal cells while waiting to be interrogated. To have one of your number taken out and marched away then returned several hours later beaten and bloodied and unable to stand never failed to sap the morale of those whose turn had yet to come.

Those fifteen, when they could stand on their feet, found others they knew – all incapacitated to some degree by the drugs that had been pumped into them. Olsen's worst fears were confirmed. The First Family had emptied death row at Grand Central. But along with those sentenced to death for their part in the blackjack operation there were Code One offenders from other

190

divisional bases. There were even some Code Two's who'd been sentenced to ten years of hard labour. Put in to make the number up.

Tough . . .

Olsen rejoined Dandridge and some of his other cronies who were clustered round a map. 'There's a hundred of us, all told. Anybody figured out where we are?'

'Yeah,' said Dandridge. 'Jerry here's the expert. If this map is kosher, then from what he can see of the lie of the land, he says we're somewhere around here.'

Olsen looked at the point indicated by Dandridge's finger. 'Iron Mountain . . .'

'North of navref Cheyenne,' explained Jerry. 'We're in Southern Wyoming. North of Colorado.'

Olsen mastered another spell of giddiness. 'You mean we're not even in the fuckin' Federation?!'

'No,' said Jerry. 'This is Plainfolk territory.'

Olsen closed his eyes. 'Shit and corruption! I knew it, I knew it!'

'The nearest way-station is Pueblo. I don't know how far that is. This map doesn't cover Colorado but it must be several hundred miles.'

'What are we gonna do?' asked Dandridge.

'Well, we can't go to Pueblo, that's for sure!' cried Olsen. 'We're under sentence of death, remember? We'll just have to make a stand right here.'

'Against what?' asked someone in the group that had gathered behind him.

'How the fuck do I know?' exclaimed Olsen. Then, addressing the group as a whole he said. 'The only thing we can be sure of is the Family didn't put us jailbirds here because they thought we needed the fresh air! I don't know how you guys feel but I vote we grab hold of as much of this gear as we can and get under cover. Find a cave, or somethin'.'

He turned back to Dandridge and Jerry the map-reader. 'Is it getting to you?'

Dandridge frowned. What?'

'The space! There's too much fuckin' sky! I can't

handle it! When I first woke up I was okay but now it's givin' me the shakes!'

'It's this dope they slipped us.'

'No, it isn't. I heard about this. Lots of guys go down with it – end up not bein' able to move.'

'We'll be okay if we stick together,' said Jerry. 'Ground-sickness can be beaten. You just gotta have the right mental attitude. Keep your eyes down. Don't take in too much at once.'

'You been overground before?'

'Yeah. Two years with Mines and Mills.'

'And you never felt bad?'

'You get acclimatized. The new guys spend the first three months on internal duties – inside the plant buildings. You work up to it by looking out of the windows and when you're good and ready you step out into the Big Open. The guys that can't handle it get reassigned'

'Well, I aint had three months to get ready! I went to sleep in my cell and I woke up here! And it's beginning to scare the hell out of me!' Keeping his eyes on the ground in front of him, Olsen pushed his way through the group and shambled across the slope to the sleeping bag he'd vacated earlier.

By the time he reached it, tears were streaming down his face. Even a prison cell, for as long as you occupied it, was your own space. Out here, there were no walls, no roofs, nothing to keep out this oppressive emptiness. The sleeping bag and the piece of earth on which it lay was the only thing he could relate to; the only point of contact with the concrete cocoon in which he spent the weeks since his trial.

He fell to his knees beside it. He had gone back to get the flak-jacket. Given the jam they were in, it made sense to put it on. Attached to the webbing straps were pouches of ammunition for the carbine, a hand grenade, machete, and battery packs to power the radio and target acquisition arrays on his visor. Once the helmet umbilical was plugged into the butt of his carbine, he'd be able to hit anything he aimed at.

Like a bunch of screaming Mutes. Out here that was the most likely thing to happen. A firing squad would have been better. Cleaner anyway. Out here, after they'd stuck your head on a pole and hammered it down so's the point came out through the top of your skull, they cut the rest of you up and turned you into smoked meat twists.

There was no point in moving camp. Best thing was to try and dig a hole under the trees. Get some earth round you and some branches over the top and hope you were asleep when it got dark. It would be a good idea to take some ration packs and –

Olsen heard someone shouting. Then other people calling to each other. He looked around and saw one of the camouflaged cee-bees standing on a rocky outcrop further up the slope. He was holding a 'scope.

Dandridge came over. 'We've spotted what looks like a bunch of renegades moving across a flat-topped ridge below us. An' y'know what? They got horses! Just like in the archives! You can't see 'em from here. D'you wanna come up and take a look?'

'What for?'

'C'mon, Jake! They're our kind of people! If we could hook up with them . . .' Dandridge saw he was getting nowhere. 'Some of the guys want to send up some signal flares.' He shrugged. 'What the hell? We might as well try. Things can't get much worse – right?'

'Right . . .'

Olsen watched his one-time associate hurry away. Good old Marv. He was doing a great job holding it down, but he'd never been overground either, and he was getting the shakes too.

A green signal flare soared into the air, and was quickly followed by several more. A dozen or so cee-bees were clustered on the outcrop, and more were scrambling up towards them.

Someone shouted: 'They've seen us! Look! They've put up a green.'

The news drew a ragged cheer from those who had found the energy and the will to get up and stay on their feet. But there were many, like Olsen, who had slumped back onto the ground, enfeebled by the drugs pumped into them, disoriented by their surroundings or simply overwhelmed by their predicament.

Zzzhhahhwikkk! Zzzhhahhwokkk!

Olsen, who had slumped down on his knees on reaching his sleeping bag and hadn't moved since, turned in time to see two cee-bees knocked off their feet. Neither had flak-jackets. And as they hit the ground, he saw several inches of metal rod sticking out of their chests.

The air was filled with blood-curdling screams and more flashing darts of silver then a horde of Mutes armed with knives and machetes burst out of the trees behind the guys further up the slope.

Ohhh, shiiiiit! Olsen's fumbling fingers searched for the safety on his carbine. *Full auto! C'mon, c'mon, c'mon!* He started to get up, bring the carbine across his body and into his shoulder. Something struck his chest knocking the breath out of him. A searing pain filled his lungs. The force of the blow pushed his head forward and as he toppled over, he saw the tail end of the crossbow bolt that had gone in at an angle under his rib cage.

Yep . . . looks like this is it, Jake. Almost . . .

Screams and shouts filled the air. People running in all directions. Guy firing. Trying to . . .

Olsen's helmeted head hit the ground. Above him was the huge clouded vault of a late spring sky. A Mute warrior leapt over him. He'd be back later. Or one of his friends would. When they'd killed everybody. That was when they collected the heads. With luck he might be dead when they got around to him. The earth felt as if it was turning under him. His dug his fingers into the soil in a desperate effort to stop himself falling towards the clouds.

If this was the blue-sky world they could . . . keep. . .

Cadillac surveyed the scene as the M'Call Bears began the grisly task of collecting the heads of the dead Trackers. The bodies had been stripped of their uniforms. These, together with their weapons and equipment were now being collected and added to the heap in the centre of the clearing.

The attack had been more successful than he had dared hope. Malone's renegades had diverted the attention of the sand-burrowers but it hadn't really been necessary. Their defences had proved absurdly easy to penetrate. No perimeter guards had been posted and many of the soldiers had only put up a half-hearted resistance.

Three Bears had died but they had been avenged by their clan-brothers. So far more than eighty sand-burrowers had been killed. The others who had fled into the trees below would be dealt with by Malone's men as they made their up in an extended line towards the campsite.

Yes. It had been easy, thought Cadillac. Too easy . . . or was that feeling due to his eternal dissatisfaction? Since meeting Steve Brickman, he had become increasingly suspicious of everyone's motives.

Two Bears, Rain-Dancer and Diamond-Head, lugged a metal box over to where Cadillac was standing and deposited it at his feet.

Rain-Dancer unclipped the hinged lid. 'There are things inside which bear the marks of silent speech. Should we carry them away?'

The outside of the box carried the legend: CAUTION/ EXPLOSIVES 12 x AP108. Cadillac hunkered down to examine the contents -- twelve flat, round metal containers about six inches across and four inches deep. Printed in yellow on the top of each dark grey container were the words: AP108 ANTI-PERSONNEL MINE followed by the instructions for arming the pressure fuse and concealing the device in the ground.

Cadillac unclipped one and looked inside. The mine, with its fusing device protected by a clear plastic cap, nestled snugly in the container. He had never seen such a device before but he had seen the destruction wrought by the explosives supplied to Steve by the Federation for use against the Iron Masters. It would be a good idea to make sure these devices did not fall into the wrong hands.

He snapped the lid shut and handed the container to Rain-Dancer. 'You have done well. Put this in your carrying-pouch'. He handed another to Diamond-Head. 'Now, as quickly as you can, find ten of your most trusted clan-brothers and give them one each. They are to place them in their pouches, as you have done, and they are not to speak about them or show them to anyone but me! Do you understand? This is a secret treasure that gives us great power! No one must know we have found it – especially the red-skins!'

Both Bears got the message. 'And the box?' asked Rain-Dancer.

'The sand-burrowers have spades. Bury it. Hurry!'

It was a close run thing. The first renegades – those on foot – came up through the trees as the two warriors appeared above the rocky outcrop and signalled the completion of their task.

Cadillac walked down to meet Malone and the other riders. Several were leading their mounts. All of them had dead Trackers hanging head down over their backs; some carried two or three.

Malone responded to Cadillac's greeting with a cursory nod and took in the scene. 'How'd it go?'

'Much better than I expected. You could almost call it a pushover.'

'Yeah, well, the discipline in these signal units ain't what it used to be. A lot of these overground boys are smoked out of their skulls.' Malone gave a dry laugh. 'Make the most of it. It's gonna be a hell of a lot tougher'n this gettin' on board Red River.'

'Can't wait,' said Cadillac.

'How many did you nab?'

'Eighty-three . . .'

'Good. With what we've got here, makes ninety-eight. Couple must have got away. Never mind. They ain't goin' very far.' Malone slapped this thigh. 'So what've we got? Uniforms? Helmets? Rifles?'

'Yep. And smoke grenades, flares, radios, maps, rations . . .'

'Anything interesting?'

'A lot of camping equipment. I imagine you could make good use of that.'

'No, plastic?'

'Plastic what?'

'Plastic explosive. Detonators.'

Cadillac shook his head. 'You'd better take a look around yourselves. None of my people would know what that looks like.'

Malone turned to his lieutenants. 'Check it out . . .'

While they searched the campsite and the heaps of looted equipment, Malone and Cadillac got one of the M'Call warriors to don a set of camouflaged fatigues, then added a flak-jacket and all the equipment. The warrior complained about the boots, and the lumps on his forehead made the helmet a tight fit but with the visor lowered, and his carbine plugged in to the helmet umbilical, he looked just like the real thing.

Malone ordered him to walk up and down, and as soon as he started to move, it was clear they had a problem. The warrior was not carrying the carbine properly, and he didn't move like a sand-burrower.

'These guys are gonna need some knocking into shape,' grunted Malone. 'This one's walking like a ruptured shitehawk.'

'Don't worry, We'll iron that out . . .'

Malone's men came back to report that no explosives had been found.

'Shame. Might have come in useful.' He shrugged off the news. 'Never mind. We've still got enough here to equip a small army.' He slapped Cadillac on the back. 'Didn't I tell you that good ole Matt would deliver the goods?!'

'You did,' said Cadillac. *And you have, my friend, you have.* . .

The small packs of plastic explosive that Malone's men had searched for in vain, a rigid wallet containing detonators and miniature timing devices lay safely concealed in his own carrying-pouch.

CHAPTER EIGHT

Five days after the M'Call Bears staggered back from Iron Mountain, dragging their share of the plunder on tracking poles, the sentinels posted to watch the north-eastern approaches to the the settlement, sighted the returning trade delegation. It included a horseman but the group itself was barely half its original size.

Cadillac was one of a large and extremely anxious posse who ran out to meet them and it was clear from the muted response of the returnees to their shouted greetings that something dreadful had happened.

As the two groups met and merged, Cadillac exchanged a perfunctory greeting with Steve then searched in vain for the familiar, much-loved face. Filled with a sudden dread, he pushed his way through the milling throng and seized Awesome-Wells by the shoulders. 'Where is the Old One?!'

His cry caused everyone to fall silent.

The elder exchanged a glance with Boston-Bruin, hesitated for a moment then said: 'He has passed over.'

Cadillac looked stunned. 'Dead?!'

The rest of the welcoming posse wailed and beat their heads and chests. 'Oyy-yehhh . . .!'

Cadillac shook his head incredulously and turned to Steve as he appeared at his shoulder. 'How did—? When—? W-Where is he?'

Steve grimaced awkwardly but didn't reply. The two elders and those around them averted their eyes and stepped back, clearing a path to the covered palanquin on which Mr Snow's inert body lay with the head exposed beneath a layer of skins.

The shock generated as the unbearable truth sank in made Cadillac go weak at the knees. He gasped as if hit by a series of body-blows. Awesome-Wells and Boston-Bruin both laid a comforting hand on his shoulders.

Moving like a sleep-walker, he allowed himself to be led towards the palanquin by the two elders then fell to his knees beside it. Lifting the furs, he took hold of Mr Snow's right hand. It was cold and stiff; the arm, bent across his chest, was locked at the elbow and shoulder.

Death now held him in its unyielding grip.

Cadillac placed a hand tenderly on the disfigured forehead. He had been the cause of many of the worry lines which had accumulated there over the years, but now death had smoothed the wrinkles away. He leant over and kissed the untroubled brow. The lifeless flesh chilled his lips. Faced with this final proof that his beloved teacher had left him forever, Cadillac howled with grief and collapsed over the body. As he tried to draw the old wordsmith into his arms, Boston-Bruin broke his grip pulled him away.

'Let him rest, young one. He died to save the Plainfolk.'

Cadillac sat slumped on his heels for a long moment then drew his hands down his face and got slowly to his feet, eyes brimming with tears. 'Save your story for the camp-fire when we are all gathered together.' His voice was choked with emotion. 'If I share my sorrow with our clanfolk, it will be easier to bear.'

Tom McFadden, Deputy-Director of AMEXICO broke the news to Ben Karlstrom when they met to review the agenda before going into the Daily Plans Conference for departmental heads of the organization.

'Dead?! When did this happen?'

'On the way back from the trading post,' said McFadden. 'We don't have the exact date. Malone called in as soon as he got the word.'

Karlstrom swore under his breath. 'Has he seen the body?'

'He's seen what's left of it, yes. Mutes on their home turf put their dead on beds of woven branches which are then raised up on four long poles. When Brickman took him up to the High Place the birds had already got to work.' McFadden relayed Malone's whittled-down version of the battle at the tradingpost. 'As far as we can ascertain, Mr Snow was killed by his own creation.'

'The tidal wave?'

'No, sorry, I didn't make myself clear. The power he summoned drained the life out of his body. Not surprising really when you consider the forces involved. Cadillac arranged for Malone to question several of the returnees. According to them the tidal wave may have killed around two hundred thousand people . . .'

Karlstrom tipped back in his chair. 'Two hun – ? Wheeee-iiouuuu . . .'

'And wrecked five of the Great lakes class wheel-boats. Lost with all hands . . .'

'Jeezuss! That's going to raise some flak from our friends over the border.' Karlstrom closed his eyes and massaged his nose for a while then sat forward again and turned his attention back to his deputy. 'So how are the M'Calls taking this?'

'The clan is in deep mourning. Everyone's walking around with their face and arms smeared with grey wood-ash. Cadillac has been formally installed as Mr Snow's successor.'

'And Brickman. You say he went to the trading post . . .'

'Arrived after it was all over. He apparently went there to warn Mr Snow that the Yama-Shita might try and get even.'

'In the hope of protecting his investment.' Karlstrom gave a dry laugh. 'Still, one has to give him full marks for trying.'

'It wasn't an entirely wasted journey,' said McFadden. 'He was able to make a first-hand assessment of the situation. He'll give us the full details when he comes in but the She-Kargo, M'Waukee and San'Paul delegations have agreed to set up some kind of loose alliance, and they may be joined by some of the C'Natti clans. It's

201

early days yet but Brickman believes it could form the basis of a mutual defence pact.'

'Leaving the D'Troit isolated . . .' The thought caused Karlstrom to pull out his bottom lip.

'Or as front-runners for the japs. I must say this alliance doesn't sound like good news.'

'No, it doesn't,' agreed Karlstrom. 'But it presents less of a danger now that the Mutes are cut off from their supply of arms. The problem is, the Iron Masters will be back in strength. They're not going to take this defeat lying down – and that could create a somewhat delicate situation.

'If the mutual trade agreement is now a dead letter, they'll have to establish a permanent hold on the Great Lakes and Northern Plains if they want to continue to exploit its resources. And that means occupying territory which they agreed was ours when we signed that secret protocol.'

'Can we stop them?' asked McFadden.

'By having a word on our private line? It's possible – but not before we've delivered the heads of what's left of the Clan M'Call. And then the Clan Kojak. Our friend the Lord High Chamberlain would like me to hand over Brickman as well but I managed to talk him out of that idea. The man upstairs has plans for our young hero.'

'I see. But now that Mr Snow is out of the frame, does the plan to use Red River to take out the M'Calls still stand . . .?'

'Yes. The terrain in Wyoming does not favour the wagon-trains and the dense tree cover prevents us from solving this problem by a sustained programme of air strikes. That's why we have to draw the clan down from the hills and into Nebraska.'

'Okay. But since Cadillac doesn't present the same level of threat as Mr Snow, we won't need to bring Roz Brickman into play. Shall I arrange to have her flown back to the Federation?'

'No, leave her out there. Clearwater too.'

McFadden made a note on his Memo-Typer. 'We've got a slight problem with Malone.'

'Go on . . .'

'When he sold Cadillac on the idea of attacking the train, it was agreed that Mr Snow would be playing a major role. When he and Brickman found out that Mr Snow had left for the trading post, he decided to back-pedal to give Brickman time to bring the old lump in.

'Basically, what Malone said was "Either the summoner's in, or we're out". Mr Snow's death has left him out on a limb. If you want this joint attack on Red River to go ahead, he needs a good reason for the climb-down. Why don't we just use Brickman and Malone to set up Cadillac and take him out with a snatch-squad? We can wrap up this whole thing inside forty-eight hours of getting the green light.'

Karlstrom shook his head. 'It's not just Cadillac I'm after, Tom. It's the M'Calls. Every single man, woman and child. Not just to please our slant-eyed colleagues but for what they did to The Lady and for being the root cause of his latest trouble. It's left the She-Kargo riding high. If we can destroy their paramount clan, it'll be a real body blow. Ordinarily, the Trail-Blazer Division would be handling this. CINC-TRAIN would like nothing better. But because of the Brickmans, the P-G has turned the heat on us.'

'I understand.'

'Good. Keep on it. And don't cut back on any of the defensive measures. I want the reception committee prepared for any eventuality. And send the same message to Malone.'

McFadden eyed Karlstrom shrewdly. 'That would seem to suggest that you don't think Mr Snow is dead.'

'Let's just say I don't trust those fuckers an inch.'

'Does that include Brickman?'

'At the moment, it's not a question of whether *I* trust Brickman, but whether the Mutes do. If you check back through Malone's signals you'll see that Cadillac voiced the suspicion that Brickman may be an undercover agent.' Karlstrom smiled. 'Fortunately, it doesn't seem to have occurred to him that Malone is not the genuine article.'

'But –'

Karlstrom cut him off. 'I know what you're going to say. If Mr Snow left the settlement before Cadillac and Brickman returned there could be no collusion between pupil and master. If his death *has* been faked then Brickman would have to know about it.'

'Unless, of course he really *is* dead.'

'Exactly. I'm confident that Brickman and his kin-sister will come through for us. But with an operation of this importance one can't leave anything to chance. That's why they will both be given ample opportunity to prove their loyalty on the day.'

Karlstrom expected the meeting to end there but his deputy didn't get up. 'You got something else to tell me?'

'Yes.' McFadden bared his teeth the way a chimpanzee does when he's trying to appease an aggressor. 'That was the good news.'

'And the bad . . .?'

'It concerns that decoy SIG-INT unit that was dropped into Wyoming. The one with –'

'Yes, yes, there's no need to explain. I set the goddam thing up. Malone led the M'Calls to them and everything went according to plan. The Mutes killed the defaulters and went away bright-eyed and bushy-tailed with the stuff they needed to attack the wagon-train.' Karlstrom paused and aimed a beady eye at McFadden. 'Or are you now going to tell me they didn't?'

'No, all that's fine, as far as it goes. It's just that –'

'Someone screwed up. Okay, who? Is this an in-house fuckeroo?'

'No. This one's down to some clerk manning a computer in the main supply depot of the Quarter-Master General.'

'That makes a change . . .'

'When the requisition order came through for the uni

204

forms and equipment for the SIG-INT unit, the people at QMGC didn't know it was for a decoy outfit staffed by Code One defaulters. They just punched up the list of hardware carried by a SIG-INT squadron on a field operation and issued everything on the print-out.'

'Didn't our people fix the air bottles and take away most of the ammunition when they set up the camp-site?'

'Oh, yes, they did all that. They laid everything out so as it looked realistic. But it never occurred to them that *all* the items delivered to the site were standard issue and . . . fully operational.'

Karlstrom sank back in his chair and pinched his nose between his right thumb and forefinger. 'Such as . . .?'

'Six packs of plastic explosive, with detonators and timers, and twelve AP108's. Anti-personnel mines with pressure fuses.'

The list lifted Karlstrom's eyebrows. 'What in hell's name does a SIG-INT squadron need stuff like that for?!'

'Well, these units are tasked with setting up radio beacons. They're issued with PX in case they need to blast out the holes for the base of the mast in rocky terrain. Once they get the mast up and braced, they plant the AP mines in a circle around it to dissuade any roving Mutes from trying to pull it down.

'Most of the lump-heads inside the Territories have learned to steer clear of the masts, but for those who haven't all it needs is for one of these goons to put a foot in the wrong place and bang! Up he goes. After that, his friends – if there are any left – tend to keep well away.'

Karlstrom had a feeling he knew the answer but he put the question anyway. 'So what happened to this stuff?'

'It seems to have gone astray. We know it was issued, and received for forward shipment by the Air-Mexico base at Dallas.' McFadden threw up his hands. 'You know what these outfits are like. They're great at covert operations but they tend to lose track of the paperwork.'

'So you can't say with absolute certainty the mines and the PX reached Wyoming.'

'We're ninety-nine percent certain. That's why I checked with Malone before speaking to you. If it *was* there, it had vanished by the time Malone came on the scene. His people made their own trawl of the camp-site but all they came up with were a few more rifles and odd bits of equipment – the sort of stuff the M'Calls had already collected.'

'Did he ask Cadillac about it?'

'In a roundabout way, yes. The Mute told him that all they'd found was on the ground – waiting to be split two ways. When Malone became more specific, the Mute appeared not to know what PX was. He couldn't press the matter too hard because his orders were to keep the Mute sweet until –'

'Sure . . .'

'Still, the thing is, Mutes can't read. So even if the M'Calls *have* squirreled this stuff away they won't know what it is.'

'Cadillac can read,' said Karlstrom. 'He also knows everything that Brickman knows about explosives. It was Cadillac who wired up the bomb that blew a big hole in Hartmann's wagon-train!'

'Christo! Yeah, I forgot about that! The lying piece of lumpshit! What d'you think we ought to do?'

Karlstrom's face darkened. 'You can start by telling Malone to find out what Brickman knows about this. If the answer's nothing, he's to check that campsite out again. Inch by inch. And meanwhile, put a couple of dozen key-pushers on the shuttle to Dallas. They're to make an inventory of every single item on that air base right down to the last blade of rainbow-grass.'

He pointed to the work-station on his desk. 'And I want the results up on this screen by this time tomorrow. Comprendo?'

'Yessir!' McFadden leapt to his feet.

'And find out which of our people processed this requisition. I expect heads to roll, Tom. I won't tolerate this kind of sloppiness at any level of AMEXICO, and I won't accept any excuses.

'SQUARE-DANCE is one operation we *cannot* allow to fail. It's probably the biggest, certainly the most complex task we've undertaken. Years of work, decades of planning, hundreds of lives – including yours and mine – are now in jeopardy and will remain there until we can establish the whereabouts of those explosives.'

'Don't worry. We'll find them.'

'You'd better. Who else knows about this?'

'Nobody apart from my assistant. She was logging the documentation on the SIG-INT set-up into the master file and just by sheer chance happened to read though the equipment list supplied by QMGC as it came up on screen. She thought it seemed a bit overloaded considering the life-expectancy of the unit it had been issued to and brought it to my attention.'

'Bright girl . . .'

'Jo-Anne? Yes, she is.'

'Get her to unpick it. Take those two items off the list, and delete them all the way back to the QMGC supply depot. That means accessing their records too. Those explosives were never issued to AMEXICO. You understand?'

'Yessir.' It wasn't the first time.

'Okay. Anything else?'

'Only what's on the agenda for this morning's meeting.'

'Good . . .' Karlstrom sighed wearily, planted his hands on the desk and levered himself out of his chair. 'Well done, Tom. Thanks for spoiling my day . . .'

Out in Wyoming, Steve decided to make himself useful by taking over the job of training the fifty Mute warriors who had been selected to take part in the initial assault on the wagon-train. Since many of the Bears who hadn't been picked were somewhat envious of those who had, Steve thought it best – in the interest of general harmony – to widen the training to include all those who wanted to take part.

It gave everyone a chance to dress up in the uniforms and deck themselves out with all the bits and bobs – something which appealed to the Mutes' love of dressing-up and putting on an extravagant performance – like they did when singing fire-songs. And it also introduced a measure of competitiveness, since Steve made it clear that only the top fifty recruits would make the final team.

There was no hope of teaching them how to use the electronic head-up displays projected onto the visor, but they had all handled the rifles supplied by the Iron Masters, and they were used to sighting and firing a crossbow from the shoulder. Since most Mutes were uncannily good marksmen, the transition from crossbow to carbine, using the basic optical sight, went relatively smoothly.

Cadillac, who had taken Mr Snow's death very badly, dropped out of circulation after his normal appointment as wordsmith and made it clear, via the warrior who barred the door to his hut, that he didn't feel like talking to anybody – including Steve.

Three days later, he turned up at one of Steve's training sessions shadowed by four warriors: Blue-Thunder, Funky-Deelix, Storm-Trooper and Twilight-Zone. Seeing him watching from the sidelines, Steve told the two Bears he'd appointed as squad leaders to carry on practising fire and movement and went over to greet him.

Steve hailed the Bears then shook Cadillac's hand warmly. 'Welcome back.' He was going to say 'to the human race' but decided it might be taken the wrong way.

'How's it going?'

'How does it look?'

'You'd better ask my clan-brothers, said Cadillac. I've never seen real Trail-Blazers in action. Have you got everything you need?'

'Yes. You guys did a good job. I never thought you'd be able to get hold of this much stuff so quickly. Y'know

208

what? I'm beginning to think we've got a good chance of pulling this off!'

'In that case, you'd better have a word with friend Malone.'

'Has he got cold feet?'

'Well, let's just say I've failed to persuade him that we can still take on Red River without Mr Snow. He says that air rifles aren't enough. We need explosives, mines – that kind of thing.'

'Which we don't have . . .'

'No. He hasn't totally rejected the idea of a joint attack. We have agreed to meet again. But he may be right. Perhaps it's time you and I faced up to the realities of the situation.'

Cadillac watched the uniformed warriors going through their paces for a moment then said: 'Anyway that's one of the things we need to discuss.'

'Sure. Can it wait – or d'you wanna do it now?' Steve saw the expression in Cadillac's eyes and turned to shout though cupped hands at his perspiring trainees. 'Okay! Break it up, you guys! Game's over. I'll catch up with you later!'

Cadillac led Steve out of the settlement. Blue-Thunder and the other three Bears followed. Nobody said anything and Steve felt a slight prickle of apprehension. If Cadillac wanted a quiet chat, what did he need the heavy mob for?

The M'Calls had pitched their huts on the same piece of turf they had occupied in 2989 when Steve had been shot down and made a prisoner. Cadillac led the way to the top of the slope above the settlement and halted on the bluff where Steve had fought a last-minute battle with Motor-Head, Black-Top and Steel-Eye. The three Mutes had caught him trying to escape on the hang-glider he and Cadillac had built. Clearwater had used her powers to help him get away. Had she not done so, he would have been a dead man.

Steve had fled because he had broken his promise to Mr Snow to stay away from Clearwater. In so doing, he

209

had also betrayed Cadillac. And here he was, back on the very spot where he'd stepped off the M'Calls' turf and soared into the air. Was he supposed to read some weighty significance into the choice of venue?

The young wordsmith invited him to sit on a rock. Two of the Bears, Storm-Trooper and Twilight-Zone positioned themselves on either side at the edge of his field of vision; Blue-Thunder and Funky-Deelix planted themselves about three yards in front of him, legs astride, arms folded across their chests.

Deciding there was nothing he could do but wait for the next move, Steve rested his hands on his splayed thighs and tapped out an impatient rhythm as Cadillac paced back and forth across the intervening space. He knew it was all part of the act, but there came a point when he felt they had played around for long enough. 'You got something to say to me? Or have we just come up here to enjoy the view?'

Cadillac stopped in front of Steve. 'It's about the Old One. Apart from the impact his death has had on me personally, it has placed us in a very difficult position.'

'You mean with Malone?'

'No. I'm sure if you put your mind to it, you could persuade him to help us. On the other hand he may be right. Maybe we should forget the whole idea –'

' – of trying to rescue Clearwater?'

'Yes. What do *you* think we should do?'

Steve shrugged. 'Not for me to say. I obviously have a vested interest but this is a matter for the Clan M'Call. You've taken over from Mr Snow. From here on in, you are gonna have to make the decisions.'

'Yes, I know, but . . .' Cadillac paced up and down again, chewing over his words then asked: 'Did you get a chance to talk to the Old One before he . . .?'

'You mean about Clearwater being on the wagon-train? Yes, I told him what happened – and that you'd decided to try and rescue her.'

'Did you tell him you thought it was a crazy idea?'

'No. I just pointed out some of the difficulties.'

'And . . .?'

'He said we should go for it.'

'Yes, but when he said that did he know he was dying . . .?'

'Dying?' Steve grimaced. 'Can't say. It wasn't his last wish if that's what you mean. He just told me The Path was drawn – and gave you his blessing.'

'Even though it means walking into a trap?'

Steve frowned. 'I'm not sure what you're getting at.'

Cadillac eyed him expectantly then said: 'I see. You didn't tell him about Malone's little secret.'

There was only one way to meet this veiled accusation. Head on. Steve glanced at the two warriors standing on either side of him then said: 'Oh . . . you mean about him being an undercover agent? Yeah, I told him.'

'But you didn't tell me.'

'I was going to. I thought I'd give you the chance to work it out for yourself. And you have. Which is great. Saves me a whole lot of trouble.'

Cadillac's temper rose. 'Just what the hell is your game, Brickman?!'

'It's called "survival"! You make up the rules as you go along and any number can play. But before this goes any further, try and grasp one simple fact – you and I are on the same side.'

'Do you seriously expect me to believe that?' Cadillac's anger exploded. 'You set me up! You and Malone were going to lead my clanfolk into a trap!'

'No, no, you've got it all wrong, Caddy. I admit it looks that way but that's not what's meant to happen. This *is* a set-up but the idea is to turn it around! It's Malone's renegades and the crew of Red River who're gonna end up as the fall guys – not us.'

Cadillac looked unconvinced. 'Easy to say that now your lies have been uncovered! Just as you have no proof that you confessed this to the Old One and received his blessing!'

Steve bit back his reply. He had suddenly realized where this discussion was heading. He decided to let it run. If he was right he could get off the hook later. It was time to go on the offensive. 'Listen! I'm not the guilty party – *you* are! None of this would have been necessary if you'd trusted me. But what did you do? You went shooting your mouth off to Malone – about how you thought I was an undercover Fed! You're lucky he's a mex! If he'd been a *real* renegade he'd have put a bullet through me. Where the hell would you have been then?!'

'No worse off than I am now!' cried Cadillac, still stricken by the knowledge that he could never again turn to his teacher and mentor for aid.

'Well you get no sympathy from me! If it hadn't been for your stiff-necked attitude I wouldn't have had to lie to you! But what happened when I suggested trying to rescue Roz and Clearwater from the wagon-train? You dismissed the whole idea, accused me of trying to sell you down the river and we end up drawing a knife on each other! Thanks to your paranoia Clearwater came close to getting killed. I didn't put her on that wagon-train – *you* did!'

'Well, that's your story . . .'

Steve ignored the jibe. 'Then what happens? Malone comes up with the same idea – strokes you up the right way – plays on your distrust of me, and you swallow it hook line and sinker!'

'You tricked me into it!' cried Cadillac. 'You put him up to it! You knew that if you said it couldn't be done, I would want to prove that it could!'

'Yes,' shouted Steve. 'That's because you always want to be Number One! You always want to do it your way, and every five minutes you want someone telling you you're Mister Wonderful! Well, sometimes you are. But most of the time you behave like a complete and utter bonzo!

'That was why I had to play it this way! Because you didn't trust me! Didn't we exchange a blood-oath with Clearwater as our witness?'

'Yes, but –'

'There's no "buts"! Now that Mr Snow has gone to the High Ground, we've got to get her off that train. After what happened at the trading post, this clan and the She-Kargo are going to need her more than ever. That's why we have to free Roz too. Not because she's my kin-sister but because she's a doctor.

'It'll take another three or four months before Clearwater is back on her feet, and during that time she'll need proper medical care. If she doesn't get it, then the whole exercise is pointless.'

'Yes, I can see that. You've reasoned this out very cleverly. But then you've always been good at wriggling out of tight spots. You're a valuable asset, Brickman. That's why your masters are prepared to go to such extraordinary lengths to keep you alive.'

'You're right. They have,' said Steve. 'Because I've managed to fool them into thinking I'm still working for them.'

'Just as you've managed to fool us . . .'

Steve's patience began to wear thin. 'That's a load of shit and you know it! Have you ever asked yourself why I've gone to such *extraordinary lengths* to keep *you* alive? No. And you know why? Cos *you're* the one who can't face up to the truth! I could have dumped you anywhere along the line and you know it!'

'Clearwater wouldn't have let you!'

'At the Heron Pool? She couldn't have stopped me! She was drained of all her power. She could barely walk! And at Long Point, when you were stewed to the gills, I could have pulled you out of that cargo hold and taken off without anyone being the wiser. Or better still, I could have forgotten to lock the hatch and slow-rolled you out once we were airborne –'

'Thanks for letting me know how your mind works. It's been most instructive.'

'You know exactly what I'm trying to say!'

'Yes, sure. And you could have let me drown in the wheel-boat. But you didn't.' Cadillac's voice lost its shrill edge and became a confident cat-like purr. A sign he now had the upper hand. 'Why? Why go to all this trouble?'

Cadillac answered his own question with a mocking laugh. 'It was all part of a plan. After you'd rushed off to the trading post and Malone – rather stupidly – gave himself away – everything fell into place. You'd been sent out to capture all three of us. When Clearwater was wounded and I was lying unconscious, you had a golden opportunity to put both of us on board Red River. But you didn't take it because you wanted to use me to suck Mr Snow into the trap!

'Bringing me back to the settlement made you a hero. The loyal friend of the M'Calls! An honorary Bear who goes to the ends of the earth to rescue his clan-brother! Who would suspect that underneath all that paint and leather was a lying treacherous toad?!'

With Blue-Thunder, and the other three armed Bears watching the whole proceedings closely, it was unwise to make any rash moves. But violence wasn't the answer. The way to destroy Cadillac in front of his peers was to hit him below the belt with some incisive syntax.

'You deserve to get your head broken for that, but I'm not gonna allow myself that pleasure. I made a promise to the Great Sky-Mother that if she spared Clearwater's life, I would never fight with you again.'

'How very noble of you,' said Cadillac. 'Can you swear in the name of Mo-Town that a plan such as I've described never entered your mind?'

'No. It did. That's exactly the line I fed to the people on board Red River.'

Cadillac caught his breath. 'You . . .?!'

'Yeah, I know what I said.' Steve waited while Cadillac cranked up a suitable degree of outrage.

'You – you've actually been *on board* the wagon-train?!'

'Of course! I had to go! I had to see Roz – find out how badly Clearwater had been hurt, and what the chances were of rescuing them both! Isn't that what you would have done?' Steve didn't wait for a reply. 'And the only way I could get *off* the train and back here was by selling them this plan to lure you and Mr Snow into making a sneak attack on Red River to rescue Clearwater.

'In reality, of course, it was to be an ambush. Once the two of you were under lock and key, the idea was to pretend the attack had succeeded so as to bring the rest of the clan into play and . . .' Steve completed the sentence with a shrug. 'I brought Malone in on the plan to keep them happy. By putting him in to work with me they figured there was no chance of, well – anything going wrong.'

'You mean they don't trust you either.'

'The man who runs AMEXICO likes to cover all the angles.'

Cadillac mulled over what he had just heard. 'What made them think they could capture the Old One? Don't they know he is the Storm-Bringer?'

'Of course they do. That's why they want him so badly. But Roz managed to convince them she had the power to neutralize his earth-magic – perhaps only for a short while, but long enough for him to be seized and pumped full of mind-warping drugs.' Steve described the demonstration she had laid on for the task force.

'Was that wise?'

'To let them know what she's capable of? Yes. They had to be convinced they had some way to control Mr Snow. Otherwise they'd never let us on board. Can't you understand? I *had* to set up this ambush plan. It was the only way I could persuade them to let a bunch of Mutes get inside Red River. And they only agreed to it because Malone was going to be holding your hand during the planning stage –'

'And he and his renegades were going to be part of the attack force . . . leading us into the trap.'

'Exactly. Just get this simple fact into your head. No raid, no rescue. D'you want Clearwater back or don't you?'

'Yes, but –'

'Then we have to go ahead with it.'

'I see. Let ourselves be herded into an ambush by Malone's renegades. Many of the She-Kargo clans use a similar technique to catch buffalo. They hem them in and stampede them over a cliff.'

'But we're not gonna be following Malone's plan, we're gonna play it *our* way – and Roz will use her power to help us.'

'You hope . . .'

'I don't hope, Caddy. I *know*. Our minds are linked, remember?'

Cadillac became irritated as he sensed he was losing the initative. 'Yes, yes, I believe you can read each other's thoughts. We wouldn't be here otherwise. The question is – how can anyone else discover what your true motives are?'

Steve's anger burst enough. He leapt to his feet. 'Aww, for chrissakes, Caddy – why d'you keep twisting everything around?! I've given you the whole set-up and been absolutely straight with you. Can't you see that?'

'It doesn't really matter now, does it? The Old One is no longer with us.' Cadillac mastered the grief which surfaced at each mention of his teacher's name. 'True or false, all your scheming and plotting has come to naught.'

'No it hasn't. We still have Roz. If we can get enough of our people aboard Red River, we can still turn this situation around.'

Cadillac looked unconvinced. 'Yes, well, you say that now, but you've concealed the truth for so long – behind so many lies and layers of deceit – I'm not sure your tongue would recognize the taste of it if it ever managed to slip through your lying throat.'

Steve realized that Cadillac was doing his utmost to provoke a violent reaction. *No, my friend, I'm not going to rise to it – because now it's clear what your game is . . .* He tuned back in on what the Mute was saying.

'. . . but even if this latest confession of yours *is* the truth, it comes too late. We can't mount any rescue attempt unless we can discover what they *really* intend

216

to do. Malone is obviously not going to tell me – and given your track record he's not going to tell you either.

'And I doubt that your kin-sister can be of much help to us. They probably distrust her as much as they do you.' Cadillac sighed heavily. 'No. Like so many of your schemes, it's far too complicated. I'm afraid we're going to have to abandon the whole idea.'

'So you're not going to try and rescue Clearwater . . .

'Let me put it this way, Brickman. I am not going to sacrifice this clan in order to further your own, rather dubious ambitions.'

Steve laid on a pitying smile. 'Know what? I've just realized what this is all about. It's got nothing to do with whether I'm telling the truth or not. You're trying to discredit me 'cos you're looking for an out! Now that Mr Snow isn't here to lead the way you don't *want* to take a shot at that wagon-train, do you?

'What are you frightened of – the responsibility? That a lot of your clan-brothers and sisters could die as a result of *your* decisions – leaving *you* holding the can? Or are you just scared to take the job in case they refuse to follow you?'

Steve laughed dismissively. 'Well, I'll tell you something. After watching you trying to wriggle off the hook I wouldn't blame them! This clan *needs* Clearwater to help them get through the bad times that are on the way. I've kept her alive, kept her within reach and set up a deal which gives us a chance to rescue her. What you should be doing is providing some real leadership! Positive thinking – some action, for crissakes! But all we've had from you are negative waves and a lot of cheap shots about my reliability.'

'Yes,' cried Cadillac. 'And considering the circumstances, they're perfectly justified!'

Steve went for the throat. 'More fancy words. But then that's your job isn't it? I may talk a lot, but at least I deliver! You? You're pathetic!'

Cadillac's right hand flashed towards the hilt of his knife. Blue-Thunder and Funky-Deelix seized his arms and locked them to his sides, preventing him from drawing the blade.

Steve raised his hands as Storm-Trooper and Twilight-Zone went to grab him and stepped out of reach. 'Uh-uh! Hold it, guys. I'm not looking for trouble.'

'We know that,' said Funky.

'Good.' Steve avoided eye contact with Cadillac and addressed Blue-Thunder. 'You can check my story with Awesome-Wells and Boston-Bruin. They were with Mr Snow when I told him about Malone and the whole shooting-match. If that doesn't clear the air, you know where to find me.'

Blue-Thunder's eyes were not unfriendly but they carried a clear signal that – for the moment at least – enough had been said.

CHAPTER NINE

Night-Fever ducked in through the door-flap of Steve's hut and knelt before him. The flickering light from the fire-stone raying upwards onto her face made it look like one of the snarling carved and coloured demons that decorated the religious shrines of the Iron Masters.

During his last stay with the M'Calls, the fearsome-looking She-Wolf had developed a soft spot for Steve and, in Clearwater's absence, had appointed herself as his cook, go-fer and bed-warmer. She had, apparently, failed to find a permanent partner during the months he had spent in Ne-Issan, and following his return with Cadillac and her journey with him to the trading post, she had prepared a hut for him with loving care.

Brought up in a society where – apart from the role of guard-mother – men and women enjoyed absolute equality (the Federation, for example, took no account of gender differences in its provision of communal toilets and wash-rooms) Steve was not used to having a female adopt a subservient domestic role.

At first, it had caused him some embarrassment, but the primitive life-style of the Mutes brought with it a host of chores that, given his Tracker upbringing, he would have preferred to do without. In the Federation, where everything was highly organized, heating came through ducts, hot food was constantly available, water was on tap, and the only life-forms moving under the bedclothes had two legs.

Out here, on the overground, the basic necessities had to be thought about *every day*. And that included choosing a spot to make your bowel movements. Apart from the last item, Night-Fever took care of everything. Steve couldn't figure out why, but he admired her dedication and showed his appreciation in every way except in the one area that might have left Night-Fever feeling totally fulfilled.

'Cadillac asks if you will speak with him.'

'Is he alone?'

'Yes.'

'Tell him I'll be right out.'

Having heard about their last angry exchange at which knives were almost drawn, Night-Fever planted herself outside the door-flap. Anyone exiting from the low huts had to bend double, or drop to their hands and knees – making it difficult for that brief moment to defend themselves from an angry caller. Such attacks were rare but they were not unknown.

On this occasion, Steve did not require the protection offered by her muscular knife-arm. Cadillac, who was no stranger to Mute body-language – had taken several diplomatic paces backwards and, as Steve emerged, he raised his hands, placing both palms together then opening them towards his rival – the open-handed greeting that was a sign of peace.

Steve stepped towards him and exchanged the ritual grips and hand-slaps used by warriors.

'I may have misjudged you,'said Cadillac, with what appeared to be genuine regret.

Steve responded with an understanding smile. 'I have a feeling both of us said things we didn't mean.'

'Can we talk?'

'Sure. Come on in . . .'

Night-Fever held the door-flap open for them. 'Shall I prepare food?'

Steve questioned Cadillac with his eyes then said: 'No. Go to your sisters by the fire-circle and wait for my call.'

Night-Fever nodded obediently, her face glowing in response to the brief smile he gave her as their eyes met. Amazing, thought Steve – how some people react to even the slightest hint of kindness or affection. If she had a tail, she'd be wagging it – just like Baz. The memory of the wolf cub's sudden end in Malone's hands flashed through Steve's mind, leaving a trail of bitterness in its wake.

Seated on talking mats inside the hut, Steve watched Cadillac stare at the flame in the firestone – and waited. With his eyes still averted, Cadillac said: 'You're right. I *am* scared they won't follow me.'

'You shouldn't be. You heard what Awesome-Wells told the clan gathering. The Old One named you as his successor and called upon them to heed your words. He's a tough act to follow, but we should do as he said and go for it.'

Cadillac faced up to Steve. 'I know! But it's not as simple as that!'

'Who said it was going to be simple!'

'Brickman, just for once, keep quiet and listen to me. And remember I know everything you've ever learnt about wagon-trains. Neither you nor I know what Malone and that bunch of killers on board Red River are cooking up. And from what you've said so far, your kin-sister doesn't have much of a clue either.

'Maybe she can use this new power she has to help us but it's virtually untried. These hallucinations for instance – can she apply them selectively? It's not going to be much use if the good guys and bad guys end up sharing the same nightmare.'

Steve shrugged. 'I don't think even she knows exactly what she's capable of.'

'Which places another question mark over the operation when what we need are answers.' He raised his hands to cut off Steve's reply. 'Okay, okay, maybe she *will* be able to help. What you haven't faced up to is the sheer size of the problem. The actual physical dimensions of the wagon-train itself, the number of people on board and its weapon-systems – especially its defences.'

'You mean the steam jets . . .'

'And the rest. Malone thought he was talking to an idiot but here's the plan he sold me. A hundred of us – fifty renegades and fifty Mutes, including you,

Mr Snow and myself – dressed up in the Trail-Blazer uniforms we captured, are going to pose as this signals outfit being pursued by a large posse of Mutes –'

'Is Malone going to be handling the radio traffic?'

'Yehh . . . Here's the picture. As the light starts to fade, he puts out a May-Day and we move in towards Red River –'

'Who drops a ramp . . .'

Cadillac's lips tightened. 'Brickman – am I telling you this story, or are you telling me?'

'Sorry, go on . . .'

'The wagon-train lays down covering fire. The pursuing Mutes fall back and fade into the bush. We go up the ramp – and all of us are wearing a coloured armband so we'll know who's who – then, when we get to the top, we split into three groups. One will hold the ramp and the immediate area around it on the lower floor, the other two will go up onto the middle and top floors and start blasting their way through to the front and rear of the train.

'Malone is going to override the ramp controls so that it stays down and deactivate the operating system that feeds steam to the jets under the wagons –'

'And Mr Snow?'

'We'd left that open. I told Malone he would do whatever was appropriate in the circumstances. He obviously wasn't going to produce a storm inside the train –'

'Wouldn't be a bad idea . . .'

'Perhaps not. But since he's dead he can't help us. Are you going to allow me to continue or not?'

'I'm all ears.'

'The immediate objective is to seize two complete wagons – so we can drop a second ramp – and get through the doors into those beyond.

'As soon as this is achieved, a group will go out through the top hatches onto the roof and release green flares – the signal which will bring the rest of the clan out of hiding and onto the train. With the steam jets deactivated, they'll come screaming up the ramps and . . .'

'Goodbye Red River . . .'

'That's what Malone would like us to think,' said Cadillac. 'Spot the deliberate mistake.'

'Mmmm, well, apart from the basic problem of how a force of one hundred men – fifty of whom are operating in a totally alien environment – can overcome a whole battalion –'

'No, that's obvious. That's why we needed the Old One.'

'Now you're interrupting me!' cried Steve.

Cadillac motioned him to continue.

'There are two major flaws in the plan. Malone *can* override the ramp controls and hold it down. That's a standard EOP. So is the steam-jet cut-off. But that's automatic. The jets under the closed wagons can still be used to pipe steam if needed but whenever a ramp goes down the jets under that wagon are deactivated. Otherwise things could get kinda messy.

'There's a cut-off button on a panel at the top of the ramp on each side. Its main function is to reassure the dog-soldiers waiting to go into action. When the ramp-master gets the green, he hits the "STEAM OFF" button and it lights up to confirm that the jets under that wagon are off line.

'That's all fine as far as it goes. But you've got problems on the roof. You can get onto it – provided you can operate the emergency hatches – but your people won't be up there long. The front and rear command cars have dorsal turrets with six-barrelled 20 milimetre Vulcan cannon covering the roof from both ends. You won't be able to knock them out unless you get into both command cars – and we aint gonna do that with a hundred men split three ways. We're already outnumbered ten to one. We don't have enough men to hold all three floors *and* every stairwell. They'll just fall back and come round behind us.'

'Precisely. And the other deliberate mistake?'

Steve laughed. 'What is this – some kind of a test?'

'Just answer the question, Brickman.'

'Even if we got onto the train, took the two wagons and lowered a second ramp *and* had Mr Snow helping us we still couldn't capture Red River.'

'Why?'

'Because both ends of the wagon-train can operate independently! All the wagon-master has to do is to activate the door seals on either side of the wagons we're in, uncouple the front and rear sections of the train and roll 'em away. We'd be left trapped like fish in a barrel!'

'So for us to have even an outside chance, both command cars have to be immobilized first . . .'

'Yeah. But you won't flatten one of those tyres with a cross-bow bolt *or* a rifle bullet.'

'I know that.'

'There's another problem. Even if you immobilised the train, knocked out the dorsal turrets and held the two wagons long enough to get onto the roof and give the green light, how are the rest of the clan going to get aboard? All the side turrets will still be working – and presumably the steam-jets. The M'Calls'll be chopped to pieces on the way in!'

'But it's getting dark.'

'The gunners have infra-red sights! And your people'll be funnelling in towards those two ramps.'

'The guns . . . are they all air-powered weapons?'

'No. The 20 and 40 millimetre Vulcan cannons use what we call caseless ammunition. An explosive charge in a closed breech drives the shell up the barrel. Like a rocket only different.'

'But they're power-operated turrets . . .'

'Yeah, they use electric motors to traverse –'

'And the six-barrels that spin round . . .'

'They're driven by an electric motor.'

'So if there was no electricity they couldn't fire . . .'

'That's right.'

'I see . . . . So if we were to immobilize the command

cars to prevent the train from splitting up and cut the steam lines and the power as we go up the first ramp, we've got a fighting chance.'

'A slim one,'conceded Steve. He laughed. 'I thought you were trying to find reasons for *not* attacking the train.'

Cadillac gestured wearily. 'I knew it couldn't be as simple as Malone made out. I wanted to hear you say it.'

'So it was a test! Goddammit, Caddy! What more do I have to do to prove I'm on your side?!'

'I don't know. Despite everything you've done there's . . . something about you that doesn't hang together.'

'What is it, for crissakes?!'

'Well, I know I'm a wordsmith but it's hard to describe. At times it's almost as if you were two people. One of you seems to be trying to help us and the other one's working for the Federation.'

'*Pretending* to work for the Federation.'

'That's what I call the good side. I think the other side wants to. On the other hand I could be letting personal feelings cloud my judgement.' Cadillac shrugged. 'Time will tell.'

'If we're gonna get our act together it'd better be sooner than later,' snapped Steve. 'Cos I'm getting mightily pissed off with all this character analysis shit! If you don't want to attack Red River tell me now and we can cut out all this frigging around! Malone can tell Mother we couldn't swing it. I'll do what I suggested earlier – go back into the Federation with Clearwater and Roz and try and get them out some other way.'

'I'm not saying I don't want to attack Red River –'

'Then what the fuck *are* you saying?!'

Cadillac became equally irritated. 'Don't get snotty with me, Brickman! You're on *my* turf! One word from me and you'll be pitched out – not on your ear, but minus both of them and with your balls stuffed in that big mouth of yours! Getting Clearwater off that wagon-train would be a high-risk operation even if the Old One was here to help us. Without him it's more like a suicide mission!

'Before I ask my people to make that kind of sacrifice – and there's no guarantee they'll follow me – I have to know what we're up against. You've confirmed the flaws I spotted in Malone's plan but that whole scheme was only to keep *us* happy – a bunch of stupid lump-heads. That's not good enough. We have to find out what the *real* plan is. Because you and I both know that none of the people letting off green flares on the roof of that wagon-train are gonna be from the Clan M'Call!'

'Sure. Even I'd figured that out.'

'The six weeks you asked for expired two weeks ago. So the reception committee on board Red River have had time to rehearse their drills.'

'Yeah, but . . .' Steve clawed air to express his frustration. 'That was all put together after I left to rejoin you and Malone. I know the object of the exercise was to capture you and Mr Snow but apart from that I'm as much in the dark as you are.'

'Not quite . . .'

'How do you mean?'

'Your kin-sister is a member of the task force assigned to look after Clearwater. She must know *something*. Don't you think you ought to get in touch?'

'I could try. But I don't think it'll do much good.'

'Why?'

'Because Karlstrom, the man who runs the outfit I work for wasn't born yesterday. Until I deliver you and Mr Snow there'll be a big question mark hanging over me. Although she's better at it than I am, they know Roz and I can communicate with each other. Which means whatever they tell her could be passed on to me. If they have any lingering doubts about my loyalty, they're going to feed her false information – stuff they want *you* to know about.'

Cadillac looked dismayed. 'But if you're to play a

226

part in our capture shouldn't you be told what's going
to happen?!'

'Yeah. They said Malone would clue me in just before
the off.'

'So Malone must know.'

'He may do. When I tried to pump him he said his
orders were to deliver you and Mr Snow and the rest of
the boarding party to the top of the ramp. From then on
the Red River team would take whatever measures were
necessary to contain the attack.'

'But he didn't drop any hints as to what form they
might . . .?'

'Nope . . .'

'And if we forced him to speak?'

'Torture him?' Steve shrugged. 'You could try but I
don't think you'll get much out of him. Agents on a
high-risk station, like Malone, are briefed on a need-to-
know basis. That way, if their cover is blown, they can't
jeopardize the whole operation.'

It was Cadillac's turn to be frustrated. 'Sweet Sky
Mother! There must be *some* way we can discover what
their plans are!'

'I'll see if I can get through to Roz. She may have
found a way to get inside other heads besides my own.
But maybe we ought to start looking at this from another
angle.'

'And what's that?' asked Cadillac suspiciously.

'Well, instead of wondering what the *other* side is going
to do *we* should make the running. Seize the initiative.
Throw *them* off balance.'

'Oh, yes. And how do we do that?'

'We've already started. They were braced to resist the
most powerful summoner of the Plainfolk – and now
Malone will have told them he isn't coming.' Steve spread
his hands. 'With just you left to lead the clan they're
bound to think it'll be a pushover.'

'Thank you. And . . .?'

'Well, this is only a suggestion but we could start by
eliminating Malone and his renegades. When we go up

that ramp we might as well take a hundred men we can trust. What's the point of going in with fifty guys we dare not turn our backs on?'

Cadillac frowned. 'But you said that Malone's participation was vital if this rescue plan was to succeed!'

'It still is – but only until everything is set up. If we can come up with a rescue package that puts us in with a chance, then we should take him out just before we start the run-in towards Red River. That's the best time to make the switch. We'll be on board before they know what's hit 'em.' Steve caught Cadillac's questioning look. 'It's okay. I don't owe Malone any favours.'

'But the other renegades . . .'

'That's the point. They're not real renegades.'

'Are you saying they're *all* undercover agents?'

'No, just some. But what difference does it make? Christopher! We're talking about seventy or eighty defaulters with close to zero life-expectancy. Piddleshit compared with the number of your people who died in order to save the She-Kargo! If you don't kill 'em some other clan or a bunch of Trail-Blazers'll hunt them down. With the trading post closed for good, they have no value!'

'Yes, but . . . they're your own people.'

'If a general thought like that he'd never send his troops into battle. You want Clearwater back, don't you?'

'Yes!'

'Then when the time comes, I'll do whatever has to be done,' said Steve. 'But before any of that can happen, you have to win over the clan – get them solidly behind you.'

'Don't remind me.' Cadillac sighed gloomily. 'If only the Old One hadn't died on the way back from the trading post.'

'Yehh,' said Steve, 'It was rather thoughtless of him.'

'That's not what I meant! If he'd died *here*, he might have been able to tell the clan to accept my leadership and have the same faith in me as they had in him!'

Steve mulled this over then said: 'He still can.'

Cadillac looked puzzled.

'Besides being a seer, you have another gift that some people might also regard as magical. A gift that saved our lives on the wheel-boat.' Steve paused, but the penny failed to drop. 'The gift of mimicry. Let the spirit of Mr Snow speak through you. If you do it right you'll have them eating out of your hand.'

Cadillac throught it through and brightened visibly. 'That's brilliant . . .'

'Yes. It is.' *Go to the top of the class, Brickman . . .*

Cadillac had already been formally installed by the clan elders as wordsmith to the Clan M'Call but the ceremony had been overshadowed by the shock of Mr Snow's death just as he, as the Old One's apprentice, had been overshadowed since childhood by his master's commanding presence. Cadillac sensed the clan felt they had been landed with the monkey instead of the organ-grinder. He had to change that perception of him – and this was probably the only chance he would get.

He looked around at the half circle of expectant faces, lit by the leaping flames of the huge bonfire. A sweet smell of pine resin hung on the night air. Behind him, flurries of orange sparks, like miniature constellations, were swept skywards on the rising air.

Steve, seated near the middle of the third row, listened with bated breath as the young Mute launched into his address. If Caddy didn't pull it off, Steve knew he might as well pack up and go home.

Cadillac was surprised to find that his earlier nervousness had vanished. He paced slowly along the front row, his gaze roving back and forth with the vaguely disapproving air of a visiting general asked to review a battalion that is not quite up to snuff. His only regret was that Clearwater was not here to witness his debut as a star performer.

He returned to the centre and began: 'As I look about me and find that your eyes, like mine, are filled with the same bitter tears, I know that your hearts are gripped by the same sorrow, that our minds are engraved with the image of one man whose name is on all our lips –'

'Oyy-yehhh . . .' moaned the clan.

'Mr Snow! The Storm-Bringer! Summoner and word-smith of the M'Calls, paramount clan of the She-Kargo! Whose mighty powers strengthened the knife-arms of our warriors, whose wise counsel guided our elders during the dark days when the greatness which is our destiny seemed to be slipping from our grasp!'

'Oyy-yehhh . . .'

'His death, his passing from this world, leaves a great emptiness in the landscape of our minds. For he towered above us like a giant tree on the the barren plains of existence. A deep-rooted tree which gave us shelter and from which we drew sustenance. From his lips flowed the fire-songs celebrating the prowess of our warriors old and new, the history of the Plainfolk stretching back to the War of a Thousand Suns, and stories of the Old Time.'

'Oyy-yehhh . . .'

'This was his gift to me! His wondrous tales, his wisdom, his knowledge of this world and the worlds beyond now reside in me! His will now stiffens my resolve! His spirit, freed from the confines of his body, surrounds me! Enters me with each breath! Possesses me!'

So saying, Cadillac turned his face upwards, closed his eyes, flung his arms out sideways and fell to his knees. His head sagged forward onto his chest, his arms dropped to his sides, then after a brief moment in which his audience watched spellbound, he opened his eyes and slowly rose to his feet. And although they were quite dissimilar in life, he somehow managed to assume all the physical characteristics of Mr Snow – chin thrust out aggressively, hands reversed onto hips, legs slightly bowed by age as he paced up and down, the quick, questioning eye movements.

And the voice. The pitch, the intonation . . . both were perfect.

'What a miserable bunch! Sweet Sky Mother! Is this what I've bequeathed my successor?! Does your backbone disappear the moment I step beyond this world? A fine reward for all my labours! Has every word I uttered been a waste of breath? If so dry your tears! It is *I* who should weep for you, who sit there trembling like lost children in a dark forest waiting for the wolves to devour them!

Steve clapped his hands together in admiration. Cadillac might be a prize bonzo but when he tried he could really put it together.

'Are there to be no more fire-songs because I am not there to put your brave deeds into words? Is the courage for which the M'Calls are renowned to wither on the vine because my power has passed over with me? Were you only shadows to whom I gave substance when danger threatened? Are you only as brave as the droppings stuck to the tail of a charging buffalo? Do you sink into a cowardly stupor when the need for heroes has never been greater?!'

'NO!!' chorussed the clan.

'No?' Cadillac tugged at an imaginary beard as he strode back and forth. 'How boldly and easily you reply! Yes – you are brave enough when you are hidden in the shadows, your voices laid one upon the other so that no one know who speaks the truth! Cadillac now wears my mantle! My knowledge of all things has passed to him. You have appointed him to my place yet you refuse to follow him against the iron-snake!'

'He is too young!' cried a voice from the darkness. 'He has no standing!'

Mr Snow's voice boomed from Cadillac's throat. 'No standing?! He inherits *my* standing! For all I was, he now is! Speak, those of you who remember! Did you not heed me when *I* was young?!'

'Yes, but he does not have the power!' protested another unidentified voice.

231

'Clearwater has that power! That is why he seeks to free her from the belly of the snake! Does he not have the gift of seership? Is he not versed in the ways of the sand-burrowers and the dead-faces? Why, he even speaks their fearful tongue! He is as brave as I ever was, and knows more than I ever will!

'Cadillac, Clearwater and the cloud-warrior are among The Chosen! They grace the M'Calls with their presence because we – among all the She-Kargo – have found favour in the eyes of Talisman! Let each man, woman and child pledge themselves anew here and now! Let them come forward one by one and say whether they will stand with Cadillac against the sand-burrowers and be the first to strike a mighty blow on behalf of the Plainfolk!

'Do this not in memory of me but in praise of him! He whom I loved and nurtured as if he had been my own blood-child! Clan-brothers! Clan-sisters! Place your lives in his hands as you placed them in mine and I swear that each one of you shall find me at your side in the hour of need! The power given to me by Talisman shall reach out to you from beyond the veil!'

Cadillac flung both arms into the air in the style of Mr Snow, spun round on his heel and became himself again. 'How say you? Are you ready to stand with me?!' The entire clan leapt to their feet in a tumultuous explosion of joy.

'Heyy-yahh! Heyy-YAHH! HEYY-YAHHH!!'

Some time later, after Cadillac had managed to extricate himself from the clutches of his admiring followers, he came over to Steve's hut and found his arch-rival sitting outside, staring into a small fire.

Through the half-raised door-flap, he glimpsed the top third of Night-Fever. The rest of her naked body was tucked between the sleeping furs. Given the general mood of celebration, she was no doubt hoping that tonight was going to be her lucky night.

Steve raised his eyes. Cadillac's face was still glowing with pleasure.

232

The Mute sat down opposite him, adopting the same cross-legged pose. 'How did I do?'

'Pretty good . . .'

'Is that all you can say?!'

'For crissakes, Caddy! What can I tell you that you haven't been told a million times already?'

'Yes, I know all that. It's just that I respect your opinion. I mean, you're not easily impressed.'

Steve sighed and threw up his hands. 'What can I say? It was fantastic, amazing. The way you transformed yourself . . .'

'Yes, even I thought I did that rather well –'

'And the voice – every nuance, every intonation . . .' Steve kissed the tip of his fingers. *'Muy perfecto!'*

'And totally unrehearsed –'

'Ahh, yes, but based on years of careful observation. And when one adds in what you had to say . . . spellbinding!'

'Ohh, do you really think so?'

I've got to stop, thought Steve, otherwise I will throw up. 'Do I think so?! I know so! I was watching the people around me. They were hanging on every word!'

Cadillac attempted a modest smile but only succeeded in oozing several more pints of self-satisfaction. 'Yes, to judge from what everyone's been saying I think I did manage to get the message across. Thank you.' He saw Steve's surprise. 'It *was* your idea.'

Steve shrugged. 'Ideas aren't hard to come by. Translating them into action – *that's* the difficult bit. And you know what?'

'I'm listening . . .'

'Watching you tonight gave me another idea. You could be Malone.'

Cadillac smiled. 'That's right. I was wondering how long it was going to take you to work that one out.'

Steve inclined his head in mock respect. 'Nice to know you're ahead of me.'

For once . . .

'Yes,' said Cadillac. 'And I've got another suggestion.

Now that you've seen my impersonation of the Old One . . .'

Steve groaned inwardly. *Christo, how much soft soap does this guy need?!*

'. . . why don't you take me to see the real thing?'

The question, coming out of left field, caught Steve totally unprepared. 'Uhh, the what?'

'The real thing,' said Cadillac patiently. 'The Old One. Don't try and fuck me around, Brickman. He's alive and well, isn't he?'

'How d'you work that out?'

'By thinking things through. The shock stopped me from doing so at first. There he was, dead, right in front of my own eyes, but part of my mind couldn't accept it. I had *seen* his dying place in the stones!'

'Yeah. According to you, he was supposed to die *last* year!'

'Have you ever tried reading a stone?' cried Cadillac scornfully. 'If you had the gift you would know that the time at which an event will take place is the hardest thing to decipher.' He paused, then said: 'How did he fake it?'

'You'd better ask him.'

'And the bodies were switched after we placed him on the High Ground. Who was left for the death-birds to feed on?'

'Some old, white-haired guy who died at the trading post. He was wrapped up in the bundle of cloth that was slung over my horse.'

'Yes, I thought it was something like that. Very clever. Do you think Malone fell for it?'

'Sure. He's never seen Mr Snow.'

'No.' Cadillac studied Steve's face then smiled. 'You can't bear me being right, can you? You just hate it when I'm out in front.'

'Not at all,' said Steve. 'It's a lot better that working with a sponge-head who keeps falling nose first into his boiled rice.'

Cadillac ignored the reference to his *sake*-sodden

234

nights in Ne-Issan. 'I haven't just *seen* the Old One's dying place, I've *been* there – twice! The pictures I drew from the stone were so clear! It was only when I ran over everything again in my mind that the truth gradually dawned on me. Yes. It was a cruel trick you played –'

'It wasn't my –'

Cadillac cut back in. 'Don't worry, I'm not accusing you. I understand why it was necessary to deceive me. I had to prove myself. Stand on my own feet. Isn't that what the Old One wanted?'

'Yes,' nodded Steve.

'Then take me to him.'

'I can't. You'll have to ask Awesome-Wells and Boston-Bruin. They're the only ones who know where he is.'

Cadillac scrambled to his feet. 'Good! Let's find them. We have important things to discuss.'

'Whoa! Slow down! They tell him what's been happening. If he wants to see you, he'll let you know.'

'But –'

Steve rose. 'Listen, Caddy. If and when we do see him, don't expect too much. They say he hasn't got long to live.'

'Long enough to take part in one last great battle.'

'The one you saw in the stones?'

Cadillac answered with a reluctant nod.

'Do you know who wins?'

The Mute shook his head, his eyes filled with tears.

How ironic, thought Steve. The one man who could save the day is lying at death's door and his successor has persuaded the clan to follow him in a suicidal attack on the wagon-train to free someone who might die if she was rescued.

When Cadillac had found him staring into the fire, Steve had been trying to piece his life back together. A little while before, Roz had come through on their private line to say that Clearwater was not well enough to be taken off the train.

235

The shattered femur in her right thigh had been carefully reassembled and pinned together but would take six months to mend, held in a hi-tech metal splint. If she did not continue to get the level of medical care available in the Federation, she could be permanently crippled or – if complications set in – might lose the leg and perhaps her life.

All his past efforts, everything he'd been working towards, had gone straight down the fucking tube . . .

CHAPTER TEN

Mr Snow had been hidden in a cave entered by a cleft in a steep jagged rock face buried in the densest part of the surrounding forest. The staggered shape of the opening meant that no light from the fire which illuminated and warmed the inside could be seen by any stray passer-by.

Access was difficult enough even if you knew where it was. The entrance was masked by brushwood piled on the narrow ledge outside, and to reach it you had clamber up a precipitous ninety foot slope.

Even the pines, packed together like giant porcupine quills, were finding it difficult to stay upright. Many of them had lost their footing and keeled over. Others, their stunted branches signalling the losing fight for air space, had died quietly in the arms of their stronger neighbours. But not all of the fallen trees were down and out: here and there, were pines whose horizontal trunks had made an incredible right-angled turn towards the sky.

As soon as the location had been pointed out to him, Cadillac steamed up the slope and disappeared into the cave a good minute of so ahead of the others.

'How d'you manage to get him up here,' asked Steve as he reached the ledge and offered a hand to Awesome-Wells.

'With great difficulty,' gasped the elder.

'He found this cave when he was a boy,' wheezed Boston-Bruin. 'And when he was a young man, he used to bring women here.'

Awesome saw Steve's puzzled reaction. 'For illicit affairs.'

Steve laughed. 'Mr Snow . . .?'

'Never stopped,' said Boston, catching his breath.

'Mack-Truck, Rolling-Stone and us two were always covering up for him.'

Awesome chuckled. 'When you weren't using the place yourself.'

'True. But then "stolen fruit is always the sweetest".' Boston heaved a wistful sigh then led the way into the cave.

To reach the cave proper, they had to zigzag between sloping buttresses of rock that in some places reduced the floor space to a V-shaped crevice. A few yards further in, the walls opened out to form a dry, roughly oval chamber with a uneven, split-level floor. The sides came together in an narrow ogee curve to form the ceiling but the rock slabs were mismatched, creating several vents through which an updraft cleared the smoke from the wood fire.

Mr Snow lay on the upper ledge, propped up on a bed of furs; a convenient slope in the far wall on which a bearskin had been laid served as a back support. To his right, Cadillac sat cross-ledgged on a talking mat, holding onto his mentor's hand like a lost child who had just been returned to his parents.

The two M'Call elders stoked up the blaze then positioned themselves by the entrance.

'Greetings, Old One,' said Steve.

Mr Snow indicated the empty mat on the left side of his bed. The movement of his arm underlined his weakened physical condition. His voice was stronger than before but speaking still required a visible effort. 'Sit here. That way I can box both your ears if you don't behave yourselves.'

Cadillac looked embarrassed. 'It was all a misunderstanding, Old One.'

'So you keep saying. Both of you still have a lot to learn. You're too headstrong, too impatient, too self-centred, too *young*! Hmmpff! You should be working together – striving for harmony, instead of constantly flying at each other's throats!'

Steve smiled. 'News travels fast . . .'

'Bad news always does,' grumped Mr Snow.

'I think Cadillac and I have both realized the error of our ways,' said Steve, generously taking a share of the blame despite believing he was the innocent party.

'Yes, well, they say miracles can happen. Let's hope at least that when you leave here you will look at each other in a different light and both be a little wiser.' Mr Snow closed his eyes and breathed deeply. He appeared to be trying to summon up the energy to continue.

'Are you able to stand, Old One?' asked Cadillac.

'I can, yes, but I'm saving my strength for the big day. Now, let's get down to business!'

Cadillac brightened. 'Are we to attack the iron-snake?'

'That's one of the things we have to talk about, yes.'

'In that case you can save your breath,' said Steve. 'Roz, my kin-sister made contact yesterday.' He looked across at Cadillac. 'Just before you came to see me. We can't rescue Clearwater. She isn't fit enough. She's gonna have to stay on the train and . . .' He couldn't bear to complete the sentence.

Cadillac did it for him: '. . . be taken back to the Federation?'

Steve nodded.

The young Mute gazed at Steve with open-mouthed disbelief then exploded. 'But this is outrageous! After all the talk, all the planning, all the arguments! After all the effort I put into rallying the clan behind me last night, are you now telling me it's all been a complete waste of time?!'

'What are you trying to do – make out that it's *my* fault?!' cried Steve.

'Well, you were the one that came up with this stupid idea!'

'I see . . . now that it's fallen through it's suddenly a stupid idea and it's all down to me! Amazing! If we'd been able to pull it off, you'd have been trampling over our backs in the rush to grab all the credit!'

Mr Snow's eyes blazed. He slapped the air in front of him, crossing his right forearm above the left in a scissor-like motion.

As he did so, Steve and Cadillac felt a stinging blow on their cheeks that snapped their heads towards Mr Snow's feet, then as he uncrossed his arms and swept the backs of his hands outwards, both young men were pounded by an invisible hammer-blow to the solar plexus which hurled them backwards against the side walls of the cave.

The impact left them stunned and winded – and not a little fearful. Clearwater had used her power in a similar way to stop their knife-fight. They both got to their knees but stayed where they had fallen, trembling with shock.

'Next time I will not be so gentle with you,' growled Mr Snow. 'A plague on both your houses! I invited you here so that I could talk with The Chosen, not to listen to the yapping of a pair of young jackals! Before you can lead the Plainfolk to greatness you must conduct yourself in a manner befitting the honour Talisman has bestowed upon you!

'What is past is past! All that matters is what happens from here on in. I don't intend to have my last days on earth ruined by a recital of your petty jealousies, so pull yourselves together!'

Mr Snow pointed to the talking mats. Steve and Cadillac moved obediently back to their places on all fours like young lions responding to the crack of their trainer's whip.

'Let us set aside the question of Clearwater and your kin-sister for the moment and concentrate on the wagon-train. Do you have a plan which will enable us to seize and hold it for several hours?'

'We're still working on that,' replied Steve. 'But I'm beginning to see a way through. A lot depends on Cadillac being able to persuade the people aboard Red River that he's someone else.'

He let Cadillac explain their basic strategy then said: 'Red River is tough nut to crack. Our only chance is to seize the initiative and throw them off balance. Your reported death is a step in the right direction.'

'If they believe it.'

'What more proof do they need? Roz will have told

240

them that *I* believe you're dead. But even if they don't trust me completely, Malone has seen the body, and will have reported that the clan are in deep mourning.' Steve smiled. 'Your clanfolk are going to be pretty upset when they find out you're still alive.'

'We'll cross that bridge when we come to it. Carry on . . .'

'We've decided to dispense with the services of Malone and his renegades,' announced Cadillac. 'I will then send false messages using his voice.'

'I see, hmmm . . . I've always thought your gift of mimicry might come in useful one day. I hope it works.'

'It already has!' exclaimed Cadillac. 'When we were –'

Steve cut him short. 'He's brilliant, believe me. But let's stick to Malone for the moment. We can talk about your impersonations some other time.'

Cadillac subsided, tight-lipped.

Steve ignored the hurt look. 'We've decided to jettison his whole plan. Originally we thought of eliminating the renegade contingent and putting a hundred Bears on board but that still meant going up that ramp into an ambush situation. The only surprise would have been our unified force instead of one in which half the soldiers were going to turn their guns on the other.'

'We would also have the power of the Old One.'

'True,' admitted Steve. 'But the crew of Red River would still be geared up ready to repel boarders. Your job as "Malone" will be to kid them into thinking that everything is going ahead exactly as planned.' He turned to Mr Snow. 'Except that it won't be. What we have to do is change both the timing and the nature of the attack.'

Mr Snow nodded. 'You mean go in early . . .'

'Yes. And in a different disguise. The ramps still have to come down because that's the only way we can get in from ground level, but apart from that we've got to come up with a whole new angle.' To help Mr Snow understand the difficulties facing them, Steve explained the physical layout of a wagon-train and the variety of defensive

241

systems its commander could bring to bear against an external attack.

'And he's backed by a battalion of Trail-Blazers. One thousand soldiers. Not all of them would be deployed in a ground action but they are all trained for combat. And they'll all be on that train. Once you get on board and cut loose I've no doubt we can hold our own. The thing is, when you start throwing earth magic around –'

'I must take care not to hurt Roz and Clearwater. That point had occurred to me,' said Mr Snow.

'Good. And on top of the basic element of surprise, which your appearance is an important part of, we've got another thing going for us.'

'And what's that?'

'Apart from their re-supply role, wagon-trains were designed for military operations against Mutes. Savages – or so they think – armed with knives, stone hammers and crossbows.'

'And renegades armed with rifles,' said Cadillac.

'Yeah, but apart from Malone's bunch – who were manoeuvred into this situation – no renegade would go up against a wagon-train. That's the point I'm trying to make. The trains aren't designed to resist an attack by *Trackers*! They're vulnerable – as Cadillac proved last year. I haven't got the whole plan worked out yet but I know exactly how we could open up that train. The trouble is, we don't have any explosives . . .'

Cadillac gave Steve and Mr Snow a thoughtful glance then said: 'We've got a box of AP108's, six packs of PX, detonators and timers. Will that help?'

Are you kidding?

Steve masked his delighted surprise behind a non-committal shrug. 'Yeah. It'll do to be going on with.' He grinned. 'Malone was wondering where that stuff had got to. Well done. You're developing into quite a cagey customer yourself.'

Cadillac accepted the compliment with a courteous nod. 'I learned at the feet of a master.'

'I asked you to work together, not form a mutual

admiration society,' snapped Mr Snow. 'Are we in business or aren't we?'

'We've got the means,' said Steve. 'We just have to figure out the ways.'

'Good.'

'Plus the really big question – "Why?"'

'Why what?'

'Why are we attacking Red River? I've already told you Clearwater can't be moved. So what's the point of risking the lives of your clanfolk. They'd be dying for nothing.'

'Not entirely. Even if we spared the part of the iron-snake which holds Clearwater and your kin-sister, we can still destroy the remainder and collect the heads of a thousand sand-burrowers!'

'Heyy-yaahhh . . .' growled the two elders.

Steve had forgotten they were there. He glanced towards the cave's entrance chamber. The two wiry old Mutes clearly found the prospect appealing. 'But at what cost?' he demanded.

Mr Snow hit the roof. 'Cost?! The honour of the M'Calls is not a negotiable commodity that can be measured out like bread-grass seed! Long ago, did I not tell you that the Clan M'Call had the courage to face its own destiny? That time draws near! It is not enough to challenge the iron-snakes. They must be defeated! Utterly destroyed! The Lords of the Dark Cities must be made to understand that they can never enslave the Plainfolk!'

'Heyy-yaahhh!' This time Cadillac joined in as the elders chorused the traditional up-beat response. And to his surprise, Steve found his lips moving silently in unison with theirs.

Mr Snow closed his eyes and sank back exhausted.

Cadillac voiced the concern Steve shared: 'Shall we return tomorrow when you have rested?'

'No . . . no . . . I have something to say to you . . . something that must be said before this battle begins.' Reaching out like a blind man, Mr Snow felt his way onto Steve's forearm then took hold of his hand and did the same with Cadillac. For a dying man his grip was surprisingly strong.

'Listen to me carefully, Brickman. I have known for a long time that Clearwater was to be taken from the land of Plainfolk. That is why you were sent to us. The Sky Voices spoke to me of your coming, and Cadillac saw your return in the stones . . . the blood and tears that would follow.'

'So Motor-Head was right. I *am* the Death-Bringer . . .'

'Yes, but you are not the enemy. It is those who seek to be your masters who are the base servants of Lord Pent-Agon, the Evil Destroyer, Sower of Hatred and Corrupter of Minds. Like us you are a pawn in a game whose scope and complexity we cannot begin to comprehend, a strolling player on a stage so vast there is room for every living creature on the face of the earth and whose back-drop is Mo-Town's cloak of stars – the heavens and the worlds beyond!

'Each of us moves along the path traced out for us. Paths that cross briefly or come together and run as one before separating again. You and I have journied together and now . . . the time of parting is near . . .'

Cadillac's eyes filled with tears.

Mr Snow tightened his grip on his pupil's hand and shook it roughly. 'Don't be such a ninny! There's nothing to be sad about. The fate of the Plainfolk lies in *your* hands! I shall keep an eye on you from up there and if I see you making a bodge of it, I shall return as a precocious little brat and follow you around making helpful suggestions. Does that remind you of anyone you know – hhmmm?'

Cadillac blinked the tears away. 'I stopped doing that years ago.'

'Yes, well, I haven't gone yet, so stop that snuffling and pay attention.' Mr Snow turned his eyes on Steve. 'We have to attack the iron-snake in order to rescue your kin-sister.'

'Roz . . .?'

'You look surprised. Isn't she the reason why you and Cadillac tried to kill one another? Wasn't it because you wanted to free her?'

'Yes . . . but that was before Clearwater was gunned down by the Skyhawk. Roz is now one of the team that is looking after her. If Clearwater has to go back into the Federation –'

'It will be *your* job to look after her. Both of you will face many dangers before you return to the blue-sky world. Your sister has already begun that journey. She too was born in the shadow of Talisman and it is time for her to take her appointed place among her own people.'

It took a moment for the full import of the words to sink in. 'You mean Roz is a . . .?'

'A Mute? Yes. Just like you.'

Steve looked across at Cadillac and saw that he was equally stunned by the news. 'But that's –'

'Impossible? You disappoint me, Brickman. A young man of your intelligence. Did you never ask yourself why you were so attuned to the overground? Had no fear of open spaces? Never became ill? You have carried the answers within you since birth – when your *real* identity was submerged.

'That is the stranger who lurks in the deepest recesses of your mind. Whose whispers have frightened you for so long! Call him! Let him emerge from the darkness into which he was cast by your masters! Face your true self! Let your soul take wing!'

Steve was gripped by a wave of panic as a babble of voices filled his inner ear, swelling and fading, reverberating through his mind. The voices became a torrent of sound. It seemed as if every word he had ever heard or uttered was being replayed simultaneously inside a vast cavern whose walls were lined with towering stacks of tape-decks.

Close to fainting, he clutched at his head, eyes shut tight, mouth open in a soundless scream. There came a moment when the cacophonous barrage reached an unbearable intensity then gradually, the atonal jumble coalesced into a number of recognizable strands which rearranged themselves into a kind of music he had never heard before but which was as much part of him as his pounding heart.

It reminded him of Mute mouth-music, but even that in all its richness was a pale imitation of the master-work which now filled his mind. The voices, touched with an unearthly purity and beauty, swelled, producing a triumphant chorus of sound, a soaring vibrant symphony that lifted his soul upwards and outwards, carrying him on a melodious wave of sound that washed against the stars.

For one exquisite timeless moment he was bathed in the crystal clear harmonies that he knew, with un-erring clarity, were at the heart of all creation. They entered every fibre of his being. He dissolved into the sound, became at one with the universe. And he sensed that Roz was there with him too. Then cruelly, the music began to fade, and with it the sense of over-whelming joy and wonder. Like a drug-addict trying to hang on to a dwindling high, he tried to fix the melodies and the feeling of exaltation in his memory but it slipped away and was replaced by a monotonous thudding beat.

Steve became conscious of his heart pounding against his ribs. He raised his head and opened his eyes to find everyone watching him intently.

Awesome-Wells and Boston-Bruin raised their right hands in a friendly salute.

Steve tried to shake some of the confusion from his mind. He caught Mr Snow's eye. 'I'm sorry. Was I, err . . . away long?'

'That's okay. The Old One smiled benevolently. 'The Federation did a good job on you. Unstitching all that must be a major trip.'

Steve nodded. 'Roz . . . She was there. She knows . . .'

'Of course she does. That's why she's on the wagon-train.'

'But how did *you* –?'

'Don't give me more credit than I deserve, Brickman. I didn't know *how* she would get here. I just knew both of you would be coming. The Plainfolk have been waiting a long time.'

'Who told you – the Sky Voices?'

Mr Snow nodded.

'I think I've heard them too.' Steve looked at them in turn. 'When did you guess?'

'There was no guesswork involved. We'd been watching the skies for some time. Cadillac knew you were on the iron-snake. He saw your presence in a seeing-stone.'

'But not your face,' interjected Cadillac, anxious to get himself back into the conversation. 'It was only when you crashed into the crop-field that I realized *you* were the cloud-warrior sent by Talisman.'

'And I realized you were a Mute from almost the very first moment I set eyes on you,' said Mr Snow. 'And it was equally clear you didn't know.'

'Or didn't want to know,' added Cadillac.

'That's not true,' protested Steve. 'Okay, I tried to suppress the mental link between Roz and myself. When you live inside the Federation, that kind of thing is bad news. But we both knew we were different. And from the moment I took off on my first overground solo I knew I belonged here, in the blue-sky world. I just couldn't figure out why.

'To be able to survive for so long without becoming ground-sick, to be able to adapt so quickly, to find that – with a little practice – I could run with the Bears . . . only a fool would not have asked himself how such things were possible.'

'Only you tried to find some other explanation.' Annoyed that Steve had become the centre of attention, Cadillac had decided to adopt the role of public prosecutor.

'Yes. But not because I would have been ashamed to discover I was a Mute. How could I feel that way when I'd fallen in love with Clearwater?'

247

'That was because you discovered she had the skin of a sand-burrower!' cried Cadillac.

'No! That's not true! Ask Mr Snow! I was smitten from the very first time I saw her. When I was made to bite the arrow! The Old One warned me off.'

'That's right,' sighed Mr Snow. He caught Cadillac's eye. 'And now that we have reached a certain level of enlightenment, let us not cloud our achievement with more of this foolish rivalry.'

Cadillac lowered his head briefly. When he raised it, his nostrils looked distinctly pinched.

Steve ploughed on. 'The reason I tried to find some other explanation was because I was looking for one that made sense! I mean I *know* who my mother was! Annie Brickman. And my father was the father of all my generation – George Washington Jefferson the 31st, President-General of the Amtrak Federation. Are you trying to tell me that they're Mutes too?!'

Mr Snow laid his hand on top of Steve's. 'The answer to that question lies at the heart of your world.'

Steve knew what that meant: the secret lay within the First Family or inside the data banks controlled by COLUMBUS. And like a moth drawn to a flame, Steve knew he could not rest until he had discovered what that secret was.

'You look troubled, Brickman.'

'That's because he can't accept it,' said Cadillac. He wasn't sure he wanted to accept it himself. Above all, he was extremely annoyed that Mr Snow had revealed the truth to both of them at the same time instead of telling him first.

'You're wrong,' said Steve. 'I'm not trying to find a way out. You and Clearwater are living proof that there are Mutes who look exactly like Trackers –'

'Shouldn't that be Trackers who look like Mutes?'

'Listen! Whatever – okay?'

Jeezuss! What a fucking nitpicker!

Steve picked up the thread: 'I don't deny feeling that coming out onto the overground was like coming home.

248

But *feeling* is not enough. Not for me, anyway. I've spent my whole life trying to control my emotions. If you want to get anywhere, you have to study the facts, reason things through.

'Cold logic – that's what counts. Emotions cloud your judgement. You can't ignore them but if you let 'em take over, it's not long before you don't know up from down. I trust you, Old One. If you say Roz and I are Mutes then I accept you sincerely believe we are. But can you prove it?'

'No, I can't, and I don't need to.' He clutched his heart. 'For a Mute, *knowing* – in here – is enough! You don't need to know why! Open up, Brickman! Sweep away all that soul-shrivelling junk that's been pumped into you by the Federation! Something happened to you a little while back, didn't it? Something good.'

'Yes, it –'

Mr Snow cut him off. 'There's no need to tell me about it. I've been there. You touched the stars. That music you heard, those strands of melody are part of the fabric of the universe. *That's* what you have to tune in to! All this so-called scientific knowledge dispensed by that electronic heap of garbage you call COLUMBUS is irrelevant! That's not what this world is about. It's weighing you down, stopping you realizing your full potential!'

'Okay, okay! I'm not running away from any of this. I – I just need time to think it through!'

'Don't!' cried Mr Snow. 'Do you remember long ago when we talked of how one might discover the truth about existence and I likened that search to climbing a mountain? What you experienced out there was that rare and precious moment. You reached the peak. And someone reached down from Heaven and offered you their hand. Don't analyse it. Grab it! Take it on trust – the way the Plainfolk put their trust in the Great Sky Mother. Make what in the Old Time was called an act of Faith.'

'It won't work, Old One. Before I can believe it, I have to know how and why.'

'Spoken like a true sand-burrower,' said Cadillac.

'Yes,' agreed Mr Snow. 'You're a tough nut to crack.'

Steve responded with a rueful grin. 'Don't worry. I'll get it sorted out. In my own way and in my own time. But thanks for telling me. It's gonna make things a lot easier when we hit the train.'

'Exactly. But in making our plans, we must not lose sight of why you must return to the Federation. The task which faces you and Clearwater is to destroy the Dark Cities from within.'

'Wowww . . . just the two of us?'

Mr Snow gripped Steve's hand. 'She has the power, and so do you, Brickman – if only you will let your mind make that leap. But let me continue. To achieve this destruction you must win the absolute trust of those who rule the world beneath the desert. You must be seen to be working hand in glove with this man Malone *against* us. And your kin-sister must also play her part in this deception. If possible, we must try to achieve *our* objectives without the Federation realizing it has been defeated. But whatever happens we must ensure that you and Roz emerge entirely blameless from this encounter.'

Steve digested this mouthful. 'Well, it's a nice idea, but . . . jeez!' He threw up his hands. 'It was difficult enough as it stood. And now you've made it just about impossible!'

'Oh, come, come, don't exaggerate! You're the master of deception, and this young pup is the man of a thousand voices. I'm sure that if you put your heads together you'll be able to come up with something.'

Such is the perverseness of human nature, neither Steve nor Cadillac emerged entirely pleased from the meeting with Mr Snow. The revelation that Steve was of the Plainfolk made Cadillac *more* bitter not less. In their struggle to become top-dog, the knowledge that Steve was a sand-burrower had sustained Cadillac in the dark moments of despair and uncertainty that engulfed him whenever his rival appeared to have gained the upper hand.

Even if Brickman triumphed, even if he had won Clearwater's heart and soul, there was always the comforting thought that Steve would always be inferior because he was a creature of the Dark Cities. But now, even that small consolation was denied him! He had sworn an oath of blood-brotherhood with someone who – on top of every other advantage he possessed – was also a Mute! Life was disgustingly unfair!

For Steve, the cold reality that came in the wake of the brief moment of rapture when the mind-blocks creating by years of conditioning were demolished to reveal his true nature was equally unpalatable. In one sense, the discovery that he was a Mute came as a great relief. It answered so many of the questions that had plagued him since early childhood, and more especially since that magical moment when he had emerged from the subterranean concrete world of the Federation and had caught his first glimpse of the overground.

There was also the added satisfaction of knowing that Cadillac was extremely upset at learning that his 'blood-brother' was a true son of the Plainfolk. But being Steve, he could not accept Mr Snow's advice. He wanted to know *why* he and Roz had been raised as Trackers. For years he had vowed to unravel the secrets of the Federation and now here was another – probably the greatest secret of all!

That was the good part. The bad part was the discovery that his kin-sister was destined to end up as Cadillac's partner and perhaps in his arms. Since the Mute had lost Clearwater, any reasonable person might have concluded it was a fair swap. But Steve was not a reasonable person.

Roz was more than just his kin-sister: their mental rapport made them psychic Siamese twins, and although he had tried to suppress it since meeting Clearwater, there was still a sexual dimension to their relationship although Steve would not have been able to express it in those terms.

Despite the frightening aspects of her newly-released

power, Steve wanted her *and* Clearwater. Not in his bed but under his control. And if that, in the case of Roz, was no longer practical, then he wanted her love and allegiance – if only to deny them to Cadillac. The thought of them together was repugnant and his distress was in direct ratio to the pleasure the news had given his rival.

Both of them had gained and lost in equal measure as a result of their inability to become true brothers under the sun.

In the weeks they had spent together, Clearwater and Roz had not spoken to each other apart from the normal patient–doctor conversations centred around the medical treatment she was receiving while in Roz's care: how well she felt, what hurt and what didn't.

Roz's attitude towards Clearwater had undergone a dramatic transformation but for the sake of appearances, she had to display a certain coldness. If Karlstrom, or one of his minions was watching the tapes, they needed to be reassured that she still regarded Clearwater as an unwelcome rival for Steve's affections.

Their non-verbal conversations, on the other hand, had become a regular feature of their lives. And it was over the mind-bridge that Roz was able to warn Clearwater that their vocal transactions were probably being monitored by a hidden video-camera.

Now, in early June, six weeks after her near-fatal encounter with the Skyhawk, Clearwater was sitting up and taking stock of the sterile, hi-tech environment which served as a prison cell. Mutes did not have jails. Prison was an unknown concept. You were either alive and free to roam the overground, or dead.

The interiors of the huts built by the M'Calls were not as large as the pale-grey sharp-cornered cave in which she had been confined, but there at least she had the constant opportunity of stepping outside. Here, in a space measuring some three paces by four, whose flat roof lay just beyond a man's raised fingertips, the sun

252

did not shine, the rain did not fall and the light that filled it was not The Light of Heaven.

The breeze which moved across her face came from a humming device with whirling arms, but it was not real. This air had not swept down the snowy peak of a pine-covered mountain, or blown across a plain of sweet-smelling buffalo grass and sage. It was heavy with strange unnatural odours fashioned in the Dark Cities.

Clearwater's heart was chilled by the thought of what lay ahead. Ever since that fateful moment when she had stood with Cadillac and Mr Snow on the edge of the bluff and watched the cloud-warrior climb steadily into the dawn sky she had known that one day she would be called upon to make the journey which had now begun.

Roz had assured her that all would be well. The cloud-warrior would return with her – but what would happen when they reached the sand-burrower's lair? Would they be separated or allowed to stay together? Would he become enmeshed in his former mode of existence? And if he did so, would his feelings for her remain the same? Most important of all, when the healing process was completed, would her powers be restored?

Mr Snow had told her she would live to see the sun again but when would that be? She was already suffering severe withdrawal symptoms and the claustrophobia generated by her surroundings had increased as she made the transition from semi-conscious invalid to a wide-awake patient eager to regain her former mobility.

Only two things helped her cope with the feeling of slow suffocation: the caring presence of Roz and the revelation that she and her kin-brother were pure-blooded unmarked Mutes like Cadillac and herself. Knowing they shared a common ancestry removed the last lingering stigma from her relationship with Steve. Their union had not been a betrayal. Cadillac had suffered but everything that had happened had been willed by Talisman. And she was further comforted by the knowledge that her soul-sister's steps were also being directed by the Thrice-Gifted One.

The realization that she too was destined to play a central role in the Talisman Prophecy had burst upon Roz when she had emerged onto the overground to make the night flight to the Red River wagon-train. Like Steve, she had heard voices, but instead of panicking and trying to shut them out, she had listened.

Her guard-mother's confession that Roz and Steve were not her natural children had helped prepare her for the moment when she would discover her true identity. It had come sooner than expected but although the moment of recognition was filled with wonder and a joyous sense of release, in a strange way it had not been a total surprise.

Ever since she had shared the visual images and emotions that caused Steve's mind to reel during his first flight, she had longed to see the overground for herself. Not only to be there *but to be where she belonged*. Her own flight, and that first unforgettable glimpse of the star-filled heavens had merely confirmed what her heart already knew: she was part of the blue-sky world and her soul belonged to the Plainfolk.

Unlike Steve, she did not seek to know the reason why. A sunrise or sunset is not made more beautiful in the eye of the beholder by the knowledge that the light suffusing the terrestrial atmospheric envelope emanates from a G1 type dwarf star, hanging in space some 93,000,000 miles away.

Knowing who she was, the intensity of feeling generated by that knowledge, the sensation of being made whole, of being truly alive was enough. Roz was content to *be*. Raised in the Federation, she found the conditions aboard Red River easier to bear, but like Clearwater, she chafed at her confinement.

The rescue flight to the renegade's abandoned campsite had allowed her an all too brief moment on the ground. Lifting her visor she had felt the wind on her face, had smelt the strange, rich, almost overpowering odours. After Clearwater had been given emergency first-aid and was being carried on a stretcher towards the waiting aircraft, Roz had dropped behind, torn off her gloves and run her bare hands over the earth, stones and grass that lay within reach. She had only been able to snatch two or three minutes at the most before her absence was noticed but it had been long enough to become addicted.

In the last eight weeks, during meal-breaks and off duty periods, she had managed to get up onto the flight-deck for a few minutes every day. As Steve's kin-sister and the guard-daughter of a noted wing-man, Roz was able to claim a legitimate interest in air operations. But it was only an excuse to drink in the beauty and variety of the landscape that lay like some exotic coral reef beneath a vast cloud-flecked ocean of ever-changing hue.

Wallis, the head of the AMEXICO task-force, had allowed her to go up on deck without an escort but Roz knew she had to ration the time spent topside and exhibit a nonchalant attitude towards the overground. No one, especially Karlstrom, must suspect that she had developed a taste for the blue-sky world and she covered her tracks by referring only to the activity she had seen *on* the flight deck as opposed to what lay around it.

In those same eight weeks, the plans for dealing with the boarding party led by Steve and Malone and the subsequent massacre of the Clan M'Call had been progressively refined, and the crew of Red River had rehearsed their battle drills.

Even though she was a member of the task-force, Roz had not been involved in either the planning or the execution. Wallis was in overall charge of her fate but on a day-to-day basis, she worked alongside the medical team and took her orders from the CMO. Her job was to supervise Clearwater's recovery. To become, in fact, her shadow. And now that she was out of intensive care, Roz was sleeping in the same ward so that she could be ready at all times to counter any threat from Clearwater's earth-magic.

There was no danger of that but Roz has not passed this news on to her superiors. Had she done so, she might have found herself declared surplus to requirements and on a plane back to Grand Central. That was the one move that had to be prevented at all costs. Roz has the means to do so, but the power to manipulate the minds of those around her had to be used sparingly and with the utmost discretion in order not to raise doubts about her reliability.

As D-Day approached, she was unexpectedly summoned to a meeting with the wagon-master of Red River, his execs and the non-commissioned officers that headed the various groups within the battalion. Wallis and the others members of the task force were there, along with the Red River Trail Boss Marvin MacEvoy whose combative style of man-management had earned him the nickname of 'Mad Dog'.

The meeting was held in one of the forward mess-decks which had been cleared and rearranged for that purpose. The tables and chairs now faced one of the large training diagrams showing a cut-away side view of a wagon-train. The twenty now serving with the Trail-Blazer Division were all built to the same basic design. An expert eye might detect variations in aerial arrays and other equipment updates but apart from the insignia and code letters the trains were virtually indistinguishable inside and out.

As everyone filed in, Wallis directed Roz to the centre table in the front row then stood alongside the train layout opposite Fargo. When everyone was seated, the wagon-master picked up a long pointing rod, acknowledged their presence with a curt nod and got down to business without further delay.

'Gentlemen . . . the latest signals from sources in the field indicate that the attack which is the centrepiece of Operation Big-Fish will be launched within the next week, perhaps as soon as seventy-two hours from now. We had been expecting two primary targets, but it looks as if the most dangerous of these will not now appear. He has apparently died, but as you know these Mutes are firm believers in reincarnation so we must be prepared for a few last-minute surprises.'

The Red River personnel, recognizing this as one of Fargo's jokes, laughed appreciatively.

Fargo continued: 'Two White House operatives, YANKEE-ZULU and HIGH-SIERRA, will lead a joint force of approximately one hundred Mutes and renegades in the initial assault on the train. This group will be disguised as personnel from the 5th SIG-INT Squadron and will be wearing the standard overground combat fatigues and helmets. They will, in other words, look pretty much like our own dog-soldiers.

'The group will be further identified by a strip of white marker tape on the upper arm, on the chin guard of the helmet and on the back visor stop. The two primary targets – or one as the case may be – will be similarly dressed. To avoid any mistakes in identification, YANKEE-ZULU, HIGH-SIERRA and six members of his team will *not*, repeat not carry white markers on their helmets and will enter the train with their visors raised. The Mutes, obviously, will keep their visors down in order not to give the game away. Any clear-skinned individual you see wearing a white chin or back marker on his helmet is a renegade and is to be shot on sight.' Fargo surveyed his audience. 'Is that understood?'

His audience responded with a murmur of assent.

The wagon-master indicated the two wagons labelled 'A' and 'B' just forward of the flight car then laid the pointer on wagon 'A'. 'In response to the May-Day from HIGH-SIERRA we will lower this ramp to allow the assault group to board the train. The bottom and middle floors of both wagons will be sealed off from the rest of the train.

'The top floor of wagon "A", and in particular the stairwells will be defended – and *held* – by ten squads under the command of Lt. Commander Torrance. A second group, led by Captain Lloyd, will hold the top floor of Wagon "B".

'Now, as you know, the plan is to create a situation which will draw the entire assault group up the ramp and into the train. We don't want any of them falling back and raising the alarm. That is why another wagon-train will soon be delivering eighty Code One defaulters to us. They will arrive kitted out in fatigues bearing the appropriate rank badges and Red River insignia, and we will use these gentlemen – who are, of course, all volunteers –'

This was another of Fargo's funnies, but this time the laughter was genuine.

'– to dress out the bottom and middle floors of wagons "A" and "B". Twelve hours prior to the assault, they will all be given a carefully measured shot of a tranquillizing drug. Don't worry, it has all been tested and timed. The defaulters will be placed in active duty work-stations and provided with the normal range of weapons and side-arms that are kept racked or carried by personnel throughout the train.

'The weapons will carry loaded magazines, but the air bottles will be empty. So our stalwart volunteers are in for two unpleasant surprises. As they start to wake up, they will discover they are being invaded by a bunch of screaming Mutes and lawless renegades and then, as they try to defend themselves, they will discover that their weapons are inoperative.'

This news was met with grim silence. As Code One defaulters, death was inevitable, but everyone in the room was glad not to be in their boots.

Fargo pointed to a plan view of the bottom floor of wagon 'A'. Two compartments on either side of the ramp access had been coloured in red.

'These two special firepoints will each be manned by eight men. They are cargo skips which have been strengthened and fitted with firing ports. The two squads will be sealed inside and will do nothing to impede the initial assault. Their task is to ensure no one goes back down that ramp alive. As you can see from the plan, they are both able to cover the ramp with enfilading fire.

'Okay. The assault is absorbed as follows. HIGH-SIERRA, YANKEE-ZULU, and the two Mutes who are the primary targets will be in the first third of the column as it comes up the ramp. They will direct their lead troops onto the bottom and middle floors, while they themselves – a party of ten made up of HIGH-SIERRA and six fellow operatives plus YANKEE-ZULU and the two targets – will make for the top floor of wagon "A" where Don Wallis and his team will be lying in wait.

'As the group reach the top floor, both targets – or one, as the case may be – will be seized. If there is only one – the wordsmith known as Cadillac – then there should be no problem. But if Mr Snow, the second and much more dangerous target, decides to put in an appearance then you, young lady' – Fargo aimed the pointer at Roz – 'will have to defuse the situation without delay.'

'I'll do my best, sir.'

'Let's hope your best is good enough, because my orders are quite specific. If this individual goes out of control, then my task is to do everything in my power to protect the wagon-train. The squads on those two top decks will be my first line of defence. It will be up to you to get out of the line of fire. You understand what I'm saying? The lives of your colleagues on the task force and those two field-operatives are in your hands.'

'Yessir . . .'

'Good. But let's assume for the moment that the targets are apprehended and deactivated.' Fargo brought the pointer back into action. 'The task force, plus HIGH-SIERRA's group will pass along the top floor of wagon "B", through the Flight Car and into the blood-wagon, where the targets will be given whatever sedation is necessar to ensure they are no danger to the train or its crew.

'The squads on the top floors of wagons "A" and "B" will continue to hold the end stairwells then move down the adjoining stairs in the centre here, where the wagons are coupled together, to clear the middle and bottom floors – working back to back and moving out towards the ends so that no one will get caught in any cross-fire.'

Fargo's pointer returned to the plan view of wagon 'A'.

'The men in these compartments will release red flares and smoke grenades onto the ramp floor to give the impression to anyone watching that a satisfying amount of internal destruction is taking place. The guns in the adjoining wagons will be swung and left pointing downwards or upwards to indicate the position has been overrun, and more smoke will be released through roof hatches.

'While this is happening, seventy line-men, wearing the same white markers and badges as the Mute assault group, will emerge at various points along the roof and dance up and down in the way these apes do, and let off green flares. They will be joined, as soon as possible, by others displaying the severed heads of some of the Code One defaulters.'

Fargo saw his audience's reaction. 'Yes, I know. A rather gruesome touch but we think it will be the clincher. This, of course, is the signal that the main group of the M'Calls have been waiting for. So if everything has gone according to plan, we would rapidly find ourselves axle-deep in Mutes.

'As they close on the train we will bring some, but not all of our guns into action and pipe steam for close-quarter protection. The ramp will be left down, but Lt. Commander Laird has arranged to by-pass the cut-out and has redirected the nozzles around the ramp to give any intruders a warm welcome.

'We will not use all our firepower because our defence must not be too robust. The image we have to present is that of a badly-wounded opponent struggling to stay on his feet. We have to draw the M'Calls' entire force into action and hold them on the killing ground until our back-up moves into position, cutting off all lines of retreat.'

Fargo laid the pointer on Roz's table, parallel to its front edge but his eyes did not meet hers. 'The result is a foregone conclusion, gentlemen, but it should nevertheless prove to be an interesting day. After the main body of Mutes has been dealt with, there will be the usual follow-up attack.'

He fixed his gaze on the two field commanders: Lt. Commander Jim Torrance and Captain Griff Lloyd. 'I'll leave you to organize that, Jim. CINC-TRAIN has asked for a clean sweep. That means every woman and child, regardless of age. And they want the heads.'

Torrance exchanged glances with his deputy then nodded. 'Roger.'

'Okay . . . The Code-Ones should be with us by tomorrow night. Fargo's eyes connected with his Trail Boss. 'Mr MacEvoy, you and I will need to have a word about arrangements for feeding and accommodation.'

'Yessir!'

'Well, thank you, gentlemen. For the moment I guess that's it.'

Everyone leapt out of their chairs, came to attention and saluted. Fargo returned the compliment then made his exit, leaving Bill Gates, the deputy wagon-master in charge.

'All ranks . . . Diss-MISS! You may return to your posts.'

Wallis approached Roz as she mingled with those heading aft. 'If it comes to the crunch, d'you think you can handle it?'

'You mean Mr Snow?' Roz smiled. 'Don't worry. He's not going to be a problem.'

'I see . . . Is this report true then?'

Roz realized that Wallis was on a fishing expedition. 'Of his death? Steve seems to think so.'

'Does that mean you're finding it easier to get through?'

'It's better than it was . . .'

'Good. How does he think it's going?'

'Don, I get pictures, sensations, not written reports.'

'I meant in general.'

'He's very optimistic. He and Malone have –' Roz stopped, then closed her eyes and stroked her temples with her fingertips. 'They're on the move,' she murmured. 'Malone's renegades and the Clan M'Call are heading towards Nebraska!'

Wallis gripped her shoulder. 'Atta-girl! Keep me posted. Boy! Are these lumps in for a surprise. What d'you think of this plan we've worked out with Fargo? Isn't it terrific?'

'Can't fail,' said Roz. Her mind was already grappling with another question: how was she going to communicate the details of Fargo's plan to Steve? He and the M'Calls had to be forewarned of the trap that had been laid for them, but as she had just pointed out to Wallis, the mind-bridge was not built to carry that kind of information you would expect to find in a video-gram.

What came across were sensations linked to visual images, but these were not the highly detailed pictures registered by a video-camera. Most had the character of surreal dreamscapes where the structure and arrangement of the elements was not necessarily logical and not every object was in sharp focus.

When Roz had shared the experience of Steve's first overground flight, she 'saw' what Steve saw, but the images were filtered through his mind, altered by his perception. On a more mundane level, she experienced soaring high above the earth but she was not conscious of being inside the cockpit of a Mark One Skyhawk. Her inner eye did not register the read-out on the altimeter, or the speedo or compass-bearing.

Similarly, when Karlstrom sought her help to discover Steve's whereabouts on his journey to the Heron Pool, she did not know the names of the places he was passing through. She did not, in fact, even look at the map. In the effort to reach Steve's mind, she had gone into a deep trance and it was her fingers, searching blindly across the map that had 'felt' his presence.

The rescue of Steve and Cadillac from the wheel-boat had been mounted with the aid of the same kind of "ball-park" imagery. Roz had been alerted by Steve's mental May-Day – a sensation of deadly, imminent danger. This was linked to the image of a wheel-boat moving towards a setting sun across an inland sea, and to another of Steve and Cadillac trapped in a dark confined space below water level.

Woven around these images had been an urgent appeal

to be rescued and this had been followed by pictures of flying shapes swooping out of the darkness, of fire – a towering wall of flames mirrored on the water and on the periphery of this mental canvas, the image of Clearwater amid a host of armed expectant Mutes.

It was only when Karlstrom had placed a map in front of her that she was able to link what she had seen to a specific area. Pin-point navigation and the nose-mounted radar on the mother-ship had done the rest.

But, as always, the link had been triggered by Steve's emotional state. His mind only seemed to open up when faced with extremes of danger or joy. It needed an emotional high or a stressful situation – such as when he had been wounded – to jolt his brain into action.

From the age of twelve, he had tried to shut her out and, to a large extent, he had succeeded – until he had emerged onto the overground. The emotional impact of that experience had blown away the barriers Steve had placed upon the mind-bridge. But not fully. For most of the time, the communication was one way. He could reach her but she couldn't reach him. The door to her mind was always wide open whereas the door to Steve's was closed or barely ajar. He only opened up when it suited him.

To Roz, it seemed as if she had been appointed to be his protector, and although he was two years older and had always played the part of the dominant elder brother, she sensed that she was, in many ways, stronger and wiser.

Since he left Flight Academy to ship out on The Lady from Louisiana, she had only managed to get through to him twice: once to warn him they were being watched, when he was being shuttled back to Grand Central for questioning after escaping from the M'Calls, and then a year later when he was on his way to Long Point and agonizing over whether to return to the Federation or remain with the Mutes.

She had told him to stay because by that time she had become aware of being transformed, mentally and

263

physically. Just as a magnet attracts a pin, an invisible force was drawing her towards the overground. And whoever was exerting that force had given her the power to manipulate the minds of those around her to enable her to break free of the Federation.

Only it was not as easy as she first thought. In the indelible moment of discovery that she and Steve had shared upon learning they were Mutes, he had warned her against acting too openly. And she understood why. She had to do her utmost to ensure that the attack by the M'Calls upon Red River succeeded without anyone knowing she had intervened.

But that wasn't the end of it. Even if she managed to escape from the wagon-train she would still not be free while Steve remained in the hands of the Federation. Karlstrom, the head of AMEXICO, had pressured him into carrying out the First Family's wishes by threats against her life. The reverse was also true: the Family could bring her to heel by threatening to kill him . . .

A strangled cry and an alarmed whinny from one of the horsess jerked Malone into wakefulness. His first instinct was to reach for the gun under his pillow but before he could move he was seized by several pairs of hands. An instant later, he found himself spread-eagled, pinioned by the wrists and ankles and with a knife at his throat – held by a grinning Mute warrior sitting astride his chest.

Glancing sideways past his five captors, he saw that the camp-site had been overrun by Mutes. The guards must have all been killed without making a sound.

Shit. How come? Mutes didn't operate at night!

By the light of torches now being held aloft, Malone saw the horses being led away. More torches were being lit from the glowing remains of the camp-fire, bathing the ground in their wavering orange glow. A lot of his men were lying on the ground where they had gone to sleep wrapped in their blankets. They'd never had a chance to defend themselves. A Grade A surprise attack. The light from one of the torches washed over someone close by. Phil Robson, one of the six mexicans who acted as his lieutenants. Robson's head was growing out of his blood-drenched chest.

Not good news. Not good at all . . .

Malone studied the Mute sitting on his chest. His ugly mug looked vaguely familiar. Trouble was, all these apes looked alike. The six golden feathers in his pebble-decked leather helmet were easier to recognize. Unbelievable. They'd been jumped by their partners in crime – the M'Calls. The suckers they'd been planning to make mincemeat of.

Malone swore through his teeth. What the hell had gone wrong? He had handled his part of the operation in his usual methodical way, applying his considerable skill and experience to cover every angle. It had looked like a sweet deal. What had happened to sour it? Sensing he might not have long to live, he racked his brains for an answer. Had he made a false move? Underestimated the guile of the opposition? Or had that painted lump-sucker Brickman sold the Federation down the river?

The answer to all three questions was 'Yes', but Malone was left to draw his own conclusions. Nobody bothered to give him a gloating exposition of the master plan and the mistakes he'd made. His captors rolled him onto his face and quickly lashed his wrists together. He expected the same thing to happen to his feet but instead he found himself gagging into his pillow in an effort to stifle the searing pain as the Mute with the knife sliced through the tendons at the back of his knees.

Yep, my friend, it doesn't look as if you'll be travelling far tonight . . .

A hand reached in and pulled the long three-barrelled air pistol from under his pillow then, as his captors hauled him onto his feet he found himself facing Steve Brickman. Malone watched him check the magazine then ease off the safety. His left knee buckled. The Mute on that side jerked him upright.

265

Malone could feel the blood from the knife-cuts running down the backs of his calves. Biting back the pain, he said: 'Seem to be havin' a little leg trouble.'

'Just as well,' said Steve. 'I've seen what those boots of yours can do.' He placed the three-barrelled pistol against the mexican's throat and thumbed the catch onto full auto.

Malone looked at him without the slightest trace of fear. The eyes said it all. 'Hope this is nothin' personal.'

'No,' said Steve. 'This one's for Baz.'

He moved the pistol up under Malone's jaw, forcing his head backwards, and held the trigger down.

CHAPTER ELEVEN

Alerted by the intermittent tone, Commander-General Karlstrom hit the ACCEPT CALL button. The Amtrak logo was replaced by his deputy's face. 'What is it, Tom?'

'I'm afraid the shit has hit the fan, sir. There's more stuff coming in but I thought you ought to know soonest.'

Karlstrom sank back in his chair, put his thumbs under his chin and steepled his fingers against his nose. 'Okay, let's have it . . .'

'Malone came through to Wallis on the open channel with a May-Day. Brickman found the explosive that sonofabitch Cadillac had purloined from the SIG-INT set-up – just as Malone suspected.'

'Go on . . .'

'Brickman loaded it onto one of the horses the M'Calls have got and was on his way over to Malone when he ran into a hunting posse. He managed to give them the slip but they raised the alarm and now the whole fucking clan has come after them with their knives out.'

'Hell's teeth!'

'Yeah, it's bad. Hold on – I just got a second decode up on the screen here.' McFadden moved off-camera briefly then returned. 'Well, it's not a total disaster. According to this, Malone's team and Brickman managed to shoot their way out. For the moment they've got no one on their tail but it may not stay that way. They're going to try to make it to Red River. Malone wants to know if we can provide air cover if they hit trouble.'

'No problem,' said Karlstrom. 'Anything else?'

'Yes. Malone figures if they can make it to the train ahead of the M'Calls, there's a good chance the lumps might come in after them. So we may get a shot at the clan after all.'

'Yes . . . but that won't give us Cadillac.'

'I know. But it may give us the next best thing – his head on a plate.'

I'm surrounded by idiots, thought Karlstrom. 'The idea was to capture him alive, Tom. Never mind. Keep me posted. Put everything up on my screens as it comes in.'

'Yes, sir . . .'

Karlstrom noted the tell-tale moment of hesitation. 'Are you saving the bad news till last?'

'That's for you to decide,' said McFadden. 'It wasn't just the explosives that Brickman discovered. Those crafty heaps of lumpshit were hiding something else.'

It wasn't hard to guess what. Karlstrom died a little inside. 'Mr Snow?'

'Yeah! He's alive!'

'And out of control! Like the rest of this operation!' This time, Karlstrom's anger was for real. 'Why the hell couldn't Brickman keep his sticky little fingers out this?!'

McFadden looked dismayed. 'B-But you . . . asked Malone to find it. And he –'

'And he fucked up, didn't he?! Too fucking zealous by half! We go to all the trouble of unpicking those requisitions and now he goes and fucking well blows everything wide open by blabbing over an open line to Wallis! What is he – out of his fucking mind?!'

McFadden said nothing. Apart from the uncharacteristic stream of expletives, he had rarely seen his director so angry – or react so unreasonably. In the search for the missing explosives Karlstrom had ordered him to leave no stone unturned. And now Malone and Brickman were in deep shit because they'd turned over the wrong one.

He waited.

Finally, when Karlstrom regained his usual icy composure, he said: 'Sanitize those messages from Wallis. And make sure he understands this. He is not to reveal the existence of these explosives to anyone on board that wagon-train or make any further reference to them in any further communication with this department. Code it "EYES ONLY". You got that?'

'I'll attend to it immediately.'

'And, Tom –'

'Yes, sir?'

'Make sure that signal self-destructs.'

'Of course.' His deputy's face was wiped from the screen.

Karlstrom, the head of AMEXICO, was a man used to dealing with complex operations but he could not remember a time when he had so many strikes against him.

The quiet revolution of the wagon-masters and their execs had seriously damaged his organization's credibility in the eyes of the President-General, along with that of the other, visible security organizations like the Provost-Marshals.

After his deputy's latest on-screen appearance, Karlstrom felt like a man hanging over a cliff on the end of a slowly-fraying rope. All it needed was a couple more strands to unwind and . . .

Normally a shrewd, unflappable man, Karlstrom found himself becoming increasingly short-tempered and venomous with his staff, and it was only by a supreme effort of will that he managed to conceal his mental disarray during his daily Oval Office meetings with Jefferson the 31st.

Thanks to Brickman's disastrous but well-meaning intervention, the lives of Malone and his team of mexicans were now in jeopardy. All overground operatives risked death on a daily basis, but Karlstrom was not prepared to stand by and do nothing. The collective expertise, the sheer overground savvy of Malone's team made them invaluable even in a training role. Every effort had to be made to rescue them. And despite his own mixed feelings, Brickman too.

With his distrust of 'earth-magic' and psionics – the Federation equivalent – Karlstrom would have preferred to dump both Steve *and* his kin-sister but Jefferson's interest in this troublesome pair made that impossible. Even though the demise of Malone's renegades had killed the plan to draw the Mutes onto the train, Karlstrom could not afford to abandon the overall objective – the total destruction of the Clan M'Call.

With a horde of Mutes in hot pursuit of Malone and his team-mates, a sky-hook – which would require putting at least two aircraft on the ground plus top cover – was a high-risk operation. Karlstrom was prepared to gamble but he preferred playing with a marked deck. Besides, there was a chance of saving his mexicans *and* saving the day. As McFadden had noted, Malone and Brickman proposed to draw their pursuers forward towards the planned rendezvous with the wagon-train in the hope of provoking the Mutes into making an all-out attack.

If Cadillac and Mr Snow – who had risen like Lazarus from the tomb – were still determined to rescue Clearwater then he, Karlstrom, was ready to oblige by offering them the bait. This time, at least, there would be no danger of a flash-flood. Brickman – via Malone – had reported that since the episode at the trading post, Mr Snow was a mere shadow of his former self. And although reports of his death had proved to be premature, it was because the summoner had exhibited every sign of being a dying man that he, Brickman, had been fooled into believing they were true.

Maybe a last attempt to use his earth-magic against the wagon-train might push the old bastard over the edge. It was a tempting scenario, but 'maybe' wasn't a word that Karlstrom liked. That was why he did not propose to alter any of the precautionary measures he had taken in conjunction with CINC-TRAIN.

The problem now was to get the President-General's approval for the fall-back plan without giving the impression that AMEXICO had lost its grip on the situation . . .

To many of those who were directly involved in fighting off the combined assault force of Mutes and renegades, the news that the turkey-shoot had been rained off was met with thinly disguised relief. Even though the containment plan had been carefully worked out to eliminate any possibility that the train could be overrun, the very idea of allowing *any* Mutes to set foot on Red River had been anathema to all concerned.

But orders were orders. Happily, they had been rescinded. The problem now was to help save the nuts of some guys whose overground operation had gone badly wrong.

What Karlstrom didn't know, as he composed himself in the elevator on the way up to the Oval Office, was that the situation he was currently coming to terms with was entirely fictitious.

Malone, his six lieutenants, and the motley collection of renegades who had been tricked into following them had become an all-day feast for a growing flock of death-birds in Wyoming.

The bulk of the Clan M'Call, in an unprecedented series of night moves had made their way towards 'Big Fork' – the junction of the North and South Platte Rivers, arriving a full two days ahead of the wagon-train. And by an arrangement which would have been utterly unthinkable before the Battle of the Trading Post, the two She-Kargo and three small M'Waukee clans inhabiting the area had trekked westwards to fill the vacuum created by the M'Calls.

The main 'battle-group' at Big Fork was led by Cadillac and Blue-Thunder. Following in its tracks was a much smaller group, consisting of Awesome-Wells, Boston-Bruin, and four Bears selected for their physique and discretion. Apart from Blue-Thunder, they were the only members of the clan who knew that Mr Snow was still alive.

The continued deception was necessary because in spite of the occasional strong rally the old wordsmith's hold on life remained precarious. Having won the clan's confidence, Cadillac did not wish to undermine his position by revealing Mr Snow's presence. If he were to do so, only to have Mr Snow die before the attack, the effects on the clan's morale would be disastrous.

The plan Cadillac and Steve had evolved was a good one. If all went well, they had a better than even chance of gaining control of the wagon-train *without* using earth-magic. If the Old One *was* able to help them with his earth-magic it would be an added bonus, but Cadillac knew they could call upon it once and once only.

He and Mr Snow were both aware that the act of summoning forth any powers greater than those held within the Second Ring would prove fatal. Mr Snow faced the prospect with a cheerful lack of concern. Having passed the baton to his pupil, he appeared not only willing but eager to die. But with only one shot left in his locker he had to conserve his energies until the critical moment.

That was why he had accepted the indignity of allowing himself to be carried into battle, and it was another reason for his secret journey. Apart from babes in arms, and comrades wounded in battle, there were no passengers among the Plainfolk. To be 'legless' meant you had reached the end of the line. The old and the infirm who were unable to walk or run never became a burden to their clanfolk. They swallowed a strong dose of dream-cap laced with a poisonous weed extract, or died from a self-inflicted knife-thrust to the heart.

Cadillac knew that Mr Snow, his beloved teacher, had chosen to make his exit in a different fashion. In his mind's eye, he carried the unforgettable pictures he had drawn from the seeing-stone: the pictures of Mr Snow's dying-place. And he remembered the sorrowful laughter with which his teacher had dismissed the news, preferring to rejoice in the beauty of their surroundings. Cadillac even remembered the exact spot where he had found the stone, on the almost flat expanse of ground south of the point where the two rivers ran side by side before finally merging for the slow journey eastwards across Nebraska to join the Missouri.

The stone lay directly in the path of the iron-snake, a

path traced by those who controlled the destiny of the Plainfolk but which the beast itself had not yet followed; its arrival on the killing-ground still lay in the future.

The terror inspired by the vision of its monstrous shape looming over him still sent shivers down his spine, and in the two years that had elapsed since his first journey to that dreadful place with Mr Snow, the feeling of suffocation upon finding himself under the belly of the wagon-train had often caused him to wake with a pounding heart and a cry of fear on his lips.

But this was not the time for timorous reflection. The die was cast. He and Brickman had evolved an audacious plan which had the blessing of the Old One. A plan in which he, Cadillac, had secured the major role and the lion's share of action. Everything hinged on split-second timing. What he needed to display now was the same boldness and resolution that he had – for far too long – envied in his rival.

Steve and his travelling companions, Night-Fever, Cat-Ballou and the small group of Mutes acting as stand-ins for Malone's team of mexicans were still in Wyoming, following the line of the South Platte River as it made its slow descent eastwards towards the state line and its eventual link-up with its northern counterpart.

Using a captured radio, Steve fed terse but graphic accounts over the voice channel linking him with Wallis, aboard Red River. Those listening were tricked into believing that the fugitives had succeeded in staying ahead of their pursuers with the aid of some of the horses given to the renegades by Cadillac.

Unfortunately, in an effort to lay a false trail, Steve and 'KYLE' – one of the dead mexicans – had become temporarily separated from Malone and the other five but had received confirmation they were in the saddle and 'walking tall'; a slang term meaning their heads were still attached to the rest of their bodies.

Although claiming to be running low on battery power, Steve obligingly kept the transmit button down long enough for Red River to get a fix on his present position. Wallis also confirmed that he had also received a couple of brief signals from Malone. They had been too brief to pin-point but the messages, garbled by static, suggested the two groups were fairly close together and heading in the right direction.

In reality, Cadillac's imitation of Malone had been broadcast from a totally different location. Steve's task was to maintain the fictional existence of the group and give the impression that the entire Clan M'Call was right behind them when, in fact, it was the other way around.

Steve had chosen Night-Fever, Cat-Ballou and the five other Mutes who had escorted him to the trading post because they had all taken turns to ride one of the horses on the way back. All of them – like Steve – were now dressed in the camouflaged fatigues and helmets acquired from the ill-fated SIG-INT decoys, adorned with four white strips of marker tape. They weren't star pupils but they could stay in the saddle and that was all he required to maintain the illusion whenever a patrolling Skyhawk swooped low overhead and waggled its red wingtips in recognition.

The M'Calls spent the day hiding amongst trees in the culverts and gullies on the northern bank of Big Fork then, when the last glimmer of light had faded from the sky, Cadillac led them across the two shallow rivers onto the killing-ground.

The mass of warriors and She-Wolves had already been divided into posses numbering five hands and placed under the command of a group-leader. Followed by these new appointees, Cadillac paced out the approximate area that the wagon-train would occupy. When this had been delineated, it was divided into sections for which the group leaders then became responsible. Before long, the posses were hard at work with primitive stone digging implements and a prized collection of Iron Master picks and shovels.

Leaving Blue-Thunder in charge of the proceedings,

Cadillac mounted his horse and rode westwards along the river to where Mr Snow lay hidden with his escort. 'How goes it, Old One?'

Mr Snow gave a tired smile. 'Well enough . . .' With the moon's sepulchral glow bathing his sunken features and white hair, he looked like a visitor from the spirit world he was soon to inhabit. 'Help me up.'

Cadillac gave him a helping hand. Mr Snow then pushed him away and tottered towards a tree some ten yards away. Cadillac hastened after him but was waved off. Mr Snow circled the tree twice before leaning against it. 'There!' he gasped. 'These idiots keep telling me I'm too weak to stand!'

'Let me help you back.' Cadillac offered his hand as Awesome-Wells approached clucking with disapproval like an agitated hen rounding up a wayward chick.

Mr Snow withdrew his elbows from their grasping hands and waved them both aside. 'Keep away! I now propose to take a dip.'

'At this time of night? Are you crazy?' demanded Awesome. 'What for?!'

'To get rid of the cramps, the pins and needles. I've been lying in that bed too long. I need some exercise!'

'Sure,' said Boston-Bruin. 'But you're not a fish!'

'Look! I know about these things! In the Old Time people swam for pleasure not just to stay afloat. It was medically recognized as an excellent way of exercising every muscle in your body.'

'It also sounds like a good way of tearing them apart,' huffed Awesome. 'Especially someone of your age.'

'On top of which you'll catch your death of cold.'

Mr Snow turned to Cadillac. 'Oh, come now. We both know how I'm going to die and it's not by drowning in this river.' He patted his successor on the arm. 'Make yourself useful. Light me a fire.'

To the rational mind, it seems incredible that Cadillac could possess the ability to draw images of the past and future from a 'seeing-stone', and equally incredible that such objects existed. But to the Plainfolk, who believed that The Path was already drawn, the past and future were merely different stretches of the great River of Time which carried the world towards the Sea of Eternity.

Past and future co-existed – like the beginning and end of all river – real or imaginary

And since in their cosmology, the natural world in its infinite variety was an ageless, sentient being in which nothing – not even the densest rock – was totally inanimate, then it was not difficult for them to accept that the earth and sky contained the knowledge of things past and things to come.

The hills, the rocks, the earth, trees and grass were silent witnesses; nothing escaped the golden glare of the sun or the pale white moon and the countless starry eyes in Mo-Town's cloak. The earth revealed those secrets to those gifted with far-sight, and to those whose inner ear was attuned to the Sky Voices that rode the wind.

The rational mind might find such notions diverting but would brush them aside. And yet, and yet . . . the map reference to which the wagon-train had now been directed – a location which, with its several approaches, had been carefully reconnoitered from the air – was the very same spot where Cadillac had found the seeing-stone with its blood-soaked images. *Two years before CINC-TRAIN chose it as the killing-ground . . .*

In some way which defied rational explanation, the earth had stored the images of the train and the carnage caused by its arrival and through the medium of the stone had passed its secrets backwards in time into Cadillac's mind.

Such was the magic and the power of prophecy.

At first light, the Clan M'Call ceased their earth-works and retired to the hiding places established beneath the trees in the culverts and gullies on the far bank of the Big Fork. Some of the warriors had been allowed to sleep through the night; these were now despatched into the nearby hills in groups of three to keep watch for the wagon-train, and two posses containing the best hunters in the clan were sent northwards in search of the nearest large herd of buffalo.

Cadillac watched anxiously as they ran off to execute their part in the plan. It was a good plan, as he kept assuring himself, but there was no fail-safe factor. It was the kind of plan that depended on the successful execution of each phase. Everything had to work perfectly, there was absolutely no margin for error. And it was absolutely nerve-racking. He looked up and watched the dawn light flood rapidly across the sky, melting the rose-tinted night clouds with its warmth. One more day, another night of preparation and then, perhaps, the fatal dawn. He settled down to wait, and when his turn came, he tried to sleep.

Roz, aboard Red River, was conscious of the gathering storm. The wall-mounted video-screens which relayed announcements and instructions throughout the wagon-train notified the crew that the train was now moving into a battle zone. An attack by a large force of Mutes could be expected at any time. As of 0900 hours, the train would go to a Level One Red Alert – the highest state of combat readiness.

At this level, all gun positions were constantly manned by shifts of gunners during daylight hours, the video-screens linked to the external surveillance cameras were individually monitored, and a three-plane standing air-patrol was put up to circle around the train as it moved forward.

All personnel were required to stay at their assigned work-stations or on immediate call. This meant that Roz could not go up onto the flight-deck even in her off-duty moments. Apart from knowing they were in Nebraska, she had no access to any maps and, as a consequence, had no idea of where the train was. Moreover, since the train was a sealed environment, and no pictures of the overground were screened in the blood-wagon, she had no way of knowing where they were coming from or going to. The vision slits which would have allowed her a glimpse of the surrounding terrain were closed and locked. They could only be opened in certain emergency situations such as a power failure when the external cover plates were automatically released and could be wound back from the inside.

As a doctor attached to the medical team, Roz was expected to take part in the normal preparations that any mobile field hospital makes prior to a major engagement. The crew on board the train were in little danger; the casualties the medical staff had to be prepared to deal with would only occur if line-men were commited to a ground action.

As the CMO explained in the standard briefing she gave on these occasions, the type of injuries they expected to deal with were relatively simple puncture wounds made by knives and crossbow bolts, plus skull and bone fractures caused by stone hammers and flails. That was the plus side of fighting a primitive enemy. The only time surgeons got a chance to deal with explosive wounding was when a line-man was accidentally shot either in a fire-fight or through the faulty handling of weapons or ordnance.

Saving Clearwater had been a real test of their medical skills which, under normal circumstances were confined to industrial type accidents and the run of injuries that occur whenever ham-fisted goons install, move, operate or try to repair heavy, hard-edged pieces of military equipment.

After Roz had given an up-date on Clearwater, the ward-sister reviewed the few cases occupying beds in the sick-bay. Decisions on who could be discharged and transferred to the daily sick-parade were quickly reached. The object was to empty as many beds as possible and to that end, the White House task-force had been prevailed upon to vacate the ward they'd been using as their base. Bunks had been found for them elsewhere, and the black boxes which gave them a secure line of communications with AMEXICO were now installed in a large, walk-in cargo skip on the hangar deck of the rear flight-car.

As the staff meeting broke up, Michelle French, the CMO tapped Roz. 'Your friend Wallis wants to see you . . .'

Jake Nevill vacated his chair inside the eight-by-ten grey-green metal compartment and motioned Roz to take his place. Wallis, seated opposite her, unfolded a map and spread it out between them.

'We need your help,' he explained. 'The Director needs urgent confirmation of your kin-brother's present position. Can you handle that?'

Roz hesitated and issued a silent call for help. 'I can try.'

'Good. Y'see, we still haven't been able to get a proper fix on Malone and –'

'I can't tune in on him. It only works with Steve.'

'I know,' said Wallis soothingly. 'We're assuming from what we've heard that they're pretty close to one another. Just give it your best shot. The Director tells me you're pretty hot stuff. If you manage to pick up your kin-brother maybe Malone will come into the picture.'

Roz nodded and closed her eyes as she mentally debated whether to sink into a deep trance state or fake it. She knew Malone was dead but she had no idea where Steve was *supposed* to be. And contrary to Karlstrom's fears, her psionic powers did not yet include the ability to read people's minds like a video-screen.

This could be a test. Wallis and Karlstrom might already know where Steve was. If they had any suspicions about what he was up to, her failure to find him would make it look as if they were working together to deceive the Federation. She was trapped. She had to make a genuine effort to find him and hope that he had foreseen this possibility.

Steve had. The knowledge that her mental map-reading powers might be put to the test was precisely why Steve had elected to stay behind and broadcast intermittent progress reports on his efforts to evade

279

the M'Calls. Since Long Point, his telepathic powers had increased or – to be more accurate – had regained some of their original sensitivity.

There was no internal bell or buzzer that went off when Roz's mind reached out towards his, but he was aware of her presence. It was like a cool breeze wafting through his brain which, during the moment of connection, seemed to contain the infinity of space and then – although it was all in the mind – a delicious physical sensation as her whole being merged with his.

It came now, as he cantered up a forested slope close to the state line between Wyoming and Nebraska. He welcomed her, and through her reached out towards Clearwater. There were no barriers between them now.

Wallis and Nevill watched with growing mystification as Roz's fingers searched blindly across the plasfilm map then gradually zeroed in on Steve's position. For a while, she sat slumped in the chair, eyes closed, chin on her chest then she raised her head. Nevill glimpsed the upturned whites of her eyes through the partly open lids as her head sagged over towards her left shoulder. Her lips moved wordlessly then in a slurred voice she said: 'Here . . . somewhere here . . .'

Wallis used a black wax marker to draw a circle round Roz's forefinger.

'A hill, with trees . . . animals . . . running. He's . . .'

'Riding a horse?' ventured Wallis.

'Yes, fast. I can feel the wind on my face. He sees . . . Malone. More riders . . .'

'Where?'

'On . . .' Roz made a scooping motion with her right hand. 'A valley. On the other side of a valley . . . horsemen.'

Her eyes fluttered open. Wallis and Nevill saw her look around in an effort to get her bearings. When her eyes met theirs it was if she had never seen them before then a moment later, her senses returned in full measure. 'Did I . . . ?'

Wallis nodded. 'Yeah, it looks very encouraging. You

even picked up Malone. And it wasn't too hard, was it?'

Darryl Oates poked his head round the entrance to the skip. 'We just picked up another sit-rep from Brickman. He has visual contact with Malone plus five. Looks like we lost one. Hope it's no one I know.'

'Did you get a fix?' demanded Wallis.

'Yeah, lemme show you.' Coates advanced towards the map. 'He's just west of navref Lagrange on a bend in the Bear River. Close to the state line.'

'In that circle somewhere?'

Coates checked. 'Yeah, look – right in the middle. There y'are, see? Lagrange. About a hundred sixty, seventy miles from the rendezvous point.'

'Thanks, Dee . . .'

As Coates made his exit, Nevill looked over Wallis's shoulder at the circled location. 'Now that, is fucking ay-mazing . . .'

'Yes . . .' Wallis sneaked a sideways glance at Roz. 'I just hope we didn't imagine this.'

Roz looked puzzled. 'Imagine what?'

'Never mind. Well done.' Wallis edged between Nevill and the table. 'I'll pass this through to Mother.' He gave Roz's shoulder a nervous pat on the way out.

Towards sunset, a runner despatched by the scouts on the high ground to the south-east, returned with news that an iron-snake had been sighted heading in the general direction of Big Fork. As instructed, the scouts were falling back ahead of the train and would send further word of its progress.

Not long afterwards, more encouraging news arrived. The hunting posses had encircled a big herd of buffalo and were shepherding it towards the twin rivers.

As the sky cooled, and the Mute's anticipation grew to fever-pitch, they sighted three high-flying cloud-warriors. Flashing silver-bright like fish in a blue rock-pool as they were touched by the rays of the setting sun, they wheeled tirelessly back and forth across the heavens until the first

281

grey-blue veil that lined Mo-Town's velvet cloak turned their shining bodies into dark bat-like silhouettes with red-eyes that blinked in time to their beating hearts.

Bunched close together like geese on the wing, they flew off on a descending curve towards the south-east then later, when the second, darker veil had been drawn across the sky, the iron-snake appeared in the distance, its head studded with glowing eyes and rows of lights along its flanks like a giant fiery caterpillar.

The feverish anticipation, which had always been grim rather than delirious, became somewhat fearful as the train's massive bulk bearing down upon its wheels caused the ground beneath to tremble. And now, to this mind-numbing vision of their possible nemesis was added the chilling dimension of sound. The drumming roar of its engines and the thunderous rush of exhaust gases exploding through the roof vents of the power cars.

The hungry, belly-rumbling, hunting growl of the iron-snake as it crawled towards its terrified prey.

The M'Calls had heard these sounds before but only in the distance. When they had attacked The Lady from Louisiana, she had been trapped silent and helpless in the flood debris of the Now and Then River. Not so helpless as it turned out but by the time the engines had been revved up for the roll-out the clan had withdrawn to lick its wounds.

The sound that was burned into the memory of the M'Calls was the gut-shrivelling scream that erupted as the iron-snake tore its attackers apart with its fiery white breath. Now, in the fading light of a June evening almost two years to the day since that bloody confrontation, another iron snake was heading towards them, filling the sky with its voice and causing the ground to shake in fear at its coming.

Cadillac, who had only ever seen a real wagon-train at a distance and in pitch darkness stared aghast at its proportions. Even though he had paced its length out on the ground, its sheer bulk was absolutely staggering. It was even bigger than the shadowy monster in the visions drawn from the stone! It dwarfed everything in sight! A few scattered trees which might have been considered to be quite large shrank into insignificance and were brushed aside or flattened and pulped beneath the huge wheels.

How could he and Brickman have been so foolish to think they could storm this armoured giant with the aid of a dying summoner?! They must have been insane!

Cadillac willed his pounding heart to slow down and tried to radiate assurance to the warriors who lay hidden on either side of him. 'Courage! The sand-burrowers hide in the belly of the iron-snake because they fear the Plainfolk! They cannot triumph against the will of Talisman! When the time comes let each one of you display the courage for which the M'Calls are renowned and remember – the spirit of the Old One will guard and guide us!'

Easy to say, thought Cadillac. He at least was one of the select few who knew that Mr Snow was still alive and gearing himself up to deliver one last stupendous burst of earth-magic. The rest of the clan, who did not share that comforting piece of knowledge, were probably wishing the old wizard had passed on the Seven Rings of Power to his apprentice instead of the gift of the gab.

Parting the feathered reeds on the bank in front of him, Cadillac saw the wagon-train roll to a stop with its nose pointing towards the river. It was parked in a straight line, more or less at right-angles to the bank on a north-south axis. The forward command car was about a hundred paces from where he lay. On its flanks, the nearest scrub was some two hundred paces away while behind its tail, the long line of white-trunked larches which formed the ragged edge of a wood was more distant still.

The wagon-train, with its gun-turrets mounted high above the ground had a virtually uninterrupted circular field of fire and the cameras mounted on the roof could see clear across both rivers and westwards towards the rising ground and the hills beyond from where Brickman was due to appear.

283

But before then, there was much to be done. Despite his unshakeable belief in his abilities as a seer, Cadillac was astounded to see that the wagon-train had stopped exactly on the spot he had chosen – right in the middle of a random pattern of shallow trenches of varying lengths, none of them more than two feet deep. The apparent aimlessness with which these trenches had been dug gave no clue as to what they might be for, and their shallowness posed no obstacle to the wheels of the wagon-train – each one of which was twelve feet wide and twelve feet high.

From his hiding place, Cadillac had a good view of the right flank of the train. A ramp had been lowered from the belly of one of the wagons aft of the flight car. He aimed the monocular viewer at the ramp and brought it into sharp focus as a couple of dozen armed Trail-Blazers emerged, their helmet visors lowered, and fanned out to inspect the ground on either side of the wagon-train.

As Cadillac expected, they spent some time studying the large number of shallow trenches and from their gestures appeared to have no idea what they were for. The M'Calls had left other items for them to find: post-holes, the charred remains of cooking fires – the kind built by migrating Mutes – animal bones, some crushed, some raw, the rotting entrails of a buffalo and several bog-holes containing human feces.

Operating the zoom on the viewer, Cadillac framed the top half of the nearest Trail-Blazer. As he turned, Cadillac caught sight of his shoulder badge – a grinning Mute skull speared by a sloping red stake. The insignia of Red River, popularly known as Big Red One. Brickman had told him what to look for. He re-focused on the wagon-train, panned left along its length to the forward command car and found three large white letters emblazoned on the side – RVR, the abbreviated code and call-sign for Red River.

On the sloping nose was a large version of the shoulder-badge. This was it. He counted the wagons . . . sixteen. One of them held Clearwater and Brickman's kin-sister.

If Brickman was right, they would be found in the wagon immediately aft of the flight car and ahead of where the ramp had been lowered.

Cadillac sent out a silent message of encouragement to his one-time soul-mate in the hope that she might pick up his thoughts and gain some comfort from the presence of her clanfolk. He did not expect a response but that did not stop him being disappointed. And once again he regretted she could not be at his side to observe the new Cadillac Mark Two, the brave, resourceful leader of his people.

Just for once, he would have liked to evoke a cry of admiration instead of exasperation – and her magic would have come in handy too . . .

Commander James Fargo and Don Wallis reviewed the findings of the line-men who had inspected the site.

'The general consensus is that the trenches were sleeping holes. If I remember my pre-history correctly, the dog-soldiers in the Old Time used something similar.' Fargo searched for the word. 'Foxholes – only they were deeper than these. But the principle's the same. Digging down gives you a measure of wind-cover and you're able to utilize the earth's internal heat to keep warm.'

The wagon-master who knew nothing about Wallis apart from the fact that he worked in the White House didn't realize that he was speaking to someone who'd got his hands dirty and his ass bitten over several years of overground assignments.

And Wallis was not about to tell him. 'Yeh . . . it's just that a collection like this has never featured in any FINTEL report that *I* ever read.'

'Me neither. But it's definitely an abandoned camp-site.'

'Yeah, absolutely. Question is – should we move 'em off it?'

Fargo grinned. He was a big man but his teeth were small and narrow and there seemed to be too many of them. Wallis didn't like being smiled at by teeth like that.

'I think the train should stay right where it is. You know what these lumps are like. They have what they call 'sacred places' – like for instance where they put their dead. Maybe this site has some kinda special significance.' The wagon-master gave a throaty chuckle. 'If our guys stay sitting right on top of it, there's a chance we might make a whole big bunch of them eye-poppin', foot-stompin' mad. And when they get mad, they keep on comin'.'

Fargo treated Wallis to another of his predatory grins. 'I tell you, good buddy, when you're behind a six-pack, belted up an' ready to let the hammer down, there ain't no better sight in the whole fuggin' blue-sky world!'

'Okay,' said Wallis. 'We'll let it ride. But tell 'em to keep their eyes peeled. If Malone and the others make it through the night, they should arrive just after dawn tomorrow.'

CHAPTER TWELVE

Around 0200 hours, when the attention of the wagon-train's night-watch was at its lowest ebb, the two Duty Vid-Comm Techs manning the screen console in the forward command-car were roused from their torpor by a high-pitched bleeper. Jeff Simons, a Master-Tech, cancelled the alarm then shared the task of checking the battery of screens with his buddy for the night, a Tech-4 called Ben Mason.

The alarm told them that one of the master-scans had been corrupted. Like way-stations, parked wagon-trains used a special computerized scanning system to pick up movement. The landscape around the wagon-train as viewed by the battery of surveillance cameras was captured and analysed by a computer. This image – 'the master-scan' – was then stored in the computer's memory and all subsequent images recorded by each of the cameras were compared with its own individual master second by second. If any of the elements in the picture moved, or a new element was introduced – corrupting the master – the alarm sounded to draw the operator's attention to what might be an incursion by hostiles – Mutes.

In this case, it was only a large, slow-moving herd of buffalo advancing diagonally from NNE, across the twin rivers towards the train. They were still some way off but there was a lot of them, and as they moved into view of some of the other cameras, it set off more bleepers.

Simons told Mason to cancel every alarm right across the board and paged the night-duty exec, Betty-Jo Aarons, the Second Systems Engineering Officer.

Two or three minutes later, Captain Aarons, a crew-cut ash-blonde with good shoulders and a boyish ass, ran up the stairs to the saddle with a towel draped round her head like a prize-fighter on his way to the ring. The front of her OD jump-suit was unzipped to the navel and there was nothing underneath but wet golden skin that was already causing the fatigues to come out in dark blotches. Her bare feet were jammed into a pair of trainers.

'You'd think at two o'clock in the morning a guy could grab a shower! What the fuggizappening? Is that May-Day unit on the line?'

'No, sir, it's buffalo.' Mason tapped the screen.

'You've got to be kidding,' breathed Aarons. She leaned over their shoulders and studied the loosely-packed mass of fuzzy green shapes picked up by the image-intensifiers. 'Doing what?'

'Grazing,' said Simons. 'But they're moving this way. If they stay on their present heading they'll pass right under the train.'

'So . . .?'

'Well, do we want that? Don't you think we should blow 'em off course with a few rounds from a Vulk?'

'Or a whiff of steam?'

Aarons eyed them both then shook her head. 'Piping steam's a job for the EO's. They're not going to be too pleased at being hauled out of bed to burn the butts of a herd of buffalo. And there are no gunners on duty. Everyone's got their heads down. Tomorrow's a big day – or hadn't you heard?'

Mason tried to be helpful. 'We could always switch on the headlight array. That should scare 'em off.'

'It would. But if you remember, the idea is not to advertise our presence any more than we have to.'

'There's nothing to stop you using one of the forward six-packs,' insisted Simons.

'No, there isn't. But I'm not going to. Christo!' Aarons pointed to the screens. 'They're just a bunch of dumb animals! If it was a horde of Mutes –'

Simons nodded. 'Yehh, sure. Just wanted to clear it with you.' He straightened up in his chair. 'Okay, Captain, if you'd just like to card in . . .'

Aarons swore quietly. Fishing out her ID-card, she ran it through the reading slot mounted on the sides of the screens showing the herd of buffalo and pressed the ACCEPT button.

It was a procedure designed to ensure that those meant to see transmitted material – be it words or pictures – left an electronic record of having done so. Its main purpose was to prevent tiresome protestations of ignorance later if the shit should hit the fan.

'And maybe you'd better call up the boys in the rear command car and tell 'em what's coming through . . .'

Aarons did so then gave Simons the beady-eye as she pocketed her ID. 'Since when did you start going by the book?'

Simons shrugged. 'These days a guy has to cover his ass.' He started pressing buttons. 'We'll strike the masters and make new ones after these dumbos have moved on.'

'Good thinking,' said Aarons. She patted their shoulders. 'I'll leave you to it . . .'

'Yessir-ma'am . . .' Mason adopted an alert position and hit a few buttons. Simons, who had his back to her, already had his eyes closed.

There was a brief high-pitched warning tone as Aarons reached the bottom step. To make life easier, Simons and Mason – with the tacit agreement of the other Vid-Comm Techs had concealed small pressure pads on the first three steps leading up to the saddle to alert them to the approach of the Duty Officer.

Anyone who'd done time up the line knew nothing ever happened at night, but some execs tended to be over-zealous – new promos transferred in looking to make their mark, and the perennial brown-nosers ever-eager to work their way up the wire. These dills spent the whole of their watch patrolling up and down the wagon-train checking the alertness of those selected for guard-duty – generally managing to spoil everybody's shut-eye and keeping the grass-heads from tunnelling out in the john.

The unofficial alarm system – switched off during the day – gave the dozing Vid-Comms time to pull themselves into watchful postures, eyes glued to the screens.

Aarons wasn't one of them. And the reason she didn't want to waste time banging away at buffalo was because she'd been working up a head of steam with a hunky jack-dandy under the shower and wanted to get back before he went off the boil.

Aarons was also right about Simons. Like most Vid-Comm Techs, he was not, by nature, an avid follower of regulations, but following the bomb attack on The Lady from Louisiana in 2990, CINC-TRAIN had issued a general divisional unit order about the need to observe proper security procedures. In the last four years Simons had seen plenty of buffalo at close quarters but he'd never known them walk towards a wagon-train and pass right underneath it as if it wasn't there.

That's why he'd alerted Aarons. Pretty soon, they'd be sitting in the middle of a sea of buffalo. Maybe it was because the train was stationary, and the turbo-generators in the power cars weren't roaring their heads off. Or maybe it was parked right across one of the herd's annual migratory paths. Tracks which, according to the archives, had been followed for centuries.

Arrgh, what the hell, thought Simons. Who cared? It was Aarons' responsibility now. She liked dumb animals. Simons could tell from the brightly flushed cheeks and the way the ID-card had trembled in her fingers that she'd been pumping some bone-headed jackeroo when he'd called her out. Everyone knew Betty-Jo Aarons liked it under a hot shower. That's why the guys called her Soapy.

Simons opened one eye and checked the screens linked to the side and ventral cameras. Buffalo everywhere you looked; a slow-moving carpet, grazing briefly then plodding on under the train towards the SSW. He yawned and wriggled down to a more comfortable position in his chair. 'Lemme know if they start eatin' the wheels . . .'

'Yeah, sure,' said Mason. He switched off one of the cameras to clear the screen and put up one of his favourite video-games.

Believing the M'Calls to be several tens of miles to the west of the train, and lulled into a false sense of security by the knowledge that Mutes – like Trackers – did not embark on warlike ventures during the hours of darkness, neither Simons nor Mason, nor the two Duty Vid-Comm Techs in the rear command car noticed the pairs of warriors cloaked in buffalo skins, moving stealthily among the slow-moving herd.

And because the side-mounted cameras were aimed outwards and not down the length of the train, they did not see Cadillac shin up a primitive ladder to reach the umbilicals linking the power cars to the rest of the wagon-train. Not just once, but eight times. And when that task was completed, they did not see him crawl under the curve of the first pair of wheels of each command car and carefully plant something in one of the moulded recesses of the tread at the point where the giant tyres met the earth.

With that crucial task completed, Cadillac made his way back through the herd to the river bank then turned north along the water's edge to where Mr Snow and his escort stood waiting in the darkness with the horses they were to ride.

'Are you ready, Old One?' Cadillac attached the leading rein of the second horse to the one he had chosen to ride.

Mr Snow answered with a reluctant nod. 'Am I going to have to get on that thing?'

'No, that's a spare in case of accidents. You're going to sit on this one with me.'

'I'd rather not . . .'

'It's really quite simple. All you have to do is hang on. I'll take care of everything else.'

Cadillac climbed into the saddle then two of the warriors hoisted Mr Snow up and helped him wriggle into position. Cadillac knew there was no point in asking him if he was comfortable. He leaned down and clasped the hands of Awesome-Wells and Boston-Bruin.

'We will return when the sun has left the eastern door. You know what has to be done. If each of us plays his part to the full, the day is ours! May the Great Sky-Mother watch over you!' He raised his fist in response to their farewell salute then urged the horses into a canter.

The darkness closed around them. The two elders gazed at the point where they had vanished into the night until the sound of hoofbeats faded then turned to face each other.

'Well, my friend, this is it . . .'

'Yes, agreed Boston. 'The big one . . .'

When the herd of buffalo finally cleared the immediate area around the wagon-train, the enveloping blackness had thinned to a leaden grey. Mason, the junior of the two Vid-Comm Techs cleared the fourth of his favourite video-games from the screen and nudged his partner. 'Sy! C'mon! Time to re-set . . .'

Simons struggled to wake up. 'Whaaa–?'

'The buffalo . . . they've gone.'

'Ohh, yeah . . . okay.' Simons stretched and rubbed his face then started pressing buttons with fluid movements of his right hand while he used the left to key himself through to his colleagues in the rear command car. A view of the senior Tech appeared on one of his screens. 'Tony? Lock on a new set of masters.'

'Wilco . . .'

The computer at the heart of the surveillance system duly recorded a new master-scan of the train's surroundings. But the procedure was fatally flawed: the system was not programmed to compare the *new* masters with the ones made the previous evening. The earlier scans had, in fact, been wiped from the computer's memory, and because the Vid-Comm Techs relied on the system, they did not remember in exact detail what they had seen on the screens. So although they could see the ground was now covered with hoofprints and scattered dollops of buffalo shit, nobody noticed that the random pattern of trenches had altered considerably.

A lot of them had been filled in . . .

Hidden from the wagon-train by a fold in the rising ground, Cadillac reined in his horse and used a Tracker torch to flash out a signal. An answering light, high up on the next slope, winked out of the darkness. 'Nearly there, Old One.'

'About time,' grumped Mr Snow.

'Don't get too excited. As soon as we get there, we have to ride all the way back.'

'Brilliant. Whose idea was that?'

'I'm doing my best, Old One.' Cadillac dug his heels into the flanks of his mount and led the trail horse up towards the flashing light.

Steve and Night-Fever stepped into view as they reached the campsite. Above them, the canopy of pines stretched away like a threadbare piece of tent cloth, black against the lightening sky.

While Night-Fever led Mr Snow away to fit him out with a set of camouflaged fatigues, boots and helmet, Steve steered Cadillac through the forest in another direction and wound up in front of a camp-fire. Several Bears dressed in captured uniforms stood around it checking their weapons.

Steve, his face and hands washed clean of dye, was already in uniform and had been for several days. Taking the offered bunch of pink finger leaves, Cadillac washed his own face and neck down to the collarbone and both arms up to the elbow. When Steve had inspected the result by torchlight and declared himself satisfied, Cadillac unrolled the bundle of clothes that had been set aside for him and started to dress.

Steve watched him pull on the red briefs and T-shirt. 'So . . . how'd it go?'

'Brilliantly. The Old One's idea to drive buffalo towards the train worked like a charm. Everybody was able to get into position and there was absolutely no reaction from the train.'

'Doesn't surprise me. When you're on the red-eye shift, that hour between two and three can be a real killer. Did you manage to get the –?'

'The PX? Yes, it's all in place.' Cadillac consulted the wrist watch he had taken from one of the SIG-INT corpses. 'Timed to explode in one hour and forty-five minutes from now.'

Steve slapped his partner's shoulder. 'Terrific. Well done. D'you want any help with that flak-jacket – or d'you know where everything goes?'

Cadillac closed the front zip of his fatigues. 'I think I can handle it.'

'Okay, I'll go and round up our pursuers for a final briefing. Excited?'

Cadillac ignored the cold ball of apprehension that had lain in his stomach ever since he had watched Red River roll to a halt. 'Can't wait . . .'

Ten minutes later, the principal players were assembled round the fire. The initial assault group, consisting of Steve, Cadillac, Mr Snow, Cat-Ballou, Purple-Rain, Diamond-Head and Lethal-Weapon were now all dressed as Tracker soldiers. The only things missing were the breast-tags bearing the names and numbers of the previous owners.

Ranged behind them was the first pursuit group, the remaining hundred or so M'Call Bears and She-Wolves who – as far as the Federation knew – had been doing their utmost to catch the runaways. Their numbers had already dwindled due to attacks by the patrolling Skyhawks whose pilots had been given the task of shepherding Malone's group to the safety of the wagon-train.

The last, smaller group was composed of elders and warriors – representatives from the two She-Kargo and three M'Waukee clan who had moved out of the area around Big Fork and were now posing as the main force of the M'Calls, moving towards the wagon-train in the wake of the first pursuit group.

With Cadillac's assent, Steve explained the set-up and the planned sequence of events then questioned the leaders to make sure everyone knew what their group was supposed to be doing – and when.

Timing, he emphasized was critical. 'I'll just go over the key action again. The horsemen will approach the train in two groups. Cadillac and I will go in first – and we will ride in all the way. The second group of four – Purple-Rain, Diamond-Head, Lethal-Weapon and Cat-Ballou – will come in a little way behind us and will complete the last half of the journey on foot.

'As they come onto the flat ground, the *last three* riders will go down.' He paused and interrogated his audience. 'Where are the bowmen?'

Twelve Bears stood up.

'Good. When you get into position, you will see two marker stakes – just ordinary branches – stuck in the ground between the foot of the slope and the wagon-train. We want you to bring the horses down somewhere between those two markers. Not before and not after. The last three horses. Is that understood?'

It was.

'Take careful aim. It's vitally important you bring down the horse and not the man.'

The bowmen nodded.

'Good. You'd better leave now. I want you in position when we ride through. Aim for the head, neck and rear flanks – and make it look good.'

The twelve bowmen melted away into the shadowy gloom of the forest and made their way towards the crest of the last slope now silhouetted against the grey-blue pre-dawn backdrop of the eastern sky. The representatives of the supporting She-Kargo and M'Wankee clans were the next to leave. And as they went off to rejoin their own people, the pursuit group retired to take up their positions for the ensuing chase.

When only the horsemen remained, Steve sent Night-Fever to fetch their visitor who, up to that moment, none of the others had seen. Cat-Ballou and the other

Bears reacted warily as Night-Fever reappeared, guiding a masked figure towards them.

'I have news that will gladden your hearts,' said Cadillac. 'Behold! The Old One has returned from the Valley of Death to be with us this day!' He drew back the tinted visor of the helmet to reveal Mr Snow's face.

The five warriors stared open-mouthed at the old wordsmith. Shock, surprise, terror, incredulity – their faces reflected the whole gamut of emotions experienced at the unexpected return of a loved one then, with a chorus of joyful whoops and yells, they rushed forward to embrace him.

Steve watching from the sidelines with Cadillac felt a twinge of envy. You had to be a pretty extraordinary individual to inspire that kind of affection and respect. And it must feel good to be on the receiving end. He saw his partner's tear-streaked face. 'Cheer up, it's not over yet.'

'Not for you and I perhaps – but this is his dying-day.'

'You think I haven't thought of that?' Steve's voice cracked with emotion. 'I don't want to lose him any more than you do but I'm saving the grief until it happens. You were wrong about the date once. You may have got it wrong this time too.'

'No. I have seen the iron-snake looming over me just like the vision in the seeing-stone. This is the place! This is the day!'

Steve hid his emotions under a cold veneer. 'Yeah, well, it's your dying-day too.' He saw Cadillac's frown and explained: 'Time for you to send your last message as Malone.'

Using the temporary video hook-up that linked the task force's base in the cargo skip to the command car, Wallis screened himself through to Commander Fargo. 'Malone just came through. His group are still in one piece. They've sighted the wagon-train and are making their run in. Can we get a camera on them?'

'We can when they break out into open-ground.'

'They've also asked for air cover.'

'No problem.'

'Good. We've got some valuable people out there. I'd hate to lose them.' Wallis rubbed his red-rimmed eyes. 'We've got to save something from this fiasco.' He heard the klaxons sounding up and down the train, summoning the crew to 'Action Stations'. 'Is there anything my team should be going?'

Fargo gave another of his skull-like grins. 'No, just relax. This could be your lucky day.'

Yeah, it could, thought Wallis. Except that you needed more than luck when you were working for AMEXICO. And there was something else which Fargo had said which struck him as rather odd. 'Just relax.' At a time like this? The man was an idiot . . .

Commander James Fargo was, of course, far from being an idiot. For the past hour, he had been privy to a piece of information that Wallis – for tactical reasons – had not been made aware of.

Leaving the horses in the care of Cat-Ballou, Steve crawled to the top of the slope with Cadillac and focused the viewer on the wagon-train. Although some of the trains were fitted with different types of external cameras and aerial arrays, they were all built to the same basic design and camouflaged in the same pattern of red, orange, light ochre and brown. But there was no mistaking the insignia on the side of the nose, and the code letters RVR.

Steve felt a surge of excitement spiced with a delicious dash of mortal danger. This was it. Big Red One. The idea that they were about to break open the flagship of the Federation really set the adrenalin flowing.

Cadillac explained where the Clan M'Call were now hiding in readiness for the main assault then said: 'I left the approach to the three middle wagons clear on this side of the train to give us room to ride in without stepping on anybody's toes. That okay . . .?'

'Yep . . .' Steve swept the whole length of the train one

more time then collapsed the viewer and slipped it back into the pouch on his left sleeve. 'I've seen all I want to see.'

'Then let's get out of here,' said Cadillac. 'Look! They've put a Skyhawk up!'

They wriggled down out of sight then got up and ran back to where the Mutes were waiting with the horses. Mr Snow was already riding pillion behind Cat-Ballou. Steve's mount was nose to tail with Cadillac's and as they swung up into the saddle, their eyes met.

'This could be tough on you,' said Cadillac, 'Are you going to be able to handle it?'

Steve shrugged. 'Had no problem at the Heron Pool.'

'Yes but they were dead-faces. These are –'

'Sand-burrowers,' said Steve. 'And we're Mutes. So let's go for it!'

The main camera towers, mounted on the roofs of the front and rear command car, zeroed in on the first two horsemen as they came over the rise and down the slope at a furious gallop. A few moments later, four more horsemen appeared. One of them had a passenger seated behind the saddle, his legs flapping as he bounced up and down.

Seven riders. Malone had started his run with eight. Who had fallen on the last stretch?

A twin-boomed Skyhawk soared into view over the slope, flew over the riders then banked right and headed west in a shallow dive.

Up in the saddle of the wagon-train, the pilot's voice came out of the speakers on the main console. 'Blue Nine to Red One. This looks like the main event. The home team has upwards of a hundred Mutes on its tail and behind them, advancing on a wide front, are at least five columns – all heading this way. They're running loose, spread out over two or three miles. If you want us to break this up we'll need more birds in the air.'

Captain Jack Cullimore, the new Flight Operations Exec, responded. 'Red One to Blue Nine Roger. We're going to nail three to your tail. Take 'em down and show 'em the town. But leave a few for us, huh? There's some guys back here just itching to get into the ring.'

This raised a few broad grins among the command staff. Cullimore keyed himself through to the flight car and spoke to Section Leader Sam Petrie. 'Sam! We got some heavy action west of here. Put up Knox, Harding and Eiger. Tell 'em to touch base with Ebbets in Blue Nine. He'll lead 'em in.'

'Yess SURR!'

'First two horsemen closing fast!' yelled a Vid-Comm Tech. 'Range now three hundred yards!'

The wagon-master turned to the First Systems Engineer. 'Lower the ramp on Number Four, Mr Wyatt.'

Steve and Cadillac saw the ramp come down and make contact with the earth. They could hardly believe their luck. The ramp was almost exactly opposite the approach avenue prepared by Cadillac.

They looked over their shoulders. The rest of the group led by Cat-Ballou and Mr Snow was about two hundred yards behind them. Suddenly, the last three horses staggered and went down, pitching their riders out of the saddle. Cat-Ballou promptly reined in his horse, dismounted, pulled his passenger off, dumped him on the ground, then ran back to the fallen riders, firing over their heads at some Mutes who had popped into view behind them.

It all looked pretty convincing.

Steve and Cadillac rode on. The air over their heads crackled and rustled as Red River laid down covering fire. An eight-man, flak-jacketed squad of Trail-Blazers came down the ramp and waved them in. Steve and Cadillac dismounted, slapped their horses' rumps to drive them away, then ran towards the ramp, raising their visors as they covered the last few yards.

They looked back at the fallen horsemen. Two were running at the double, carrying a limp figure between them, one was giving covering fire, and the fourth was hobbling on a damaged left leg.

The squad leader waved Steve and Cadillac up the ramp with his rifle. 'C'mon you guys! Get your asses outta here! We'll bring your buddies in!'

Cadillac checked his watch and exchanged glances with Steve. This was something they hadn't planned for. Standing at the top of the ramp in full combat gear was someone Steve recognized. 'Commander Moore!'

'Brickman! What the heck have you been up to?! I heard you were coming in. Just couldn't believe it!' He hurried them over to the stairwell. 'This way. You're wanted in the saddle.' Moore aimed a finger at Cadillac. 'Is this Mister Malone?'

Steve was tempted to say 'Yes', but didn't. Someone on board might know Malone. Might even know – or have viddies of – *all* his team. But that was a chance they had to take. They were relying on speed, and the tenseness generated by a ground action to carry them through.

Best to stick with the script . . . 'No. This is Barney Kyle, one of his side-kicks!'

'Okay. Follow me.' Moore went up the stairs two at a time. 'We'll take a wheelie!'

As they neared the top floor, they saw a group of soldiers heading down. The stairwells linking the three floors of a wagon-train consisted of short flights with landings that made right angled turns around a fire-man's pole. To avoid a traffic jam, anyone in a hurry ran up and slid down.

That was when Steve got his second surprise. Coming onto the top floor one step ahead of Cadillac, he found himself eyeball to eyeball with a uniformed Jodi Kazan as she stepped out and grabbed hold of the pole.

'Steve?!' – 'Jodi?!' The names collided in mid-air. In that same fleeting moment, Steve saw Jodi's eyes switch onto Cadillac, saw the brief nano-second of puzzlement then the flicker of recognition as she slid downwards and was followed by the next in line.

Mouth agape, Steve leaned over the rail and watched her go. This was absolutely disastrous! With Kelso dead,

300

Jodi was one of only four people who could recognize Cadillac – and the *only* other Tracker still alive in the whole of the Federation to have seen Mr Snow.!

What the fuck was SHE doing here?!!

A shout from Commander Moore broke the spell: 'BRICKman!! Get the lead out!!'

'YESSURR!!' Steve leapt onto the wheelie, dragging Cadillac with him. The Mute looked stunned.

'Did you see who that –'

'I know!' hissed Steve, hoping like hell that his voice was masked by the general hubbub and the whine of the wheelie. 'And d'you know where she's going? Outside to help bring in –'

'Ohh, no –!!'

Moore looked over his shoulder and smiled cheerfully. 'Guess you guys have had a pretty bad time, huhh?'

'Yessir,' cried Steve. *And it was getting worse by the minute.* His head snapped round and practically came off his shoulders as another familiar face stepped back into a side passage to let the wheelie through. It was Big D. Buck McDonnell . . . Trail Boss of –

Had he been transferred to Red River along with Commander Moore –?

Cadillac checked his watch again. Barely fifteen seconds to go. The wheelie sped through the top floor of the power car between a maze of pipes and the drumming exhaust vents and stopped inside the command car where the Junior Field Commander – a guy whose breast-tag gave his name as Drysdale – was waiting.

'Brickman and Kyle!' shouted Moore. 'Take 'em on up! I'm going back to the ramp. We may have some trouble getting the others in in one piece!' Moore spun the wheelie around and sped away.

Drysdale led Steve and Cadillac along the last few yards of corridor and up the steps to the saddle. He paused at the top to salute. 'With your permission, Sir – Brickman and Kyle.'

'Bring them aboard, Mr Drysdale . . .'

That voice . . .

301

Drysdale beckoned to Steve and Cadillac.

Steve stepped up onto the saddle on leaden limbs. Rising to greet him from the wagon-master's high-backed chair was 'Buffalo Bill' Hartmann – commander of The Lady from Louisiana. And more than half of those manning the screens and control panels were people he had known and served with before being shot out of the sky.

They were attacking the wrong train!

He founds his heels coming together. Transferring his carbine to his left hand, he snapped off a parade-ground salute. Cadillac did the same.

Hartmann responded more casually. 'We'll save the welcome till later, gentlemen. What can you tell us about these Mutes?'

As he uttered that last fateful word, there was a series of muffled explosions, then two louder ones from almost directly underneath. The command car shuddered then tipped forward as the front tyres collapsed, throwing those who were standing off balance.

Steve and Cadillac had been braced for the impact. Twelve charges of PX had exploded within milliseconds of each other. Four, each reinforced by an AP mine, had blown out the front tyres on both the forward and rear command cars; the other eight had severed the life-giving umbilicals on both sides and at each end of the two power cars. Eight explosions that cut all electrical power to the command cars and the other wagons, deactivating the gun positions and plunging the entire train into darkness.

But only for a second. Emergency batteries in each car cut in, restoring the lighting and power to the external cameras, screens and radio communications equipment.

It was that second that made the difference. When Hartmann and his command staff recovered from their surprise, they found themselves confronted by two faceless camouflaged figures with closed helmets, firing from the hip as riot gas grenades rolled along the floor and exploded.

Steve dropped another down the stairway followed by

302

a standard fragmentation grenade then, while Cadillac continued to sweep the saddle with fire, he stepped over the bodies in front of him and dropped into Hartmann's seat. Holding his carbine ready in his left hand, he searched for and found the Emergency Fire Control Panel. Lifting the cover, he activated the alarm by means of a switch and hit the button.

The cover and switch were designed to prevent accidental use. When pressed, the button triggered shrill warbling alarms that signalled a major uncontrollable fire hazard warning. Signs lit up, ordering the crew to evacuate the train and every boarding and escape ramp was automatically lowered.

Steve had twice taken part in practice drills at Fort Worth. The ramps could be lowered using the emergency battery supply but once down they could not be raised without mains power. The belly of the wagon-train was now open from end to end, and with all the system lines severed, steam could not be piped through the jets to defend it . . .

Outside the wagon-train, in the closing seconds before the PX charges exploded, another part of the master-plan misfired. The timing had always been perilous since none of the Mutes involved had been able to grasp the notion of time as displayed on the digital watches taken from the dead defaulters.

The aim had been to arrive at the top of the ramp just as the PX charges exploded whereupon Mr Snow – protected by his escort – would use his powers to cause the maximum disarray inside the train in the seconds prior to the main assault – which was to be launched when all the ramps came down.

To create the illusion that the 'renegades" lives were under threat, Steve had arranged for three of the horses to be brought down by the bowmen. This would provide a convincing delay enabling Steve and Cadillac to get to the saddle, take over, and activate the ramps. As bonafide Mutes, Cat-Ballou, Mr Snow and the others could not enter the train before that moment of confusion because their real identities would be revealed as soon as they raised their visors – which they would have been expected to do. The plan called for Cat-Ballou and Mr Snow to dismount and rally the fallen who between them would shoulder the old wordsmith, then limp – but not too slowly – towards the open ramp, arriving in time for the big bang.

Unfortunately, the well-being of their riders is not always uppermost in the minds of horses fatally wounded in mid-gallop. They tend to jerk and stagger then founder untidily, crashing and rolling – usually on top of something breakable like the legs or back of their passengers.

With no experience at being pitched from the saddle, the Mutes did not know how to fall, so when they picked themselves up, they didn't have to *pretend* to be hurt. The damage was for real and it was only their in-born resistance to pain that kept them going.

No one had anticipated that their display of fortitude under fire would cause two squads of Trail-Blazers to come down the ramp, one to guard it while the other eight ran out with four stretchers to carry the 'walking-wounded' on board!

Before the five Mutes had time to work out how to cope with this unforeseen departure from the script, Mr Snow had been transferred to a stretcher then, as he was hurried away with Cat-Ballou running alongside, Purple-Rain, Diamond-Head and Lethal-Weapon were invited to adopt the same mode of transport. Which – after a brief hesitation – they did.

With their visors closed and their hands concealed in gloves, no one could tell they were not Trackers, but their real identity could not be concealed for long. Conscious that they must not ruin the element of surprise – at least until they reached the ramp, the three Mutes lay back clasping their rifles to their chests and allowed themselves to be carried feet first into battle.

Things were unravelling even faster for Mr Snow. Jodi Kazan was part of a third combat squad that had now joined the Blazers guarding the bottom of the ramp, and as his stretcher was carried towards it, Buck McDonnell, the Trail Boss of The Lady, ran down to take charge of the situation.

Ignoring the breathless requests to lie down, Mr Snow had hoisted himself into a semi-sitting position on the swaying stretcher in order to appraise the situation. Seconds later, the lead stretcher-bearer made a sharp right-hand turn up the ramp. The soldier manning the poles behind Mr Snow's back stumbled over the toe of the ramp as he swung left to get into line, tripped over his own Size 12's and went down – *whump!* – on both knees. He held onto the stretcher but the momentum gained in the turn toppled Mr Snow sideways to land in a heap at Jodi's feet.

Laying down her rifle, Jodi moved in smartly with the stretcher-bearers to pick him up. Cat-Ballou, sensing danger, backed off, fingering his rifle nervously. Mr Snow, who had been seized with a feeling of suffocation ever since he'd been obliged to shut his visor, wrenched the badly-fitting helmet off his head as he was given an underarm lift.

'Enough of this farce!' Mr Snow kicked away the hands trying to lift his feet back onto the stretcher, forced himself upright between the two surprised bearers and broke their hold on his arms. 'Clumsy oafs!'

Jodi rose to find herself looking into the deformed, angry face of a Mute with white hair and a – 'Christo! Buck!' She levelled an accusing finger. 'It's Mr Snow!'

McDonnell, moving faster than he'd ever done in his life, was already in action. He'd seen Cat-Ballou back off suspiciously and now the helmeted figure was about to bring his rifle up into the firing position.

Raising his own rifle across his body, McDonnell pumped four triples into Cat-Ballou's chest at close range. Continuing the same swift movement, he rammed the hard rubber butt forward, hitting Mr Snow right between the eyes as those same eyes widened and blazed.

Kerr–runch! The wordsmith's head snapped back-wards. An instant later, the twelve charges placed by Cadillac during the night exploded in quick succession – *B-B-B-B-BA-BA-BBOOOMMM!!*

McDonnell saw the lights above him go out then blink on again a second later.

One of the Blazers standing clear of the train pointed to the smoke and steam billowing out sideways from the front end. 'The forward power car's blown!'

'They both have!' yelled someone else.

There was a burst of confused shouting from people at the top of the ramp and a lot of things happened at once –

The three 'renegades' on the incoming stretchers rolled off and came up on one knee with rifle raised and started shooting at their startled bearers as they themselves were gunned down by the Blazers guarding the bottom of the ramp.

'Cover me!' McDonnell tossed his rifle to Jodi, grabbed hold of Mr Snow's baggy uniform in two places and ran him up the ramp like a half-filled sack of potatoes.

Unable to resist a fire-fight, Jodi loosed off several vol-leys but by the time her rounds struck home, the three attackers were dead several times over. She backed up the ramp and as she caught up with McDonnell her ears were assaulted by a high-pitched warbling alarm. War-ning panels lit up and started flashing –

'EMERGENCY! MAJOR FIRE/EXPLOSION HAZ-ARD! EVACUATE TRAIN!'

There was a rumbling roar and a winding-down of gears as the ramps came down along the whole length of the train. And as the rubber-capped toes hit the earth with a dull thud, the ground on both sides of the train erupted to reveal a horde of screaming Mutes armed with rifles, knives and crossbows.

Each of the shallow trenches that had been sur-reptitiously filled in during the passage of the buffalo under and around the train, concealed a Mute warrior. With the stillness only primitive hunters can attain, they had lain silent and unmoving under a covering of earth and scrub for over three hours, waiting for just this moment. And now, as they hurled themselves towards the foot of the undefended ramps, the crew of The Lady, responding to the evacuation order started down and ran slap into trouble.

Jodi stared aghast as the line-men below her gamely fought off a swarm of Mutes. She clutched at McDonnell's sleeve and pointed to the unconscious Mr Snow. 'Buck! It's not just him! Brickman had another smart Mute with him! He's the clear-skinned guy I told you about –'

'WHAA-ATT?! And you let him go up to the command car?! The guy was festooned with grenades! Fer crissakes, Jodi! Why the fuck didn't you blow the whistle?!'

'I just caught a fleeting glimpse of him! I couldn't believe it! It was only when I spotted Mr Snow that it hit me!'

Still clutching the limp body of Mr Snow, McDonnell threw himself towards a wall-mike linked to the PA system and punched it into life. 'Hear this! Hear this! The fire hazard warning is a false alarm! Repeat – FALSE ALARM! The Lady is under attack! Stay on board and hold the ramps!'

The banshee warbling of the alarm continued and the warning panels continued to flash, and the conflicting information the crew was getting seemed to add to the general confusion.

'Can't you turn that fire warning off?!' shouted Jodi.

'Only from the saddle! The whole fucking system's shot to hell. C'mon! Let's get this joker out of here!'

McDonnell hoisted Mr Snow over his shoulder, turned aft into the next wagon and ran up forward stairs onto the second floor. Pulling out a smart key-card made of red plastic, he opened the door to a small narrow cubicle.

It was a punishment cell. A bare-metal bunk, table, chair, wash-basin and toilet all folded away into the walls. You either slept, sat, washed or shat. There wasn't enough room to do more than one thing at a time.

McDonnell pitched Mr Snow onto the bunk then stepped outside and pushed Jodi into the cell. 'Stay with him. I'm gonna lock you in, okay?' McDonnell pulled out his hand-gun. 'Don't worry, I won't forget where you are.' He found time for a reassuring grin. 'And by the way, well done. You may have saved our asses.'

The door started to close.

'Buck! Wait! What do I –'

'You've got the rifle. Don't hesitate to use it.' McDonnell closed the door. The mechanism locked, pushing the red key-card he'd inserted to the mouth of the slot leaving one of the short edges protruding by one eighth of an inch. The slot had two finger-sized scoops, allowing the card to be grasped and withdrawn. And this was what he proceeded to do with his left hand – since the pistol was in his right.

In the brief moment of time it took to raise his left hand, McDonnell's brain was evaluating the situation and working out what to do next. An inner voice told him that Hartmann was probably out of action. The explosions that had cut the power and steam lines was the work of someone who knew about wagon-trains. Those smart Mutes who had hit The Lady the previous year had pulled another fast one and this time, Brickman was definitely in on it. *Fuggin' lump-sucker* . . .

Shouts and animal-like screams, the thump of bodies locked in combat, the clash of steel and the characteristic sound of compressed air exploding from rifle barrels filled the air as Blazers on the floor below tried to beat back the invading Mutes.

McDonnell was faced with three choices: (a) to stay where he was and organize the local defence, (b) to try and find out what had caused Commander Hartmann to go off the air and, if possible, retake the forward command car or (c) make his way along the top floor to the rear command car where Lt.Commander Jim Cooper, the deputy wagon-master, was no doubt trying to hold the fort.

The fire alarms had been silenced and the signs

308

switched off, and it was Cooper's voice now that was coming over the PA system, telling the crew to stay on the train, seal the lower wagon access doors and hold the middle floor.

It made sense. If the Mutes could be boxed in and kept on the lower deck the train could be held until help arrived. Fortunately there was no ramp under the flight cars – but there *was* one under the blood-wagon. Bad news . . .

The Trail Boss decided to make contact with the deputy wagon-master. He had to tell him Brickman had gone native, and that he and a clear-skinned Mute were running wild in the forward command car. That news had to be gotten back to Grand Central fast –

The decision was never implemented – and the key-card was never taken out of the slot.

There was a sudden burst of firing to his left. Three unarmed Blazer technicians staggered backwards into the corridor from the passageway to the next wagon. McDonnell spun away from the cell door, around the corner of the passageway and onto the down flight of stairs to get out of the line of fire. As the techs fell dying to the floor, a howling Mute exploded through the doorway, rifle held high.

McDonnell brought him down with a triple head shot. Deciding the extra firepower would come in handy he reached for the fallen rifle but before he was able to pull the barrel from under the warrior's body, he glimpsed a movement on the stairs below him right at the edge of his vision. Without letting go of the rifle, he aimed his pistol blindly and fired volley after volley –

Chu-wii, chu-wii, chu-wii, chu-wii, chu-wiii!

The needlepoint rounds sliced into the warrior's body, knocking him back against the wall. But they did not kill him before he fired his cross-bow. As McDonnell got a one-handed grip on the rifle and brought it to bear on the warriors now surging through the doorway, the bolt shot upwards between the stair rails and struck the exposed right-hand side of his throat, pinning his tongue to the roof of his mouth on its way through his brain.

The impact caused his fingers to tighten round both triggers, killing a second Mute on the stairway below and the first man through the doorway above.

In the seconds before McDonnell's death, Lt.Commander Cooper, the deputy wagon-master had also perished. The rear command car had been specially targeted, and as the ramps came down, a hand-picked posse of Mutes armed with Tracker rifles burst from their hiding places in the ground and stormed onto the lower floor.

The crew, who were still recovering from the impact of the disabling explosions and confused by the evacuation order, proved easy meat. Moving ahead of their leader, Spandau-Barry, six Bears shot their way up onto the second floor, then the top, clearing the way to the saddle with a continuous stream of fire as Spandau-Barry bounded up the steps with an AP108 mine in each hand.

Cooper and the saddle staff of the rear command car – among them Betty-Jo Aarons – were already reaching for the available weapons as the screaming, wide-eyed Mute warrior burst into view.

They were too late. His outstretched hands were already coming together as the first rounds from several hand-guns struck home.

Time slowed, and in the instant before death overtook them, they saw with horrifying clarity that the pressure-sensitive fuses of the AP108's he held were about to impact on one another. As some tried to dive for cover and others stood frozen to the spot, the top half of the Mute's body disappeared in a blinding sheet of flame and –

From the trees to the south of the rear command car, from the twin rivers and both flanks, the rest of the M'Call clan burst forth and rushed across the open ground towards the stricken wagon-train. The side guns which had fired at the Bears pretending to pursue Steve, Cadillac and the other disguised riders had fallen silent.

The danger – and it was considerable – came from the six arrowheads that had swept away towards the west and were now returning.

In the short interval between the first explosions and Spandau-Barry's *kamikaze* mission, the deputy wagon-master had succeeded in getting a message to the airborne patrol, telling them the wagon-train had come under attack.

The command staff aboard Red River were also listening out on the same channel. While Wallis passed the news back to the White House, Fargo had made repeated attempts to contact Hartmann but so far there had been no reply. And now Cooper had gone off the air.

In the same short span of time that encompassed the death of McDonnell and the staff of the rear command car, the hand-to-hand fighting continued throughout the length of the train and at the front end a posse of Mutes stood ready to repulse any counter-attack on the command car.

Up in the saddle, among the litter of dead bodies, Steve sat slumped in Hartmann's seat, his head in his hands while Cadillac rummaged through the racks of drawers under the table section of the main video-screen console. Eventually he found what he was looking for – a batch of cassettes labelled with the name of the dead wagon-master, the daily record of his radio conversation with Red River and CINC-TRAIN.

'The bastards,' muttered Steve. He raised his fists and bared his teeth at the ceiling. 'The BASTARDS! Oh, Roz! How could you let them DO this?!'

Cadillac, who was listening to the play-back of Hartmann's voice through a light-weight head-set, lifted one of the ear-pieces. 'Do what?'

Steve swore violently. 'Don't you realise what's happened?! This isn't Red River! This is the Lady from Louisiana!'

His partner swivelled round to face him. 'But the letters – the insignia – the aircraft –'

'All faked!' cried Steve. 'Just like we've been pretending that Malone was still alive! Roz and Clearwater aren't ON this train!'

'Calm down!'

Before leaving Big Fork, Cadillac had entrusted Blue-Thunder with the delicate task of storming the blood-wagon. His orders were to seize and hold everyone they found until Steve and Cadillac arrived on the scene. Only those who refused to surrender were to be killed. The assault was still in its infancy. Less than ten minutes had elapsed since boarding the train and Brickman, the super-hero, was losing his grip.

Hahh, If only Clearwater could see her Golden One now . . .

'There's no need to go overboard. We haven't even looked for her yet!'

'I don't NEED to look!' shouted Steve. He swept a hand over the bodies lying around the saddle. 'I KNOW these people!'

'And there's no possibility they could have been transferred?'

'One or two perhaps, but not the whole fucking crew! Whassa matter – you dumb or somethin'?! We've been shafted! The M'Calls are making an empty sacrifice! Your people are dying for nothing!'

To vent his anger, Steve attacked the video screens and the control panel on Hartmann's console with the butt of his carbine. 'What the fuck are we gonna do?!' He glared across at Cadillac.

The Mute had turned back to the main console and was concentrating on the voice coming through his headset. Steve leapt out of Hartmann's chair, strode over to the main console and shot out several of the screens. 'ARE YOU LISTENING TO ME!!'

Cadillac eyed him calmly then removed the headset and stopped the tape. 'No. I'm listening to Hartmann. I take it he *is* the commander of this wagon-train.'

'Yeah.' Steve regained a measure of self-control. 'The Lady from Louisiana . . .'

312

'And this man Fargo I've heard you mention. He's in charge of Red River?'

'Yeah. And Wallis is the head of the AMEXICO team – but it's called the White House task force. I can see how they did it now. Wallis handled the communications with us and kept Fargo in the picture. And Fargo and Hartmann must have been working in concert, sharing the same radio channels. We thought we were dealing with Red River but it was The Lady – in disguise – that was making the moves!'

'So where *is* Red River?'

'How the hell do *I* know?' cried Steve. 'It's Karlstrom who's behind all this! Slimy sonofabitch!' He banged the butt of his carbine on the table. 'Why the hell didn't Roz tell us what was going on?!'

'Maybe she didn't know. If Karlstrom has gone to this much trouble maybe he let the people on board Red River think they were going to be attacked – to fool Roz and prevent her from *warning* you.'

'Yeah, maybe . . .' Steve rubbed his face wearily. 'Nyehh, what the hell . . . doesn't really matter. I've blown it. Not just for you and the M'Calls, but for Roz, Clearwater . . . everything!'

'Not necessarily,' said Cadillac. 'We might still be able to salvage something from the wreckage. I think it's time your masters heard what a good job you're doing – helping to defend this wagon-train.'

'You mean –?'

'Yes. I'm going to pretend to be Hartmann *and* Malone. If they ask to speak to you, try not to give the game away. Just tell them everything is going splendidly.'

Steve eyed him. 'You've got a fucking nerve . . .'

'Well, at the moment, it's certainly holding up better than yours.' Cadillac rose to his feet.

'Wonder what's happened to Mr Snow?'

'Never mind about that! The Old One can look after himself! Just show me how to work the radio. Can we alter the quality – y'know with that crackling noise you get? I don't want it sounding too clear.'

'Jeezuss! Any more requests?! I'm not a Comm-Tech, y'know! Just count yourself lucky I know how to switch the thing on!' Steve looked around the saddle and got his bearings. 'C'mon, it's over here. Let's hope it's still working . . .'

Roz came through. It was like a cool, calming hand on his brow. *Too late, little sister. TOO LATE . . .!*

CHAPTER THIRTEEN

At 0530 Standard Time, fifteen minutes after the initial explosions had crippledd The Lady, Karlstrom passed through the turnstile into the Oval Office. The President-General, summoned from his bed by the first news of the assault, was – as always – impeccably groomed and exuded the businesslike air of a man who had been at work for hours.

He greeted Karlstom by the 'stile. 'I can't believe this is happening, Ben. Hartmann must be the unluckiest man alive.'

'Either that or the dumbest. Never mind. Perhaps it'll teach the wagon-train division not to back a loser. Have you seen the map projections showing our units and where this is taking place?'

The P-G nodded. 'While I was dressing.' He steered Karlstrom over to the chair facing the desk then seated himself behind it.

'We've had two messages from Hartmann, and Wallis, my task-force leader, has spoken with Malone. He and Brickman made it to the train but the rest of the team didn't make it. Red River received a report from the deputy wagon-master about some shooting incident on the ramp. He also said he'd lost touch with Hartmann. Since when *he's* gone off the air and Hartmann's come through saying he's lost contact with the rear command car.

'Sounds very confusing . . .'

'It is. Here's the situation. Shortly after Malone and Brickman arrived, there was a series of explosions which immobilized the train, cut the power to the guns and caused a systems failure which lowered all the ramps. You can imagine the situation.'

315

'Christo! I didn't realize they were that easy to crack.'

'I don't think anybody did.'

'But can't Hartmann raise the ramps?'

'Not without mains power. It's a major flaw in the operating system. The designers never envisaged a simultananeous breakdown in both power cars.'

'No . . .,' mused the P-G. 'And of course the umbilicals are on the *outside* of the train.'

'That's right. They're in protective trunking which up to now have been invulnerable but –'

'Not to explosives . . .'

'No. It's something CINC-TRAIN's going to have to get on top of pretty fast. Anyway – that was when the Mutes attacked.'

'Which Mutes are these? The last air reports put the M'Calls several miles to the west of Malone's party.'

'That's right,' said Karlstrom. CINC-TRAIN is still trying to sort that one out. This may be the work of another clan – perhaps more than one. Brickman did warn us that the She-Kargo had agreed to support one another following the defeat of the Iron Masters at the trading post.'

'Is that where they got the explosives from?'

Karlstrom had been prepared for this one. 'It seems the most likely source. The big wheel-boats carry upwards of sixty cannon.'

'But it would still need expert knowledge to disable a wagon-train. So who – Cadillac?'

Karlstrom nodded. 'He wired the bombs that blew The Lady apart last year. We have to assume he lifted the information he needed about the train out of Brickman's head. That Mute has some extraordinary capabilities. Jodi Kazan, for instance, told us he left Ne-Issan able to read and speak fluent japanese – without a single lesson!'

'And what else, I wonder . . .?'

Karlstrom moved the conversation on. 'The how and why can wait till the post-mortem. The important thing is to help Hartmann turn this situation around.'

'Agreed . . .'

'Thing's aren't too good but the situation is recoverable. Hartmann has an unconfirmed report of an internal explosion in the rear command car and that's been sealed off. The Mutes control the ground under the wagon-train and now hold most of the lower floor and the middle floor of *some* wagons.

'Hartmann's battalion is holding the flight car and blood-wagon, the power cars, most of the middle floors and the entire top floor – except at the rear. That includes the flight-deck and the roof of the train. It's a little iffy, but it's still possible to get a plane off and land-on.'

'What's happened to the air component?'

'There were six planes in the air when the Mutes hit the train. Three were on their way back after making strafing runs on the columns of Mutes moving in from the west. They handed the job over to the second flight – which meant that when the Mutes made their assault on the train, the only planes in the air had no ordnance and empty guns!

'The Lady told them to divert to Red River and recalled the second flight but by the time they arrived overhead, most of the Mutes were either on or under the train. The power loss interrupted communications for a while and now most of the Comm-Techs on the command staff are engaged in defending the command car so apart from Hartmann there's been no one to handle the radio traffic.

'The second flight have been circling the train but have hesitated to attack it. Their guns are no good against the Mutes already inside and they don't want to use what napalm they have while there's a whole battalion of Blazers on board.'

'That's understandable. What about our other units?'

'They're moving into position.'

'Has Hartmann requested any specific type of assistance?'

'Yes, he has.' Karlstrom shifted uneasily on his chair

317

as he came to the difficult bit. 'The Mutes have brought a summoner on board.'

'Mr Snow . . .?'

Karlstrom threw up his hands. 'Can't say – but whoever it is, is making life very difficult. Our boys are battling against gale-force winds gusting down the passageways and they're being bombarded with seats, helmets, airbottles, hatch-covers – you name it. The bastard is levitating everything that's not screwed down and turning it into a missile!'

'So what does he propose?'

'He's asked for Roz Brickman to be flown over from Red River so that she can, well – use her powers against whoever's doing this. He says if they don't nail this guy they may lose the train.'

'Mmmm . . .' The President-General turned his attention to his right hand, drummed a brief rhythmic tattoo on the top of his immaculate desk then fixed Karlstrom with a penetrating stare. 'And how do you feel about that?'

'It's why we put her on board Red River. Clearwater's given no trouble.'

'True. But that may be due to her injuries. Do you really think she could handle someone like Mr Snow?'

Karlstrom shrugged. 'We won't know that until we try.'

'And we could end up losing her *and* the train . . .'

'There *is* that risk, yes.'

'And we also have to think about what Clearwater might do if Roz wasn't around. I'd hate anything to happen to Red River.'

'I know how we can cover that. I think we should transfer Roz to The Lady – but only after Brickman and Malone have flown to Red River. That leaves us with one bird in the hand and it gives us leverage against Clearwater. She won't do anything that'll put her boyfriend in danger.'

The P-G nodded. 'That's good. Well done, Ben.'

Karlstrom smiled. 'Yeah, I think it's rather neat. But we'll have to move fast if we're going to turn this situation around. Can I take it I have your approval to make the transfer?'

Jefferson gazed at him for a moment then spread his hands. 'You're the head of AMEXICO, Ben. She's part of the team you sent out to Red River so . . . I guess that makes it your decision.'

Karlstrom jumped to his feet as the P-G levered himself out of his chair. 'Yes.'

And it's your ass that's on the line, Ben, ole buddy . . .

There was nothing else to say.

'Keep me posted as things develop.' Jefferson broke off eye-contact, leant towards his video-console and pressed the key which brought the head and shoulders of his senior private secretary onto one of the screens. 'Nancy – could you come in for a moment?'

'Yessir!'

Jefferson turned away to admire the computer-generated sea and cloudscape projected onto the screens outside the curving window of the Oval Office. One of the P-G's favourite places: Cape Cod.

Karlstrom, who could read the signs, let himself out through the turnstile as Nancy came in.

Leaving Cadillac to handle the fake radio traffic, Steve poled down to the bottom floor of the command car. Picking up a quartet of Mute warriors – to avoid getting killed by mistake – he went down the ramp and aft under the belly of the train to look for Mr Snow and Jodi Kazan.

Near the foot of the original entry ramp he found the bodies of Cat-Ballou, Purple-Rain, Diamond-Head and Lethal-Weapon. None of the other uniformed corpses belonged to Mr Snow. And Jodi wasn't there either.

With his escort boxed around him, Steve went up the ramp and into the train. Scattered pockets of Trail-Blazers were holding out on all floors throughout the length of the train but contrary to what Karlstrom had been told, the flight car and blood-wagon had both fallen to the M'Calls.

319

Inside, compared to the charnel-house calm which had descended on the forward command car, the situation in the rest of the train could be compared to a vicious chaotic race-riot fought in the sewers of a space-age city.

The air was filled with the noise of battle: angry screams, shouts, yelping and whooping war-cries, splintering crashes, thuds, thumps, the thunder of running feet and the muffled whump of fragmentation grenades. And there was blood everywhere. The corridors were littered with dead bodies of Blazers and Mutes – which live warriors, bright-eyed with blood-lust, used as stepping-stones in their race to get to wherever the fighting was fiercest.

Few could be persuaded to stop. Those that did only had time to shout 'No' to the question 'Had they seen the Old One?' and were off again before Steve could ask if they had seen a female sand-burrower with a slab of pink scar tissue down the left-hand side of her face. He asked one of his escort to go back down the ramp and see if either were to be found under the aft-section of the train.

Within seconds of the warrior's departure, Blue-Thunder, the M'Calls' paramount warrior, came into view from the direction of the flight cars, toting a Tracker carbine with a blood-streaked bayonet attached. He was sweating and smeared with blood.

'We cannot find Clearwater, our clan sister!'

'I know,' said Steve. 'But never mind. Cadillac will explain that later. Have you seen Mr Snow?!'

Blue-Thunder shook his head. 'I thought he was with you!'

'No. He's disappeared!' Pulling Blue-Thunder with him, Steve stepped back against the brass slide pole in the centre of the stairwell to allow a large group of warriors to pass along the corridor. Many of them carried severed heads on bayoneted rifles.

A drop of blood trickled down the back of Steve's raised hand. Looking up, he saw a helmeted body slumped forward against the stair rail leading to the second floor, with one arm hanging down parallel to the brass pole. The blood had drained out of a neck wound, along the angled shoulder and down the limp arm.

Steve recognized the powerful hand and thick fingers before catching sight of the broad red diagonal rank stripe outlined in black. The arm belonged to Buck McDonnell. He'd glimpsed Big D heading aft just after he'd run into Jodi. Had they both died in sight of each other?

Motioning Blue-Thunder to wait, Steve clambered over the dead Mutes lying on the stairs and reached the Trail Boss. The barbed point of the crossbow bolt sticking through the crown of his helmet said it all. More dead Mutes lay in the passageway above. Higher still, on the top floor, there was a firefight in progress.

Steve signalled his escort to cover the stairs and the pass-way to the next wagon then stepped over McDonnell and up into the corridor.

Several doors to the side compartments hung open, some with bodies lying across the sill. There was debris scattered everywhere. The door to the first compartment on his left was closed. He moved past it without thinking then remembered his interrupted conversation with Blue-Thunder. As he turned back to see if the warrior had followed him up the stairs, his eyes were drawn to the sliver of red plastic sticking out of the lock of the closed door.

He withdrew the card. It was a high-security key-card. The kind that a Trail Boss and other senior non-coms like Battalion Master Sergeants would carry. And it had been inserted in the lock of a punishment cell. Steve tested the door with the tips of his fingers. It was shut fast. The cardholder had either had no time to open it, or had forgotten to withdraw his card after locking it. Which meant there could be someone inside.

Steve silenced Blue-Thunder and his warrior escort with a warning finger then put the key-card back into the slot and pressed a button on the COMMS-LOCK panel set at shoulder height in the door surround.

A miniature black and white tv screen flickered into life. Linked to a fish-eye camera in the roof of the cell, it revealed Mr Snow sprawled unconscious on the bunk with his head towards the door. Jodi Kazan was down on one knee in the far corner with a rifle, ready to fire at whoever came in.

Steve invited Blue-Thunder to view the scene but it only left the Mute totally perplexed. Like his companions, he had never seen a video-screen image before and since this one was a top view of a small room distorted through a wide-angle lens he didn't know what to make of it

'The Old One is in there,' whispered Steve. 'Can you not see him – lying on the bed?'

Blue-Thunder studied the image again and gave a perplexed frown. 'But . . . he is no bigger than a beetle!' The mute tapped the tiny screen. 'Has he been trapped in this stone by dark magic?'

'Forget it. Just leave this to me.' Steve pushed him aside and put his mouth to the speaker grille. 'Jodi . . .?'

Having journeyed back to the Federation in a similar cell on the same train the previous winter, Jodi knew the setup. Keeping the rifle aimed towards Mr Snow and the door, she straightened up and addressed the camera lens behind the small clear panel in the ceiling. 'That you Brickman?'

'Yeah, now listen – we need to talk.'

'So talk.'

'No. Face to face. I need to explain things. But first I want you to understand you're not in any danger. Just slide that rifle under the bunk and clasp your fingers together on the back of your neck. I promise you won't come to any harm. You have my word on that.'

'Oh, yeah?' Jodi took a firmer hold on the rifle and placed the barrel against Mr Snow's midriff. 'Your word ain't worth shit, Brickman. I saw who you came in with

322

– Cadillac. The scumbag that killed Dave and blew half The Lady apart. And if it hadn't been for Buck McDonnell, I'd have gone sky-high with the rest!

'An' you know what? I got the blame! I was the one who got thrown in the slammer and –' She gave a harsh laugh, '– here's the biggest joke of all. I stood up for you, swore you had nothin' to do with it! And all the while you were tucked up tight with these lump-shits! Now I know why they hit me with a Code One!'

'So what are you doing here?'

'They gave me a chance to redeem myself by fingering your Mute friends. When I came on board I was supposed to be kept under close arrest but Buck McDonnell persuaded Hartmann to put me back on the team while I was on the train. For old time's sake. Not flyin', of course, but regular duties alongside the other Blazers. Nice gesture, huh? Didn't know it was going to end in a shoot-out with you.'

Steve spoke with a new urgency. 'It needn't, Jodi. We can work something out.'

'Yeah? Like what – the length of the pole you're gonna stick my head on?'

'No! You'll be safe with me. Just put the rifle down and listen! I'm going back to the Federation. You can come with me if you want. We can cover for each other. I can help you beat the rap!'

Jodi answered with a mocking laugh. 'Where you been living, Brickman – fantasy-land? You been smokin' too much rainbow grass! D'ya know where I was before they put me on the train? Death Row! Being around you is bad news, honeybun!'

Steve tried a softer line. 'This is getting us nowhere, Jodi. You can't stay in there forever.'

'I'm staying until Buck McDonnell steps through that door. If anyone else comes in this old lump gets blown away! And that goes for you too. Comprendo?!'

It didn't seem like a good time to tell her that the Trail Boss was lying on the stairway with his brains leaking out the top of his head. And with the rifle barrel aimed point blank at Mr Snow it was too risky to burst in. He'd be dead before the door opened up far enough for them to shoot her down.

It was at this point that Mr Snow chose to open his eyes and take in his surroundings. He clutched his bruised forehead and groaned. 'Sweet Sky-Mother . . .' He looked down the barrels of the rifle then fixed Jodi with his faded blue eyes and chuckled hoarsely. 'Goodness me, that looks rather dangerous!'

Jodi shrank back into the corner and aimed the rifle at his head. 'Stay down! If you try to sit up I'll shoot!'

Mr Snow raised his head a little further then fell back with a gasp of pain and covered his face with his hands. 'I can assure you that's the last thing I feel like doing.' He coughed and retched as if he was at his last gasp.

Steve saw Jodi's rifle waver then, with a movement that was too quick to see, Mr Snow's left hand flashed out and grasped the front of the rifle, deflecting it away from his body. His uncovered eyes blazed. The outstretched arm connecting him with the rifle was like a steel rod, every sinew and muscle taut and unyielding. A lightning conductor.

Jodi's two-handed grip on the rifle tightened, every muscle in her body contracted as the current ran through her. Her lips drew away from her clenched teeth and her eyes dilated as she was hit by a series of convulsions; five massive shocks that jolted her from head to toe, followed by a sixth that slammed her lifeless body against the back wall of the cell.

Steve unlocked the cell door and rushed in as Mr Snow tried to sit up. 'Are you all right?'

'No, I'm not!' snapped Mr Snow. 'On top of everything else, some great oaf tried to take my head off! If it wasn't for these he'd have knocked my brains out . . .' He fingered the broken skin on the ridged front of his skull then said: 'How's it going?'

'Don't ask,' said Steve. He looked down at Jodi's crumpled body and heaved a sigh of regret. This wasn't how it was meant to be. 'Come on – I'll take you to Cadillac.'

In the saddle, the young and the old master embraced each other warmly.

'Easy, easy,' grumped Mr Snow. 'I'm feeling a little fragile.' He sank into Hartmann's chair and gazed at his surroundings with a mixture of curiosity and disgust. 'What a strange world. How could anyone in their right mind want to live in a place like this?'

'We'll have to save the philosophical questions until later,' said Cadillac. He squared up to Steve. 'Good news and bad news. Your friends aboard Red River have agreed to fly your kin-sister over here to deal with the summoner that's causing so much havoc.' He glanced across at the semi-recumbent figure of Mr Snow.

'The bad news is they want to exchange her for you and Malone. And you have to go there first. I'm planning to dispose of him on the way to the flight-deck during a gallant rearguard action. But we don't have any steam. Can we get a plane off?'

'Yes. Each catapult is fed from a reserve tank that's kept topped up by the system. Even with the lines down they'll be good for a couple of launches before the pressure falls off.'

'Good. Okay, you'd better show me how it's done.'

Steve looked surprised. 'I've got to leave now?'

'Yes! They're waiting!'

Mr Snow rose to meet Steve as he came over to say goodbye. As they clasped each other's hand and wrist, the old wordsmith's grip was reassuringly strong.

'Farewell, Old One. Would you believe me if I said it grieves me to leave you – especially at a time like this?'

'This is how it was meant to be, Brickman. You've come a long way to find your true self. You're close to the top of the mountain. Don't fall!'

'I'll try not to . . .'

Cadillac and Steve climbed out of a duckhole onto the flight-deck. M'Call warriors armed with rifles and dressed in captured uniforms manned the other duck-holes to fool the circling wing-men into thinking that Hartmann's battalion still controlled the top of the train.

A Skyhawk Mark 2 was parked on the deck with its bubble canopy open and tail booms folded. It had taken several hits from crossbow bolts but none of them had hit anything vital.

Cadillac peered at the exposed joints of the wing and tail booms. 'How do we unfold these?'

Steve was momentarily flummoxed. 'Err, shit, hang on a minute. Lemme see . . .' He peered at the exposed wing joints then slapped his forehead. 'Idiot! Of course! It's hydraulic! You work it from inside the cockpit once you've started the engine.' He leant into the cockpit and pointed out the control levers. 'You push that one for-ward and lock it – so, and the other raises the tail.'

'Okay. Let's get you hooked up.'

'Hang on, there's a couple more things I need to show you.' Steve led the way aft to the rear port duckhole and showed Cadillac the control mechanism that raised the arrester wires which engaged the landing hook of incoming planes.

'Brickman, I know all this. I've learned everything you've learned.'

'Yeah, like how to unfold the wings of a Mark 2.'

'Even you were hazy about that.'

'Yeah, well there's no harm in making sure. It's the cleverest people who make the stupidest mistakes. Like attacking the wrong wagon-train.'

Cadillac turned his face to the sky. 'Sweet Sky Mother . . . are we never to hear the last of that?!' He turned to Steve. 'Don't you understand?! Talisman guided us! Your masters tried to trick us but they played into our hands!

'If we had attacked the *real* Red River every person on that train would have had to die leaving only you and

326

Clearwater alive to tell of how your kin-sister was carried off into the hills. Reflect on that for a moment. Are your masters so foolish? Your treachery would soon have been exposed!'

'You're right,' admitted Steve.

'Of course I am! This way, your kin-sister is released as the Old One wished, and you will return a blood-stained hero! A loyal soldier-citizen of the Federation who did his utmost to protect his comrades-in-arms.'

'Yeah . . . C'mon.' Steve quickly ushered Cadillac to the forward duckhole on the starboard side and explained the launch control panel for the steam catapult.

'Yes, yes, look, it'll be quicker if I tell you,' said Cadillac. 'That's the steam-pressure read-out. The top button raises the catapult, the second fires it, and the third one lowers it back into the deck. I'm having to revise my opinion of sand-burrowers. Like all the systems on this train, this was designed to be idiot-proof – something which most of you clearly are!'

'You've forgotten something,' said Steve. 'I'm a Mute.'

He vaulted up onto the deck and climbed into the cockpit of the Skyhawk. As soon as the engine was running, he unfolded the outer wing panels then raised the tail. The twin booms which were folded forward under the wings, dropped down on parallel swing links then were brought up into line with the trailing edge of the wing by hydraulic rams. A small illuminated diagram on the instrument panel confirmed both wings and tail had locked into place.

Cadillac and another Mute warrior came forward to hook the Skyhawk onto the launch cradle as Steve taxied forward onto the catapult.

'D'you want any help?!' shouted Steve.

Cadillac popped up beside the open cockpit. 'For heaven's sake, Brickman – just GO!' He smiled and offered Steve his hand. 'Take care of our sister!'

'I will,' said Steve. 'Make sure you take care of mine!'

Cadillac dropped the cockpit canopy into place and gave it a goodbye slap.

The wing-man circling immediately above the wagon-train pressed his transmit button. 'Blue Three to Red River, we have one bird on its way.'

'Red River to Blue Three, Roger. Any update on your last sit-rep?'

'No. The Blazers are still holding down the roof and the Mutes are under the train. Over.'

'Roger, Blue Three. Take out as many strays as you can. Let 'em know you're there. But try not to damage the train. We want to get that Lady back on the road.'

'Blue Three, Roger, Wilco. Listening out.'

Roz, Don Wallis, Jake Nevill and the rest of the task force scrambled up onto the flight deck as Steve landed. Red River ground crew quickly manhandled his battle-scarred Skyhawk onto the rear port lift as the first two out-going planes came up on the forward lifts and were lined up on the catapults.

Wallis ran his eyes over the protruding crossbow bolts then turned to Steve as he emerged from the cockpit. 'This doesn't look too good . . .'

'Don't worry,' said Steve. 'We're holding the line. If we weren't, I'd never have gotten clear.' He paused then said: 'Did you get the news a –'

'About Malone?' Wallis's face tightened. 'Yeah, Hartmann . . .' He shrugged off the rest of the sentence.

'Losing him was a real blow,' said Steve. 'He was a great guy.'

'The best . . .' Wallis buried his feelings and became the brisk team-leader. 'Okay, guys, off you go.'

George Hannah and Cal Parsons hurried towards the aircraft that was now hooked up and ready to go.

'Jake! Let's go wind up Number Two!' Wallis gripped Roz's arm. 'You got one minute!' He strode off with Nevill.

Darryl Coates and Tom Watkins headed across the deck towards a third Skyhawk, complete with buddy-frame that had just come up on the rear starboard lift.

Roz and Steve hesitated for a moment before throwing themselves into a warm, rocking bearhug. When they separated, they held onto each other's arms. The slip-stream from the propellors flattened their clothing and snatched the words from their mouths.

'Why's this happening, Roz? Where're you gonna go? What're you gonna do?'

'I can't say!' she cried. 'I'm just glad to be part of it – aren't you?'

He tightened his grip. 'I'm scared. Are you sure you're not hiding something from me?'

'No. Wait – did you pick up my message about Annie?'

'Annie . . .?'

'Yes, ages ago. I obviously didn't get through. She wasn't our mother, Steve.'

'Yeah, well, with what we know now that makes sense . . .'

'But don't you see what it means? You're not my brother and I'm not your sister!'

'There's no need to sound so happy about it.'

'I'm happy because we're both *free*! Free from the guilt and the pressure of that relationship. Free to give expression to that love we felt or give it to someone else. To follow The Path, Steve!'

'Oh, jeezuss! I don't want to lose you, Roz!'

'You won't lose me, Steve. Our lives are bound together by a power and for a purpose far greater than our need for each other.'

Steve nodded. 'How come I get the feeling you're suddenly a lot smarter than me?'

'I always was, little brother!'

Steve ruffled her hair playfully and hugged her again. 'Look after yourself. It's a rough world out there.'

'You too . . .'

They looked along the flightdeck. The five mexicans were clustered around Wallis. He looked towards Roz and beckoned her forward. Roz signalled she was on her way.

'Do those guys know what they're doing?'

'They think they do.' Roz kissed him quickly on the mouth then broke away. 'Look after Clearwater!'

'I will.' *If they let me* . . . Steve followed her along the flight deck. 'Listen! I know this is a stupid question but . . . will we see each other again?'

Roz favoured him with another enigmatic smile. It was getting to be a habit. 'That depends on you.'

Steve stood on one side with Wallis as Roz wriggled into the prone position on the buddy-frame then had the flight-bag zipped shut around her. It was like a wind-proof sleeping bag with a clear plastic ventilated hood covering the head and shoulders.

Hannah and Coates went away first, then Nevill's Skyhawk was hooked up. The engine went to full revs, there was a tremendous *whoooshh!* then Roz was gone, leaving wisps of steam curling from the vents in the catapult rig. Gone without an answering wave.

Steve let his hand drop, and swallowed the lump in his throat. The third Skyhawk with Cal Parsons on the frame and Watkins at the controls was brought forward and went off in its turn.

When the three Skyhawks carrying Roz and the five mexicans aarrived over The Lady from Louisiana, they found a reassuring number of camouflaged and helmeted Trail-Blazers on the roof. Hannah, flying the lead aircraft, made a low pass alongside the train to check the state of the flight-deck before landing with Parsons. Wallis had ordered them to go in first to make sure everything was okay. On receipt of their signal, Nevill would then bring Roz in, followed by Watkins and Coates.

Mr Snow, who had been cajoled into wearing another Tracker helmet, crouched in the duckhole with Cadillac as the latter, using his normal voice, talked the Skyhawk down onto the wire. Along each side of the flight deck, M'Call warriors dressed up in Tracker uniforms stood ready to pounce.

Mr Snow gazed at his protégé admiringly. 'You amaze me. Where did you get all this knowledge from?'

'Lots of people – but mainly from Brickman. We're lucky he had an enquiring mind. Now – for the last time – close that visor!'

The three Skyhawks from The Lady's own flight component which had been circling the train and making the occasional strafing run, came in ahead of Hannah's aircraft in V-formation as he made his final approach. The two wing aircraft strafed the ground on either side of the train to prevent any Mutes taking a pot-shot at Hannah and his passenger as the Skyhawk floated in over the rear command car with its flaps and arrester hook down.

Cadillac leapt onto the flight deck and ran forward while two warriors hauled Mr Snow out of the duckhole. Taking care to keep clear of the whirling propellor, Cadillac freed the snagged cable then assumed the role of deck marshal, signalling the pilot to fold his wings and taxi towards the forward port lift.

Mr Snow and a hand of disguised warriors caught up with Cadillac as Hannah parked on the lift and cut the motor. To the mexican, the Blazers around the flight-deck seemed strangely disorganized but at that point in time he had no reason to suspect there was anything wrong. This was, after all, no ordinary fire-fight.

Unzipping the flight-bag, Cadillac glimpsed an unmistakably male figure inside. Parsons. By this time Hannah, his partner, was out of the cockpit.

'Where's the Brickman girl?' demanded Cadillac.

'Up there.' Hannah jerked a thumb skywards as he helped Parsons extricate himself from the buddy-frame. He glanced at the masked figures crowded round the airplane and wondered why they weren't facing outwards ready to gun down any Mutes who poked their nose from out under the train. 'Who's in charge here?'

'I am,' said Cadillac.

Parsons, now standing by his partner's side, coughed. Covering his mouth he turned in towards Hannah. 'Check the badge . . .' he whispered.

Hannah's eyes fastened on Cadillac's uniform and saw

it carried a badge of the 5th Signals Intelligence Squadron. The decoy outfit that had been jumped by the M'Calls and Malone's renegades. 'So what's happened to the crew-chief?'

'He's been wounded. He's in the blood-wagon.'

'Then where's the Flight Ops Exec?' demanded Hannah.

'He's dead.'

'Aww, shit – Pete Carmichael?!'

'Yeah . . .'

Hannah took a step back. Parsons was seized but before anyone could reach Hannah, his pistol was out of its shoulder-holster and pointing at Cadillac's face.

'You just struck out, good buddy! That's the wrong name and you're wearing the wrong uniform! What the fuck's going on?!'

Mr Snow raised his visor and pushed aside the warriors who were shielding him. 'A battle, my friend! Which YOU are losing!'

The pistol wavered in Hannah's hand as he tried to control an unreasoning urge to throw it away. His brain was telling him that it wasn't a gun he had in his hand at all. It was a snake – coiled around his fist!

With a horrified yell he jerked his hand open and flung the hideous thing away. And as the pistol clattered across the flight deck, a voice filled his mind, banishing all other thoughts and feelings.

Do whatever is required to bring the girl to us . . .

Moving like a sleepwalker, Hannah reached into the cockpit and plugged himself into the radio circuit.

Circling above the train with Roz lying alongside his cockpit, Jake Nevill heard the hiss of static in his earphones as Hannah came through.

'White Knight One to Mother Hen. The perch is green and clean. Bring the bird home to roost.'

'Mother Hen, Roger.' Nevill glanced over his right shoulder towards the Skyhawk flown by Coates, tucked in behind and below his starboard wing. 'White Knight Two. Do you copy, over?'

'White Knight Two. Roger. Will follow you in.'

Filled with a great sense of well-being, Hannah pulled off his helmet, dropped it onto the pilot's seat and stood erect, ready and willing to face whatever lay in store. Parsons had also ceased to struggle. They were like poultry which, when seized by the feet and upended, accept the inevitable and go unresisting to their death.

'Take them below.' Cadillac turned to Mr Snow as the mexicans were led away. 'Wait here!'

He ran back down the flight deck and jumped into the Deck Controller's duckhole and plugged himself into the radio linking him with the aircraft overhead. 'Lady-Lady to Mother Hen. Surface wind bearing two-seven-five, speed one zero. Call finals. Over.'

'Mother Hen, Roger. Two seven five, speed one zero.'

Cadillac watched the Skyhawk bank left onto the short crosswind leg over the forest of larches beyond the rear command car. The third aircraft piloted by Coates was coming downwind west of the train to make the same turn.

'Mother Hen turning finals, over.'

Cadillac was gripped by a rising sense of excitement. Everything was working out beautifully. And only *he* could have done it! And with Brickman gone there was no chance of anyone else stealing the limelight.

Once again, the three patrol aircraft swept in ahead, clearing the way as Nevill landed on. Then as White Knight Two, carrying Watkins and Coates, turned over the forest of larches, the trio of Skyhawks banked round over the twin rivers and swept back towards the train and the incoming aircraft.

On the flight deck, helmeted Blazers in full combat gear unhooked Nevill's Skyhawk and waved him forward. Two soldiers were already peeling open the flight-bag as Roz eagerly unzipped it from the inside.

Nevill cut the motor, threw open the cockpit cover and started to climb out. 'Don't bother with that! Let's get this heap out of the way first! There's two other guys on their way –'

A savage knife thrust to the heart, delivered by one of

the masked uniformed figures, stopped him in his tracks as the three patrol aircraft zoomed overhead.

Exercising the same power that Clearwater had employed in her earlier battle against The Lady, Mr Snow reached out with his mind and filled the formation leader with an overwhelming unreasoning desire to destroy the plane now in his sights. It became the focus of everything he hated.

Coates, at the controls of the incoming Skyhawk, expected the formation to break away on either side of him. Instead, a hail of fire from the six-barrelled gun under the nose of the lead aircraft exploded through the windshield and punched a gaping hole in his chest.

Watkins, on the buddy frame, could do nothing but hang on helplessly, braced for the crash he was unlikely to survive. The pilotless plane side-slipped into the roof of the wagon-train, lost its starboard wing as it bounced off and cartwheeled messily into the ground.

Petrie, the bewitched patrol leader, pulled up into a tight loop, half-rolled off the top into a diving right-hand turn that brought him around onto the port side of his startled wingmen and pressed the gun-button. Nothing happened. The low-level strafing runs and the frontal attack on Coates had left him with an empty drum.

But both pilots, stunned by his downing of the Skyhawk, knew something had gone badly wrong. Petrie had flipped. But they had run out of ammunition too. And now that he was flinging his plane around the sky in an effort to ram them, the only thing they could do was split – and fast. Separating out, they opened the throttle and went down to treetop height where they were harder to spot and sent a May-Day to Red River.

Petrie followed. With each succeeding mile, the desire to destroy all blue flying objects faded, vanishing completely by the time he reached Red River. But by that time, the damage had been done: Mr Snow had achieved his objective – to empty the skies above the wagon-train.

Roz, stepping onto the flight-deck, knew who Mr Snow was before he cast aside his suffocating helmet, and as she clasped his outstretched hands their minds were instantly attuned. He looked incredibly old, his face was haggard and drawn, but there was still plenty of life in his eyes.

'I thought you'd never get here.'

Charmed by the mischievous smile, Roz tightened her grip on his thin bony fingers. 'We have waited a long time, Old One.'

'Too long, my child. This tongue that greets you must bid you farewell with the same breath.'

Roz removed her helmet and brushed her fingers through her short auburn hair. Throwing her head back, she breathed deeply, relishing the cooling touch of the wind upon her face then, as her eyes opened, she found herself looking at Cadillac.

He too was bare-headed – and seemed to be struck dumb. For a moment their eyes remained locked together then Roz turned to Mr Snow.

'Is this the warrior who is to become known as the Sword of Talisman?'

Mr Snow, amused to see that Cadillac had temporarily lost command of the situation, smiled broadly. 'He has the makings of a warrior. With you at his side he may even become a great one. But for the moment, he is known as Cadillac.'

The old wordsmith beckoned them to step nearer. Without being bidden, they took hold of each other's hand and knelt before him. Watched by a silent circle of warriors, he laid his hands on their heads and raised his face to the sky and uttered a silent prayer for divine guidance.

When it came, he closed his eyes and lowered his head. Roz and Cadillac felt their scalps tingle beneath his hands. 'It is the wish of Talisman that you be joined together, in blood and breath, body and soul, for you are The Chosen, destined to raise his banner high and accomplish mighty works in his name! May his blessings be upon you from this day forward. I hereby bequeath to you all that was mine and entreat you to open your minds to the powers which only he can bestow.'

Opening his eyes, Mr Snow waved them to their feet. 'Enough!' He pushed them towards the Skyhawk that Roz had just arrived on. 'Go! Before it's too late!'

'Go?! Go where?!' cried Cadillac.

'Go west, young man! Into the hills! Towards a new beginning!'

'But . . .' It was all happening too fast for Cadillac. He was already trying to cope with the revelation that this striking young woman had been chosen by Talisman to be – assuming he had interpreted the Old One's words correctly – his life partner! Admittedly with her very first glance, she had reached into the depths of his being but even so . . . A commitment like this should not be rushed into. She had, quite literally, entered his life and his heart like a bolt from the blue but she was . . . Brickman's sister! And now, on top of all that, the Old One had given his tail another unexpected twist –

'But . . . my blood-brothers and sisters! This may be *your* dying place, Old One, but what is going to become of them?!'

'Take a look around you!' Mr Snow flung out his arms and swept the horizon.

Cadillac gazed around him and felt his blood run cold. Close enough to be seen by a sharp-eyed Mute but still a long way off were four more wagon-trains – moving in from the north, south, east and west. The clan could not retreat. It could only stand and fight.

'It grieves me to go against you, Old One, but if I honour your wishes I shall be without a shred of honour myself. I brought our Bears and She-Wolves to this place. I cannot run from here and leave my clanfolk to die.'

'"I-I-I this, I that"! Can you think of no one but yourself?' cried Mr Snow. 'Talisman has given this star-child into your care! The Path is drawn, Follow it and don't look back!'

'But –'

Mr Snow slapped him hard on the chest, forcing him to step back towards the Skyhawk. 'The Clan M'Call is not *going* to die! It is going to become immortal! When

the history of the Plainfolk nation is written – as one day
it will be – our sacrifice here today will be remembered
as one of the first glorious steps on the road to final
victory!'

'HEYY-YAHH!' chorused the listening warriors.

'But you still haven't told me what I must do!'

'Exactly! I'm through giving advice! Stop thinking
about yourself and listen to the Sky Voices!'

Cadillac and Roz found a score of willing hands to
help them position the Skyhawk on the unused catapult. Hannah's craft parked on the adjacent lift proved
to be in the way and was promptly tipped over the
side. Cadillac checked the steam pressure read-out and
explained the control panel to Mr Snow.

'Are you sure you know which button to press?'

'I'm just *old*, not feeble-minded, you impudent rascal!
Don't let this promotion go to your head!' He accompanied Cadillac back to the Skyhawk; Roz was already
in place on the buddy-frame but she had not closed up
the hood of the flight-bag.

'Does he know how to fly this thing?'

'Oh, yes. That's the problem. He knows a great many
things but not enough about the things that really count.'
Mr Snow squeezed her shoulder affectionately. 'I'm
relying on you to drum some sense into him.' He moved
round the nose of the aircraft to bid Cadillac farewell.

'I shall miss you, Old One . . .'

'Nonsense! If that were true, it would mean you were
not ready. Are you trying to tell me that all the years I've
spent teaching you have been wasted?!'

'No, but –'

'Then be off with you!' cried Mr Snow, hiding his
deep love for the wayward, gifted child whose mind he
had nurtured from the age of one. 'We've got work to
do!'

The command staff of True Grit, the wagon-train now
rolling westwards along the far bank of the North Platte,
saw the Skyhawk leave the deck. Tracking it through a

telephoto lens, they watched it gain height in a climbing turn towards Wyoming.

The Flight Ops Exec tried to contact the departing aircraft on the standard frequency but there was no reply and it vanished in a bank of dense low cloud before one of their own Skyhawks could be put up to intercept it. The four approaching wagon-trains had been ordered to keep their aircraft grounded so as not to alert the M'Calls to their approach. CINC-TRAIN wanted to nail every single one – not send them running into the hills.

Aboard Red River, currently a hundred miles to the south east beyond the Nebraska/Kansas State line, Wallis was becoming increasingly worried. Fargo's staff had been relying on Hartmann's radio messages to tell them how his battalion was coping with the attack and now he had gone off the air.

His disappearance had coincided with the arrival of Roz Brickman and the team from the White House. Nevill had set down after getting the all-clear from Hannah and Parsons then things had gone haywire. There had been an inexplicable incident involving Petrie – one of the Red River wing-men loaned to The Lady to train up her own pilots on the Mark Two aircraft. An incident which had cost the lives of two of Wallis's colleagues and had almost claimed two more.

The stunned Petrie, faced with the testimony of his fellow wing-men, could offer no explanation for his behaviour. There was a total blank in his memory starting when he began the run in towards the wagon-train. The next thing he could recall was tailing one of his wing-men back towards Red River and receiving orders to land on. Pending further investigation of the incident, Petrie was formally relieved of his duties and thrown in the slammer.

James Fargo, the wagon-master of Red River, could make neither head nor tail of it. Wallis, on the other hand, had been given access to the record of Jodi Kazan's debriefing. The similarity between Petrie's behaviour and the incident surrounding her pick-up by aircraft

338

from The Lady were too striking to ignore. This was earth-magic. The work of a summoner. Probably Mr Snow. Had he also overcome Roz? They wouldn't know the answer to that until someone on The Lady came back on the air. Or until – as seemed more likely – the four Trail-Blazer battalions now being carried into action by True Grit, King of the Pecos, Sands of Iwo-Jima and Overland Raider had retaken the stricken wagon-train.

By the time that happened, Red River would be even further from the scene. CINC-TRAIN had already ordered her to roll south and off-load Brickman and the injured Mute at Monroe/Wichita for forward shipment to Grand Central. The signal had caused Fargo and his crew considerable distress. This was the first time they had been ordered away from a fight. What made it worse was the fact that they had been ready and willing to take this cocky bunch of Mutes apart for more than eight weeks only to learn twenty four hours before the expected attack that The Lady from Louisiana – a real nothing train to nowhere – was going to act as a decoy!

After giving the command staff of Red River a report on the general situation aboard The Lady up to the time he'd left, Steve was handed over to Wallis for debriefing on the more sensitive aspects of the operation.

Steve stuck to the scenario he and Cadillac had concocted. After two hours of patient questioning that ranged from the battle at the trading post to Malone's death while attempting to reach the flight car, Wallis indicated that he had enough material for his preliminary report but warned Steve he would be required to cover the same ground in greater detail when they reached Grand Central.

Until then he would be required to remain close to Clearwater and use his 'best efforts' to prevent her from becoming a threat to the security of the wagon-train or its crew.

In a somewhat blunter vein than usual Wallis said. 'The word is you've developed a relationship with this lump. I

339

don't know how much influence that gives you, but you should make it clear to her that if she steps out of line, *you* will be held responsible.'

'I don't think there'll be any problems, sir.'

Wallis's face creased with anxiety. 'I can't understand why Jake hasn't reported in. I hope they're okay.'

Steve shrugged. 'They flew into a tough situation. Hartmann's boys were doing a good job when I left but they were only just holding their own. That's why I suggested calling in Roz. Wish I hadn't now. If I'd known you weren't going to let me stay and help look after her I'd have kept my big mouth shut.'

'In this game you do what the big man says. I have to follow orders too.' Wallis eyed him, then said: 'Have you, ahh . . . heard from Roz?'

'No, sir.'

'Don't you find that kinda strange, in the circumstances? From what I understand, your mind-contacts are stress-related.'

'With her they have been. It doesn't always work the other way around. There's nothing *strange* in not hearing from her – but it *is* worrying.'

Wallis appeared satisfied with this explanation. 'But if she *does* come through . . .'

The lie came easily. 'You'll be the next to know . . .'

Wallis slapped the table top. 'Okay, listen, I'm assigning you to the blood-wagon. Report to the CMO – Michelle French. You'll be quartered with her staff until we reach Monroe-Wichita. The night duty-staff will keep an eye on your patient but otherwise she's all yours.'

'Thank you, sir.'

'Don't take your eyes off her.' Despite his anxiety, Wallis managed a grin. 'Having taken a look at her myself I imagine that won't cause you too much hardship.'

'No, sir.'

'Okay, get on it . . .'

Clearwater opened her eyes to find Steve sitting by her

bed, freshly scrubbed and in a clean set of fatigues. 'At last . . . How d'you feel?'

'Better for seeing you.'

'The doc tells me your arm will be out of that cast soon and that in a month or two you'll be on your feet again.' He touched the back of her hand. 'When I think of how you looked when . . .' He waved the thought away. 'But that's all over now.'

'For you, perhaps. Tell me, Cloud-Warrior – why did your masters save my life when, as we speak, they are killing my clanfolk?'

'That's because you're important. They hope to discover the secret of your power.'

'I am merely a channel. The power belongs to Talisman.'

'Yeah, well, that's their problem.' He took a firmer grip on her hand and gave her a warning glance. 'We've got other things to worry about.'

'Where is your kin-sister?'

'She's gone.'

In his mind's eye, Steve looked down at the M'Calls, settlement as he circled it like a bird. Flames and smoke from burning huts rose into the air. Many were already rings of grey ash. Around them lay the bodies of the nursing mothers and the young children the clan had left behind with a posse of She-Wolves to guard them.

The only moving figures wore camouflaged combat fatigues; a unit of Trail-Blazers had descended without warning to complete the destruction of the clan. And as the flying eye swooped lower, some of them turned their faces towards the sky and waved triumphantly.

Steve shared with Roz the sense of utter desolation. He lowered his head and pressed a thumb and finger against his closed eyes in an effort to wipe away the haunting images but they were branded on his soul.

This was all his work. This was why he had been called the Death-Bringer. Oh, Sweet Sky-Mother! When would it stop?!

Clearwater saw the pain in his eyes. 'I see it too,

Cloud-Warrior. I share your grief. But these are things we cannot speak of.'

Steve got the message, 'No. So . . . from now on, it's just you and me.'

Against the might of the Federation . . .

Not *just* you and me, thought Clearwater. But that news could wait. She nodded and squeezed his hand. 'The journey begins.'

'Yes . . .' *But how would it end?*

Despite Brickman's cooperative attitude, the debriefing failed to provide Wallis with an answer to the one big question. Whatever the final outcome of the present engagement, the Mute attack on The Lady had obviously been carefully prepared. But how had they known so far in advance where the wagon-train was going to be?

Brickman, outwardly none the worse for wear, was unable to add anything of significance to what Wallis already knew from the radio signals he and Malone had sent while on the run. He claimed to have done his utmost to warn them of the impending attack and although he repeatedly expressed the wish to have done better, could offer no explanation as to how the Mutes came to be lying in wait for The Lady.

The young man had suffered a double trauma – the assault on the wagon-train crewed by many of his former comrades and officers, and the loss of Malone and the other mexicans. Crushed by the guilt which haunts all survivors, he felt personally responsible for both and in an effort to unburden himself he confessed to not having reported that the M'Calls believed Cadillac was able to predict future events.

Wallis struck this veiled and somewhat embarrassed reference to seers and seeing-stones from the record. Even though he had been given access to what COLUMBUS knew about Mute summoners, Wallis shared his director's scepticism. The subject of 'gifted' Mutes and psionics was a speculative quicksand into which a rational man ventured at his peril.

In time, Brickman's mental scars would heal. He would come to realize that the responsibility for such disasters could rarely, if ever, be laid at the door of a single individual. The system might need to find a scapegoat but investigations showed it was a series of actions and decisions – often apparently unrelated – by a large number of people that created the circumstances in which something like this could occur.

Wallis counted himself doubly lucky – first, because he had been ordered to hold the fort instead of flying to the embattled wagon-train with the rest of his team and second, because the order to transfer Roz Brickman had come direct from Karlstrom's private terminal. With Nevill watching, Wallis had translated the coded letter strings into a clear on-screen message, then he had logged it into the comms-system memory to build up a complete record of the operation. When you were working on something this sensitive, it was always advisable to cover your ass.

A niggling thought triggered by the continuing silence from his men aboard The Lady prompted Wallis to double-check the log. It proved impossible to retrieve the record of Karlstrom's signal ordering Roz Brickman's transfer to The Lady. With growing desperation, Wallis spent several hours trying to coax the fateful order from the system's memory but-it was no longer there.

There were only two explanations for its disappearance, and both cast a dark shadow over his career prospects. He had either been the victim of another stunning illusion created by Roz Brickman or shafted by his superiors. Perhaps the message he and Nevill saw had only existed in their imagination for the length of time needed for them to act upon it. The alternative was altogether too depressing.

Ray Ramsay, the Red River Flight Ops Exec knocked on the outer wall of the skip and put his head around the open door. 'A message for you from the wagon-master. It looks as if we may have lost Hartmann's battalion. The Lady is ablaze from end to end.'

'Jeezuss!' Wallis drew a hand down his face.

'We don't know the full score. The support units that went in are still mopping up. Commander Fargo asked whether you would like to join him in his quarters to hear the news as it comes in.'

'Thank you. I'll be right along. Just got a little business to attend to.'

When Ramsay had gone, Wallis thought over all the moves, then closed the door to the cargo skip, sat down in front of the blank screen, switched his pistol to Full Auto, placed the barrel against his chest and shot himself.

CHAPTER FOURTEEN

'It's over. I just got word from CINC-TRAIN.' The President-General invited Karlstrom to take a seat by the blazing log-fire. The logs were modelled in cast-iron, the glowing ashes were flakes of mica, and the flames were fuelled by a gas line but the effect was real enough.

Karlstrom wondered why this news hadn't reached him through his own information network. He hated surprises. 'And The Lady?'

Jefferson stretched a hand towards the flames. 'A total loss I'm afraid. A lot of her crew ended up with their heads on sticks. The Mutes – and it has now been confirmed it *was* the M'Calls – formed up around the train and charged the Blazer battalions as they closed in for the kill.

'With the supporting firepower from the trains it was over in minutes, but as the Mutes went down, the wagon-train went up. Nobody quite knows how. The suggestion is a combination of napalm, fuel and explosives taken from the stocks on board. They must have laid it from end to end of the train . . .

'Anyway, it started a fire-storm that completely gutted her from end to end. Then she just . . . blew apart.'

'And Mr Snow?'

'No trace. But then there was virtually nothing left of the hundreds who must have died on board. Strange though . . .'

'Why?'

'When the final explosion occurred, it was accompanied by a severe earth tremor. The earth split four ways, with deep fissures running out towards True Grit and the other trains –'

'Oh, shee –'

The P-G held up his hand to quell Karlstrom's anxiety. 'It's okay, they didn't reach them. But it was enough to throw people to the ground . . . and there was some structural damage.'

'But nothing serious . . .'

'We'll get the score-sheet after they've been checked over at Fort Worth. We won't release this news of course. But what I wanted to tell you was this – when The Lady fireballed and the earth split open, a shaft of white light fringed with rainbow colours shot out of the middle. The trains caught it on their cameras. They reckon it was about two hundred feet high. Seemed to flash upwards then vanished –' Jefferson snapped his fingers. 'Curious, eh?'

'Very. Let's hope it was him. What about Cadillac and Roz Brickman?'

'No trace of them either. But since our young hero shows no visible signs of distress we must presume that she, at least, is still alive. A Skyhawk was seen to leave The Lady just before our counter-attack. We know that Cadillac can fly . . .'

'Ye-ess . . .'

The P-G raised his eyebrows expectantly but Karlstrom did not respond to the prompt. 'Assuming there was no prior collusion, they must have reached, ahh – how can one put it – an understanding? From what you told me about that young lady's abilities it's unlikely she would allow herself to be coerced.'

'No. But "understanding" might be putting it too strongly. Given the situation she was, quite literally, catapulted into, she may have decided to take the least line of resistance.'

The P-G chewed this over. 'You think she's still working for us . . .'

'I think we should assume that until there's evidence to the contrary. Brickman did his utmost to warn us that things had gone wrong and both Hartmann and Malone praised his efforts to help save the wagon-train. I think we should give them both the benefit of the doubt.'

346

'Mmmm, yes, I'm inclined to agree. There's just one thing I'd like to clear up. How, in the light of all this, did she come to be transferred to The Lady?'

Karlstrom spread his hands. 'I can't tell you, although I hope to have an answer soon. As you know I consulted you on this as a matter of some urgency. Wallis was pressing me for a decision. My orders were quite specific. Brickman and Malone were to fly to Red River and give us a complete sit-rep *before any further action was initiated*. I wanted to establish that whatever was left of Hartmann's battalion was still being properly led and capable of organized resistance.'

'Wise move. But you didn't okay the return trip . . .'

'No. You can imagine how I felt when I received a signal from Wallis confirming that Roz had been landed on The Lady.' Karlstrom gestured frustratedly. 'I just can't understand what got into him. And I still haven't had an adequate explanation.'

The P-G gazed into the fire for a moment then said: 'You're unlikely to get it. Wallis shot himself.'

Karlstrom hid his relief behind a look of total consternation. 'Wha-aat?! When?!'

'A few minutes ago . . .'

'I don't understand.' Karlstrom added a flash of anger. 'Why wasn't I told?!'

'Calm down, Ben. Isn't it obvious? With Wallis gone and the rest of your team missing, Fargo didn't have a direct line to you. No one else on Red River had the codes to operate that equipment.'

'No, of course . . .'

'He had to go through CINC-TRAIN. I told them I'd break the news. But it means we'll never know what prompted him to make that decision. Still, these things happen. We've got Clearwater, Brickman's back on the team, Roz – we hope – is well placed to put Cadillac in the frame, Mr Snow may have finally shot his bolt and we've taken out the M'Calls.'

'You're right. It's not all bad news.'

'Except for the fact that it cost us a wagon-train.' The

347

P-G's face clouded. 'Well, we can live with that – and thanks to your clever little scam it wasn't Red River. That really *would* have been a disaster.'

'Nevertheless we did lose a whole Trail-Blazer battalion.'

'Hartmann's battalion. There were some good men in it but that's how it goes. They ran out of luck from the first day they ran into the Plainfolk. Let's hope their demise will make the other wagon-masters realize there's no mileage to be gained out of supporting lost causes. If his Blazers had been on the ball, that train could never have been taken.' Jefferson's mouth tightened. 'But it seems we won't ever know how that happened either.'

'Looks that way . . .'

'Never mind. I refuse to be downhearted.' The P-G rose from his chair. 'We may have fumbled a pass but we're still in the game.'

And I'm still on the team, thought Karlstrom, already on his feet. How long, he asked himself, would he be able to conceal the full story of his own involvement in this semi-fiasco?

The chain of administrative orders which had led to the issue of the explosives used by the M'Calls against The Lady had been 'sanitized'. With the train now a shattered, burnt-out shell in enemy territory, no one was going to be checking it for tell-tale clues that, under other circumstances would have pointed to the use of Federation PX and not the black powder used by the Iron Masters.

Unfortunately, other people in AMEXICO had been involved in covering those tracks. Could they be relied upon?

With the order to transfer Roz from Red River to The Lady, Karlstrom knew he was on firmer ground. The message, routed directly from his own computer terminal to the comms-system operated by Wallis, had contained a code-virus which caused the message to self-destruct when it was transferred into memory. When Wallis keyed in the instruction 'SAVE TO DISK', the order concerning Roz disappeared from the screen and – despite the visual confirmation that it had been safely transferred to the hard-disk – vanished into thin air.

Despite the risks, the opportunity to swap Roz for Steve had been too good to miss. Karlstrom didn't want Roz and her so-called psionic powers back inside the Federation. And especially not anywhere near AMEXICO. If she intended to betray the Federation then it was better to deal with her at a distance. If, on the other hand, she was as loyal as she claimed to be, there was always a chance that someone else might use her mental abilities to spy on him.

Someone like his cousin George Washington Jefferson the 31st. Karlstrom, a voracious reader, was aware of an ancient quotation which – as head of the secret organization dedicated to the protection of the President-General – was directly applicable to just such a situation: *Quis custodiet ipsos Custodes?* – Who is to guard the guardians themselves?

No. Steve Brickman might be devious but he was not a threat. The young man was brave, resourceful and gifted – but he also had a certain weakness which Karlstrom believed could be exploited to keep him in line until – like most pawns – he became expendable.

Five days later, Karlstrom found himself back in the Oval Office with the young man in question. And this time, there was no trace of the Mute whose painted presence had so disturbed the wagon-master of Red River. Brickman, immaculately dressed in a blue wing-man's uniform, clear-eyed and clear-skinned, with his blonde hair trimmed into a regulation crew-cut would have been a credit to any passing-out parade. To have turned this half-breed into a Tracker from head to toe was an amazing feat . . .

Karlstrom tuned back into what the P-G was saying.

'. . . while the operation could be said to have mis-fired, the failure is not yours, Steven. Overall, taking into account that this was your first assignment, we think your

349

performance has been outstanding. Your achievements in Ne-Issan deserve special commendation, and it gives me great pleasure to be the one to tell you that as from today, you have been promoted to the rank of Captain.'

Brickman who had been sitting rigidly to attention, with his parade cap aligned neatly on his knees, jumped up from his chair. 'Sir! I, uhh – thank you sir!'

'Thanks don't come into it. You deserve it. Right, Ben?'

'Yes, sir . . .' Karlstrom rose as Jefferson came round his desk, took hold of Brickman's hand and shoulder. The fatherly gesture that never failed.

'Steven, I don't want any secrets between us. That's why I'm going to tell you that there were times when we had grave doubts about you. We have never thought you would deliberately betray the Federation but we were worried that your mind might have become contaminated by some of the experiences you have undergone. Experiences that might have affected your judgement – altered your perception of the world we're trying to build.'

Jefferson injected a more cheerful note. 'But that's all in the past, isn't it Ben? This young man has been given a clean bill of health!'

'Absolutely . . .'

Jefferson firmed up his grip on Steve's shoulder as he accompanied him to the 'stile. 'We are going to give your life a new dimension, Steven. You will find that loyalty, allied to the courage and ability you have displayed is handsomely rewarded. And it is my belief that you will prove worthy of the confidence we have in you. Keep the faith, Steven. Never falter in your devotion to the First Family!'

'I won't, sir!'

When they emerged into the outer suite of offices, Karlstrom turned to Steve and offered his hand. 'Congratulations. How do you feel?'

'About the promotion and everything? It's incredible, sir. But I still feel bad about Roz. If I'd stayed with her –'

Karlstrom cut him short. 'You were following orders.

350

It was my people that fouled up. And the real sickener is we'll never know why. Even so, it's not all bad news. Since you're looking bright and healthy that would seem to indicate she's still alive. Right?'

Steve didn't hesitate. 'They both are, sir.'

'Is Cadillac holding her prisoner?'

'He thinks he is.' Once again he didn't bat an eyelid.

'Good man . . .' Karlstrom patted Steve's arm. 'Stay in touch.'

'I will, sir. What about Clearwater, sir?'

'Keep up the visits. Unless you have other duties, you have unlimited access, day or night. You're an essential part of the get-well programme.'

'Thank you, sir.'

'Did, ahh – Clearwater give you the good news?'

'Sir . . .?'

'I see. She didn't. I wonder why? Well, there's no point in keeping you in suspense. The surgeons on board Red River managed to save the baby.'

'Baby . . .?' The news took Steve completely by surprise. 'I – I don't understand –'

'Ohh . . . isn't it yours?'

Steve felt totally confused. A confused babble of distant voices filled his brain and were submerged by a roaring sound. He felt the blood pounding through the arteries close to his ears. 'No, sir! I – I mean . . . how could it be?!'

It was the President-General who was the sole progenitor of humankind . . . the father of all life within the Federation . . .

Karlstrom smiled. It was not often he managed to unsettle this artful sonofabitch. 'You've only just begun to discover what you are capable of. That's why you're on the Special Treatment List. Do you think everything that's happened to you so far is due to good luck and your winning smile?'

'Uhh, no, I – I had no idea, sir!'

'Well, you've managed to get this far, don't jump the rails. There are interesting times ahead.'

'Will I still be working for, uhh – your department, sir?'

'Yes, you will,' laughed Karlstrom. 'You and I still have a great deal of unfinished biz –' He broke off as his eyes were drawn to someone behind Steve's shoulder.

Steve turned to see a dark-haired woman walking towards them. She wore the silver grey and blue uniform that marked her out as a member of the First Family.

It was the young President of the Board of Assessors that had tried him for desertion. The woman who had stripped him of his wings and sentenced him from three years to life in the A-Levels. He had guessed that she was Family during the trial and he was right. The trial, the sentence, the early reprieve, the chance to win back his coveted wings . . . it had all been a set-up. Nothing was what it seemed.

Steve jumped to attention and threw a parade-ground salute as the woman with the grey eyes, the oval face and the wide firm mouth reached him. Her sleeves carried the stripes of a commander topped by the inverted chevron – an exclusive mark of the First Family which conferred automatic seniority over the commanders of ordinary Federation units.

She acknowledged his salute with the casual assurance of someone who knows there is not the slightest chance of being hauled up on a charge of indiscipline and turned to Karlstrom. 'Ben, I'm sorry! I was held up!'

'That's okay. Let me introduce you.'

The grey eyes fixed on Steve's. 'We've already met, haven't we Captain?'

'Yesssir-ma'am! I believe so!' News travels fast, thought Steve. The extra stripe he'd been awarded was not even on his sleeve.

'Yes, but he doesn't know who you are.' Karlstrom did the honours. 'This is Commander Franklynne Jefferson. She will be your host and guide over the next few days.'

'Yess-SURR!'

'Fine. We've completed the formalities. Now relax.

You're among friends.' Franklynne Jefferson offered her hand. 'It's Steve, isn't it?'

'Yes, sir-ma'am.'

'Oh, dear . . .' She sought help from Karlstrom. 'What does one have to do to get this man to unbend?'

'Give him time . . .'

She tried again. 'We're going to a place called Cloud-lands, Steve. And by the time we get there, I shall expect you to call me Fran. Think you can manage that?'

Nothing in his wildest dreams could have prepared Steve for what was to happen following that encounter outside the Oval Office. After an elevator ride which his stomach told him was in an upwards direction, Steve stepped out into a large lobby with several exits – the walls and doors of which were covered with panels of wood similar to Karlstrom's office.

The first surprise was finding the lobby manned by two smooth-skinned Mutes dressed in dark clothes cut in a style Steve had never seen before. Both Mutes had vari-coloured skins but were straight-boned, with no cranial lumps. Yearlings. One male, one female.

The male – whose greying hair was cut short and brushed flat across his head – wore three pieces of black clothing – trousers, tucked into calf-length boots, and a long kind of tunic, with a tighter-fitting tunic with a V-neck underneath. This garment, buttoned down the front, reached to just below the waist and had broad diagonal gold stripes woven into the black. Instead of the universal T-shirt, he wore a shirt of white material drawn into a high tight band around the neck, with a looser, curly piece of the same material running from the throat down into the V-neck of the gold-striped tunic, and cuffs that poked out from the sleeves of the long, open garment covering it.

The clothes of the female Mute were equally strange. She wore a cap of white cloth which covered most of her hair, and an elaborate curly-edged spotless white apron – a fancy cousin to the straight-cut style worn by kitchen staff on the mess-decks – and fastened at the back with a wide bow. Underneath she wore a black, sleeved garment puffed out at the shoulders but tight on the rest of the arm. The tunic had a similar high collar but in black with a frilly white liner. The waist was drawn in then came over the hips in a slim bell-shape and went all the way down to the floor.

Extraordinary . . .

Fran addressed the male Mute. 'Joshua, this is my guest, Captain Brickman. Will you help him change into the uniform I gave you this morning, then show him upstairs?'

The Mute inclined his head respectfully. 'My pleasure, ma'am.' He indicated a door on the far side of the lobby with a white-gloved hand. 'This way, Captain . . .'

Steve hesitated, seeking guidance from Fran.

She smiled. 'Go on. Off you go. I'll see you later.'

The changing room had a marble floor and walls and the luxurious fittings and furniture he had seen in the Oval Office and the adjoining suites and corridors of the White House. Steve showered and dried himself on large soft white towels then emerged to find a new set of clothing laid out of him. The pale grey briefs were familiar enough, the T-shirt was replaced by a sleeveless under-garment with a curving neckline. Mid-grey socks. A white shirt similar to the one Joshua was wearing but with just a neat high collar band. So far so good . . .

Next came a pair of mid-grey trousers with a line of yellow braid running down the outside seams. Then a long grey tunic with an overlapping rear split and a high collar that buttoned down to the waist. The sleeves were decorated with captain's rank stripes in the same yellow braid as the trousers. And then there were the boots, of soft black leather.

Joshua coughed politely. 'The trousers go outside, Cap'n.'

'Got it. Thanks . . .' Steve corrected the mistake then reached for the grey stetson with the yellow crossed swords parade badge of the Trail-Blazer Division and placed it carefully on his head with the aid of a mirror.

'If I may, sir . . .' Joshua adjusted the tilt, then went over to the table to fetch the sword and helped Steve fasten it around his waist. It resembled the sword on his hat badge but Steve had never seen a real one before.

'What is this?'

'It's a cavalry sword, Cap'n.'

'Looks pretty old.'

'It is. Been in the family for centuries.'

'You look pretty old too, Joshua. How long you been here?'

'Me, Cap'n? I was born here in Cloudlands.'

Steve checked himself in the mirror. 'I have to tell you this feels very strange. What is this outfit I'm wearing?'

'That's what we call Confederate grey, Cap'n. The uniform of a southern officer and gentleman.'

Steve shook his head. 'Can't say I'm any the wiser.'

'That's as may be, Cap'n. But you look mighty fine to me. And I'm sure that Missy Fran, she's going to be real proud to be seen walking on your arm.'

Joshua ushered him back into the lobby and led the way towards a set of double doors which, when opened, revealed a flight of wide marble steps. Inviting Steve to follow, he led the way to a similar set of doors at the top then through into a spacious room filled with light from tall white-framed windows. Huge clusters of what looked like ice crystals hung from the high, sculptured ceiling. There were carpets covering sections of the gleaming wood floor, ornate chairs covered in richly coloured cloth, a magnificent marble fireplace, framed portraits and mirrors on the patterned walls.

Steve turned full circle, head raised, mouth open like a first time tourist in the Big Apple. He gestured towards the trees and flowered gardens beyond the windows. 'Columbus! Is that computer-generated?!'

'I don't understand, Cap'n.'

Steve stepped towards the open glass panelled doors and peeked outside. There was no screen. What lay outside was part of the overground. Neat, sculpted, ordered – but beautiful nevertheless.

Joshua smiled at Steve's evident bewilderment. 'Make yourself at home, Cap'n. Take a seat – or maybe you'd prefer to walk on the verandah.' Joshua indicated a polished table with bottles and jugs of liquid and cups made of the same sparkling ice-crystal material. 'May I offer you some refreshment?'

'No – but those cups and bottles . . . are they made of clear plastic?'

Joshua chuckled. 'No, Cap'n. Them cups you're referring to is what we call glasses. Same stuff as in them there windows only this –' He picked one up and turned it so that it caught the light, '– is much prettier and finer. It's what they call cut crystal – see?'

'Yeah, thanks, Joshua. Must seem kinda stupid.' Steve swept a hand around the room. 'This is all so new.'

'New?!' Joshua chuckled again. 'This ol' place's been standin' close on two hundred years!' The Mute indicated a circular button push on the wall. 'With your permission, Cap'n, I'll leave you be. If you want anythin' just ring.'

'Oh, yeah – thanks . . .'

The Mute bowed. 'Missy Fran'll join you shortly. She'll be in the yellow I expect.'

Joshua, who had served Fran's family since she was a child, was familiar with the routine that accompanied the elevation of tall, strong-shouldered young men – Fran called them her 'beaus' – from the subterranean world to the elegance of Cloudlands.

When she appeared, she *was* dressed in yellow, but the transformation was so startling she was not immediately recognizable. The silver and blue uniform had been replaced by a frilled and layered costume which gave prominence to her breasts, hugged her rib-cage, squeezed her waist then flared outwards with draped folds to the ground. An outfit which, a century and a half before the Holocaust, was known as a 'walking dress'.

She also had a lot more hair. The neatly combed bob

had been augmented by matching braids, ringlets, and a soft bun extending onto the nape of her neck. Her face looked softer, her eyes larger, her lips redder.

Fran twirled around in front of Steve. 'How do I look?'

Steve eventually found his voice. 'Amazing . . .'

'And so do you, Captain Brickman. Raise your right elbow.'

Steve offered it to her awkwardly.

Fran unfurled a matching parasol, took his arm and led him towards the verandah. 'Come . . . walk with me.'

Yes sir-ma'am. . .

Anyone with access to the cinematic archives of the 20th century – a privilege enjoyed by members of the First Family – would have immediately recognized Steve's surroundings. Walking into that light-filled room with its sumptuous furnishings was like entering one of the interior scenes from 'Gone With The Wind'.

Like the closely-guarded domains reserved for the top brass of pre-Holocaust Russia, Cloudlands was a vast chunk of real estate reserved for the exclusive use of the First Family.

But this was no space-age colony shielded from overground radiation by protective bubbles. On these landscaped acres, the First Family had lovingly recreated the mid-19th century sugar-plantation splendour of the Deep South. Pristine white mansions, with colonnaded porticos, nestled among trees and lakes, surrounded by immaculate lawns, formal gardens, arbours, fountains, drives and shaded avenues, tastefully furnished in a style that echoed the French colonial past of Louisiana and Mississippi, and staffed by an army of servants, grooms and retainers; liveried Mutes – the 29th century equivalent of the negro slave.

There were no wheelies here. Horses, and horse-drawn carriages with Mute drivers carried the privileged inhabitants wherever they wanted to go. Pride of place was given to the railway with its hand-built replicas of period locomotives and rolling-stock spanning the glorious days of steam. But they weren't the only anachronisms: the background lighting was powered by electricity, tv screens and computer keyboards were artfully concealed in antique cuboards and desks, and the open skies were patrolled by First Family wing-men flying silver Skyhawks.

On the ground, however, authenticity was the keynote. The men were dressed in uniforms of the Confederate Army and the women as 'southern belles', but both changed clothes to suit the occasion or the time of day, donning what they called 'evening dress' when the sun went down.

For the men this meant a more decorative uniform in sober colours, or dark 'civilian' clothes; the women emerged in off the shoulder dresses with deep neck-lines that exposed the tops of their breasts, layered elbow-length sleeves and long gloves. The lower parts of these evening dresses were even more extravagant in their detailing and dimensions – wide, sweeping skirts with trailing extensions at the rear, supported by layers of hooped petticoats.

Fran was an immensely agreeable and informative guide but it was a lot to take in all at once – even for Steve.

The contrast with the uniformed monotony of the underground Federation could not have been greater. Steve had to keep reminding himself that this wasn't a dream. This was for real – and yet this reality was tinted with a kind of madness.

How long had this been going on? Was this what count-less generations of Trackers – including Poppa-Jack – had sweated, slaved and died for? So that an already over-privileged elite could enjoy a lavish fantasy existence while the rest of the population lived in neon-lit concrete burrows where the biggest event in the calendar was a trip to the walled-in acres of John Wayne Plaza? Compared to Cloudlands, the fabled Plaza was nothing more than a marbled prison exercise yard.

Steve kept his feelings to himself, but with the knowl-edge of who he now was, he couldn't help identifying with the smooth-boned Mutes who did the fetching and carrying, who were ever-present but whose quiet-mannered discretion rendered them almost invisible. Part of the woodwork. Compared to the Iron-Feet, their Plainfolk brothers in Ne-Issan, these Mute yearlings were in a gilded cage, but one day they too would be free.

Oh, yes, brothers . . .

But now it was time to watch and to listen. There was much to see and a great deal to learn . . .

Like on that first evening when Steve found himself invited to sit next to Fran at a long cloth-covered table decorated with bowls of flowers and silver candlesticks, sparkling glassware, polished metal knives and forks and ceramic plates with coloured patterns round the rim. The chairs around the table were occupied by twenty men and women the nearest of which addressed Steve with an easy familiarity. The food was good, the wine – quite different in taste to *sake* – was agreeably liberating, the company convivial and when Fran revealed that he had been to Ne-Issan on 'Family business', they listened with genuine interest to his descriptions of life in the Eastern Lands.

By the end of the evening, his feelings of hostility had waned considerably. Steve had not abandoned his desire to pierce the innermost secrets of the First Family. The truth had to be revealed. After Mr Snow's revelations, they were not just the top layer of an oppressive regime, they were the enemy. They and everything they stood for had to be swept away, but that was an immense undertaking that could not be accomplished overnight. In the meantime, however much he might deplore the flagrant unfairness of the system, it would be foolish not to take advantage of what was on offer . . .

Around eleven pm, the after-dinner conversation groups broke up. As the guests bade each other goodnight and departed to their own rooms or to other houses, Joshua, the Mute servant, led Steve upstairs to the large bedroom which had been set aside for his use. The curtained windows opened out on the front lawn, and through them, Steve saw a coach and pair, with bright yellow lamps, rattle away down the curving gravel drive. Animated voices floated up from the porch below. He caught a glimpse of someone in a yellow dress and thought he heard Fran laughing . . .

A log fire like the one in the Oval Office blazed cheerfully in the hearth. The large bed, which had a post at each corner and a cloth canopy, looked soft and inviting. There would be no bug-uglies in that.

After Steve had donned a bathrobe, Joshua took his uniform away to be freshened and pressed, leaving what he called a dressing-gown and a nightshirt laid out neatly on the foot of the bed. Crystal decanters of wine, peach brandy and a smooth, amber-coloured alcohol called Southern Comfort stood on a silver tray with a selection of glasses.

Steve went into the bathroom and took a shower. As he stood under the warm spray, his body suffused with a sense of well-being, he reflected on the time he had spent among the Mutes and the Iron Masters, the pleasures and privations of life on the overground and within the Federation.

It seemed incredible that four different worlds with such contrasting life-styles could co-exist within a few hundred miles of each other: hi-tech gadgetry and stone-age savagery, total freedom and slavery, individuality and restrictive conformity, equal rights and overbearing discrimination – sexual *and* racial, rigid hierarchies and relaxed anarchies. Why did people have to choose one over the other? Why was there no middle way?

When Steve emerged from the shower, he found Fran occupying the left hand side of the bed. Her head and naked shoulders were propped against two of the four over-sized pillows. One hand held a glass of brandy, the other held a smoking reaf. The soft insistent beat of a blackjack tape floated out of a hidden speaker. Below ground, people went to the wall for peddling this kind of shit.

'Surprised . . .?'

'Not really.' Steve searched for a suitably ingratiating

follow-up. 'I can't think of a better way to end an unforgettable day.' *Yukkkk-hhh* . . .

'It's just the beginning, Stevie.' Fran patted the empty place next to her.

Steve walked around the bed and reached for the night-shirt.

'You won't need that.'

'Just clearing the decks.' He gathered up the long loose shirt and the dressing-gown and put them on the low wooden chest at the foot of the bed.

Fran proved to be an ardent sexual partner. Their coupling reminded him of his solitary encounter with Donna Lundkwist. Donna whose life had ended with a kiss and a knife in her throat. And like Donna, Fran started out making all the running, but when Steve delivered the goods, she ended up tender and grateful.

'How did it feel, Stevie?'

'Well, ma'am, I –'

'Fran!!'

'Sorry! I –'

'Never jacked up a member of the First Family before.' Fran treated him to a conspiratorial smile. 'No need to answer. I know everything there is to know about you.'

I wonder . . .

She pulled his head closer and whispered in his ear. 'What was it like with her – Clearwater? The same? Better?'

'No . . . just different.'

'In what way? What did she do that I didn't do?'

'Nothing, it was –'

'Tell me! Ohh, I can feel you getting hard again! Are you thinking about doing it with her? Oh, come on! Give it to me! Oh, yes! She squeezed you like that, Stevie?'

Almost, almost . . . Christo!

'Why was it different? Was it because she said she loved you? Is that it, Stevie? Do you want to be loved? Would you like me to say I love you?'

361

That question, that word, on *her* lips, sent a shiver through him. He raised himself up and began to withdraw.

Fran locked her legs across the small of his back, and hung on tight round his neck, thrusting her pelvis hard against his. 'No! Stay there! If you knew how long I've waited for this! Hooh, baby! C'mon, give it to me! Gimme all of it!'

Steve suppressed the feelings of self-loathing and betrayal.

Yessir-ma'am. If this is what it takes to get where I want, you GOT it!

An hour or so later, when they'd screwed each other to a standstill, and she'd explored every inch of his body with her lips, tongue and fingers, they lay in each other's arms, their skin glazed with sweat. Steve was having difficulty staying awake. Fran brought him back to life with a playful bite on the shoulder.

'Jeezuss!'

'It's all right. I haven't drawn blood.' Fran kissed it better. 'Mmmm . . . you smell and taste like a man should.' She offered her throat. 'Taste me.'

Steve took a sample. Honey with a dash of salt . . .'

'Do you like it?'

'Yeah. Tastes good.' He put his cheek against hers and buried a yawn in the pillow.

Fran took hold of one hand and slid it between her thighs. 'And did you like this?'

'Delicious . . .' *Didn't this dill ever stop?!*

She twisted her body around so that she was looking down on him. 'Did it shock you – me talking about love? It's a word the Mutes use, isn't it?'

'Yes. But it wasn't so much shocking as, well . . . unexpected.'

'Because of who I am?'

'That was part of it, yes.'

'Call me Fran. Say my name! Keep your hand there and whisper it in my ear.' When he had repeated it several times with as much feeling as he could muster, she said:

'I love your voice. You know that? Can't you feel what it does to me?'

Steve didn't answer. He knew he was in bed with a member of the First Family. Not just *any* member of the First Family – a Jefferson. This kookie was related to the President-General! This couldn't be just a reward for services rendered. What the hell was going on?

'Do you think I'm beautiful?'

'Uhh, well, yehh, y'know –'

'That's another Mute word, isn't it? I bet you know lots, mmh?'

'I was out there for quite a while . . .'

'You'll find we use lots of Mute words up here, Stevie. And quite a few I bet you've never heard of.'

'Always willing to learn . . .'

'Good. I'll teach you things you've never dreamed of.' Fran brought her mouth to his for a last tender, teasing kiss. 'Did you enjoy doing it with me?'

'Yeah, it was terrific.' *What the heck was he supposed to say?*

'Would you like to do it again?'

Aww, jeezuss . . . 'You mean now?'

'No. But soon. And *often*. She gave his starting handle an affectionate squeeze then leapt out of bed and went into the bathroom.

Steve heard the swish of the shower. He pulled the bedclothes over his nakedness and reflected on what was happening to him and what might happen next. The session with Fran, although enjoyable on a purely physical level – which in the past was all that any Tracker would expect – left Steve feeling empty and vaguely ashamed of his opportunism.

In the Federation, the sexual act was one of the few things to which no guilt was attached. No involvement was expected by either party beyond the brief physical proximity required for the act to take place. Mutual consent was all that was needed; desire, the need to temporarily relieve the basic sexual drive, was the only emotional element.

It had been different with Clearwater. The intensity of his feelings – feelings which she returned in equal measure – had given a new dimension to their physical relationship, enriching what, for him, had previously been a meaningless exercise involving his body but which, until then, had never engaged his heart and mind.

Jacking up Fran had merely served to remind him of what he was missing. Clearwater had never claimed exclusive rights to his body. Indeed, for her, possession of the body was of minor importance. What counted was to whom you gave your heart and soul. And it was true – although it hadn't stopped him hating the idea of Clearwater allowing Consul-General Nakane Toshiba to instal her in his island love-nest.

Maybe it *was* the will of Talisman. Her liaison with the jap had certainly led to their escape. But it was good ol' Brickman S.R. who had blown the Consul-General out of the sky. Watching his smouldering body fall to earth had been a sweet moment. Yes . . .

Clearwater would not have felt the same need for revenge against a third party. She had never probed the intimate nature of his relationship with Roz. She was too wise. She had a serene confidence in the power of Talisman, in the pre-destined, ordered nature of existence.

In her world, human frailty – except where it flagrantly transgressed a blood-bond sealed before the elders – was overlooked or generously forgiven. What counted was the purity of the spirit, the nobility of the soul. Which was fortunate, because it let Steve off the hook.

Trackers were totally promiscuous, but due to the nature of their society, the word 'promiscuity' had been stripped of any moral connotation. In the pre-Holocaust world, copulation may have been raised to an art form and accorded the status of an inalienable civil right for commercial and political reasons, but in the Federation its importance as an essential activity was on a par with evacuating the bowels and was usually discharged with a similar lack of ceremony.

By demoting sex while allowing a continued free-for-all, and by removing the word-concept 'love' from the Tracker vocabulary, the First Family effectively eliminated the basis for personal relationships between individual men and women. Widespread and persistent sterility had already destroyed the nuclear family; what remained was a collective identity based on the squad, the block, the battalion, the division. Loyalty, a sense of comradeship and allegiance, was directed upwards through the system towards the figure at the pinnacle of power – the President-General.

Because of this, Steve was not burdened by guilt but he felt diminished. He'd been given a privileged glimpse of the system from the top down – a system that was not only harsh and unjust at the bottom, was not only built on lies, but whose leaders now stood revealed as corrupt and crazy.

For centuries they had held out a dream of a bright future and here they were living in a self-deceiving dream-world that belonged to the distant past! And his sense of shame was increased by the knowledge that if Fran required his services again, he would answer the call without hesitation. Would do whatever had to be done.

The idea that jacking up a high-flying member of the First Family could lead to advancement seemed, on the face of it, preposterous, but if that was part of the deal – what the hell?

The higher he got up the wire, the more chance he would have of getting even with those who had helped to shaft him. And to that list were now added those who had manipulated his life and twisted his mind. Yes . . . given time, he'd get them all . . .

When the hospital orderly left after cleaning her room, Clearwater noticed that the wheeled table carrying the computer terminal had not been pushed back into its proper place. It now lay within reach. Leaning sideways, she stretched out her good left arm, caught the edge of the table with her fingertips, pulled it towards her then manoeuvered it round until the keyboard and screen faced the bed.

Thanks to Steve's winter schooling she could now read and write. And on the wagon-train and now, in her new home which her senses told her was not far underground, she had watched medical staff tap the keys to call up or record information. This machine was part of a spider's web of power that gave life to the Federation. And at the centre of this web lay something or someone called COLUMBUS. She knew this because the Cloud-Warrior had talked boastfully of these things to Mr Snow.

Before his eyes and heart had been opened . . .

She studied the keyboard and pressed the HELP button.

Letters appeared on the screen: DO YOU WISH TO (A) TRANSMIT DATA (B) RECEIVE DATA (C) USE MATH FUNCTION (D) CONSULT LOCAL ARCHIVES? – SELECT LETTER AND PRESS ENTER.

Clearwater selected (A) – Transmit Data.

The screen cleared and a new message appeared: ENTER NAME OF RECIPIENT, UNIT, DEPART- MENT OR DIVISION AND ADDRESS CODE OF RECEIVING TERMINAL.

She tapped out the letters carefully: C-O-L-U-M-B-U-S . . .

There was a pause then: THE CENTRAL CORTEX CANNOT BE ADDRESSED FROM THIS WORK- STATION WITHOUT AUTHORIZATION CODE. INSERT ID-CARD OR ENTER PASSWORD.

T-A-L-I-S-M-A-N . . .

THE SYSTEM RESPONDED: PASSWORD NOT RECOGNIZED. ENTER FULL NAME AND NUMBER.

T-A-L-I-S-M-A-N . . .

A NEW MESSAGE FLASHED ON TO THE SCREEN: UNAUTHORIZED SYSTEM ACCESS IS A LISTED OFFENCE. THE LOCATION OF

THIS WORKSTATION HAS NOW BEEN REPORTED. TO AVOID A MORE SERIOUS CHARGE YOU SHOULD REMAIN THERE AND AWAIT THE ARRIVAL OF INTERNAL SECURITY.

CLEARWATER SIGNED OFF: G-O . . . T-O . . . H-E-L-L . . .

An insistent bleeper alarm began to sound. Not deafening, but loud enough to be heard in the corridor outside.

Clearwater pushed the trolley away from the bed and pretended to be asleep as a medical orderly came in and swore quietly under her breath. 'The idiot . . . why can't he leave things the way he found them?'

Another medic poked her head round the door. 'Trouble?'

'That bloody cleaner!' said the first. 'Look at the way he's left this! And I see this thing's playing up again.' She cleared the screen, switched the terminal off and straightened up the table then came to check on Clearwater as her eyes fluttered open.

'What's happening . . .?'

'Nothing. Relax. Just let me fix your pillows . . . There. You all right?'

'Yes . . .'

'Good. Go back to sleep.'

Contrary to the stern warning displayed on the screen, the incident had not been reported, and the bleeper alarm was programmed to turn itself off after sixty seconds. Centuries of experience had shown that only a minority of youthful pranksters were frozen into fearful immobility by the order to remain by the computer terminal. Everyone else promptly left the scene.

Like the tacit approval of rainbow-grass, the computer network controlled by COLUMBUS also acted as a safety-valve. The number, provenance and frequency of nuisance calls were noted for statistical purposes but the manpower and other technical resources needed to follow up the thousands of violations were simply not available.

The efforts of the Federation's computer security units

were directed towards the apprehension of those trying to penetrate or corrupt the data and control circuits as part of a purely criminal conspiracy, and 'moles' – political subversives living inside the Federation but outside the eco-system maintained and policed by COLUMBUS: people who were trying to access services to get what they needed to stay alive while evading the checks and controls that would have brought the Provos down on their necks.

For the moment it did not matter that the first attempt to contact COLUMBUS had failed. The terminal in her hospital room had enabled Clearwater to sense its all-pervading presence, its purpose, its power, its intelligence.

This was why she had been sent into the dark world of the sand-burrowers. First, she had to regain her strength and then, in a way which would be revealed to her, she had to make contact with this soulless entity and destroy it.

Karlstrom watched the President-General walk to the high curving window behind his blue leather-topped desk.

In front of the centre curtains, a large eagle with out-spread wings, carved out of gleaming rosewood, was poised on a waist-high plinth. Between the eagle and the blue curtains were two crossed poles draped with the flag of the Amtrak Federation and Old Glory.

Jefferson rubbed his hand over the eagle's head as one might touch a good luck charm, gazed briefly out of the window at a stunning view of Kentucky Blue-Grass country then waved Karlstrom into his usual seat.

Karlstrom hovered, waiting for the P-G to sink his solid rear end into his high-backed chair. In the Oval Office no one sat while the P-G was standing.

'Sit down, Ben. Let's skip the protocol. I need to walk around for this one.'

Karlstrom subsided, and watched Jefferson gaze out across the wooded slopes towards the sunlit hills. The clarity of the image was amazing. This was the way America had once looked. Green and beautiful.

'Ben, I'm going to tell you something which may put your mind at rest. You must have wondered why we've invested so much time and resources in young Brickman and his sister – which, by the way, she isn't. With people dying for the Federation every day, two more, two less – what's the difference? Well, they're something of an exception and I think it's time you joined the club.

The P-G began to pace slowly to and fro, circling the desk and Karlstrom's chair. Karlstrom followed him with his eyes.

'As you know, we've been breeding Mutes for ex- perimental work at the Life Institute for close on a hundred and fifty years. The stated objective was to find the genetic key to their longevity and immunity to radiation in the hope that we could transfer those benefits to our own people. If we could increase the average life expectancy from forty to sixty years it would give us a fifty per cent increase in our skill base and productivity – and that would release more people for overground operations.

'Since you're one of the Family and bright enough to be the head of AMEXICO, it probably won't come as much of a surprise when I tell you that over the years we've fed a large number of what we call farm-boys into the units engaged on overground operations – the Trail-Blazer Division, QMGC, FINTEL, SIG-INT and AMEXICO. Not yearlings – super-straights, smooth-boned and clear- skinned. Just like you and me.

'When I say a large number, don't get the wrong idea. The percentage of farm-boys – and girls – in these units has always averaged less than ten per cent. We've always put the cream of the crop through the Flight Academy. The best of the rest have gone onto the wagon-trains. That's why people like Brickman have performed so well.

'The overground is in their blood. They can handle the vast open spaces and they don't pull TRICS. But

369

sometimes the conditioning fails and they get the urge to cut and run. They become renegades. But they're the lucky ones. Ordinary cee-bees who go over the side eventually succumb to radiation-sickness.'

'But we don't . . .'

'No. But then we're Family.'

Karlstrom nodded. 'Right. So the overground is still radioactive.'

'Oh, yes. The level of contamination is less than it was a century ago, but it's still dangerously high. Even if they could overcome their fear of open-spaces, extended exposure would prove fatal for the majority of our present population.' The P-G smiled. 'Did you think this was just another lie – like pinning the blame for it on the Mutes?'

'No,' said Karlstrom. 'But it's a useful control mechanism. If the atmospheric radiation dropped to a safe level tomorrow, I certainly wouldn't tell anybody, would you?'

The P-G smiled again. 'That's why you and I get on so well, Ben.' He sat down in his high-backed chair, laid his forearms on the table and clasped his hands together.

'What I have to tell you relates to OPERATION SQUARE-DANCE. Some of our home-baked super-straights have also been "gifted".'

'Steve and Roz Brickman . . .'

Jefferson nodded. 'They're among the most out-standing examples to date, but the research programme has been running for several decades. And as a result of intensive investigation of their physiology down to the molecular level and beyond, we've discovered certain "markers" in their genes. We still don't know the how and why of Mute magic but we can now identify those individuals who have the potentiality to become wordsmiths, summoners and seers.'

'Or all three . . .'

The P-G nodded approvingly. 'You've got it in one, Ben. We believe we now know the genetic markers that the Talisman would have to possess. Now that does not necessarily mean that someone with these markers will *be* the Talisman, but they would have the *potentiality*.'

'I think I see where this is leading . . .'

'Do you? I wonder. We've known about Steve and Roz's genetic make-up since Day One, and now we have Clearwater's. Tissue samples were flown to the Life Institute soon after the Red River medics got her on the operating table. The unknown element is Cadillac. But he may still fall into the net. Neither Steve, Roz nor Clearwater have all three markers but we ran their data through COLUMBUS and fed in some variable combinations for Cadillac.

'The result was two interesting matches. Steve and Clearwater could produce a child with the potentiality to become the Talisman, and so could Roz and Cadillac. Both children *could* possess all three "gifts".'

'And we already have one of them under our control . . .'

'That's right.'

'And you think that Cadillac may pair off with Roz . . .'

'It's not inevitable, but it's a possibility we have to consider. We don't know the full story behind her unauthorized transfer to the The Lady. She may have engineered it. The rational part of me says it doesn't make sense but we can't ignore the accuracy of the Talisman Prophecy. And its force, Ben. We're up against something that is . . . beyond our present comprehension.'

The P-G brushed aside the metaphysical dimensions to the problem and got back to basics. 'It's quite possible to imagine Cadillac jacking up Roz just to get even with Brickman.'

'Yes . . . interesting situation.'

Jefferson studied Karlstrom. 'What plot are you hatching now?'

'I was wondering if we could get Brickman to open up the way Roz did.'

'You mean give us a map reference, plus what she was thinking and feeling?' The P-G considered the possibility. 'There may be no limit to what he might do – given the right inducements.'

371

'I thought we were already providing them.'

The P-G responded with a tongue in cheek smile. 'Fran has always had a weakness for young studs like Brickman. But if he proves more than a passing fancy we can always build her into the package. As you know, the Family is always prepared to support worthy causes.'

'Indeed . . .' Karlstrom expanded his initial suggestion. 'If Brickman *can* establish contact, there's a chance he'll be able to give us a rough fix. Now that we've eliminated the clan, they're on their own. We can snatch them any time we want. Failing that, Brickman should – at the very least – be able to tell us if she's pregnant. Given their past relationship his reaction to that news should be very interesting.'

'Go on . . .'

'The child that Clearwater is carrying. Is it possible to run those tests you mentioned while it's still in the womb?'

'That's something I'd have to check up on. But for the moment, let's say yes.'

'Then if the test proves that Brickman's child *doesn't* have all three markers, it's possible that Roz – if she became pregnant – might give birth to the Talisman.'

'She might. I think I know what you're going to say but tell me anyway.'

'Psychosomatic wounding. The involuntary telepathic link which caused Roz to share the mental trauma and enabled her body to mirror the wounds suffered by Brickman. *Real* wounds – even if the phenomenon was only temporary. If we wanted to eliminate Roz and her unborn child all we would have to do is kill Brickman.'

'If – for the sake of argument – he fell down one of the deep ventilation shafts and her mind and body shared the experience, there's no way that child could survive even if, by some miracle, she did. The shock would cause her to abort.'

'You're right. That's worth bearing in mind. However I don't think I've explained why we've developed these conditioning techniques and what we've aiming to do.

These farm-boys, the smart Mutes we're raised . . . the programme is designed to turn their heads around, to change their whole nature, to make them into *Trackers*. To own them, body and soul – so that even if they somehow discovered they were Mutes, they would still remain loyal to the Federation and the Family.'

Jefferson stood up. 'And despite the odd mishap, we're almost there. Earth magic still eludes us. Clearwater may help us with that. But we've got the secret of their longevity, their resistance to pain and wwe're close to reproducing the brilliance of their wordsmiths and the ability to read the stones.

'We can take that Mute clay and mould it any way we want. We can transform it into a *human being*. That's why we been searching for the Talisman, Ben. We don't want to kill him. We want to make him one of us.'

THE AMTRAK WARS

Book 1: CLOUD WARRIOR
Patrick Tilley

The first volume of a futureworld epic.

Ten centuries ago the Old Time ended when Earth's cities melted
in the War of a Thousand Suns. Now the lethal high technology
of the Amtrak Federation's underground stronghold is unleashed
on Earth's other survivors – the surface-dwelling Mutes. But the
primitive Mutes possess ancient powers greater than any
machine . . .

0 7221 8516 2   GENERAL FICTION

Book 2: FIRST FAMILY
Patrick Tilley

The second volume of a futureworld epic.

After countless years of fighting – of pitting sophisticated
technology against the primitive surface-dwelling people who
seemed to possess supernatural powers – the Federation was still
no nearer to ending the battle with the Mutes. But then a lone
flier was hauled into one of its underground bunkers – a man
whose very existence was a challenge to the all-pervading wisdom
of the First Family. A man whose destiny would determine the
future for both the Federation and the Mutes . . .

0 7221 8517 0   GENERAL FICTION

THE VISIONARY CHRONICLE OF THE ULTIMATE STRUGGLE TO RULE THE EARTH . . .

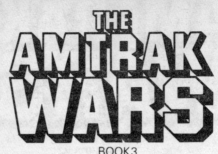

THE AMTRAK WARS

BOOK 3

Iron Master

The third volume of a futureworld epic

PATRICK TILLEY

The year: 2990 AD. The centuries-old conflict between the hi-tech underground world of the Trackers and the primitive, surface-dwelling Mutes continues with unabated ferocity. Steve Brickman, a Tracker wingman whose heart and mind is torn between the two cultures, embarks upon his most dangerous mission yet: the rescue of Cadillac and Clearwater, two Plainfolk Mutes held captive by the mysterious Iron Masters. It is a nightmare journey into the unknown . . .

0 7221 8518 9 GENERAL FICTION

☐	THE AMTRAK WARS 1	PATRICK TILLEY	£4.50
☐	THE AMTRAK WARS 2	PATRICK TILLEY	£4.99
☐	THE AMTRAK WARS 3	PATRICK TILLEY	£4.50
☐	THE AMTRAK WARS 4	PATRICK TILLEY	£4.50
☐	THE AMTRAK WARS 6	PATRICK TILLEY	£3.99
☐	THE ILLUSTRATED GUIDE	PATRICK TILLEY	£5.99
☐	MISSION	PATRICK TILLEY	£3.50

All Sphere Books are available at your bookshop or
newsagent, or can be ordered from the following address:
Sphere Books, Cash Sales Department,
P.O. Box 11, Falmouth, Cornwall TR10 9EN.

Alternatively you may fax your order to the above address.
Fax No. 0326 76423.

Payments can be made as follows: Cheque, postal order
(payable to Macdonald & Co (Publishers) Ltd) or by credit
cards, Visa/Access. Do not send cash or currency. UK
customers: please send a cheque or postal order (no currency)
and allow 80p for postage and packing for the first book plus
20p for each additional book up to a maximum charge of
£2.00.

B.F.P.O. customers please allow 80p for the first book plus
20p for each additional book.

Overseas customers including Ireland, please allow £1.50 for
postage and packing for the first book, £1.00 for the second
book, and 30p for each additional book.

NAME (Block Letters) ....

ADDRESS ....

....

☐ I enclose my remittance for _____

☐ I wish to pay by Access/Visa Card

Number   ☐☐☐☐☐☐☐☐☐☐☐☐☐☐☐☐

Card Expiry Date   ☐☐☐☐

interzone

SCIENCE FICTION AND FANTASY

Monthly   £1.95

- *Interzone* is the leading British magazine which specializes in SF and new fantastic writing. We have published:

BRIAN ALDISS	GARRY KILWORTH
J.G. BALLARD	DAVID LANGFORD
IAIN BANKS	MICHAEL MOORCOCK
BARRINGTON BAYLEY	RACHEL POLLACK
GREGORY BENFORD	KEITH ROBERTS
MICHAEL BISHOP	GEOFF RYMAN
DAVID BRIN	JOSEPHINE SAXTON
RAMSEY CAMPBELL	BOB SHAW
ANGELA CARTER	JOHN SHIRLEY
RICHARD COWPER	JOHN SLADEK
JOHN CROWLEY	BRIAN STABLEFORD
PHILIP K. DICK	BRUCE STERLING
THOMAS M. DISCH	LISA TUTTLE
MARY GENTLE	IAN WATSON
WILLIAM GIBSON	CHERRY WILDER
M. JOHN HARRISON	GENE WOLFE

- *Interzone* has also published many excellent new writers; illustrations, articles, interviews, film and book reviews, news, etc.

- *Interzone* is available from good bookshops, or by subscription. For six issues, send £12 (outside UK, £13). For twelve issues send £23, (outside UK, £25). Single copies: £2.30 inc p&p (outside UK, £2.50).

- American subscribers may send $22 ($26 if you want delivery by air mail) for six issues; or $40 ($48 air mail) for twelve issues. Single copies: $4 ($5 air mail).

To: **interzone** 124 Osborne Road, Brighton, BN1 6LU, UK.

Please send me six/twelve issues of *Interzone*, beginning with the current issue. I enclose a cheque / p.o. / international money order, made payable to *Interzone* (Delete as applicable.)

Name _____

Address _____

_____